THE STORM GOD'S GIFT

JERRY AUTIERI

1

Lightning scraped the black clouds and thunder exploded in its wake. Rain and wind bent the line of pine trees like slaves under the lash. Audhild staggered forward, head and shoulders pointed into the gale. Her doeskin boots sloshed with mucky water as she fought to open her eyes against the rain slapping her face. A sealskin cloak was the only protection against the storm she had taken. Her cold, shaking hand wiped aside a lock of hair plastered to her cheek and she pushed ahead.

Another blast of lightning divided the world into white and black shapes. The field and surrounding pines momentarily resembled the wood carvings that had adorned the lintel of her father's hall. Then midnight darkness swept back over the land and a crippling boom staggered her. Audhild felt it in her chest. Thor was raging tonight, battling the giant serpent Jormungand and quaking the world with blows of his hammer. When lightning flashed, she looked skyward. Roiling clouds showered rain into her eyes. She did not find what she hoped for.

She heard her name called, a small and desperate sound in the swell of the storm. It galvanized her onward. No one would stop her tonight. If this was the night the gods sent their gift, then she would be present to receive it.

Her next step was into a rut hidden in the darkness and she pitched onto hands and knees in the muddy grass. Another lightning strike and thunderclap gave her pause, then she began to stand. The voice calling her name closed the distance in the moment she had fallen.

"Audhild, by all the gods, woman! This is madness. Get back to the hall."

Regaining her feet, she searched the sky and ignored the man, Gudrod, closing behind her. She staggered forward, clapping the mud from her hands. The black outline of the Frankish tower on its high cliff emerged against the ultramarine dark of the stormy sky. Her steps remained quick and sure, even after having fallen.

"Audhild, we must go back. Do you want the Franks to capture us?"

She snorted at the threat, as if any Frank would be out in such a storm. All men were hiding from Thor's battle, and only she had the courage to come seek the reward he would offer the brave on this night.

At last a strong hand seized her shoulder, arresting her aimless plunge forward. She whirled on Gudrod, shucking off his grip with a snort of disgust. "Do not touch me again. If you come to witness the gift, then so be it. But do not hinder me."

Gudrod's face was lost in darkness, revealed only in stark angles of white and black when lightning struck again. She saw the rainwater pouring off the edge of his hood, him standing bent in the rain as if he had been punched in the gut. He inhaled as if to reply, then held up a hand in apology. She used the moment to push on.

There was no sign of anything but rain and misery falling from the sky, yet Eldrid had foreseen the storm god's gift. Perhaps it had already fallen and she had not yet discovered it. A sudden chill spread through her guts. What if Gudrod's presence offended the gods and they withheld from her?

"We're getting too close," Gudrod shouted from behind. "The peace was only just made. The Franks won't be above taking us for slaves." Again Gudrod's hand caught her shoulder, and again Audhild shoved it away.

"Touch me once more and I will have Eldrid turn your stones to nubs. You are interfering with the gift. Eldrid said I was to find it myself."

"That's not what she said." The rest of Gudrod's protest disappeared under a ground-shaking thunderclap, and Audhild smiled. It seemed the gods had no ears for his insolence.

The high tower, already a mighty structure of wood and stone, loomed even higher on its rocky ledge. The tower monitored the land in every direction. If the gods would send a gift, this was a fitting spot. Gudrod shouted after her.

Then she was weightless and her world milk white. Her ears filled with a keening ring. Cold rain pelted her face. She became aware of a muddy sound, viscous and slow. Something clamped to both her shoulders and shook her.

It was Gudrod. In an instant, she could see and hear again. The ringing still prevailed over all other sounds and her vision was bleached white, but she now realized she was laying face-up in the mud with Gudrod's hooded shadow hovering over her.

"Are you alive?" he asked, his voice cracking with fear.

She nodded. "Let go of me."

Gudrod paused, rivulets of rainwater flowing over his shoulders onto her body, then backed away. "You were almost struck by lightning."

A joyful warmth spread through her and she scrambled to her feet. Gudrod tried to assist, but she fought aside his quaking hands. Where the lightning had struck a pine tree was now flopped to the ground and sundered in two. Bits of bark and pine needle were in her hair and wood splinters scattered the ground. She began laughing and pointed at the tree.

"What is there to laugh at?" Gudrod followed her pointing finger, but only looked back at her.

"The gods have marked where they will place their gift. It is as Eldrid foretold. I have found it."

"Then can we get out of this storm before the gods mark us as well?"

Audhild turned her face to the sky and let the rain wash over her.

The gods would grant their boon, and her future, the future of all her people, would be safe.

2

FRANKIA 895 C.E

"The fools chose to fight," Ulfrik called to the ranks of mail-clad warriors as he strode back across the fields from the parley. Coarse laughter met his announcement, and he muttered out of the side of his mouth to Gunnar who walked beside him. "No Frank ever has the sense to know when he's beaten."

"He knows when I've beaten him," Gunnar answered. Einar, who followed behind with Ulfrik's banner, laughed.

The warriors were already straightening their lines and touching their battered round shields together as the three men rejoined them. Dozens of shield designs in as many colors bobbed along the front ranks. Ulfrik unslung his own green and white shield as he turned to face the Franks assembling across the dew-laden grass. They were assembling their own lines, comprised of a bushy black slash of inexperienced fighters under one veteran man-at-arms too proud to back down from a force outnumbering him three to one. Of course, their farms and homes lay behind them and Ulfrik had come to plunder as he did each summer, so he understood their reluctance to stand aside.

"Archers forward?" Einar asked as he helped Gunnar bind his shield to the stump of his right arm. Ulfrik watched the giant man pull straps tight over Gunnar's forearm.

"Save the arrows. We're going to blow through these bastards like wind through the trees."

Einar nodded, then thumped Gunnar on his helmet once the shield was secured. Gunnar's eyes were already far away, and he saw the killing fever rising in his son. Their eyes met, and Ulfrik acknowledged his son with a slow nod. Gunnar took his spot behind Ulfrik, his sword white fire in his left hand. He could not stand in the front rank because his shield did not match with his sword-brother's, nor could he stand behind another and step into the front rank for the same reason. Therefore, he stood behind Ulfrik in support until the enemy lines were broken. He had grown into Ulfrik's height and strength, while his curling dark hair and eyes marked him as his mother's son. On the battlefield Gunnar was unlike either of them, becoming a savage and bloodthirsty force more akin to a berserk than a disciplined warrior.

The morning sun had finally pierced the sullen clouds, speckling the Franks with blots of light. The grass was a rich blue-green that offset the faded yellow surcoats the Franks wore. Sunlight flared on their conical helmets or their spear points. Their lines grew still and quiet, and Ulfrik shook his head. "It is an ill-done thing to kill children. But they are in the way."

"And they're pointing spears at us," Einar added. The giant man shook out Ulfrik's green banner, showing the black elk antlers that been his father's standard in what felt like another lifetime. The cloth cracked and snapped and galvanized Ulfrik to begin his attack. The Franks wouldn't move and he had not patience to prod them into a charge.

His voice boomed out for his men's attention. "There is victory waiting across this field, then the spoils in silver and slaves beyond. These Franks are not prepared for us. Remind them why they must never grow lax, nor deny us what our might entitles us to take. Go forward and make widows and mothers' tears. Forward to death and glory!"

A roar went up and the men banged weapons against their shields. The line lurched ahead with Ulfrik pointing the way with his drawn sword. Gunnar shoved at his back and the men at his sides raised shields. Ulfrik judged the moment to begin the charge, leaving it to the exact moment he saw their few archers tip their bows toward the sky.

"Arrows!" he yelled and began to run. Shields slid overhead as the first shafts splattered across the wide ranks. Wooden thuds echoed all around. Einar's shield tipped as an arrow slammed into it.

The first volley was not even noticed, and Ulfrik's artful timing left the Franks no space for another. His massive line was already swarming the Franks. Across the field he saw their white eyes peering over teardrop shields. Only their leader owned any boldness, swearing like a drunk for someone to challenge him. The front rank of Franks knelt to brace their shields and the second rank set their spears. It was a stubborn display but unfit to deter furious Northmen hot for the slaughter.

The clash of shield upon shield was like a thunderclap, and the flash of striking iron like the lightning that birthed it. Ulfrik kicked into the shield blocking him, and used his own shield to deflect the spear aimed at his face. Gunnar's short blade darted beneath Ulfrik's legs to jab the Frank his father had just toppled. Screams began, both sides spilling blood and breaking bone. Ulfrik shoved into the gap he opened, his own sword snapping forward and returning red. A flurry of faces collapsed under his shield as he drove forward, Gunnar and three other ranks behind him relentlessly pushing him through. The familiar reek of blood and urine wafted up from his feet. Pressed as close as lovers, he killed each Frank that opposed him with ruthless efficiency.

Then he was free. As expected, Ulfrik had marched his men completely through the weak Frankish line. In a space of minutes he had defeated the enemy with one strong push. Franks were scattering and the neat ranks were unfolding in pursuit. Einar, his ax dripping blood, planted the banner, and Ulfrik stood beneath it to accept any who would challenge it.

It took only a moment.

The man-at-arms dashed screaming across the short space between them. He had lost his shield and held his sword overhead with both hands. His face was red with shame and his mail red with blood. He leapt the tidemark of bodies where the first line of Franks had resisted, and slashed at Ulfrik with a wild, hateful swing.

Deflecting it easily, Ulfrik drove his shoulder into the leader and set him sprawling. The ground was wet with blood and he struggled to regain himself. Ulfrik could have run him through, but he waited. As the leader scrambled to his feet, Ulfrik kicked a lost shield across the grass to him. When he stood, he stared dumbfounded at it.

"Pick it up," Ulfrik said in his poor Frankish. "Then try that again."

"My thanks," said the leader as he warily retrieved the shield. It was one of Ulfrik's, a chipping white paint job decorated with black scroll work. It looked out of place on the arm of a Frank.

The two regarded each other a moment as the battle milled around them. Einar stood in a crouch, watchful for interlopers. In the moment of inattention, the Frank struck at Ulfrik.

Barely catching the strike on his own shield, he instinctively chopped down to cut the Frank's hamstring. They continued past each other, whirling about to face off anew. The blow had only been a gash, and the Frank registered no pain. Ulfrik crouched and resolved to end it.

His strike was explosive, using his shield and superior strength to fold up the Frank's shield and expose his side. Ulfrik's blade rammed into the leader's kidney and he crumpled with a wail. Drawing out the blade as the enemy collapsed, Ulfrik swiftly struck the back of the neck. The head did not come free, but he delivered the swift death he wanted. "Foolish but brave," he said to the crumpled body of the dead leader.

A motion caught his eye and he looked up to see a Frankish spearman charging him. His shield came up and he jumped aside, but the Frank did not charge home. Instead, when he saw the dead leader at Ulfrik's feet, he fell to his knees and threw down his spear.

"Mercy, I beg you, my lord!"

Here was a man no older than Gunnar, perhaps eighteen or nineteen winters, though he had a child's face. His eyes were filled with tearful hope. Ulfrik pointed his sword at him. "You should die."

The Frank cried out and threw himself flat. "Mercy, please!"

"What ransom will you fetch? Better a slave maybe?" Ulfrik was not above selling or buying slaves, though he seldom did. He no longer needed the wealth, and housing them before their sale was troublesome. He considered giving the Frank over to a hirdman. "Get up and start running. If you're caught again, don't seek mercy."

The Frank looked at him in astonishment. He didn't move.

Ulfrik kicked him. "Then it's death you want?"

The Frank scrabbled to his feet and began to run. At a safe distance he turned and waved his thanks to Ulfrik.

Ulfrik removed his helmet and wiped sweat from his eyes. In every direction men were running down fleeing Franks.

"He'll be caught again," Einar said as he joined Ulfrik. "Then he'll tell how you freed him once before."

"So let me be accused of mercy," Ulfrik said, idly prodding the dead leader with his foot. "Men follow me for victory and gold, not bloodshed alone."

They surveyed the carnage surrounding them, Ulfrik tracing a stream of wrecked bodies, lost shields, snapped spears and bent swords to where his men had broken into small combats. He found Gunnar standing over a man on his knees, arms raised in surrender. Gunnar did not hesitate to ram his sword through the surrendering Frank's face. When he collapsed in death, Gunnar placed his foot on the man's sword arm and hacked off the hand.

"No one will accuse him of mercy," Einar said dryly.

Answering with a long puff of breath, Ulfrik shook his head and approached his son. In the years since losing his hand, Gunnar had dedicated himself to overcoming that handicap. The fanatical effort had paid off, for now he could do as well or better than a man with two hands, but the cost of recovery had been more than the effort of relearning with his left hand. A part of him had changed forever.

"A trail of handless bodies follows you across every battlefield," Ulfrik said as Gunnar wiped his sword on the dead Frank's surcoat.

"And what trail do you leave? Footprints of the men you let run?" Gunnar sprung to his feet, standing a hand's distance from his father. "What was that I saw? You let the enemy go?"

"The Franks are broken. We'll have their land, their women, all they own by nightfall. I did not need to kill him to claim what I want."

Gunnar scowled. His dark eyes flashed with the anger and stubbornness of this mother's side. With his hair curling from sweat and his chin tipped out, he reminded Ulfrik so strongly of Toki that the name nearly came to his lips.

"Your anger is useful, Gunnar. Guide it, but don't let it rule you. You've done well today, killed many a foeman. No man will doubt your prowess."

He knew Gunnar was not listening. His son was already scanning ahead, looking for the next enemy to kill. A dark knot of men hailed him, his closest friends, and he ran after them without another word to Ulfrik.

"Shall I sound the horn to call them in?" Einar said as he rejoined Ulfrik. "This battle is won. Time to grab the rewards."

Ulfrik nodded and watched Gunnar stoop down to hack off another sword arm.

"Some battles are never won," he said to himself.

3

Ulfrik waved to the crowd that had flooded out of Ranvdal to greet his returning army. He rode at the front, only a dozen others privileged to accompany him on horseback riding close behind. The black stockade walls of his fortress were sharp against the summer blue of the sky, and the sun washed the land and people in dewy brilliance. His warriors snaked along on foot behind him, and then the baggage train as well as wagons of loot and prisoners. At the rear of the column came the carts of the fallen. While each man was laid out with all dignity, the dead were never a good thing to present first to the crowds.

"The people love you," shouted a lantern-jawed hirdman. "Look, that woman is holding her baby up to see you."

"Maybe she thinks the babe is his," Einar said then laughed.

"Doesn't look like me," Ulfrik quipped.

"Not ugly enough to be one of yours." Einar began to guffaw at his own joke, then stopped. "Of course I didn't mean offense by that, Gunnar."

Ulfrik twisted over the back of his horse. Einar was red-faced, but Gunnar only smirked.

"I'm not the one who can't laugh at himself. That's my father's problem."

"Respect, young man." Ulfrik pointed at him, and Gunnar bared his teeth in response.

The crowds grew closer, and hirdmen broke off to keep the overzealous at bay. Cheers and praise flowed after Ulfrik, but as he rode past, the people sought their loved ones in the crowd. Homecomings were always a drizzle of pain in the joy of reunion. Men would find their waiting lovers or families and break away with them, dwindling down to a forlorn group that would throw themselves tearfully on that final wagon of the dead. Ulfrik was relived he rode at the front of the column for that reason.

The north gate had been opened, and the few guards left behind flanked it. A group of figures were framed within, and Ulfrik's heartbeat hastened. He had been gone a month whipping the countryside and trimming the Franks from his borders. The work had left him scant room for thoughts of those remaining behind, but since he began the march home, they were all of his thoughts. He leapt off his horse.

He took two bounding steps before he schooled himself. Eyes were still upon him, always judging, and he assumed a more dignified stance. He strode with confidence, flipping his cloak over the shoulder and straining to not look too carefully at his wife and sons. Standing before them was his fort commander, Konal. His burn-scared face twisted in a half smile as he awaited Ulfrik's approach. When he arrived, Konal went to his knee.

"All is well in Ravndal, Jarl Ulfrik." Konal raised his bowed head, his voice rough and strained from his old burns. "You return in victory?"

"Did you expect otherwise? Now off your knee, you bastard." Ulfrik extended his arm and Konal took it. He pulled his commander close and slapped his back in greeting. "Thank you for protecting my home and family. I know it was hard to stay behind."

"It is an honor to stand beside your family. But I expect to hear a good story or two tonight." Konal had lost all of his family including his beloved twin brother during a hall burning in Ireland. His only son was Aren, born of an affair between Konal and Runa. Ulfrik forgave him and to his mind time had cured any awkwardness.

Ulfrik turned to his family. His boys, Hakon and Aren, stood attentively with white-haired Snorri resting a hand on each of their shoulders. His adopted daughter, Kirsten, stood next to them, pale and delicate hands folded at her lap. At seven years she was too young to feign indifference and smiled broadly, daring a small wave. Ulfrik matched it and slipped a brief smile.

Before all was his wife, Runa. Age may have stolen the luster from her hair and sprayed it with gray, and worry may have creased the corners of her eyes, but it had not bent her back nor weakened the fierce pride of her gaze. Yet more than her beauty was her constant companionship down all the long years. A bond forged in so much shared tribulation could never be broken. Ulfrik went to her first.

"Here I've been sweeping the land for its treasures, only to find the greatest of all was in my home all along." He took her hand and kissed it, her skin warm and smooth against his lips.

"So you were hit in the head again? I told you that helmet is too old to protect you." She withdrew her hand with a laugh.

"You deal me a harsher blow." He put his hand over his heart and Runa rolled her eyes, then shared a kiss before turning to his children.

Kirsten was first into his arms, being the youngest. Ulfrik had never wanted a daughter until he adopted Kirsten. She was a constant source of surprise and joy. She had survived the loss of her father, Toki, then her mother Halla's madness, and finally the death of her older sister to the pox, all without diminishing her spirit. Her thin arms around his neck squeezed and he told her how much he had missed her.

"Have you made us safe now?" she asked, her blue eyes wide and bright.

"You will always be safe here, little one."

Both Aren and Hakon had grown into boys equal to the role of a jarl's son. Hakon approached him first and embraced his father.

"Welcome home, Father, and congratulations on your victory. You bring honor to our family and glory to your name." He smiled hopefully.

Ulfrik paused, hands on both of Hakon's shoulders. Doubtlessly

Hakon had labored over his words all night, testing them on his mother and brother. Ulfrik had seen him do it a dozen times for more trivial matters. Today he had stuck a note too formal for the occasion, but Ulfrik had no heart to correct him.

"Your words brace me, young man. I hear the heart of a skald in them. It is good to be home and to see you." Hakon's smile escaped and Ulfrik laughed.

Finally Aren came forward. He was as grave as ever, growing into a face and body that resembled none of his family. The pox had nearly killed him the prior winter as it had half the children of Ravndal, and scars marred an already unattractive face. He embraced Ulfrik with a hug strong for his young frame.

"You have been good for your mother?" Ulfrik knelt to Aren's level and the boy nodded. "And you've kept watch on things for me?" Again he nodded. "This pleases me."

He ruffled Aren's hair and stood. Gunnar now repeated the same welcoming, starting with his mother. He noted the wince in Runa's expression upon seeing Gunnar splattered with dried blood. He and his friends held a foolish notion that washing off the blood of an enemy before returning home was bad luck. Ulfrik knew it was only a youthful attempt to look fiercer for the veterans. Yet it only made them look dirty.

The rest of the morning was spent in reunions and trading news. The day passed for Ulfrik in turns of joy and sadness, for eventually the corpse wagon rolled in with its sad followers. Names of the fallen had to be memorized, widows and mothers consoled, and old fathers assured the blood-price of their dead sons. Runa no longer organized the welcome feasts, and Ulfrik felt the cooking poorer for it. She had finally surrendered to her station as the jarl's wife, in fact now a Hersir's wife given the number of men and farms under his command. Still, she had disappeared into the hall to oversee the preparations and terrorize the women with her suggestions.

By late afternoon the air was full of savory scents from the mead hall, and Ulfrik was not alone in anticipating the celebration. Now he had wandered to the blacksmith's forge, where Trygg examined

Ulfrik's helmet and swords. Ulfrik leaned against a workbench, idly playing with a file when Konal and Snorri walked into the forge.

"Please, I had hoped to find some peace listening to Trygg bang iron for a while. Your faces have the look of unhappy news."

"My face has been unhappy news since the fire destroyed it," Konal said in his whispering rasp, joining Ulfrik at the workbench and nodding to Trygg.

Snorri hobbled next to him, now depending on his staff to walk. The light behind him turned his wispy hair to a halo of white fire. "Lad, glad you're home. But there's news that can't wait."

Ulfrik returned the file to the workbench, then stood straight. He glanced at Trygg, who nodded. "I can strengthen the helmet, Jarl Ulfrik. I'll just check on the materials."

All three watched Trygg leave, and Konal began. "Jarl Hrolf the Strider is coming."

"By the gods." Ulfrik turned aside. "Now's not the time. I've only just returned."

"His messengers are already staying at the hall," Snorri added. "He's coming for his share. Bringing the wagon."

"Of course he is." Ulfrik rubbed his face. "I thought he was in the north, making trouble in Amiens?"

Both Konal and Snorri shrugged. An uncomfortable silence bloomed. Ulfrik was loyal to Hrolf, and he had prospered under him better than he could have ever imagined. Still, Hrolf's visits portended new directions and usually new battles. Ulfrik had learned that being Hrolf's so-called "luck" was a demanding role.

"There's no time to hide any of the loot from this raid," Konal said. "He's counting on a good share."

"So say his messengers?" Ulfrik asked. Both men nodded.

"Lad, word is some fellows representing a jarl from south of the Seine accompany him."

Ulfrik folded his arms, Hrolf's plan crystallizing in his mind. "So he needs gold and guts for an adventure in the south, and he's coming to me for it."

"Seems like it," Konal said.

They stood a while in silence. The adventure was welcomed, even if he had only just returned. No one could fight the Franks as well as he could. It was only natural to seek him out. The gold bothered him, for he understood a large part of it to be funneled back to the Franks in Rouen as part of Hrolf's attempts to buy a safe haven at his back. Ulfrik kept hidden stashes of treasure buried in places only he knew, but he couldn't hide everything. Hrolf would have his share.

"Thanks for letting me know," Ulfrik said at last. "I cannot change what Fate has set in motion. We will welcome Hrolf with another feast and do as he asks of us."

4

The big red-bearded man had wrestled his opponent to the ground, one muscular arm wreathed with faded blue tattoos and white scars locked around his head. The circle of men tightened and both cheered and cajoled the wrestlers. The smaller man being choked turned red and his hands flailed at his opponent. It was Hrolf's man and he was losing badly.

"You can pay your loss from your share of the treasure," Ulfrik said to Hrolf. "Your man is as blue as a peacock."

Hrolf the Strider stood beside Ulfrik, towering above all with arms folded and face drawn into a frown. His clothes were newly sewn and finely made, but he bore little adornment beyond gold armbands and a silver charm of Thor's hammer. He grumbled at Ulfrik's jibe, watching the match intently.

Ulfrik's man was waving to the crowd with his free arm, a gap-toothed smile radiating his confidence. His opponent seemed to give up, nearly choked into unconsciousness, then his hand reached down behind him. Now the big man suddenly began to scream, though he did not relent on his grip. The choking man had found the crotch of his opponent and was crushing his balls.

Men cringed in sympathetic pain, including Ulfrik, but the big man held on until the clamp on his balls overwhelmed him. When he fell back the crowd exploded in cheers. Hrolf's small man was suddenly atop his opponent and battering him with rapid blows to the face.

"More like a raptor than a peacock," Hrolf said, and sniffed. He stole a glance at Ulfrik with a wry smile on his face. Ulfrik shrugged and watched the man he had bet on lose the match under a storm of face-bloodying strikes. When he finally conceded, the small man sprung up into the waiting arms of his supporters while the big man rolled over holding his crotch.

"There'll be some high notes in the singing tonight," Ulfrik said. "You have a knack for knowing where to bet, Jarl Hrolf."

"I look beyond what is in front of me to see the potential inside a man. The big one has probably won every fight in his life. He was blind to the killing spirit of his smaller opponent, only seeing what he expected. The man's cockiness was plain. He never considered it possible to lose everything in one instant. Now his pride is crushed."

"Along with his stones and my gold," Ulfrik added, and both men laughed.

"EXCELLENT GAMES AND FINE MEAD," Hrolf said as the two turned away from the circle of men settling their bets. "And a feast tonight. I must visit you more often than I do. You have done well for yourself. Men might soon call you a king."

They strolled in companionable silence, guards following them close behind. Even within Ravndal, particularly after the incident with Throst and Hakon three years ago, Ulfrik maintained a guard for himself and his family. Hrolf had his men, but Ulfrik only trusted his own. Who could say if a spy had infiltrated Hrolf's ranks, but of his own he was certain of their loyalty. As they drifted away from the center square where the games continued, key men lingered at their periphery. Einar and Gunnar followed for Ulfrik, and Gunther One-Eye and Mord followed for Hrolf, along with two others who had not been introduced.

"We shall discuss business after the feast," Hrolf said, sensing the encroaching followers. "For now, you and I should speak."

"What news have you to share? I thought you were trying your luck in Amiens?"

Hrolf shook his head and growled. "I've not the success you enjoy when it comes to breaking the Franks. I was turned back, as much as I hate to admit it. I saw no profit in pushing deeper, not without a proper army, which would mean calling you and all your jarls to my banner. That'd leave my borders full of holes."

"Odo squabbles with King Arnulf in the East and Charles in his own territory." Ulfrik scanned his walls, where men kept watch even during the celebration. "He's distracted enough to let me crisscross his lands and take what I will. I've captured more land for us north of Brunn. We only need to garrison it to make it permanent."

"No, that fight with Arnulf is ending. I have it on good authority that Arnulf summoned both Odo and his lap dog, Charles, to Worms, but Charles did not go. He sent an emissary, which angered Arnulf enough to get back in bed with Odo. The problem for us is he ceded land to Arnulf as a show of loyalty. I'd rather fight Odo than Arnulf, but that land is right on my north border. I can't vacate this area, not with that warhound Arnulf sniffing at my hall doors."

Hrolf halted their walk and rubbed the back of his neck. "I fear the easy years are behind us now, and regret I didn't do more with that time. Without the distractions of fighting Charles and Arnulf, Odo will be able to make a solid push to reclaim territory."

"He won't come after us. We're too strong. He'll seek the easy victories over the small raiders and petty jarls."

"We are not so strong; otherwise we'd be having this talk in Paris instead. The small victories hurt as just as badly as a direct attack. What we need to make our lands here permanent is a unified force. Right now our brothers are scattered everywhere, and each man calls himself king of wherever he's shitting that day. How easy it is for the Franks to pick off these pockets until we are the only targets left. If we were to unite under a single banner, the Franks would never expel us."

Ulfrik studied Hrolf's pensive face and realized he was worried for the future, something Ulfrik had never seen before. The candor surprised him enough to rob him of a reply. He looked around as if the answers were waiting to be grabbed, then he saw the two visitors who had accompanied Hrolf. They clung to the shadows of homes lining the boardwalk roads of Ravndal, awaiting a cue to bring them forward. Both turned aside when they realized Ulfrik was staring.

"So you plan to add these scattered banners under your own," Ulfrik said, a smile forming as he realized Hrolf's plans.

"That has always been my goal, and now it has become urgent. With Odo ready to turn his army back to fighting us, we must consolidate before theses smaller settlements disappear under Frankish flags."

"And establishing a disposable buffer around the core of your territory is another smart move. Particularly south of the Seine, where we have nothing to trade for peace but our own land."

Both Hrolf and Ulfrik smiled. Hrolf said nothing, but instead resumed walking, his hands clasped behind his back.

"When are you planning to bring in the two guests who are following us?"

"They are a discussion for later tonight. For now, I think you understand what is needed after hearing my news."

Ulfrik nodded. "I understand. All too well."

5

The feast was a great success, as Ulfrik had expected. Though Runa no longer personally cooked the meals, she ensured servants delivered a feast worthy of her reputation. The hall overflowed with carousing warriors, their families, and slaves. The hearth glowed and rendered the smoke crawling along the ceiling in golden hues. From the high table, Ulfrik raised a mug to each of the dozens of men who toasted his victory. By now he had to draw lightly on the warm, foamy ale or he would be dumber than a lamb for the late-night meeting.

Hrolf sat across the table from him, the endlessly replenished mug at his right hand seeming to be no burden on his mind. He regaled the table with war stories from his adventures in Frankia, England, and even from his old home of Norway. Though noble-born and richly adorned, Hrolf spoke with the plain force of a shieldwall veteran. More than once someone at the table forgot he spoke to a lord and was gracefully yet firmly reminded of his mistake. Ulfrik admired that casual ease and saw firsthand how it inspired men to serve and sacrifice whenever he asked.

At last, when singers began to forget their songs and others crawled under the table for sleep, Hrolf nodded to Ulfrik then waved closer the visitors who had been relegated to the far end of the high table. Runa gave Ulfrik a brief kiss then gathered both Hakon and Aren from the table. Gunnar remained, along with Einar, Konal, and Snorri, all of them closing around Ulfrik like a group of conspirators.

"Now for that discussion I promised," Hrolf said. Gunther One-Eye, grayer and thinner than years past but still able to drink an ocean of mead and walk away, stood to allow the guests to slide into his place. His son Mord had fallen beneath the table some time ago and his drunken snoring filled the brief silence.

"An incredible feast tonight," said the first guest. His name was Hrut Magnusson. He had a face too small for his head and a nose that had been broken too many times.

"Yes, I have tasted no better fowl anywhere," said the second guest. He was called Stein Half-Leg, presumably for his short height. Ulfrik had deduced him as the senior man of the two, both for his less damaged features and the gold armband on his arm. He seemed to always be trying to touch his head to an invisible ceiling.

"Let no man leave my hall with an empty stomach or an empty mug." Ulfrik winked at Gunnar seated beside him, then ceased the formalities. "But I assume you have not traveled so far to follow Hrolf the Strider to his next meal. So what is your intention, and why do I feel you and Hrolf have already involved me in your plans?"

Ulfrik laughed to ease the bluntness and all joined him, though Stein's eyes showed no mirth even as he tipped his head back in laughter.

"Ever to the heart of the matter," Hrolf said, leaning forward across the table. "Of course I've brought these men here with a purpose. We could've discussed this alone, but I thought you should hear directly from them."

Hrolf sat back and with an upturned palm invited Stein Half-Leg to speak. Shadows thrown by the hearth and table lamps flowed into the recesses of his eyes and hollows of his cheeks. Stein licked his lips and stifled a glance at his companion, Hrut, before he began. His stubby fingers played with his empty mug as he spoke.

"It's true we're not here to follow Hrolf from one feast to the next. We have dared the journey from south of the Seine. Gunnolfsvik. Have you heard of it?"

Ulfrik shrugged. "I watch the north and east. Gunnolfsvik would not be in my line of sight, but it's familiar."

"It should be familiar." Stein stopped rolling his mug and set it with a hard clack on the table. "Gunnolf was with Sigfried at Paris, and he took his men south when the siege failed. He settled a crew of thirty men, and every year he has drawn thirty more. By now we've got two hundred crew, along with the lands and farms to support them. Like you, I'll come to the point. The Franks attacked at the start of raiding season. They surprised us. They're also a lot better than before, more organized and more of them."

Hrolf leaned on his elbows and gave Ulfrik a knowing smile. Stein continued.

"They're beating us. All summer, we've been on our back foot. The border is like a shieldwall ready to collapse. We're trying to negotiate a peace that lets us hold onto what we have. Men have taken wives and started families here. We can't get back in our ships and sail for easier lands anymore. We don't expect the Franks to agree, so my father, Gunnolf, has sent me to Hrolf for aid. We need help, men to stick in our lines and leaders to show us how to break the Franks."

Ulfrik held Stein's unwavering gaze, finally breaking it by draining the dregs from the bottom of his mug. He then scanned the faces of his allies. Konal, Einar, and Snorri had noncommittal expressions, but Gunnar's lips twitched with his desire to speak.

"I don't have the men to send you," Ulfrik said, pulling back with arms folded. "This border has only been stable for the last three years and I expect the Franks will make a stronger effort against me now that Odo has settled his worries. I've captured farmland to the north that needs consolidation. That's where I'll put my men if they must go anywhere. I'm sorry, Half-Leg."

Stein Half-Leg and Hrut Magnusson shared a pained glance before both looked to Hrolf. He too had folded his arms and regarded Ulfrik with an expression of a father irked at his son's pointless obstinacy, tongue probing his cheek. Ulfrik returned a smile he hoped communicated that his words were true. Someone dropped a stack of wooden plates behind Ulfrik, providing a welcomed relief from the long stares as all turned to the noise. A drunk had knocked over a servant attempting to clean up.

"I will send the men," Hrolf said. His expression of exasperation did not alter. "Your dedication is admirable, but I'd have thought after our talk you'd understand the benefits of aiding our brothers."

"I understood. Understanding doesn't mean agreement."

Hrolf bristled at the public challenge, eyes narrowing and lips bending into an angry wedge. Gunther One-Eye, standing behind him, slowly shook his head. Ulfrik felt heat on his face as he realized too late he had overstepped himself. Ale may have freed his tongue but it would not excuse embarrassing his oath-holder.

"But I also have to see beyond my borders and protect all of our brothers." Ulfrik forced a smile, hating the toadying words falling out of his mouth. "If you send men, how can I help?"

Hrolf relaxed and Gunther One-Eye gave an approving nod. His old friend and benefactor knew better than anyone how to tread around Hrolf's moods. For as Ulfrik had rose ever closer to his king, he discovered Hrolf's temper once aroused was hardly ever quenched without violence.

Sweeping his palm across an imagined landscape, Hrolf spoke. "This land has been paid for with our blood, and we are on the brink of losing it to an organized Frankish resistance. There is no greater power in the western Seine, either north or south of it, than me. It is right that Gunnolfsvik seeks aid from me, and once we have secured victory it is also right it unites under my banner. This is how we keep the land out of the hands of our enemies, through combined strength. Ulfrik, you may wonder why I have chosen you for this duty, but you should not. None among all the jarls sworn to me have had your success. The gods are ever on your side, and they will bring you success against the Franks and glory my banner. For you travel in my name, with my authority. While you forge alliances in the south, I will secure the north and our power grows along with those who join us."

Stein Half-Leg sat up like a dog expecting table scraps. He jumped into the opening. "Your success against the Franks is famous. Everyone knows how you trapped them in your own hall and slew them to a man. You threw an ax to cut off the Frankish baron's head in a single go."

"I doubt he was a baron," Ulfrik said, but Stein did not hear him.

"We need that kind of cunning. Our most cunning warriors are either old or dead. The rest of us have done our share of fighting, but mostly easy raiding. Nothing like what you've done. You lead armies to victory. It's what we need."

"You only have farmers left to fight?"

"Not at all," said Hrut Magnusson. "We've got a strong core, but our ranks are filled with inexperienced men. Neither Stein nor I have led an organized force against such a concentration of Franks. If Hrolf will send men and you lead them, we will have a chance."

"And my father, Gunnolf, has promised to swear an oath to Hrolf," Stein Half-Leg added.

Hrolf raised a brow and smiled at Ulfrik. "And Gunnolfsvik would be placed under your territories to rule in my name."

Ulfrik turned to his own side. Gunnar, red-faced with drink, nodded vigorously. He only need hear the promise of killing Franks to agree. Einar and Konal were more thoughtful, but in turn each nodded. Only Snorri frowned.

"You think they should be asking you to lead," Ulfrik asked and drew a few chuckles. Snorri's smile was as short-lived as the first snowflake of storm.

"Doesn't feel right, lad. No insults to our guests; it's not them. Just something in these old bones of mine aches at the thought. Something bad hangs over this. Call it an old man's hunch. I get to have those at my age, don't I?"

"You do," Hrolf said, slapping the table with a new smile on his face. "And never let it be said I don't understand the wisdom of tired, old men who have hunches. But as we just learned, understanding doesn't mean agreement."

Ulfrik shrunk in his seat, realizing Hrolf was not going to forget his misstep.

"Twenty of my best men will go, and if Ulfrik agrees, they will defend him as they would me. Stein, your father must understand that Ulfrik must have complete command of all your forces." Hrolf pointed a thick finger bearing a silver ring at Stein. "There can be no success if leadership is divided."

"Honestly, we'd be glad to have someone like Jarl Ulfrik leading us. We're struggling as it is." Stein nearly leapt off his bench to hug Hrolf, but Hrut put a hand on his shoulder.

Ulfrik unfolded his arms, shook his head at Snorri, then turned to Hrolf and Stein. "I pick the twenty men, and I'm back before Yule even if the Franks haven't broken. The other details of treasure and spoils will have to be worked out. But if I'm leading, I get the leader's share. Agree to this and you'll get my help."

"No arguments from us," Stein said with a look to Hrut, who also agreed.

"It's a fair arrangement," Hrolf said. "Details can come tomorrow, but tonight let's drink on it."

Ulfrik called for more ale, rousing a serving girl to fetch a pitcher. Soon she was spilling drink into raised mugs. They drained the ale and banged the mugs down on the board. The malty taste filled Ulfrik's mouth and nose, and he wiped his beard with the back of his arm. They raised mugs again for another round, all but Snorri who limped down from the high table massaging his wounded leg and shaking his head.

6

With twenty warriors selected and gathered on the north bank of the Seine, Ulfrik prepared for departure. The late summer dawn had turned the sky pink, setting golden sparkles on the brown water of the river. Stein Half-Leg's longship leaned on the small strip of muddy bank. Ulfrik's nostrils flared looking at the faded red of the sail and the patchwork shades of wood strakes. He was thankful only river travel awaited, for one gale at sea would send the ship down to Ran's bed beneath the waves.

"We make the sacrifice now," Ulfrik said to Einar, who stood by his side. With a whistle and snap from Einar, a Frankish slave boy led forward a ram. Runa followed with a bowl of silver, which she handed to Ulfrik. He let his hands touch hers as she released it to him, but her eyes fell away and she returned to her sons. Ulfrik sighed and drew his knife. He directed Einar to hold the ram and the twenty crewmen gathered close.

"Thor Lord of Storms, Meili Lord of the Long Road, see this sacrifice in your names. Grant us fair weather and safe travel. Shelter us from ill-fortune so that we may bring doom to our enemies and glory to your names." Einar pulled the ram's head back and Ulfrik sawed open its throat. The beast thrashed and another man grabbed its legs as hot lifeblood splashed into the silver bowl. When the ram sank down in death and the bowl quivered with blood, Ulfrik lifted it overhead. "Our blood is as pure as our sacrifice. Gods grant us your favor."

He dipped his hand into the hot blood, scooped out handfuls, and splashed all the travelers and the bow of the ship with the offering. Men nodded in satisfaction as Ulfrik completed the blessings. Finished, he handed the bowl to Einar then lifted off a thick chain of gold from his neck. His bloody hand dripped as he twirled the chain overhead, then cast it far into the murky Seine. "Ran, take my gold and spare us from your frightful bed. Be pleased with our offering."

With the sacrifice complete, men began to load their gear aboard the ship. Stein and Hrut organized the effort, finding places for the extra twenty men. They had arrived with only eight crew, and stuffing twenty more aboard was desperate work. Ulfrik had considered taking his own ship, but chose to keep them at Gunnar's disposal. Longships were the fastest travel down the Seine and he did not want to deny Ravndal any if they were needed during his absence.

Studying the men he would soon command, he deemed them lax and undisciplined. Already he had reined in a half dozen urges to shout them into form. Hrolf had assigned this burden when he was expecting to spend time in his own hall. His frustration at that could easily be dumped on the new men, and so he held his tongue. Hrolf has left him little choice in this matter, and Ulfrik's review of options all resulted in openly defying his oath-holder. Yet Hrolf was as famous for his pragmatism as well as his prowess. Offering Gunnolfsvik as part of Ulfrik's holdings made the mission far sweeter. It was outside of his borders and he expected challenges in keeping the local jarl in line. However, the increase in tribute would be welcomed along with the glory of holding more land. Further, a holding south of the Seine offered both protection and a staging ground for battle with the Franks. After a night of deliberation, he had settled his doubts. Success in Gunnolfsvik was best for him and his dependents.

"You shouldn't be taking an old man with you," Gunnar said, hiking his thumb at Einar as he approached them.

"If he's old," Ulfrik asked, "then what am I?"

"A fool for not taking me," Gunnar answered. He laughed as he threw both arms wide for his father. His stump hand was wrapped in clean cloth, and it caused Gunnar no shame or shyness. It had been Ulfrik's great fear that the loss of his hand would make him timid, but instead it seemed to have emboldened him. Father and son embraced on the banks.

"Mother's still angry with you for leaving so soon," Gunnar whispered as they slapped each other's backs. "Try to say something nice before you leave her. No more fighting, eh?"

They stepped apart, Gunnar with his face red for admonishing his father and Ulfrik feeling heat in his own cheeks. Gunnar was referencing the colossal argument that followed Ulfrik's announcement of his journey. He was certain even Hrolf had heard it through the walls of his private guest room at the front of the hall. He met Gunnar's eyes and nodded.

"You will have complete command while I'm gone, but you're to leave the Franks alone. Konal will advise you on the hirdmen, and Snorri can help you with nearly anything. Listen to the old man, except when he's talking to himself. Your mother's a smart one, too. Lots of wisdom to support you while I'm away."

"I'll be fine. You should be careful. Only twenty men with you, that's hardly enough."

Ulfrik dismissed Gunnar's worry with a wave of his bloody hand, then wiped it off with the hem of his cloak. He waited as Einar said good-bye to his wife and daughters, then, once all were aboard the ship, he gathered his other children for their farewells. He had brave words for his sons and gentle assurances for his daughter. At last he came to Runa, who smiled sheepishly.

"It is the memory of that smile that will keep me until I return," he said, flashing his own smile. Runa covered her mouth, then leaned into Ulfrik. He folded his arms around her and buried her face in his shoulder.

"One day, you will not return. What will I do then?"

"Don't curse me, woman."

"Every man dies one day. But men who stand in front of enemy spears die sooner. How many more times before that spear pierces your heart?"

"Fate is everything. It can't be changed no matter how hard we pray otherwise. If an enemy spear is destined for my heart, it will find me whether I stand in the shieldwall or lie in my bed. I won't take foolish chances, nor make grand battle plans that risk my life. This is not my war, only my duty. I'll do it well, then come home."

"I know." She pulled back, her eyes glittering with tears. "But Snorri has an ill feeling in his heart."

"Not so strange for an old man's heart to feel ill."

"He saw two black ravens perched atop our hall the day Hrolf came with these two." Runa swept her hand toward Stein and Hrut's ship. "They lingered on the roof all day."

"The gods send us signs as sport, just to see what men will read into them. They must wager on who will create the scariest omens."

She thumped his chest and clucked her tongue. "You see favorable signs all the time, and you've been right. Don't dismiss the ones that trouble you."

"That's it; I'm not troubled." Runa cocked her head and squinted. Rather than let her vent any more worries, he grabbed her close and kissed her long enough to draw calls from the waiting men. She struggled, then relinquished. When they drew apart, she touched his cheek.

"Be safe, and I will be waiting for you," she said. "No later than Yule. That's your promise."

"One I will never break." He turned from her, winked at Gunnar who gave an approving nod, then finally met Konal and Snorri at the gangplank to the ship.

"No more bad omens," he said to Snorri. "You'll drive my wife mad."

"I see what I see, lad."

"Fine, but don't speak what you think, at least not about my doom. Now, watch after my family, old friend."

"And you watch after my son. He thinks he's too tall to get his head knocked off."

They embraced, then he gave his final instructions to Konal.

"Burn the ram once we're launched; share the meat however you want. Make sure Gunnar doesn't pick a fight with the Franks while I'm away. Gunnar's in charge, but I'm counting on you to keep his head straight."

"It'll be straighter than a plumb line, I swear." They laughed and embraced, then Ulfrik trotted up the gangplank. Men on shore launched the boat into the water, and, since they traveled against the current, oars extended out the tholes like the legs of a giant water bug. The blades swished into the river and Ulfrik watched his family from the aft.

Seeing Runa gathered with all his children, Snorri and Konal joining their huddled group, he suddenly felt as if he were leaving them forever. Konal placed a hand on Runa's shoulder as they waved a final time, and Ulfrik's ship disappeared around a bend in the Seine. He leaned against the gunwales, listening to the oar blades slap the water and thought of Snorri's two watchful ravens waiting atop his hall.

7

The ship nosed toward the riverbank, Hrut aiming for the dark group of figures on the shore. They were ragged and sodden, obvious victims of the raucous thunderstorm of the prior night. Their grim shapes caught an errant glint on patches of exposed mail from the pallid light suffusing the sky. Ulfrik stood by Hrut, hands eager to lay on the tiller. He had been so long landlocked that even a river journey excited his lust for the sea. However, the gathering of men held his attention.

"You're certain they're yours?" Ulfrik asked a second time.

"This is our territory," Hrut said, eyes never leaving the water. Men took up the long oars and prepared to prod the riverbed for rocks as they closed to the bank. "If they were Franks, we'd be filled with arrows now, wouldn't we? Besides, those are Gunnolf's colors on their shields. The yellow-haired giant is Kleng Flat-Nose, leads our scouts."

Folding his arms, Ulfrik said nothing more. A giant like Kleng seemed a poor choice for a scout, but he trusted Hrut's word. Stein Half-Leg was already waving at them from the bow. He supposed whatever news these scouts possessed would be worth hearing. Better he knew the situation before arriving in Gunnolfsvik.

Ulfrik had spent three days sitting on a chest lodged against the mast. Stein and Hrut took turns at the steering board, but it was easy work navigating a river. The rowers alternated their duties and thereby ensured swift progress. They had traveled west until reaching the Eure River confluence, where they turned south. The shallow draft of the longship meant it could sail in water shallower than the height of a man's knees. The rivers of Frankia were the Northmen's roads. Ancient Frankish kings had built low bridges to stop them, but on this journey Ulfrik noted at least three burnt-out ruins that must have once been these bridges and their towers, one only a few miles behind them.

Men prodded the riverbed with long oars as the ship safely navigated to the bank. The crew tossed ropes to the scouts, who hauled the ship onto the muddy sliver of bank. A gangplank splashed into the shallows and Stein Half-Leg jogged down to embrace the tall man named Kleng. Ulfrik shared a glance with Einar, and both gathered their cloaks tighter. Ulfrik touched the hilt of his sword, brushing the reassuring hardness of the pommel, then followed Stein off the ship.

Arm-clasping and back-slapping each man, Stein paused to introduce Ulfrik and his crew. Kleng inclined his head to Ulfrik, but guarded his welcome. He seemed more intent on sizing up Einar, who was his better in height and strength. "We heard you made the deal with Jarl Ulfrik," he said.

"News travels so fast?" Ulfrik shared an amazed look with Einar and Stein. "Then the Franks have heard as well."

"No doubt they have," Kleng agreed. His expression was solemn and he glanced at his companions. "There's news on that score. It's why I wanted to meet you here."

"Let's hear it, brother," Stein said. He waved Hrut down from the ship.

"We clashed with the Franks two days after you left for the north. Was a surprise attack on Gunnolfsvik. We beat them, as good a blood-letting as I've ever seen."

"That's great news," Hrut said as he jaunted down the gangplank to join them. "With our reinforcements, we can push into them instead of holding the line."

Kleng bowed his head. "We've made a truce with the Franks.

That's why we've been watching for you; don't want you clashing if you run into them along the way."

Ulfrik's stomach began to burn thinking of the wasted time and trouble he spent to travel south. He scowled at Stein, but he was intent on Kleng. His face was bright with bemused confusion.

"Why would we make peace if we bloodied them? Why not cripple them instead? It makes no sense, brother."

"Aye, well, it will in a moment." Kleng rubbed the back of his neck, and Ulfrik already anticipated the next words. He nearly matched in his mind what Kleng said next.

"Gunnolf was killed in the fighting, and your brother too. He died the next day. We won, but we gave our best to do it. We needed to call a truce until we knew of your success with Hrolf."

"Father is dead?" Stein asked, his voice rising. He grabbed Hrut's arm, who also stiffened at the news. "And Arni died with him?"

Kleng gave a heavy nod and his companions stared at their feet. Ulfrik turned to Einar, who let a brief grimace escape to confirm he shared the same doubts Ulfrik did. They both let a thick silence rule the moment, the croaking of frogs and the buzz of insects filling in. After a respectable pause, Ulfrik interjected.

"With Gunnolf and his son gone to the feasting hall, who negotiated the truce with the Franks?"

Stein looked up sharply at the question, a frown overtaking him. "Yes, who made that foolish choice?"

"It was Bjorn Hairy-Cheeks. He took over when no one else knew what to do?"

"Bjorn, small wonder." Stein spit the words like spoiled ale. "That coward was ever prepared to wave a hazel branch and beg peace. That's not how my father would've wanted it. My mother would've told him so."

Kleng straightened at the mention of Stein's mother, but no one else seemed to notice his worry. Ulfrik already mistrusted Kleng, and now he knew something else was bothering him.

"We should hurry home," Hrut said, gently shaking Stein's arm. "You can settle matters with Bjorn and Jarl Ulfrik can take over. Come on, we'll be home before nightfall."

The group broke up, and though Stein offered to take Kleng and his men aboard, they declined. They noted the crowd watching from the deck and decided they preferred the open air. Kleng helped launch the ship back into the river, and soon Hrut was steering it toward Gunnolfsvik.

In the final leg of the journey, Ulfrik spotted a wooden tower perched atop a cliff in the blue distance. Pine trees grew beneath it like dragon's fangs. Einar whistled, and Hrut laughed.

"It's the Frank's idea of a fortress, just a tower for them to frown down on us. We never let them build the rest of it, and once we surrounded them up there they gave up. It's empty most days."

"You could see for miles up that high," Ulfrik said. "You don't occupy it yourselves?"

Hrut shrugged. "Franks trap us in it just as easily. Maybe now that there's a truce, we can safely get up there. I'll take you to the roof if you like."

"I would," Ulfrik said, imaging he could see to the edge of the world from such a height. "Once I'm in command, we're going to burn it to the ground if we're not going to use it. I can't see the reason for letting our enemies have a stronghold so close to ours."

Hrut shrugged again and spit over the side. The remainder of the trip, Ulfrik spoke encouragement to his men and prepared them for their arrival. He wanted a sharp display of discipline that would inspire confidence, and encourage Bjorn Hairy-Cheeks to embrace Ulfrik as leader. He pulled Einar aside for a final word as Hrut glided the ship into the docks of Gunnolfsvik.

"If this becomes a spat between Bjorn and Stein's followers, we're leaving. We'll take this ship as payment for our troubles."

Einar smiled. "Neither will be pleased with a stolen ship, and one of them might have sense to guard it."

"Then we will go burn up that truce with the Franks and lead them back to Gunnolfsvik. That'll settle their differences for a while. And did you notice how Kleng seemed to be keeping something back from Stein? There's more going on than we know. Keep the men ready and near the ships until we know what's happening."

Dockhands caught ropes tossed to them and pulled the ship to its berth. Two other ships sat at dock, and berths remained for two more. Trees had been cleared back from the surrounding lands, creating a wide swath that swept back to stockade walls much like the black walls of Ravndal. Though only gone three days, the similarity summoned a pang of homesickness. Happy curls of smoke rose above it and birds circled overhead in a scene of perfect peace. If a battle had been fought, Ulfrik noted little in the way of damage or death. He guessed the Franks must have attacked from a different approach.

A throng of warriors awaited them, word having traveled ahead of their arrival. A tall but frail man with a beard that seemed to weigh down his head stood before them, and Ulfrik guessed he was Bjorn. Stein leapt the rails and stalked straight for the man, and Hrut followed in such haste that Ulfrik had to secure the steering board for him as he followed his master.

"Bjorn Hairy-Cheeks, what is this about a truce with the Franks?" Stein Half-Leg punched the air to emphasize his frustration. Bjorn had opened his arms in welcome, but quickly dropped them as Stein drew up to him. Their height difference made it seem like a child scolding his father, as Stein continued to holler. "You disgrace my father's and brother's deaths with your cowardice."

"Keep our men aboard ship," Ulfrik said. "I'll go down alone."

Bjorn and Stein exchanged calmer words once Hrut intervened, and Ulfrik could not hear them as he climbed the rails off the ship. Stein's crew followed, men sharing wary and confused glances with each other and the dockhands. All of them approached the waiting group as if approaching strangers. One crewman had his hand on his sword hilt, and Ulfrik began to consider there was more tension here than just upset over a foolish truce.

"It's not a permanent peace," Bjorn said as Ulfrik joined Stein's side. "Now that you have brought us Lord Ulfrik, we can renew the fight. It's nothing to be so angered about."

Bjorn turned a bright smile to Ulfrik and bowed with a grandness that betrayed its insincerity. In other circumstances Ulfrik would have rebuked the man, but given the bridling emotions, he only grunted at Bjorn. Instead, he focused on Stein. "There is never permanent peace with the Franks. Your servant is right."

He glanced at Bjorn when he called him a servant, but noted no change in the thin man's expression. It was a cold mask of a false smile buried under thick beard.

"We've given them time to recover. I want them smashed for good," Stein said, bordering on a whine. The note of petulance in his voice made Ulfrik wince. He had not considered that Stein might be a spoiled son of a petty jarl, and only now began to see a streak of immaturity peeking through his otherwise competent demeanor.

"Now that Jarl Ulfrik and his men are here we will burn out the Franks from this land." Again, Hrut put his hand on Stein's shoulder and shook him gently as he spoke. "For now, think on your family and the families of the men who died."

Stein paused, a slight color in his cheeks. "Of course. What would I do without you, Hrut? My brother and father must be laid to rest, and my poor mother needs me."

Bjorn lowered his head and the men with him shifted uneasily. Stein picked up on it, demanding to know what had happened.

"Your mother was so distraught at the death of your father and brother, she died upon hearing the news."

Stein stood with his mouth hanging open. No one knew what to say, least of all Ulfrik. He reflexively gripped the Thor's hammer amulet at neck, a shock of cold surprise filling his gut.

"That's impossible," Stein said. "My mother was stronger than that. She can't have died."

Bjorn did not answer, nor did any of his followers. Stein searched everyone's face, his eyes growing red and watery. Hrut placed two hands upon his shoulders and began to guide him away. He leaned into Ulfrik as he did.

"I will take him to the hall," he said. "Bjorn will see that you and your men are lodged in a clean barracks. We were to have a feast tonight, but perhaps we shall only have a light meal given this news. Forgive our rudeness."

"Do not trouble yourself with it," Ulfrik said. "See to Stein and do not worry for my comfort."

As Hrut left, he met Bjorn's expectant gaze, the sycophantic smile returned to his mightily bearded face. "Yes, don't worry, Jarl Ulfrik. I will see to you and your men."

But Ulfrik did worry.

8

The barracks were exclusive to his men, but far from clean. The musky scent of the last inhabitants lingered thick in the air. Even the sharp notes of fresh-burning logs in the central hearth did not dispel it. Lice crawled in the beds and the straw was rotten. All people lived like this, but Ulfrik had long grown accustomed to better beds with fewer bugs. He curbed his disdain, not wanting to appear above his men in their hardships. Yet he soon realized the men did not consider lice-ridden beds stinking of another man's sweat and piss as hardships. They flopped down their bags and themselves, tearing off boots and cloaks with exaggerated yawns.

"I've forgotten what it is to itch with lice," Einar said. "I should've thought to bring extra combs."

"And no women to help us pick out the bugs," Ulfrik said. "So I've got to settle for your fat fingers running through my hair. This is going to be a long campaign after all."

Einar snorted and swept the rotten straw off the bed. "They've been fighting the Franks. We can't expect them to have prepared anything better."

Ulfrik paused, drawing Einar's attention with his silence. He stuck his chin at the open door. "Come outside with me a moment."

Beyond the door, the fresh air hit him like a wet hand. The storm of the prior night had scrubbed Gunnolfsvik, leaving behind a fresh earthy scent. The townsfolk were at their business for the most part, though the majority seemed to be converging upon the mead hall atop a short hill. Einar gave him a quizzical look.

"Do you see any signs of this surprise attack that Kleng claimed happened recently?"

Einar stood straighter, scanned the buildings while his face grew more disbelieving. Ulfrik gave a weak smile.

"You don't see anything either. I've been telling myself the Franks hit from either the south or eastern approaches, but there are just too many trees there."

"We don't know the land," Einar countered, and Ulfrik shrugged in agreement. "They must have fought outside the walls."

"Then where are the bodies, the piles of broken shields, spear hafts, and bent swords? There's the smithy, but I don't see anything stacked outside."

"So it's around back. What are you saying?"

"I'm saying that my eyes do not see what my experience says I should. If we're being lied to, I want to know why. I'm going to demand a look at the battlefield. Let's find Bjorn."

Ulfrik started to move but Einar's hand restrained him. "Is that wise? Maybe we should see how things develop. Stein and Hrut have a lot to work out and our making trouble might set off more problems."

"We'd not be making trouble if there's a battlefield to show us."

Einar and Ulfrik stared at each other, but Ulfrik relented. The truth would likely not be anything more than a misunderstanding. "All right, we will wait to be summoned. But have a care for what goes on here and keep your sword ready. The death of Stein's family creates a gap for someone to grab leadership for himself. We don't want to be involved with it."

"Agreed. I'll make sure a watch is posted at every direction."

They continued to settle into their barracks and Ulfrik passed the afternoon conversing with his men while surreptitiously checking the main hall for any sign of activity. Not until late evening did Stein and Hrut return together. Seeing them approach with calm confidence released a knot that had held Ulfrik's stomach all day. He met them with Einar outside the barracks.

"Sorry for the rough quarters," Stein said. "You will be a guest in the main hall, but right now everything is—confusing."

"You have much weighing on your mind," Ulfrik said. Stein's gaze drifted past him to the horizon as if he were watching for something. Ulfrik followed his gaze, which caused Stein to shake his head.

"And sorry for my distraction. I can't believe what has happened while I was gone."

Ulfrik said nothing, hesitant to overplay his sympathy. If he were to make an army of these men, a soft demeanor would work against him. Instead he shifted his attentions to Hrut. "I want to see the battlefield where Stein's father bravely gave his life. Can that be arranged?"

"Why?" Hrut's brows drew together.

"Answer me without asking a new question." Ulfrik folded his arms, and Hrut exchanged a bemused glance with Stein.

"I'll ask Bjorn to take us tomorrow morning."

Satisfied, Ulfrik nodded. Einar shifted his stance and cleared his throat. "Was the battle fought at your walls? Kleng said it was a surprise attack."

"I wasn't there, was I?" Hrut replied, folding his arms as well. "But I heard it happened farther afield. Scouts picked up their approach and our men caught them in the open, out by the tower."

"A foolish risk to leave your walls," Ulfrik said.

Hrut and Stein both had no answer. Stein promised cooks to be sent to down to the barracks for the night and the next day they would hold a proper feast in the hall.

The meal was average and the women who served it were old, disappointing Ulfrik's warriors. The night passed without event, though Ulfrik found sleep difficult even with posted guards. Another terrible thunderstorm kept him awake. He had only begun to sleep when roosters crowed and announced the new day. He took the morning to tour Gunnolfsvik and was satisfied to find wreckage of battle: broken weapons and mail all piled up for repairs near the blacksmith's forge. During the tour, Ulfrik realized a young woman had been following him. When he decided to confront her, she darted away.

By midday Hrut had come prepared to show Ulfrik and Einar to the battlefield. They met outside the barracks where Ulfrik watched his men drill, more to dispel their fatigue of inaction than the need to practice.

"I will wear my war gear. Give me a moment to prepare." Ulfrik turned to enter, but Hrut grabbed his arm.

"If we leave now, we will still have time to climb the tower before dark. We should hurry."

Ulfrik frowned at Hrut's hand upon his arm until it fell away like a dead leaf from a branch. Without another word, he donned his mail and helmet and strapped on shield and sword. He would not be seen as anything less than a war leader, particularly not on a battlefield. He also suspected Franks could be in the area looking to recover bodies or gear, and did not want to be unprepared for a fight. He emerged from the barracks with Einar and another man named Hogni, who was nearly equal to Einar in height if not in strength.

"We'd provide an honor guard for you, Jarl Ulfrik." Hrut's eyes widened at the two giant men flanking him in their freshly scoured war gear.

"Then provide them. I will take whom I please."

The trek to the battlefield took little time. The battlefield was a clearing in the trees the Franks had to cross and stood in the shadow of the great hill and its jagged side. The tower seemed impossibly high from the ground. Stein wanted to see the spot where his father and brother had died, and one of the men showed him the ground. Ulfrik satisfied his doubts with a glance. Arrow shafts crisscrossed the grass; rust-red stains blotted the ground; water from the prior night's storm filled the ruts and holes where men had dug in their feet to hold their ground.

"If this is an approach the Franks use, then we must take care to have it watched once we renew our attacks." Ulfrik's obvious statements drew flat nods from Hrut and his men. Stein was still kneeling in the mud where his father had fallen.

"There's time still to climb that tower," Hrut offered. "Maybe we should allow Stein some time with his thoughts while we go."

Ulfrik had not been so high since walking the cliffs of his old home in Nye Grenner and the Faereyjar Islands. He relished the thought of seeing to the edge of the world, like he had on a clear day in Nye Grenner. "Is Paris visible from its height?"

"So they say," Hrut answered. "I've only been to the tower once and I didn't get to the roof. I'm as eager as you are to see it."

Sharing a smile with Einar and Hogni, he patted Hrut's shoulder. "Then let's be quick."

Two men remained with Stein, whose eyes were red and wet as he walked the battlefield that had claimed his kin. Three accompanied Ulfrik to climb the hill and reach the tower. Crumbled stone walls outlined the failed attempt at fortifying the location. The tower was backed up to the cliff, but he knew all too well from the siege of Paris that a tower like this was easily blockaded. The door had been removed from its hinges, ensuring no one would hole up in it. Hrut claimed patrols kept it clear of bandits and animals, though a bear had supposedly adopted it for a home one winter.

The inside was dark and empty. The bottom floor was of pounded earth, but subsequent floors were of old, stained wood. A moldy scent enveloped the place and the rain of the last two days had worked its way inside. At last they came to the top floor. The square room had one window to let in light, but it faced away from the high view. A single wooden ladder stood at the center to access the roof.

"Still glad you wore your mail for this climb?" Hrut smiled and Ulfrik laughed with him.

"I could swim the Seine in my mail," Ulfrik said, then cheerfully punched Einar in the shoulder. Despite his strength, he was red-faced and sweating after mounting the fourth floor.

"You first, Lord Ulfrik." Hrut held the ladder for him.

Wiping his forehead with the back of his hand, he set his shield aside then began to climb. Once within arm's length of the top, he pushed open the trapdoor and white light bathed him. "That air feels good," Ulfrik said as the clean smell of pine mixed with the stale interior.

He glanced down and saw Hrut just below him with Einar waiting to climb. As he continued, his hand gripped the final rung and felt something cold and gritty. Stopping, he looked at his palm. It was mud.

"Up you go, Lord Ulfrik," Hrut said cheerfully, but the push from below was anything but friendly. Hrut grabbed both his legs and shoved him through the hole. He landed half outside the trapdoor.

A shadow hovered over him, and he instinctively pulled himself through and rolled out of its way. White sunlight peering from behind dark rainclouds obscured the form closing on him, but he clearly saw the trapdoor slam shut and the figure stand atop it. Muffled shouts came from below.

Ulfrik was leaning on his sword arm, and rolled to free it. When he did, he could now see who stood over him.

For the first time in long memory, Ulfrik's guts turned to ice and he froze in place.

He knew the man, and knew death was at hand.

9

"Surprises like this come but once in a lifetime. A gift from the gods." The man's drawn sword flashed in the milky evening light striking the top of the tower.

"Throst! You gutless bastard! I've dreamed of your death a hundred times over." Ulfrik scrabbled away from Throst's feet. He heard the muffled combat below, clearly hearing Einar's voice.

"Have you enjoyed your stay in my new hall? Too bad it will burn down with your men inside." Throst's feet widened into a fighting stance and his sword lowered. He wore no mail nor carried any shield, not even a cloak. He was stripped to deerskin pants and a gray linen shirt. His bright face had acquired new scars and sharper features. Ulfrik remained on his back and had no chance to stand before Throst's sword would skewer him.

He rolled to his side, wishing he had taken the shield rather than leaving it below. As expected, Throst struck like a snake, but Ulfrik's mail turned the blow. Space on the roof was tight and the floorboards beneath him sprang like loose decking as Throst's foot landed next to him.

He lurched upright, hand searching for the sax sheathed at his lap. It was still hooked into the sheath and the moment he took to flick it free was enough for Throst to spin with animal ease, a deadly white line of his blade leading.

Flexing back, Ulfrik stumbled into the rail atop the tower. An idea flashed in his mind. If he let Throst charge him, he would step aside and throw him from the tower.

But instead of charging, Throst backed up with his sword lowered and maneuvered so the sun swallowed him from behind. He laughed and teased Ulfrik forward. "Come now, mighty Jarl Ulfrik. You showed me your plan when you stared at that railing. Did you think I would plan this far ahead only to be stupid enough to be thrown from this tower?"

"You were foolish enough to make me your enemy, and now Hrolf the Strider as well. I'll be doing you a favor when I slit your belly."

A horrible scream came from beneath the trapdoor. Ulfrik could not think on that battle, needing only to win his. Throst only laughed and continued to back up to the center of the square tower roof.

"Hrolf is not long for this land. I've no worries. The Franks are uniting and I'm on the winning side. Getting you in the bargain was a boon I could not pass. I'll be sure to send your head back to your wife. She can put it next to your son's severed hand."

Ulfrik roared and charged forward, sax held low in a double grip. Throst crouched as the sax stabbed up for his gut.

Throst kicked back with his leg, his heel catching a thin rope that now pulled taut across Ulfrik's path. It caught his legs as he drove his strike where Throst had stood. Careening forward, it was as if the world moved ensconced in ice. He felt his feet lifting off the ground, his free arm wheeling for balance. He staggered as he landed, and he forced his legs to pump back lest he crash on his face. He dropped his sax as his arm reached forward to keep himself upright. It all moved in crystal, icy slowness.

Then the world flipped and time resumed.

He had pushed too hard and now stumbled for the rails. He crashed into it, breaking the weather-beaten wood and plowing through it. His stomach lurched and his groin ached with the terrifying feeling of being in the air over a massive drop into dark treetops.

Both hands grabbed the edge of the roof before he plummeted. His arms felt like they would rip from his shoulders and his face slammed against the wooden side. For a moment, he held his breath and pressed his face to the rough wood. His hands were filled with splinters and he already felt them sliding away. He tried to pull up, but his mail coat was like another man clinging to his back. Unless he had help, he could do nothing but fall. Tilting his head back, his helmet had twisted on his face so that only one eye could see through the face guard.

He saw Throst squatting over him and laughing.

"Not what I had planned, but it will do. Death is death. I'd invite you to grab your sword before I send you to Valhalla, but I can understand why you wouldn't feel inclined at the moment."

"You fucking worm! Pull me up and finish this like a man. You've no honor, no pride at all?"

"Honor and pride? Interesting words and often inconvenient ideas. I was hoping to flatten you and put my sword through your back. Shattering you on the rocks below will have to do. Unlike what you think, I have plenty of pride. Long ago, you took my father from me, you took my home, you took my place in your hird. No one takes what is mine and gets away with it. So think on that in whatever time you've left."

"You'll never get away with this. Hrolf will crush you. My sons will be avenged."

"Your sons will have to live long enough for that, wouldn't they? Right now, a bunch of boys waving their wooden swords is not concerning. I have to admit, speaking to you like this has been more rewarding than my original plan. I'm glad we've cleared up matters. Now you die."

"I'll be avenged! You will—"

Throst's sword thunked into the wood of the tower and severed the little finger of Ulfrik's left hand. He lost his grip as he howled with pain. His right hand alone could not support his weight, the chain shirt an anchor stone that wanted to sink to the bottom of the sea. His hand came free and his guts felt as if they had piled into the back of his throat.

He plummeted down the cliff side, blood streaming from his left hand as it searched for his sword hilt.

Death awaited below in the crowns of dark pine trees.

10

In what seemed a lifetime ago, Ulfrik had fallen out of tree while playing with his brother in the woods surrounding his father's hall. The image of that day crystallized in his mind. He was no older than ten winters, still a lithe boy with no cares of the world beyond his forest playground. Sun shined through the canopy in blots of golden light. Birdsong filled the green spaces. His brother, Grim, clung to the foot of the tree too afraid to climb and Ulfrik had teased him. He reached for a limb that had seemed sturdy until he pulled on it. Suddenly he was plunging headlong to the ground with the limb in his hand. At the time he only remembered lying on his back, but now memory revealed how his hand flailed out to grab other branches to slow his fall. He had gashed his cheek on an exposed root, but his worst injury was the derisive laughter his brother had poured out over him.

Pain exploded across his shoulder, jarring him out of his dream. He was falling and struck the side of the cliff.

The pine treetops were flying at him like green spears.

Then his left leg caught an outcrop of rock and it crumbled like an old tent pole. He heard a snap and his vision went white. When it returned, he was plummeting into the pines face-first.

He remembered to extend his arms like he had a lifetime ago. A handful of pine branches tore through his grip as he rushed through the tops of the trees. The crack and rush of the top branches filled his ears.

Heavy limbs came next.

Crashing into one, he bounced like a leather ball into the trunk of another tree. He screamed, feeling a broken branch impale the meat of his left calf. His head clunked on the trunk, helmet taking the blow and spinning off his head.

The next branch caught him on his hip, but the velocity of his fall had already been broken. Rather than crash through it, he bounced to another branch that failed to hold him. He dumped the final distance down the long trunk, enduring a hundred rends and cuts to his exposed skin. His mail prevented his body from becoming impaled but had done nothing to lessen the crushing power of thick branches battering him.

He crashed to the ground on his left side, the branch driving deeper into his shoulder. He rolled a short distance until he slammed into the stump of a fallen pine tree.

The sky above had grown dark purple as the sun retreated and storm clouds threatened. Had the fall taken all afternoon? His vision blurred and his ears filled with a high-pitched ringing, and he realized he had passed out. Judging from the sky, he had been unconscious for hours, though to his mind no time had passed at all.

Nothing hurt. He struggled to raise his head, but he had sunk up to his ears in thick muck that sucked at him as he tried. It took nearly all his strength and raising his head made his head swim. The scene took a moment to understand. His left leg was bent above the knee and a dark stain appeared on his pants. His right leg seemed normal, but he could not move it. He could rotate his right ankle slightly, but his leg seemed unable to lift.

Bits of broken branches stuck out of his mail shirt, and both hands were ragged with bloody cuts. His left hand was completely coated in blood, and something about it bothered him. He could not think of what.

Overall, he was not too bad for such a fall. He expected he should get back to Einar and tell him all about it. He probably would not believe it either. With a sigh he attempted to sit up again.

Vomit ejected over his mail shirt and he fell back and turned his head to the side to expel the rest of it. He could not get up. He remembered his leg. Was something wrong with it? Yes, he had fallen and broken it.

What was he doing here looking at the ever darkening sky? Nothing made sense. He had to get back to Einar, that was his only thought. Einar needed him, but for what?

A burning scent wafted through the air. It was a light, pleasant scent. Ulfrik imagined a cozy hearth fire, so much better than the damp muck and wet pine needles encasing him. A fire. What about a fire?

It all flooded back in an instant: Throst, Einar and Hogni ambushed in the tower, the promise to burn Ulfrik's men in their barracks. He lifted his head again, only high enough to see the stump of his little finger. He dropped his head back down.

Voices. Distant voices drawing closer.

Throst had come looking for him, to find his body and hang it on the walls of Gunnolfsvik as a trophy. He tried to raise his head, to search for a weapon. He had lost his sax and sword in the fall. Throwing axes had been in his belt, but he could not move his right arm. He clawed the earth with his left hand, searching for a rock in the mud, anything for defense.

"Right where the gods marked," a voice exclaimed. Ulfrik lay flat, hoping no one would see him. It came from behind his head. "Do you see him there?"

It was a woman's voice, light and flush with excitement. A moment of relief drained away when he heard a man speaking as they drew ever closer.

"It's true. By the gods, Eldrid was right." The man's voice was even more astonished than the woman's.

Two faces crowded overhead. They were indistinct, wreathed in shadows, nothing more than human blurs. The woman ran her hands along his body, stopping at the lump in his broken leg.

Ulfrik opened his mouth and began to demand their names and intentions.

"I think he is trying to speak," said the man. He leaned his ear closer to Ulfrik's mouth. "Speak again, friend."

"Get back, Gudrod," the woman said. "He is worse than I imagined. We must bind his leg now."

The woman shoved the man called Gudrod aside, and her cool hands touched Ulfrik's face. She still remained indistinct, and the ringing in Ulfrik's ear was loud enough to overpower her voice. She pulled back the lids of his eyes, moving her head aside to let the light strike them and blind Ulfrik.

"His wounds have dulled his senses," she said, taking the hem of her cloak and wiping the vomit from Ulfrik's mouth. She continued to examine him. "This chain shirt is in the way. I need to see if he has any wounds on his back."

Ulfrik was vaguely aware of hands prying him out of the mud. His tongue was like swollen leather in his mouth and he could not form any words. He caught a flash of the woman's face. She was young, firm-jawed with smooth skin and a pixie face. Dark blond hair fell loose around her shoulders. She met his eyes for a moment as she worked on cutting away his pant leg with a small knife. A ragged white scar ran through her left eyebrow.

Hands let him down gently. "His back looks fine. No blood or anything stuck in him."

"This bone has to be set and braced before we can move him. His other leg is also broken. He's a mess. The two of us can't move him alone."

Their conversation echoed in his head as his eyelids began to droop. Sleep was overtaking him.

"Why move him at all? The gods can't have intended to send us a broken man."

A long silence ensued. He was about to drift into sleep when a terrible pain lanced through his leg. A muddy, hot hand had been clamped over his mouth to muffle his scream. His broken bone had been set, the only thing painful enough to cut through the numbness enveloping him.

Consciousness bobbed like driftwood on a choppy sea. Hands worked over him, binding and patching injuries, searching his body. At last the woman leaned close enough for him to kiss her.

"You will live," she said. "You are too heavy to move. I'll be back with help. We are going to cover and hide you. Anyone else who comes is an enemy. Make no sound or I assure you it will be your last. The jarls of Gunnolfsvik are dead. Some of our own betrayed us. Trust no one but me."

"Who ... you?" Ulfrik managed to croak the question.

"I am Audhild Brandsdottir. You are the storm god's gift to me and my people. We will see you whole again, I promise. For now, be patient."

She pulled back and dripped water into his mouth, only enough to wet his parched throat. Placing her cloak over him, she stood and the man named Gudrod began to cover him with pine branches. For a moment, Ulfrik felt like they were building a pyre for him, but the wood was wet and thick with sap. The cloying pine scent nearly gagged him.

"He just can't be the one," Gudrod said, the disappointment clear in his voice. "He's almost dead."

"Cease your questioning," snapped Audhild. "You heard Eldrid. Now let's go while there's still light to see. We can't leave him here much longer."

Footfalls across the branches and sucking mud retreated into the distance. Beneath the cloak and pile of branches, Ulfrik could hardly move. He imagined a mountain of limbs piled over his head and wondered how Einar would find him. Scrambled thoughts rose and fled through the ringing emptiness of Ulfrik's head. Nightfall was at hand, but his own darkness came before it.

11

In the depth of the night when crickets chirped and owls called, Ulfrik awoke to a flaming, body-encompassing pain. He cried out, forgetting the admonition to make no sound. A thousand needles sewed agony up both of his legs. Every beat of his heart pulsed suffering into his limbs. His head and eyes throbbed, and he felt as though wire had been wound tight over his brows.

He was still stuck in the mud and buried beneath branches, and he grunted as he struggled against the haphazard pile. Pine needles fell into his eyes and mouth and he cursed, then stopped for fear of drawing wolves to himself. Despite the cloak he was cold. The damp of the earth seeped up through his mail into his body, which absorbed it like a rag left in a puddle. In this moment of clarity, he realized Einar and Hogni were dead. All twenty of his men were burned alive, just as Throst had promised. Hadn't the woman named Audhild confirmed it for him? He had smelled the smoke of the burning hall.

Worse now than any pain was the thought of the men he had led into a trap. Einar had been like son to him. He cursed his wakefulness and wished for the bliss of dreamless sleep. Better still, he wished he had died if it somehow could have spared his men, or Einar at least.

Tears leaked down his face, rolling into his ears as he lay facing the patch of stars visible through the lattice of branches.

Eventually his wakefulness faded again, and he passed out. Just as suddenly his eyes fluttered open. He did not remember closing them. A myriad of triangles and rectangles of faint light hovered over his eyes. The predawn light seeped through his blanket of pine branches.

Sounds of cracking branches drew nearer, and Ulfrik held his breath at murmured voices gathered over his pile. Branches lifted away, dropping more needles onto his face and releasing the cloying pine scent to escape. Cool air washed over his skin, but instead of refreshing him it heightened the ache permeating his body. The woman from the prior day reappeared over him as indistinct voices spoke behind his head. Her cold hand touched his cheek and she smiled at him. Her voice was a whisper.

"I've brought something to ease your pain. We are going to move you before the Franks come searching at first light."

She searched through a hide pack at her side, producing a wooden bowl that she placed to the side. Ulfrik could hardly turn his head to see what she placed in it, but he heard fluid splashing. He felt the press of others standing close to him. A man's voice, hoarse with the effort of keeping it low, spoke just over his head.

"Are you sure about this one?"

"He came from the sky as Eldrid foretold." Ulfrik saw the woman whose name he could no longer remember pause to jab a thin finger at the tower. "The gods marked this place. Gudrod knows. We do not question what the gods chose to send us."

No more voices protested, but others continued to lift away branches. He heard one voice mention covering their tracks from the Franks. Another mentioned Ulfrik's helmet. The swish of the branches overpowered their conversations. He guessed there were at least four other men accompanying the girl.

"Drink this," the woman said, and proffered a bowl as she gently cupped his head forward. It smelled like bile and Ulfrik recoiled. Her hand did not yield. "The pain will be great when we move you. This will dull it. Drink."

The cold fluid was bitter and slimy in his mouth, but he gulped it.

He had no choice other than trusting these people; they could do no worse to him than Throst would and seemed determined to keep him alive. Almost instantly his tongue and lips numbed, and he grew weak and heavy. The woman monitored his face beneath her furrowed brow, the white scar above her eye pulling down. She was not as young as he had thought, but a woman of at least nineteen or twenty years. He had no more time to judge her appearance, for whatever she had fed him made his body melt. His head fell back and his jaw slackened.

"That's good," the woman said, carefully placing his head back into the muck. "He's ready. Let's be quick."

The drink had rendered him limp and numb, but he was aware of the activity around him. He felt hands working at his belt, pulling down his pants. True to the woman's word, he was numb but not without pain. As someone worked his pants off, both legs blazed in hot agony. He wanted to scream but found himself unable to form more than a gurgle of protest. Cold air washed over his exposed leg as the woman examined his naked lower body. She tightened bandages and checked the splints on his legs. Ulfrik hadn't realized his legs had been braced, even if crudely done with branches and linen.

The sun was approaching the horizon and now Ulfrik could see the men surrounding him with greater clarity. One stood waiting at Ulfrik's feet, staring pensively at him. He wore the clothes of a slave, but was strong and tall and with a full head and beard of blond hair that had grayed at the temples. The woman moved in between them, and she began to lift away Ulfrik's chain shirt. The pain jarred him as she wrestled with it.

"This shirt has been a burden from the start," she muttered. "Help me get it off."

Hands lifted Ulfrik on both sides, and his head flopped forward like his neck had broken. Drool spilled out of his mouth as he struggled to lift his head, but had no power to do it himself. His shoulder burned deep in the tissue as the woman and another man worked off the shirt. It caught on his face, the scent of iron thrusting into his nose as they finally lifted it off. The shirt crunched into the mud beside Ulfrik's head, and they laid him back. They stripped him of his armbands, rings, even his Thor's hammer necklace. He was completely naked now, and no one thought to cover him. A desperate cold filled him as the group sorted out his clothing.

"Take off your clothes," the woman said to the slave. "Put on his. The mail, too."

The slave stared at her a moment, then moved out of Ulfrik's sight. His heart pounded in his chest, confused at what these people had planned for him. He stared at the stale sky above, until the woman leaned next to him and whispered in his ear. Her sweet scent was a welcome relief from pine and mud and her breath was wet against the side of his face.

"We must leave the Franks something to find, or they will know you survived the fall. Wait a moment longer, and all will be clear."

She gingerly positioned his head for him to see the slave struggling to wear his armor. Two men helped with it, and another stood by with a sharp rock held low in both hands. When the shirt was in place and the belts strapped around the slave's waist, the woman hung Ulfrik's necklace over his head. They worked on arm bands, and one of the men corrected the number and placement on each arm. Rings were slipped onto the correct fingers. When finished, Ulfrik wanted to sneer at the man. He looked like a slave wearing his clothes. Did these people think mail and gold armbands made a jarl of his standing? They were sorely wrong.

The man dressed as Ulfrik knelt in the mud. "You will keep your promises?" he asked. "My sons will be freemen?"

"They will," said the woman, and the other men nodded in agreement. Nothing more passed between the slave and the others.

The man with the rock hoisted it overhead and stepped behind the slave. He slammed it down on the slave's head, collapsing him to the ground. The slave's head bent sideways and blood flowed out of his nose. Immediately the other men began to beat him with heavy limbs, clubbing him like a seal stranded on a beach. The slave suffered the injuries with nothing more than a moan. Ulfrik wanted to turn his head away, but was powerless to do more than stare and drool as this man died. The killing of a slave did not disturb him, but what it portended for his future with these people did.

"That looks like he fell through the trees," said the man named Gudrod. The woman watched impassively, but said nothing. She swept the men aside with an outstretched arm. She held a freshly broken branch in one hand.

"The wounds have to match the blood on his clothes." Gripping the spear-like branch with both hands she rammed it into the slave's leg. He jerked with the pain, apparently still alive. The woman did not stop, but leaned with both hands on the branch to drive it through the meat of the leg. Ulfrik was suddenly glad he had only broken his leg rather than suffer the impaling he witnessed now.

She stepped back, out of breath. The slave's hand was balled tight, though Ulfrik did not think the others saw it. She gave a tired gesture to the man with the rock. He straddled the slave and lined up his rock to his head.

Then he bashed the man's face into bloody pulp. When finished, blood and brains had splattered over his arms and chest. The others watched as they erased the man's identity, making it easier for Throst to believe that it was Ulfrik's body and not a replacement. Ulfrik considered it might work, now that the head was little more than a collapsed pocket of hair and gore.

The group raised Ulfrik out of the muck and began to dress him in the slave's clothing. As cold and sore as he was, he welcomed the rough wool over his body. He was still numb and had no control over himself, but he felt the cold as sharply as a blade to his flesh. Once they had finished, the men lifted him onto a litter they had set beside him. The sky had brightened considerably, and while Ulfrik heard nothing, all of the men turned as one toward a point beyond Ulfrik's vision.

"This is earlier than expected," said Gudrod. "Move fast."

"We've got to cover these tracks. The damned mud—"

"Do your best," said the woman. "Get this body into the hole."

Ulfrik heard her grunt as she helped move the body, presumably into the hole he had made in the soft earth. He heard the mail crunch as the body rolled into it.

"We didn't cut off his finger," the woman said, her voice flat. "He's missing the little finger of his left hand."

"Gods, they're coming straight here," said Gudrod. Ulfrik still could not hear anything, but everyone had grown agitated, their movements hurried. They constantly looked over their shoulders at the same direction.

"Shit, my knife is too dull," said the woman. "Give me something sharper. Quickly."

Gudrod shook his head and stomped out of Ulfrik's sight. Two other men each lifted an end of the litter and began to jog away.

"Forget it," he heard Gudrod say. "It's close enough. We've got to cover these tracks now or we're done."

"We can't risk something so obvious," the woman said, but the litter bearers carried him beyond hearing the response. He jostled along, watching the sun stain the gray sky as the argued details of his faked corpse faded away. While in as much danger for being caught as the others, his numb state made him feel more like an observer than anything else. He hoped his rescuers would get away, but if they did not then it just did not matter. Ulfrik realized he was dead either way.

12

Sleep and delirium were Ulfrik's twin keepers. A terrible, winter cold set him shivering from the inside. Ice water poured from his skin. He fell endlessly from the tower, slamming into the cliff face, smashing through branches, and plowing into the mud. Over and over. His guts lurched and his body wailed with the pain each time he fell. Sometimes, he was not falling from the tower. Instead, he plummeted off the walls of Paris, forced over the sides by pig-faced demons in Frankish surcoats. Other times, giant sea gulls picked him off the cliffs of Nye Grenner and dropped him into the sea. Still other times he fell through total blankness, never landing anywhere.

Hot, smooth hands touched his face. He opened his eyes but saw nothing but muddy darkness and vines of smoke growing among rafters above him. Cold fluid slipped from a bowl held to his lips as a woman's voice whispered in his ear. Then numbness and the relief of dreamless sleep.

How many days fled in dark and madness, he could not reckon. Fractured scenes of faces staring into his, men and women studying him like he was either a mound of gold or a heap of trash. Sometimes he awoke to find children staring at him. Once he swore Aren and Hakon stood at his bedside, if indeed he was on a bed—he did not know—and they shook their heads in silent reproof. Aren placed a rock by his bedside, as he had done for Gunnar when he had lost his hand. In a blink his sons were gone and he was staring at the rafters once more. A dream.

In a moment of clarity, or at least a moment without confusing visions, a group of people appeared around him. His body pulsed with pain, which he had rarely felt in his delirious condition. Mournful, grave faces ringed him and were lit only with the dancing light of a candle held outside of his view. The shadows danced around their frowning mouths, adding a judgmental cast to their expressions. The woman who had saved him, Audhild, stood at his feet. She was dressed in fine clothes of russet and green, and silver rings glittered from her hands folded at her lap. A string with a key hung from her belt, a symbol that she ruled the hall and was most likely the wife of a jarl. She did not smile when his eyes met hers, only reflecting a yellow point of flickering candle flame back at him.

He realized he had moved his head to see her, something he had not done since his fall. The effort of holding his head up exhausted him, and he let it fall back into a pillow. Next he tried to move his legs, but found them too heavy and painful to shift. A blanket covered most of him and it felt as heavy as lead. He started inventorying the rest of his body, flexing his hands and feeling the burn of where his finger had been severed. Rotating a shoulder to have it burst into hot agony.

All heads turned to face a sudden light, and Ulfrik heard a door open. He let his head flop toward the source, but a woman blocked his view. Two people stepped away, and into their place came another woman. She was willow-branch thin, dressed in an ill-fitting gray wool dress cinched at the waist with a frayed leather strap. A necklace of bones clattered across her chest as she leaned over Ulfrik. A bony, blue-veined hand extended to his arm and lightly brushed his skin. He was cold, but she was colder still. His eyes were now hot and watery, blurring the scene into a smeary haze. Yet he did not doubt what he saw. The woman's eyes were covered with a dirty binding of gray cloth which disappeared beneath long, greasy locks of faded blond hair. Then he noted a staff clutched in her other hand. She was blind.

A long hiss escaped her thin lips as she moved her hand along Ulfrik's body, touching his injures beneath the blanket. Her fingers lingered over his broken legs and her head cocked as if listening to distant voices. Sometimes she nodded as if agreeing, and other times she waved her hand as if shooing away a fly. Ulfrik was too weak and too painful to inquire. His mouth was full of wool and he wished for nothing more than a drink as the woman examined him. The other figures around the bed waited in silence. At last, she stood back and rested on her staff.

"He is the one from my visions," she said with a firm but rough voice. Ulfrik was reminded of barnacles being scraped from an old hull. The men and women exchanged cautious glances, and several stole looks at Ulfrik staring up at them from his bed.

"Eldrid has verified this man," intoned Ulfrik's caregiver, Audhild. "He was at the place Thor marked. We will have success."

A weight seemed to lift from the room, and Ulfrik noted how some postures relaxed and heard a woman standing behind him let go of her held breath.

"You did not say the gods would deliver a broken man." The protester's voice was familiar to Ulfrik, the same man who had argued with Audhild beneath the tower.

"Gudrod, you lack belief," the blind woman, who Ulfrik guessed was Eldrid, tipped her staff across Ulfrik's body at Gudrod opposite. "Yet here is exactly what I promised: a champion thrown from the sky, delivered by the storm god Thor, to lead us in safety and bring us the favor of all the gods. With this one among us, we cannot fail."

Voices murmured approvingly, but Ulfrik was already slipping away. Sounds echoed in his head as he strained to listen and his blurry vision grew darker. Audhild watched him as if she did not recognize his suffering, merely tapping a silver-ringed finger on her arm as she observed. She now was a smear of brown and green with gleaming splotches in his vision. Still her echoing voice was clear when she finally interrupted the general chatter.

"Broken or not, Eldrid has foretold all this. His fever must break before we can move him, but while we wait I expect all of you to prepare."

"What is his name?"

Heads turned to Eldrid, who stiffened at their stares. "The gods speak through me and their visions grant me no rest. You must fulfill what the gods have shown, or perish in the attempt. Do not trifle with small matters. Names are unimportant."

"Ulfrik," he managed to squeeze out his name. While he had his mind and strength, these people needed to know him. He prayed they would recognize they could claim a reward from Hrolf for returning him home. Had they wanted a bounty from Throst, they would have left him beneath the tower.

The blind woman Eldrid lowered her head to his ear. A scent of ale was strong on her wet breath. "Save your strength, champion. The gods will reveal their purpose for you soon enough." She placed thin, pale fingers over his neck and dropped her voice even lower. "If I say names are unimportant, then they are unimportant."

Her ragged, chewed nails dragged across the coarse flesh of his neck as she straightened herself. Though blindfolded, she appeared to stare at him through the dirty cloth. "We are done here. Let our champion take his medicine and rest."

13

Days and nights were erased. Ulfrik knew only restless dreams or painful wakefulness, which rotated in a maddening cycle. Men and women attended him, feeding him beer and broth, changing buckets of his waste, and rotating him in his bed. Always Audhild came with that terrible brew that rendered him numb but motionless for hours at a time. She also oversaw the progress of his wounds and ensured bandages were changed on schedule. This all happened in a timeless space where he floated in a bed, alternately staring at rafters or at a wall remarkable only for its lack of any features.

When he could speak, no one answered his questions. Some of the women recoiled at his attempts, dropping whatever they were doing to fetch Audhild who came with her brew. Despite fighting her, she managed to force him to take enough to slacken his resistance, then she would coo to him like a child. If she intended it as a reward for his compliance, it only fired his rage at being helpless. The relief from pain was welcomed, but not the destruction of his will.

Today no one came to him and the numbness and stupor induced by Audhild's brew retreated. His eyes were still clouded and a wailing ring still afflicted his hearing, but his senses lifted out of the fog for the first time since falling from the tower. It was as if a heavy cloth that had wrapped his body uncoiled and fell away. Immediately he was aware of a tremendous soreness in both legs. He raised his head to look at them, but the shifting of his body made both legs feel as if a spear had been driven through each one. Water came to his eyes and he flattened himself again. The wracking pain coursed through his hips and down into his toes. After a few moments it subsided and his breathing normalized. He dared a careful peek at his left shoulder, which was bandaged with a clean white cloth dotted with brown spots. His left hand also throbbed, but he had no desire to see his missing finger.

Now his consciousness spread. The house was no longer a void that held only a bed, but a lived-in place. Signs of previous lives were everywhere from the square hearth filled with ashes to the table laid with plates and mugs and a flickering fish oil lamp. A child's toy spear, capped with a leather head, lay forgotten in the dirt floor by the side benches. Hanks of animal hair curled into balls that hid in corners and beneath benches. Daylight registered with him. The smoke hole flap was tied open and yellow light flowed in. He had just noticed, though the opening had been uncovered since he had awoken.

Taking note of such simple things renewed him. Still too painful to move, he at least realized he was not careening through the darkness alone. His bed was actually a table made more comfortable with a padded down blanket beneath him. His broken legs ensured he would never move enough to fall. A section of table had been broken away between his legs, presumably for him to eliminate waste. Overall, the people caring for him understood exactly what he needed. Once recovered and returned to his family, he would reward them for saving his life.

Through the log walls, Ulfrik heard voices. Audhild's brew had dissipated enough for his awareness to extend beyond the tight circle around his body. He relished the sounds of a village about its business. A dog barked, and Ulfrik realized it was just outside his door. Perhaps a guard? Then the door, which was behind his head, opened and he heard a man and woman speaking hurriedly. He decided to feign sleep and learn what he could.

The first voice was Audhild's. "You must never speak of this to your masters. Do you understand?"

"Don't lecture me on loyalty," answered a rough, time-worn voice. Not daring to open his eyes, Ulfrik imagined a gruff veteran with a face craggy enough to match his voice. "I came to you, didn't I?"

A short silence followed, and Ulfrik felt the two of them come to his side. Audhild eventually spoke, "I'm sorry. You're right of course. So, this is the one."

"Is he dead?"

Audhild laughed. "He's asleep. His wounds are horrible. Look at the swelling." Ulfrik felt Audhild's cool hands lifting away his blanket to display his legs.

"Can't even see where his knees are," the man said. Ulfrik consoled himself knowing he no longer needed to struggle to see them.

"This one is broken in two places, but this one the bone cut through his flesh. There are broken ribs on his left side, and his shoulder was dislocated. His left hand is missing a finger. He was riddled with splinters."

The man whistled through his teeth. "What's this supposed to be, his face?"

Audhild laughed. "Don't be cruel. The swelling will take time to go down. He might be a handsome man when it does."

"I doubt that. He's old, but tough. Look at the scars. He's witnessed a fair bit of fighting. Either that or he once fell into a pile of swords."

Again they laughed, and Ulfrik calmed himself at the jokes made at his expense. Only now did he realize how puffy and heavy his face felt. He imagined looking like a bruised walrus. They sat quietly until the man spoke softly.

"Is this really what you want to do?" Ulfrik heard a rustling he took to be Audhild nodding her head. The man sighed. "The Franks have left you alone longer than they've wanted. They're coming tomorrow and taking your menfolk."

"We're not ready. He's not ready to be moved."

"Then leave him."

"The gods have decreed otherwise. He must remain with us, and he cannot be moved without risking more injury."

Again a silence stretched almost to the point where Ulfrik opened his eyes. Then the man shrugged. "Girl, I've done all that I can for you. I'm with the Franks now, like it or not. Your father would've been proud of your spirit, but he'd tell you what I'm telling you now. Do not trust the words of the gods, even if you hear those words for yourself. They never give a gift. There is always a price."

"Eldrid has foreseen all of this. Right to the very place I found him. The price the gods demand is we take their worship to new lands, out of this place that the Christian god wants for himself. Away from any master but ourselves."

"And Eldrid."

"Don't mock me, Uncle."

Ulfrik could no longer resist peeking, but found the other man out of his sight. He closed his eyes, hoping to learn more of his situation. Yet their discussion ended abruptly.

The dog began barking wildly only moments before the door crashed open. Ulfrik opened his eyes out of reflex, in time to see Audhild leap back with her pale hand over her chest. Men were shouting at each other in confusion, all behind Ulfrik's head. He struggled to turn to the sound, but the pain in his shoulder and legs arrested him.

"And here is your real leader," said a familiar voice. "Along with an unexpected visitor."

The rough-voiced man grunted. "Visiting my niece, is all."

"Strange timing," said the familiar voice. "I picked the same day to visit."

"I tried to stop him," interrupted another. Ulfrik recognized him as Gudrod. He hissed at the pain and braces preventing him from facing the people behind him. Only Audhild remained in his sight, and her eyes were wide with shock and staring at the others. Voices jumbled together in a loud argument that was finally settled when he heard the rasp of a drawn sword.

"Enough of this!" the familiar voice shouted. "Your decision to visit your niece," the words were twisted into a curse, "made me decide to step up my plans. You can help me recruit the men of this village to our forces."

"No, you cannot do that," Audhild said. Ulfrik noticed as she held the speaker's gaze she surreptitiously guided her hand to the table and grabbed a knife that had been under Ulfrik's leg. She palmed it flat to her hip in a smooth motion, her eyes never flinching.

"This sword and my men say that we can. This village has sat on the border for too long, and we need men to fill the ranks. Anyone over the age of fourteen is coming with me. Now."

"We will never work for the Franks," Gudrod said. He heard feet shifting across the dirt floor, and heard two more swords drawn. He had no idea how many men were above his head nor whose side they were on. Again he cursed his immobility.

"You will work for Throst. He's no Frank."

A fire ignited in Ulfrik's gut at the name. In the same instant he recognized the voice, the man leaned over him and stared into his face.

"What happened to this one?"

"A bear attack," Audhild said.

The man staring down at him grimaced in disgust. "Looks more like an anvil was dropped on his face."

He turned aside, and the tension drained out of Ulfrik's body. Standing just inches from him, back turned to Audhild as she began to raise her knife, was Hrut Magnusson: the whoreson who had betrayed Ulfrik to Throst and who deserved an ignominious, painful death.

"If the broken man lives we'll come back for him. Otherwise, round up the others. You too, Uncle."

Audhild struck with bared teeth. She brought her knife around Hrut's neck, digging it up to his throat. "Anyone moves and I'll slit him open."

Hrut laughed and began to step out of her feeble grip, which he could have done easily. Two more blades suddenly rested on his gut. He had not even worn his mail, such was his arrogance. Hrut stopped and raised his hands.

"Tell your men to stand down," Gudrod said. Ulfrik could not see beyond Hrut, but the dark wave of fury on his face was a balm to the fiery anger Ulfrik felt. After a tense pause, Hrut gave a curt nod and he heard two swords drop. Audhild stepped back, but kept the knife at the base of his spine.

"Uncle, you've decided to come with us after all."

"Not without my family."

"You'll pay for your betrayal," Hrut said. Now Gudrod stepped into view and dragged Hrut's arms behind his back, where Audhild wound bandage cloth around his arms to secure him. All the while, a sword point poised at this throat. Audhild's uncle said nothing.

In moments, Hrut and his men were bound. Audhild stood over Ulfrik, as if recognizing him for the first time. She whispered to him. "We must move you now. The pain will be great."

"I will be fine," he said, his voice a hoarse croak that surprised even him.

Audhild shook her head. "Drink the medicine, if only to easy your pain this final time. There will be no more of it once we leave."

Gudrod interrupted, pulling her up. "I can have the ships loaded and launched by midday, but we've not gathered everything we'll need."

"No time," Audhild said. "Why have you not prepared as I asked? We should be ready for this, not scrambling at the last moment."

Blushing, Gudrod mumbled something about secrecy making his life too hard. Audhild had no patience for it, and pushed him away.

"Excuses are worthless to me," she said. "We leave now, with whatever we can carry. I will ask Eldrid to beg the gods for a favor."

"I thought that was his role," Gudrod stabbed an accusing finger at Ulfrik, but Audhild only glared at him. Hrut climbed out of his purple fury to stare at Ulfrik with a raised brow. Gudrod shook his head and left.

"Uncle, I'm sorry for this." Audhild and her uncle bound Hrut and his three men to support beams while fresh guards with spears entered after Gudrod exited. One held a snarling dog by a rope. It snapped at Hrut, who spit in return.

Once they were secured, Audhild assured Ulfrik she would fetch his medicine. She left him with the guards and Hrut. Ulfrik stared hard at the treacherous bastard and dreamed of cutting out his heart. He could neither speak nor move, but his mind was alive with promises of vengeance. *I hope they keep you well, Hrut. Just live long enough for me to cut out our lying tongue before I pop your eyes and open you from crotch to neck.*

Hrut stared blankly back at him, not recognizing the swollen, smashed face of a man he believed he had killed.

14

True to her promise, Audhild administered a draught of the slimy, bitter medicine that removed all pain but plunged Ulfrik into stupor. While he waited for this medicine, he learned little more than he already understood: a long-standing plan for the villagers to flee had to be stepped up. Hrut had arrogantly arrived with only a handful of men, anticipating a compliant if surly crowd. He had not expected an organized resistance that had been armed and forewarned. "Your ships won't make it to the open sea," Hrut said. "We'll run you aground and cut off your heads before nightfall."

"That's why you'll be a hostage," Gudrod had explained. "We'll drop you ashore once we're certain no one is following."

The consternation etched into Hrut's face was the last satisfying sight Ulfrik could remember before Audhild coaxed the medicine down his throat.

A series of bright lights and hard bumps jarred him soon thereafter. A dull ache penetrated the heavy numbness induced by the medicine. Awareness extended to a circle at the edge of his body, and when he finally regained himself after what could have been days or only hours, he was tied down to a litter that had been secured to the decking of a ship. Clouds glided overhead and dark tree branches sped through the periphery of his vision.

Again he tried to lift his head, but a bolt of pain shot through his legs and he stilled. He decided rushing things was pointless with two broken legs and a wrecked shoulder. Instead he rotated his head slowly to judge the size and condition of the ship. The deck planks were bright and close-fitting. High sides and a wide belly indicated he was on a knarr, a ship built for trade and ocean travel. He heard the splashing of oars and one deep snort of air filled his nose with the wet earth scent of a river.

Before he could determine more, his stomach lurched and he barely turned away to eject watery vomit on the clean deck. The constant stream of medicine made his guts bloat and gurgle. Judging from the odors in his beard, he had vomited previously but had no memory of it. A rough voice cracked a laugh.

"So the first stain upon your deck is a swine-herd's puke. Fits you fools perfectly."

Ulfrik spit the last from his mouth, a string hanging from lips to the deck. He grimaced at the ripples of pain washing over him from the stress of vomiting. He grunted, angry that even throwing up was too much of an effort. When recovered, he rolled his head to the other side and saw Hrut seated against the high sides of the ship, both hands bound behind his back. He stared at that pinched face and fat head with its flattened nose and wondered how he had never seen the deceit radiating from it. If the gods had ever chosen to demonstrate the countenance of mistrust, it would be small-faced Hrut. Ulfrik blinked and looked away.

"You are awake." Audhild's voice was thin in the open air. She knelt beside him, and dabbed a rag at the corners of his mouth.

"How long?" he struggled to ask.

"Long enough to kill me through boredom," Hrut answered. "My brothers' vengeance will be doubly violent for it."

"I'll replace the gag if you don't still your tongue. Remember our deal." Audhild met Hrut's gaze over Ulfrik's body. He could not see Hrut's reaction, but silence ensued and Audhild returned to cleaning Ulfrik. A soft murmur of voices came from behind, though the loudest sounds still remained the rowing. He was in the prow of the ship, the crew and passengers all behind his head.

"How many?" Ulfrik could not complete his question, and she tried to calm him with a hand on his chest. He insisted on asking again.

"Sixty-two in both ships, plus livestock in the other. For all you don't know, that's a strange question. Why?"

Ulfrik shrugged. He did not know. In truth, it was the shortest question he had strength to ask that provided information. The medicine still clung to him like a bad dream and he was not yet fully in the world. The pain in his legs was only a dull ache and the throbbing of his body was less pronounced. His mind was not yet his own, and random thoughts still blotted out his waking world. He slipped into a momentary daydream of playing in the forest when he was a child. Boughs passing overhead reminded him of it and soon his thoughts were gone. When he came around, Audhild was already stepping away.

He lay on the deck, enjoying the fugue state between his medicine wearing off and the waking world. When the last of it surrendered its hold over him, the pain from the rocking deck hit him. Such gentle swaying would not bother a normal person, but shattered bones of an old man were like shards of glass in his legs. The stabbing agony cycled in and out, and for a long time he fought to make peace with it. From past experience tending the wounded after battle, he knew a serious break would be months in healing, and at his age might never heal at all.

Finally a shadow draped him and he opened his eyes to find the blind woman standing over him. She wobbled with the rowing, using her staff for balance. Ulfrik chuckled, knowing if the woman could not handle river travel the sea would send her sprawling. Then the thought of sea travel hit him, and the thought of traveling anywhere by boat concerned him. Where were they taking him and why? That was a better question to ask Audhild.

The blind woman—Eldrid, he recalled the name out of the fog of recent memories—smirked as if she had read his thoughts. Ulfrik considered maybe she had.

She leaned forward, blotting out the sun behind her so that she seemed a giant black shape of wild hair and rags. Her voice was low and rough.

"You are the one from my visions. Yes, I am blind, but the gods allow me to see all manner of things. Things no small mind like yours could ever understand." Her arm swept over him as if she were swiping away clutter between them. "They showed me the plan for our people in that vision."

A dozen questions crashed behind Ulfrik's clenched teeth. The cycle of pain hit him again, worse than anything he had felt in days. It was a horrid spike of agony that lanced up his body to coil around his mind. He arched his back in the struggle against it. Eldrid continued, her voice dropping lower.

"You must obey me as all others obey. You must serve the gods that speak through me. To defy me is to defy them. Ask Audhild if it is not so. Ask your shipmates what curses await those who do not heed me. The gods have decreed that the man from the sky must forever remain with our people. Odin spoke to me through the fishes of the river, and said as long as the sky-man's heart beats among his people so will prosperity follow in all they undertake. Heed me well, sky-man. The gods demand it of you."

The coiling pain released, and Ulfrik realized Eldrid had been leaning her staff on his broken left leg. He wanted to growl in fury and crack the staff over the woman's head. Instead he flattened against the litter, sweat oozing from his flesh and breath ragged. He felt as if he had pushed a boulder up a mountainside. Once she had shuffled past him, Ulfrik again faced Hrut who stared back at him with eyes wide and mouth closed tight. Their eyes remained locked until Hrut dropped his head and shook it.

"Seems like you're a special man. Not that I envy you being that crazed bitch's pet." Hrut laughed, which turned to a phlegm-thickened cough.

Ulfrik looked back at the sky sliding past him. A black dot of a bird fluttered in a lazy circle before leaving his field of vision. These people had more than kindness in their hearts when they rescued him. Audhild, Gudrod, and all the others were helping Eldrid fulfill her vision, whatever that entailed. He closed his eyes and listened to the creak of the new deck and the splash of the oars. The rowing was too slow for pursuit. He wondered where they planned to take him and why the gods had decided he must live with them. Whatever Eldrid had envisioned, the gods had not shared with him. Never one to offend the gods, he had no plans of forever remaining with these people no matter what they had done for him.

He had to escape. Until his legs healed he would be at their mercy, and he could go along with their illusions. When his strength returned, he would leave for Ravndal. The simplicity of the idea calmed the tension of Eldrid's visit, though it was short-lived. They had faked his death, and judging from Hrut's reaction, he seemed to believe Ulfrik was dead. Now he frantically tried to recall what they had done. A slave of roughly his size and age had been killed and his face demolished, yet he would not have his scars. Runa would certainly know the body for a poor replacement. Then he thought of Throst and of Einar and all his men burned alive.

Facing Hrut again, he found him working against his bonds. Ulfrik called to him, making Hrut's face flush red with anger.

"All right, I'll be good. Don't call your friends over." He shrugged. "I'll be getting off this damn boat soon enough."

"Ulfrik Ormsson?" he strained to ask. Hrut stilled at the name, face suddenly cold and wary. "Dead?"

"What do you know of him?"

Ulfrik shook his head, and Hrut continued to stare at him as if seeing him for the first time. His small face displayed a swift range of thoughts, from wrinkled brows, distant eyes, and finally a satisfied smile. He leaned back against the gunwales. "Ulfrik's dead. Saw it myself. Was he a friend of yours? Didn't think he mixed with scum like you."

Being called scum made Ulfrik narrow his eyes at Hrut, but then he realized his slave's clothing and battered face did little to mark him otherwise.

"Not a friend," Ulfrik managed to say. Words were coming easier as he spoke, the pain and the vestiges of medicine receding in equal measure.

Hrut grunted and laughed. "Wasn't one to me either. Good man, really, but has powerful enemies."

"Who? Throst?"

"Look, just because I'm tied up here doesn't mean I'm answering all your questions. Piss off." Unable to stomp off in anger, Hrut did his best with a violent sigh and looking up at the clouds. After a while, Hrut's face softened into something more pensive and his brows pulled down in consternation. Ulfrik waited until he lifted his eyes back to him.

"What do you know about Throst? I thought a bear ripped you up. You've been keeping up on Gunnolfsvik while hanging onto your life?"

Ulfrik smiled wanly. He had to get his name out, even if only to his enemies. Eventually his allies would hear it and know the reports of his death were false. Hrut was the only one capable of carrying away the message. The rest of these people seemed intent on keeping him prisoner long after his legs healed.

"Not a bear attack. A fall from a tower." Ulfrik's voice trailed off as Hrut leaned forward against his bonds. "Trapped there with Throst. I fell."

"I saw Ulfrik's body, found it in the mud. He's dead."

Shaking his head with a hateful smirk, Ulfrik cut in. "Not me. A slave's body in my clothes. Look at my eyes. I'm not lying."

Hrut's mouth hung open, and suddenly he was wrestling with his bonds like a rabid guard dog. "We hung your body from the walls. Sent your head and helmet back to Hrolf. They're celebrating your death in Paris, you prick. I'll kill you myself!"

Ulfrik closed his eyes, imagining the grief and horror Runa and his children would experience thinking he was dead. He might still die if his legs remained broken when Hrut returned with a warband. He had to take the chance.

Gudrod and two other men now ringed Hrut, and when he refused to calm they pounded him down with the butts of short oars they had carried for that purpose. Soon, Hrut was collapsed against the gunwales. Gudrod gave Ulfrik a cursory examination and returned to his duties.

"I will kill you." Ulfrik hissed across the deck to the piled up form huddled in the gunwales. "Be sure to tell Throst we have a fight to finish."

Hrut did not stir, and Ulfrik closed his eyes and waited for time to pass.

15

Crickets chirped along the river banks, and dark shoulders of forests rose out of the night-blue landscape farther upland. Ulfrik was no longer tied to the litter on the deck. The cool damp of the night air was a welcomed relief though mosquitoes tormented him through the gaps in his shabby clothes. He stared up at the full moon, where the god Mani's face was lost in its brightness. Ulfrik considered the god's face was only visible in the crescent, but hidden in all other forms. It was like his situation, visible to all yet unseen. No one had paid Ulfrik any mind despite his supposed importance. Like the god Mani, his face was lost in plain sight.

He propped himself on his right elbow, a flash of pain in his opposite shoulder protesting. Hrut remained tied to the gunwales and two men flanked him, leaning on the rails. One man was hardly grown into full beard, and neither seemed confident in themselves. If Hrut were ever freed, he would break them like dry branches. They were not warriors, and few on these ships besides Gudrod were.

Flattening himself again, he heard the oars splashing in the night. Shifts of rowers had taken the ship far down the Seine without stopping. The blind woman Eldrid was preaching to them, shouting about gods and visions and great destinies. Ulfrik struggled to ignore it. The people paid her great respect and seemed to believe her visions. Certainly, they believed what she had said about him. People had avoided him, restricting themselves to whatever was necessary for his care and nothing else.

Burping up the broth he had been fed earlier, a sour taste of river eel filled his mouth and he frowned.

"Is your stomach settled?" Audhild asked as she sat next to him. Moonlight ringed her head in silver and filled in the stern contours of her face. He admired the clear, youthful power of the lines drawn by the play of light and shadow.

"It growls for more than broth and beer. I need real food to heal properly, woman."

"Call me Audhild. I'm not your woman."

"I wouldn't have you for one, either." Ulfrik narrowed his eyes at her and scowled. "You made a great show of helping me, but you want to keep me weak and dependent. You're no friend."

Expecting her to protest, she shrugged at his accusation. "Neither are you."

"But I'm your gift from the gods, am I not? I'll keep your people safe in their new homes."

"Yes, but that doesn't make you a friend. It makes you a vessel for the will of the gods."

"Odin's balls, woman. The gods let me live a good thirty-nine winters without telling me about it. I'd say your blind hag has been sipping from the medicine cup you've been feeding me."

Audhild pulled back, her face disappearing into shadow. Her hands pulled into her body, and Ulfrik reflexively reached for a sword he no longer possessed. In any case, he was too weak to threaten anyone. Yet Audhild did not draw any weapon, merely hovering in a silver-lined shroud of night. Even without her face visible, Ulfrik imagined the angry expression. He turned aside with a grunt.

"I didn't mean to insult you."

"You insult the gods with your clumsy words. Don't apologize to me."

The silence grew between them, and as Eldrid finished her

speech with a mad howl, those not occupied with rowing applauded. Ulfrik shuddered.

"Who leads these people? It's not her, but Gudrod doesn't seem to either."

Audhild paused and began to rub her arms.

"I lead them."

Ulfrik blinked in the darkness, his mouth open. This woman was a healer, not a leader. Yet, what did he know of her? Only recently had the hazy stupor muzzling his senses released. Until now, he had no sense of her as anything but a smooth, cool hand on his face or a strong arm to brace him as others changed his bandages.

"We are a village of farmers, not a band of noble warriors," she said. "My family owned most of the land and so the community looked to us for decisions. After my father died, I continued on. It comes naturally to me."

"What of Jarl Gunnolf and Stein Half-Leg?"

"We gave whatever they demanded," Audhild said, then faced Hrut and lowered her voice into a harsh whisper. "But Gunnolfsvik never cared about us. Only ever saw them when they came to take."

"And so you built ships in secret, and planned to break with them."

"I see the fog is lifted from your mind," she said. "We would've departed earlier but the encroachment of the Franks delayed us. I suppose I can thank Throst for settling with them and giving us this chance."

"Any friend of Throst's is an enemy of mine. So be careful who you thank." Audhild laughed and Ulfrik's body tensed at her reaction. "You think I joke with you? Do you know who I am?"

"I see what you have become. It will be a long time before you can stand again, and longer still before you are independent. You are in my care, Ulfrik Ormsson. So, yes, I've learned who you are. Your wargear and gold alone marked you for a great lord. Yet one more sign that the gods have gifted us with you. Anyway, you've told me enough about yourself while in your fevered state. Runa must be your wife, yes? You've called me that name enough times that Gudrod even calls me it."

Ulfrik went limp at the mention of Runa's name. He had avoided thinking of her and his family, knowing it would bring him only suffering. Now his eyes saw a different place, a warm bed with his wife laying beside him in peaceful slumber. "No," he said quietly, shaking his head. "I would never mistake you for my wife."

Audhild remained hidden in darkness, and placed her hand on his chest. "I am sorry it has to be this way. Fate is cruel and unknowable, but you belong to us now. Take solace knowing that as your wife mourns your passing, your very life ensures the safety of scores of people. One life for the lives of many, a fair exchange."

"Madness!" Ulfrik shouted. He jerked up, but the sudden rush made him dizzy and he collapsed just as fast. Audhild's hand snapped back and she recoiled as if from a snapping dog. "What possible good can I do? I am a burden in this condition, not a savior. The gods laugh at your foolishness."

"Be quiet. They can hear you clear to the other ship."

"Do I care? Everyone should know what you are doing." He raised himself again, and began to shout to the rowers and the people sleeping on the deck. "I am a great jarl, and any who help me escape will be rewarded with more gold than you'll see in a lifetime. Name your ransom and it will be paid."

Heads turned to face him and the rowers looked at him with blank expressions. Audhild stood, pulling her cloak tight against her body. In the same moment he saw two men approaching from the stern, Gudrod and another. As they loomed over him, in his weakened condition Ulfrik suddenly felt like a mouse under a falcon's talon.

"Told you to gag him until we're at sea," Gudrod said as he gestured to the other man.

"Then do it," Audhild said, voice rich with scorn. "I had only hoped he'd accept his duty to the people who've rescued him from his enemies and spared his life."

The man pinned Ulfrik to his litter, and his feeble effort to fight back drew derisive laughter from Gudrod. He forced a strip of leather into his mouth and tied it at the back of his head. The pain of being jostled set his legs and shoulder aflame and he surrendered to the attack. Once secured, Gudrod stepped back and admired his work. He gave a satisfied nod to the other man.

Hrut began laughing, then called for Gudrod. "Put him ashore with me. I promise you won't be pursued. Throst will pay good gold for the chance to kill him a second time."

Gudrod shook his head. "He stays with us. If your friends are following, then they've lingered well enough behind for us to not see them. We'll be at sea by tomorrow morning, and we'll let you ashore then. It's a long walk home for you now."

The jab silenced Hrut, and Ulfrik glared at him. The small-faced man smirked, then turned away. Suddenly a cold hand grabbed his chin and yanked his head over. Audhild frowned, her moon-bright locks of hair fluttering in the night breeze.

"Take a look at yourself and ask if anyone will believe your promises. A broken, old man in rags is what they see. The gods say you are our savior, but outside of us you are nothing. Be grateful to me and my folk, and to Eldrid for finding you. Otherwise, the head Throst sent back to your family would've truly been your own."

She shoved his head back, and a jolt of pain lanced his shoulder. Stalking away, she revealed Eldrid standing behind her and leaning with both hands wrapped around her staff. Her blindfolded eyes stared straight over him, but a wicked smile shined in the night. She too turned away.

For a long time even the splashing of the oars plying the ship through the night seemed dampened. The leather gag was tight around his head, and spit began to leak into his beard. He considered Audhild's words, and the awareness of his impoverished clothing made his whole body itch. His racing heart settled only after he had counted a hundred strokes of the oars.

Hrut hissed for his attention, and Ulfrik ignored it. Persisting until Ulfrik turned to him, Hrut leaned forward to whisper. His guards had both sunk down to the deck and were asleep. "You had better find a way to delay these fools or your end will be miserable. If you come with me, at least I can give you a warrior's death. I've heard where these people are going. Do you know?"

Ulfrik shook his head. His stomach tightened as Hrut's smile widened. "If you think to slip them after your legs heal, forget getting back to Ravndal. You're going too far for that."

He paused and checked the guards beside him, as if his next words might startle them from their sleep. Satisfied he could continue, he licked his lips then raised his voice.

"They're headed to the top of the world. Iceland."

16

The salt air awakened Ulfrik. Not only from fitful sleep but also from a land-bound torpor. The sounds of ocean waves slapping the hull echoed through the deck. Above him clear blue sky stretched out, disrupted only by the billowing sail snapping into his view. Gulls screamed in the distance, and their melody lifted Ulfrik up from his litter. His heart lightened knowing he was once again on the ocean.

Drawing a deep breath, even if his ribs ached from it, filled him with joy. The leather gag had been removed to feed him the night before, and Audhild had not bothered to replace it. He was grateful for the taste of the air on his tongue, and it flooded his memory with a hundred youthful adventures. The world fell away and he saw himself at the tiller, Toki at his side and sea spray in his face. A fierce crew sat upon sea chests filled with plunder and rowed for foggy shores, singing bawdy songs in time with their stokes. His eyes dampened at the memories, for all the years gone, and for all the days locked into ceaseless land wars. Even as a prisoner, the flavor of the sea was good.

Memories shattered with the shrill screech of Eldrid. She strode into the prow as confident as any sighted woman and raised her arms above her head, one hand holding her staff. She screeched again, but now addressed the waves.

"Gods above, we are freed! No more jarls to tax us or steal our children. No more wars to bleed us. Freedom! Rejoice!"

Ulfrik estimated more than thirty people filled this ship, and guessed the second ship held as many again. The vastness of the sea weakened Eldrid's voice, but sixty people shouting to the sky made an impression. Everyone stopped and threw their arms wide and stretched out to the heavens. He had never seen such an act. Audhild and Gudrod, the two most familiar faces, both imitated Eldrid and closed their eyes as if savoring the moment.

Hrut, still tied to the gunwales, spit on the deck. Ulfrik shared a confused shrug with him. These people believed in gods Ulfrik did not recognize, nor understand. The ship rocked and Eldrid wavered. Ulfrik hoped she would pitch into the water and drown, but she merely stumbled back and nearly tripped over him. Her staff whisked around to get her bearings, colliding with his head and drawing a protest from him. Eldrid laughed and struck him again, leaving no doubt she intended it.

As she exited the prow, everyone returned to their duties. Ulfrik remained alone with Hrut for a moment.

Ulfrik wasted no time. He had plenty of idle time to perfect his offer. Catching Hrut's eye, he nodded him closer.

"It's not like I can take a quick walk over," he said, arms pulling at the cords lacing him to the gunwales. "At least they roll you over and move you. My ass is killing me."

"We're at sea now, so they'll be letting you ashore. Looks like no one followed you after all." Ulfrik smiled. The strain of sitting upright drew sweat to his brow, but he fought to appear unperturbed. Hrut frowned and turned away. For a moment, Ulfrik saw a spoiled and jealous child sitting in Hrut's clothing. He wondered if Hrut had sought Stein's seat but lost it to Throst. He let the consideration pass.

"You have a long walk home after all. Realize you're in Hrolf the Strider's lands now. The Franks here love him; gods know he's done much to make their lives easy. Don't suppose you're going to find many friends here."

"You got something to say, dead man? I'll get back fine, but you'll be rotting at the bottom of the ocean before Yule. These fools don't know what they're doing. Put all their trust in the gods, and we both know what that gets a man." Hrut squeezed out a twisted smile.

"It gets him whatever the gods are giving out," Ulfrik said, scanning for the approach of others. Eldrid braced herself against the mast and shouted at a boy working the back-stay. Gudrod and Audhild were in the stern and all others were preoccupied. "Throst has abandoned you, and for good cause. You betrayed Stein Half-Leg easily enough, so can't be trusted. You'll be the next body flying off that tower if you go back to Throst. He was going to kill you anyway, but your disappearance suited him just as well. You're not so stupid to believe otherwise."

Hrut frowned and stared at the deck.

"So join with me. Only you know I'm alive and what I'm worth. Get a ship to follow, track us down and save me. Ransom me back to my family."

"Sure, I'll pick up a crew of fifty warriors and we'll overtake this ship by tomorrow." Hrut rolled his eyes and looked to the sky. "I'm no better off than you. Do you think I carry my fortune in my pack?"

"Pay your men out of the spoils, just like any raid. You'll capture these two ships, for the love of the gods. Offer them that much. You don't even have to reveal my identity, just claim me as your reward. Take me home and you will be paid and forgiven. No fear of revenge, I swear it. I'm saving it all for Throst."

Hrut mulled the offer, his tongue prodding his cheek. "Hrolf'll want his revenge, though."

"Returning his favorite jarl from the dead will earn his forgiveness. No one knows what you did. We'll tell him our own story."

"Not so." Hrut shook his head. "We sent Einar back with what we thought was your head. I gave it to him."

Ulfrik stopped with his mouth open. He blinked and his heart fluttered, weakening him so that he sloughed down to the deck. Knowing Einar lived felt as good as if his own body had been made whole again. He closed his eyes and summoned Einar's memory. A sickening wave overcame him, knowing how badly he would blame himself for the death of his jarl.

"How did you defeat him?" Ulfrik asked in a whisper like dead leaves in the wind.

"Bashed him in the head before we took out the other man. He went down readily enough. Anyway, he won't let me off if he sees me again."

Shaking his head, Ulfrik refocused on the moment. "Einar will do what I say, and you will be rich enough to travel far from his reach or mine. Do not fret the details of something so distant. Your other choice is not so good by half. Do you want to start over from nothing? Risk being captured by Franks or Danes looking for slaves to row their ships? At the least you realize Danes have marked two new ships filled with women and children leaving the Seine for the open sea. I don't need to see it to know it has happened. They'll be racing to capture these ships and take slaves. Join them, capture me, and your life will be better for it."

For a long time Hrut remained gazing at his boots. A big toe poked through a hole in one of them. Ulfrik left him to his thoughts, but knew sense would prevail. Ulfrik did not want to end up with raiders boarding this ship. Seeing him broken up and in rags, they would toss him overboard as nothing more than trash. Whether he liked it or not, becoming Hrut's captive was now his best chance to return home and was also Hrut's best option. Even if he did not answer, Ulfrik assured himself Hrut would come for him.

The rocking of the deck and the gull-song above soothed Ulfrik so that he had dozed. He jolted awake as men filled the prow, the sudden motion flaring his shoulder and legs. He struggled to raise himself, then Audhild knelt to aid him. "Don't move too fast; you'll pull the stitches in your leg. Let's move you away from this spot."

Shifting positions was a welcomed relief, but the crowd of people in the prow confused him. Audhild held him under his arms while another man lifted his litter and glided him aside. A ring had formed around Hrut, and Gudrod was untying his bindings. When his arms came free he flopped forward with a gusty exhalation. "Gods, what a welcome moment. Help me stand, will you?"

Gudrod and another boy guided him up. From his seat on the deck Ulfrik could not see over the high sides of the ship. Audhild shoved a chest behind him for support, and while she did he noted a young man worked the tiller in Gudrod's absence. He seemed to be maintaining course rather than steering for shore.

He looked back at Hrut, who briefly met his eyes and gave the slightest nod. Ulfrik smiled, knowing Hrut had accepted his offer. But the smile was fleeting.

The crowd parted and Eldrid stood before Hrut. The cloth wrapping her eyes was fresh white and she wore a white smock over her plain dress. Hrut flinched at seeing her, raising his hands only a fraction before Gudrod cracked the back of his head with a wooden mallet. Hrut collapsed to the deck with a grunt.

Eldrid threw her head back and produced a dull gray iron knife. "Let this sacrifice of blood please the gods and grant us safe passage to our new homes. May this warm flesh fill the cold sea with the glory of our offering."

Hrut had castled himself on hands and knees, spit hanging from his gaping mouth as he struggled up. Gudrod grabbed his hair and yanked to expose his throat. Eldrid's free hand fumbled across Hrut's face as she oriented her blade on his neck. The knife slashed, spraying bright red blood across her white smock. Gudrod fed the deck Hrut's blood, holding back the slashed throat as Hrut's legs flailed and hands grasped at the air. Eldrid screeched again, holding both arms out to the sky and smiling in rapture. More blood sprayed her as both Gudrod and another man heaved Hrut's twitching body over the side.

The splash receded as the ship glided past.

Ulfrik watched, eyes wide and mouth agape. His last hope had went overboard, leaving only a puddle of scarlet blood on the deck. Gudrod wiped his hands on a cloth as if he had just slaughtered a lamb.

"Why?" he whispered, and was shocked when Audhild whispered her answer.

"Because Eldrid said he knew too much to let go. What if he decided to gather men and come after our ships?" Ulfrik slowly turned to face Audhild, who stared back at him, her scarred eye brow raised. "He served us better as a sacrifice."

They stared at each other in silence, until Audhild stood and left him facing the dangling cords where Hrut had been tied.

Eldrid dipped both palms into the blood and smeared her cheeks with it, then stood and began spinning in a circle as she turned her bloodied face to the sky.

"They are all mad," Ulfrik muttered. "And I can't escape."

17

Ulfrik sat upright against the gunwales in the fore of the ship. His free arm was draped over the anchor stone, a smooth edged rock the size of a cow's head lashed into a wooden frame. Morning sun had brightened the sky and signaled the changing of the crew. He watched men kick themselves out of their leather sleeping sacks, stretch, then take their positions. Gudrod relieved the man at the tiller with a slap on the back. The bailer in the lower cargo hold in the ship's center extended his arm to be helped out of the recess. Though a new ship, water leaked far worse than some of Ulfrik's oldest vessels. The bailer was hard pressed to keep the water in check, and it signaled to Ulfrik that either caulking or construction had been rushed.

His stomach growled and his gaze drifted to where the rations were stored. An appetite was a positive sign of recovery, though he regretted he could not heal fast enough to reverse his fortune. He watched Audhild extract herself from her sleep sack. Her dress had rolled up to reveal a strong curve of white calf, and Ulfrik burned with shame for noticing. She's the enemy, he reminded himself, she and this whole ship of fools. Audhild smoothed out her skirt, combed her hair, then attended Eldrid. The blind woman slept more than the ship's cat, but was nowhere near as useful. She waved Audhild away with a thin arm and rolled over in her sleep sack.

The hull creaked as the ship cut the rolling waves and the sail cracked overhead. Ulfrik heard the gulls, and reckoned they were not far off the Frankish coast headed north. However simple these people seemed, Gudrod and his companion were able navigators. Iceland remained a myth in Ulfrik's mind, but he had heard of people willing to seek it out. People who sought it were never heard from again, though Norse traders swore men lived there. If he were making the journey, he would sail directly north to Norway, find his bearings along its coast, then turn straight west until landfall in Iceland. Gudrod likely had the same plan.

Once Audhild stuffed her belongings into her sleep sack, she cinched it closed and smiled at him. Had he known better, he might have mistaken it for something genuine. She gathered white cloth into her arms and started toward him. She staggered with the sway of the ship, and the bailer nearly doused her with sea water as she skirted the cargo hold. He waited, unable to do anything. Gudrod stared after her like a hound leashed to a tree.

"Good morning." Her voice was as clear as birdsong. "Time to examine your wounds."

"Such a smile and I'd almost believe it sincere." Ulfrik leaned back, anticipating the sting of the bandages coming apart.

"But I am sincere." She peeled the first layer of wrapping from his leg, then paused. "I am happy to be at sea. Been a long time in planning and it has gone beautifully."

Ulfrik looked at the brown stain of Hrut's blood and kept his silence. Everyone judged beauty in their own way. A young girl came with a bucket of sea water and placed it next to Audhild. The girl avoided Ulfrik's gaze and scurried off.

"You're not going to clean me with salt water?"

"Just around the wound. Fresh water is precious, at least until we can resupply." The cold water still worked into the cut and the sting made him wince. She was unapologetic, but worked with more care. They remained unspeaking as she worked. Ulfrik focused on the people behind her, families and single men all attending different tasks for sailing the ship. Some were competent, most made mistakes that worried Ulfrik. One boy, trying to skirt the open cargo hold but encountering traffic on the deck, decided to jump along the railing to scoot past. He succeeded, but such a foolish risk would set off a chain of disasters were he to fall overboard. He imagined trying to wrench the ship around in time, a gust of wind forcing the already-leaning ship over, and a host of other similar mishaps. The stories were all too familiar and all too likely with a green crew.

"Ouch!" Audhild got his attention as she prodded his shoulder. "The bones are still broken, if you were wondering."

"Sorry." She continued her examination, and once satisfied replaced the wrapping. "By the time we make landfall in Norway, you'll be able to stand with support."

"That will ruin all your plans."

She sat back on the deck, flopping her hands on her knees and sighing. "No one wants you to be crippled. We are your family now, and we want you whole."

"When I am whole, I'll be leaving this family." He twisted the last word into a curse. "And you won't be able to stop me."

Expecting defiance, he was disappointed when she shrugged and stroked the amulet of Thor's hammer hanging at her chest. "Maybe so. The gods sent you for a purpose and when it is finished they could send you away."

"Gods be cursed, I'll be taking this ship back to Frankia as soon as I am whole. By summer I will be gone."

Again she did not argue, but tightened her grip on the amulet. She turned to face the others at work. Ulfrik noticed how Gudrod eyed him from the tiller, as if it took more strength to stay away than it did to steer the ship.

"You will sail this whole ship alone for so far? Maybe you will offer men gold in return for aiding you. Every great man thinks gold can buy a solution to his worries. No reason you should be any different."

"My gold pile would fill the cargo hold. I've no trouble parting with it to get back to my life." Ulfrik's free hand rubbed his upper arm where gold bands had adorned it not long ago. Now only scratchy wool covered it.

"Then you have nothing these men desire. What do you know of us?" She faced him now, levelly holding his eyes. Her scarred brow cocked as she tilted her head. "You assume we're all mad because we've listened to our gods. Not so. Everyone here has more to gain than just bending to Fate's plan. These people, nearly all of them, are slaves or servants. Surprised, but why? Surely a man so great as you had halls filled with slaves? Not everyone here is from my village, but they're all here because freedom awaits in Iceland. For their sacrifices, they will become freemen, landowners, and masters of their own halls. Run off with you, and they get a handful of silver bits and nothing more."

"They would be welcomed in my hall. I'd give them lands, flocks, anything they wanted." Ulfrik reined himself back, detesting the desperation he heard in his own voice. Audhild was already shaking her head.

"Not the same, and you know it. In your world, a jarl will sit above them. In Iceland, they will be masterless and free. You cannot give them this, and once they taste it they will not follow you back to servitude."

"And you will not sit above them?"

Audhild shook her head. "There will be no rulers, only the community. We will make decisions as a group, help each other as a family, and above all make our own ways through this life. The gods have shown us this vision, and I embrace it. They do too."

Ulfrik snorted. "They embrace it or Eldrid the miserable blind bitch will cut their throats in the night."

Though he spoke in low tones, he watched for Eldrid's reaction. She stirred in her sleep sack as if in a terrible dream. Maybe she had heard him. He was convinced she had overheard his talk with Hrut. In the days afterward, he had cursed her under his breath and dared her to hurt him. Though the curses should have been out of earshot, without fail she would come to him within the hour and utter cryptic threats or press her thumb into his stitches.

"I've warned you about how you speak of Eldrid." Audhild

straightened and a look of fear and anger passed across her face. He had seen that look in the faces of men across the shieldwall, ready to fight and die but scared to do either.

"You know she torments me when you turn away. The more tenderly you treat me, the harder she presses my wounds."

"Enough," her shout drew stares from the entire deck. Gudrod strained against his invisible leash. Face flushing pink, she waved absently as if dispelling a foul odor. "You've not the strength to fight with your hands, so you strike with words. I'm a fool to listen."

She continued to inspect his other cuts and began to replace the wrap on his forearm. He sat in silence, realizing he was driving off his sole ally. Her commentary on his strength was devastatingly accurate; his body had withered from inaction and a diet of soups and meat scraps. He had to regain strength before he could do anything under his own power. With the world considering him dead, he had no hope for aid. Far worse, he had a greater chance of being captured at sea and killed out of hand. The bitch Eldrid's prophecy may in fact be his only hope at eventual escape. Without belief in his divine purpose, he was nothing more than a burden to be discarded. All Eldrid had to do was proclaim a new vision and he would end up like Hrut. His stomach burned at the thought. He needed an ally to prevent Eldrid from changing her mind.

Pursing his lips, he considered a new approach. "I am sorry. I've not been so helpless since—I can't remember when. I've been ungrateful." *I've also been a prisoner, but I'll ignore that for now.*

Audhild nodded, slowly folding the last of the bandage over his arm. When she did not respond, he continued in the most contrite voice he could muster.

"And to be honest, I've not been so scared in all my years."

She thrust the used bandages into her bag, wrinkling her nose at him. "Scared? Of what? Eldrid? Really?"

"Of course not." He had expected more sympathy instead of her disgust. "I'm just, well, I am completely at your mercy."

"And my mercy frightens you?"

The sneer on her face told Ulfrik he had steered into the rocks. Vulnerability seemed abhorrent to her, which suited him. He could not maintain that act for long. He decided to appeal to her maternal side.

"Bah, you can't understand. Forget about me for a moment, and consider my family. I've three sons and a daughter who think I'm dead, and a wife who is faced with raising them alone. Just to think upon them—"

Audhild's hand landed square over his mouth, clamping into his cheeks. She leaned over him, raising one slender finger in warning.

"No more about your fears and helplessness. No more about your family or wife. You belong to us now, and you have a duty to me for saving your life and setting your bones. That is what you think about as you lay here and eat my food. When I bring a bucket to haul your piss and shit, you remember to be grateful. When I turn you so sores don't form on your legs, you remember who is caring for you. When I clean you and do every other damn thing because you are as helpless as a baby, you remember me. Forget everything else. Do your part. Show your gratitude."

She stood, hands on her hips. Others had paused in their work to watch. Ulfrik averted his eyes.

"And your spine was not broken in that fall. So use it."

He kept his head turned, too humiliated to face anyone. He heard her footfalls as she left him and murmurs from others.

At least he had learned what infuriated Audhild, and had a far better idea of how to ingratiate himself with her. More than bones had to be broken before he could escape. He would have to break his pride as well.

18

On dry land after weeks at sea, the people of both ships staggered as they milled about the shore. Two men had borne Ulfrik's litter to the shore, neither much older than his first son, Gunnar. They had placed him in the grass, where the sweet smell of rain from the night before clung to the blades and emanated a soothing coolness. The colorless sky still threatened rain, but the wind was low and birds still winged above him. No storm was coming. Having been divided by two ships, people came together on land in cheerful conversations. Their thin, high laughter spread out over the gentle slope. Only the occasional screech from Eldrid marred the pleasant landing.

"Have Gudrod and the others returned?" Ulfrik asked one of his minders, the boy who had helped carry him ashore. His name was Lini, and over the weeks at sea was the first new person willing to speak with him. He was good-natured but timid, barely grown into a loose, red beard. He had a strong face obscured by a violent splash of freckles and unruly hair.

"Not yet," he said, seated beside Ulfrik in the grass. He was picking at the blades, twisting one between his fingers. They sat in silence for several moments.

"No one you want to see from the other ship?" Lini shrugged, threw the grass aside. "No girl to sneak off with like your other friend?"

"How'd you know he did that?"

"My bones are broken, not my ears. They're just over that rise, rolling in the grass. Thought maybe you'd want join in."

"Audhild said to stay with you."

"That frightens me, Lini. A willing girl in reach, but you'd rather sit with a broken old man?"

"Didn't say I'd prefer it. Said Audhild ordered me." Both Lini and Ulfrik chuckled, and he pulled out more grass to study. "Besides, Thorir doesn't like sharing his girls."

"Not much of a friend, is he." They both laughed again, their voices joining the general positive spirit infusing the landing.

The weeks at sea had been monotonous, worsened from being an invalid, but his dire predictions of raiders had never materialized. Only one tense encounter occurred with passing traders, and the worry was mutual. Both formations skirted each other, but exchanged friendly signals. Eldrid had proclaimed her sacrifice of Hrut's life had banished all evil from their path. Everyone had readily accepted this as the truth. Ulfrik had called it luck, but kept the thought secreted. Once he had learned the art of silent acceptance, Eldrid had become more tractable. She spouted her wisdom and promises in between long periods of sleep, and had stopped tormenting Ulfrik. However, Audhild had been cold to him since his failed attempts to manipulate her feelings. Potentially her coldness also calmed Eldrid's hostility. He had begun to think Eldrid worried for the two of them forming an alliance against her. It made no sense to Ulfrik, but he could not guess what made sense to the mad, blind prophetess.

A large wave crashed on the beach, rocking both ships and drawing Ulfrik from his thoughts. Lini craned his neck forward but just as quickly lost interest.

"I want to stand," Ulfrik said. He turned to Lini, who sat frozen with a long blade of grass between his fingers.

"That's not what Audhild told—"

"Forget her," Ulfrik commanded like he stood at the front of a shieldwall. "I need to stand, if only for a moment. It's a small thing for you, but it has become a dream for me. I can do it with your help."

"But your legs. You're not set up for standing. What if you fall?"

"Then I fall and I'll cry and curse, but will be no worse than I am now. But if I stand, if only for a moment, then my life will have meaning again. You are a good man, Lini, and I want you to be the one to help me. Please."

Lini stared at him, his green eyes wide and the blade of grass fallen from his fingers. He searched over his shoulder as if his father might catch him playing with a sword he was not old enough to handle. "I'm not sure how to get you up."

"My legs are locked in place. Take my arm and heave me up like a log. Let me balance against you, and get some weight on my legs. I've not moved in a month, and my muscles are like mushrooms. I've got to build back the strength in small steps. You help me, and I'll be in your debt. Hurry, before Audhild returns."

He wanted to do this on his own terms, and to be standing when Audhild returned. He would show her the strength she believed he lacked and demonstrate he did not rely on her for everything. Reaching out his good arm, he waited for Lini to take it.

"You sure about this?" His head swiveled in search of someone to stop him, but when no one came, he grabbed Ulfrik's forearm in sweaty hands.

"Pull hard and catch me when I'm up."

The pain was more than expected, but Ulfrik gritted his teeth as Lini yanked him up. The moment he was on his feet, bolts of pain shot up his legs but the wooden braces lashed to either side held his limbs rigid. He wobbled then continued forward, but Lini butted his chest against his to prevent him from stumbling. "How does it feel?"

"Like my legs are breaking again."

"Then get back down."

"No!"

For endless minutes he quivered and the pain lanced through his joints and hips. He crushed his eyes shut and grimaced, clasping his good arm to Lini's. Holding close to the boy, he slowly opened his eyes and viewed the world upright. Before him was the rolling iron-gray sea and two ships leaning on the beach.

"You're standing," Lini exclaimed. "You did it."

Ulfrik forced a smile through the pain, but could not speak. He feared even to turn his head or lose his balance. Tears flowed down into the tangle of his beard, and the simple victory of standing under his own power filled him with hope again. If he could walk, then he could return home again. Behind his gritted teeth, in the depth of his heart, he vowed to escape. Runa, I will stand beside you again. I swear it before all the gods. I will sit in my hall once more.

"What are you doing?" Audhild's voice broke into his thoughts, and at last he smiled. The gods had sent her back in time to witness his daring. She was as flustered as he had hoped. "He's not ready to stand."

"But he is standing," Lini said. "I'm just helping balance him."

"Until his legs give out and he collapses." Audhild was at his side now, and she grasped his other arm. "What are you doing?"

"Standing," Ulfrik said. "You promised I would be able to by Norway, and here we are."

Lying down again was not as easy as he had hoped. Lini and Audhild placed him like a log on a woodpile, Audhild stern and worried but Lini smiling and excited. Ulfrik winked at his new friend.

As soon as he was laid out, Audhild grabbed Lini's shirt in both hands. "You were to watch over him, not risk breaking his bones again. What kind of fool are you?"

"I made him do it," Ulfrik protested. "Leave him alone."

"Made him? You are little more than a sack of bones. How could you make him do anything?"

"A friend cannot grant a favor to another? Or do you only understand force? I used our friendship to get what I wanted. I'm sorry, Lini, if I've caused you trouble."

"Not at all," he said. "I can't believe you stood on two broken legs."

Audhild inhaled to unleash a renewed tirade, but she stopped when Eldrid and Gudrod arrived. Others maintained distance at the edges, but leaned in to see. Eldrid's screechy voice grated on Ulfrik's ears.

"What has happened? Why the anger?"

Lini explained to both Gudrod and Eldrid. When finished, Eldrid fingered the bones of her necklace and remained silent. Gudrod frowned at him, but gave more attention to Audhild. He touched her arm tentatively, and she pulled aside.

"Standing is good," Eldrid proclaimed at last. "The gods will have more use for him if he can stand and walk."

A chill ran through Ulfrik's back at the words. Had Eldrid intended him to remain crippled? The consideration made no sense, but in light of her proclamation it seemed to have been her plan. Audhild meekly nodded, and he wondered if she also had conspired to keep him weakened. Eldrid thumped her staff on the ground and turned away, as if closing a meeting. For a blind woman, she moved with ease over the uneven ground. Ulfrik hoped she would trip and break her teeth.

Audhild dismissed Lini and began fussing with Ulfrik's braces, tightening the bindings and straightening the wood slats.

"How did the meeting with the townsfolk go?" He decided not to press his victory too much, unsure if he could even consider it as such. Instead, he had another plan he hoped to set into play.

She twisted her mouth to the side as she roughly checked his other wounds. "Not as we had hoped. The local jarl is willing to allow us to trade and buy what we need for the voyage, but ship repairs will take too long. He's afraid we'll remain here all winter."

"We should. Ouch, the stitches are not ready to come out. Don't pull them." He raised his head, and Audhild was plucking at the thread holding together his thigh where the bone had punctured.

"Winter anywhere is difficult, so may as well begin it in our new home. The Franks and your friend Throst forced us to action before we would've liked. We were going to set out next year."

"You'd have never kept two ships secret for so long. Who built them anyway? Some things could stand to be better crafted, but overall our ship at least is sturdy."

"Gudrod and his crew. They were ship builders by trade, worked for my father. Those ships that took you to Gunnolfsvik were made of my father's hand." Audhild faced the beached ships, a small sigh escaping. "Of course, no one needs ships when all the battles are fought over land these days. Would that he had relocated to a port or England, he'd be alive today."

"Were it Fate's plan to end his life, no matter where he went death awaited. I take it he fell in battle? There's no more honorable way than to die a hero."

"Cut in battle, yes, but the bending sickness overtook him. He became locked like an iron bar and died worse than a mad dog. Nothing heroic in that."

Ulfrik turned away, too familiar with that horrid manner of death to want to know more. Audhild remained staring at the sea, and Ulfrik decided he had to advance his plan now while she was willing to speak with him.

"I can do nothing right today," he mumbled. She did not acknowledge, but remain twisted toward the sea. "I'm sorry the locals won't look at our ships, but without repairs, I fear our journey will be more dangerous than it already is. The caulking on our ship alone is poor or there is a structural problem. In either case, one good storm will make bailing impossible and we'll be swamped. Eldrid's sacrifice has held us to this landfall, but will it be enough to carry us from here to Iceland?" He closed his eyes, hating the credit he gave to Eldrid. For now he had to act complacent or risk finding himself at the bottom of the ocean.

"Are you suggesting we find another man to sacrifice? Human blood is the most potent gift. Why would it not satisfy any longer?"

He thought human sacrifice was detestable to the gods, for what glory was there in killing a helpless person in their name? Would a man be honored if a caged rat were drowned in his name? If any man's blood were to be spilled for the gods, it was better done on the battlefield. Such considerations were not shared by many, and clearly not among his so-called new family. "How do I know what pleases the gods? If I did, I'd not be lying here and dressed in rags. No, the repairs are my concern. Listen, how much do you know about me?"

"You were a Hersir over many jarls and sworn to Hrolf the Strider. You defeated the Franks inside the walls of your own fortress. I guess you thought yourself a mighty man." She turned back to him, and again raised her scarred brow. The gesture was beginning to irritate him as much as Eldrid's piercing voice.

"So before all of that, I lived here in Norway. My accent should've told you as much. When Harold Finehair decided the jarls of this land must bend a knee to him or die, many people fled. That's when I met Hrolf. Other men fled to the Faereyjar Islands, which lie upon our route. The people there are peaceful and their land is nothing but mountains and wide plains of grass. Some are ship-builders who did work for Hrolf. If they will not let us winter on their lands, then I'm certain they will be willing to trade for repairing our ships. Unlike the people here, in the Faereyjar people need to trade for what they lack."

Audhild's mouth twisted again and her cocked brow dropped. "Gudrod mentioned these islands on the way back. You say Hrolf had worked with them before?"

"He has, though I was merely part of his crew. There are many islands, most of them empty. I can show Gudrod where the major settlements are and where we can barter for repairs. Places without many people are more likely to allow us to winter on their land. I understand winters are actually mild in those islands."

Standing and slapping away the wet grass from her skirt, Audhild smiled. "I'll talk with Eldrid and Gudrod. What is the name of this place?"

Ulfrik frowned as if in a great struggle to summon the name from memory. "I'm not sure. I believe it was called Nye Grenner."

19

"There it is." Ulfrik stuck his chin at the blue strip rising out of the horizon. Though it pained him to sit, he had endured it to help guide Gudrod the final distance to his former home of Nye Grenner. In his weakened condition every swell threatened to pitch him off the crate he had placed beside the steering board. With his left arm still in a sling, he dared not release his other hand from gripping the rails.

"These islands all look the same," Gudrod muttered. "You sure this is the place?"

"Bet my beard on it," he said, focusing on the distant cliffs. He had sailed these waters too many times to count. Sea birds and whales showed him the path, along with the currents and craggy islands dotting the approach. To the untrained eye it was empty sea and sky, but to him it was a well-trodden road. He could not reckon the years it had been since he had traveled the path, but he had never forgotten it.

Cold sea spray prickled his face as the ship cut the choppy waves. Oars had been shipped and men now worked the sails in response to the wind. He remembered how welcoming the winds were in this leg of the journey home. He used to think it was the gods whisking him back to his hall. It had not always been in glory, but now Ulfrik's memories had acquired that golden glow that comes with age. Barely holding on to his seat, bones broken and braced, his mind dwelt in a completely different world—one where he was young and strong, the master of his hall and ship, and leading men to riches and adventure. His smile trembled as he dreamed.

"How close are we?" Eldrid's screeching voice blasted into his reverie. She stood before Ulfrik, legs thrown wide to balance herself on the rocking deck. Her knuckles were white clutching her staff, and seeing it broadened Ulfrik's smile.

"With these winds, we'll arrive soon," he said. Gudrod grunted in agreement.

"They better welcome us like you promised." She tried to raise her staff to menace him, but could not balance herself otherwise.

"I'm the storm god's gift, am I not? Don't doubt me."

She scowled but moved off to harass the bailers, who were resting against the sides and out of breath. The ship had taken on so much water that two bailers had to work nonstop. Bailing was a normal function on any ship, but this bordered on swamping. They had to empty the hold to prevent damage to their cargo, and the deck was overcrowded with people, sacks, boxes, and barrels. They needed to repair at Nye Grenner or the ship would be lost in the first storm it faced.

Ulfrik had other plans.

No one on this ship realized who he was and his relationship with Nye Grenner. He would exploit that. As the high cliff walls drew up out of the distance, he came ever closer to a place where he still ruled. In truth, he had long ago abandoned this land to its fate. Yet he had built it from nothing, and cultivated a community that for a while was the pinnacle of power in these islands. The earth here had been watered with his blood. The people would not forget him, or his sacrifices. They would save him from captivity, and restore him to his rightful place. For all he had done for them, no matter how much time had passed, these people owed him a debt.

Even so, a fire smoldered in his guts. How much could he trust the memory of the people?

In the last stretch, he guided Gudrod through a treacherous

current that dragged unsuspecting ships into the cliffs. They approached from the south, following the high brown cliffs into the calm waters that broke on a beach of smooth rocks. He expected to see docks, but instead found only a single piling sticking out of the waters, like an old tree too stubborn to collapse.

"They'll have spotted us from the hall long ago," Ulfrik said, hemming in the excitement that had slipped into his voice. Gudrod seemed too intent on steering to notice. "You should send a party to speak with them while the other ships anchor a safe distance away."

Gudrod spared a tired glare while hauling on the tiller. Men shouted to each other as they worked the rigging, trimming the sails to slow their approach. Ulfrik craned his neck to see who had come to greet them, but the grassy slope remained empty.

The ship thumped into the beach, expertly landed with a great smile from Gudrod. "That's how it's done," he said to Ulfrik. "Slide like ice right up to shore."

"Where's everyone?" Audhild joined them, one hand shielding her eyes against the sun. Their only reception was from sea gulls squawking on nearby rocks and seals barking farther down the shore. "There's hearth smoke."

Ulfrik stared across the deck, up the slope to the hall he had built with Toki and Snorri and dozens of others whose names had gone on to the feasting hall. Nye Grenner still stood, its roofs of green turf like furry green hats. That had been a change from the original construction, but was better suited for this climate. Boat houses and barracks he had built were no longer there, at least as far as he could see. A tear came to his eye as he rejoined the land where he had taken Runa for his wife and his sons had been born. Atop that hill, in a hall where another man now ruled, he had once lived a life of simple pleasures. Where had it gone? Why had it gone?

"Bring me ashore," Eldrid screeched. "Let me kiss the rocks and feel the dry earth under my feet."

"Where's everyone?" Audhild asked again, as if no one had heard her the first time.

"Two ships out of the morning sun make people wary," Gudrod said. "They're either in the hall or all fled."

"They should arrange themselves on slope before the hall. The approach is a killing field for archers." Everyone paused at Ulfrik's observation, and he realized he had revealed too much. His mind was still wrapped up in the past. "That is what Hrolf said of this place. Very defensible."

He was readily dismissed, and Gudrod was already strapping on a sword in preparation. No matter how peaceful intentions were, men were expected to bear swords but leave them sheathed. As he fastened the buckle around his waist, he asked Ulfrik, "What's the leader's name again?"

"Gunnbjorn Red-Hand, last I was here. He should still lead, or his kin. He was the son of Frida Styrdottir, a respected name here. Mention any one and you should get their leader. You're taking me along, of course."

Gudrod laughed until he choked, then left without answering. Audhild gave a smile reserved for young children. "What possible good will you do us? You'd have to be carried. How would that look?"

"Like we come in peace, that's how. What's less threatening than a wounded man?"

"Stay on the ship," she said. Her hand brushed his cheek and her smile was more sincere. Ulfrik leaned away, absently touching the spot she had. "You are too important to risk moving around unnecessarily."

She joined Gudrod and two other men who bracketed Eldrid as they led her down the gangplank. Ulfrik had wanted to protest, but the surprising tenderness had stunned him. Audhild had been moody and cold since he had stood on his own. By the time he had recovered his senses, she was already halfway up the slope with the others. Figures had emerged from the hall to greet them, a knot of hesitant dark shapes that clung to the walls.

Watching alongside his shipmates, he could not determine who had come to greet them. They were all men, about six of them, and they moved cautiously down to Gudrod. Ulfrik shook his head at the fear he saw in the people of Nye Grenner. Had they forgotten how well he had positioned their hall against raiders from the sea? He had held off armies from that slope and littered it with corpses. What was wrong with these people?

The exchange seemed friendly enough, though his sight was no longer as sharp as it had been years ago. He could not see expressions, but the postures seemed open and less guarded. Eventually, his red-bearded, wild-haired friend Lini sought him out. The young man was the only one brave enough to speak with him, and that was only for fleeting moments when neither Eldrid nor Audhild watched.

"I hope they agree to let us winter here." Lini stood beside Ulfrik and leaned on the tiller, idly toying with the loose handle. "I've never seen the likes of those cliffs. You could see to the end of the world from there."

"Not so far as that, but other islands are in view when not smothered in fog."

"You know a lot about this place." Lini continued to play with the tiller, as if he were imagining steering the ship through a gale.

Ulfrik nodded in answer to his question. All eyes were turned toward the meeting on the shore, and Ulfrik decided he had to make good use of his time with Lini. "Audhild is a tremendous healer. I wonder how she learned such arts?"

Lini shrugged, more interested in the tiller and the cliffs.

"Only someone acquainted with battlefield injuries should be able to dress wounds like that. Did she serve Gunnolf at some point?"

"Never, her father was Jarl Gunnolf's ship-builder. Maybe they hurt themselves a lot while building ships."

Ulfrik smiled. Of all the people on this boat, the simpleton had to befriend him.

"I suppose so. I thought since her father had died from fighting the Franks, she might've had such experience."

"Her father died in a fight with a relative. Something about honor. I don't know the details and it does not matter. Eldrid foretold her father's death. That I remember." Lini stopped playing with the tiller and stared as if looking into the past. "Eldrid's words always come true."

Blinking at the revelation, Ulfrik stole a glance toward Eldrid in the distance. It was ludicrous to think she could hear him, but somehow she had unnaturally sharp hearing. "Eldrid said Audhild's father would die? Why?"

"He was her father, too. Eldrid and Audhild are sisters. I don't remember why she said it would happen. The gods show her things, like how she said you'd come from the sky to lead us to safety in a new land."

Questions stacked up on each other, but Ulfrik had to stop with the return of Gudrod and the others. Lini left him before they boarded the deck. When Eldrid stumbled the final steps over the railing, suddenly she did not seem as old as he had thought. Her bony arms and fine, fair hair made her look older, and her ragged voice was that of a hag's. She was a strong counterpoint to Audhild.

"We've been invited to their hall, and are free to make our repairs and trade," Gudrod announced. Cheers came up from the rest of the people. "I haven't mentioned anything about wintering here, so not a word from any of you."

Gudrod stared at Ulfrik as he made his request. A slight smile played on his lips. He did not care at all, for as soon as he could he would meet with Gunnbjorn and arrange for his freedom.

The process of disembarking took longer than Ulfrik would have liked. He was eager to see a familiar face, but the men who came to help were unfamiliar. He felt useless and forgotten, having been laid flat again like a piece of cargo. Not until the last moments did Audhild come with bearers to fetch him. In light of Lini's information, Ulfrik now saw the similarities in the shape of Audhild's and Eldrid's faces and the severity of their mouths. Eldrid was irredeemable, but Audhild need only smile to cure the meanness of her features. As the men bore him over the side, she spoke to him. "You were right about these people. They are friendly and willing to trade. I'm so glad that I convinced Eldrid to listen to you. Imagine if we tried to finish this crossing without stopping here?"

Her unusually animated talk further confused Ulfrik to silence. As bearers carried him down the gangplank, and then up the slope toward his old hall, her words faded off. Such a strange way to return home, and to a hall filled with unfamiliar faces. He had nearly given his life for this patch of land, and he prayed the people who remained would remember it.

Most of Audhild's people were gathered outside, now sharing news with the bewildered inhabitants of Nye Grenner. Curious children came to stare at and poke Ulfrik, and one asked if he was dead. Rather than leave him under the sun, Audhild asked to place him in the shade of the hall. A dark-skinned man with a coppery beard twisted to a braid answered her. "You will all be welcomed to my hall, but I fear I lead a humble life and it is a poor place for guests. Still, we will welcome you as friends and are eager for news."

This was Gunnbjorn, who had been a much younger man when Ulfrik had seen him last. Now the sun had cooked his skin and time had bent his back. Though he was a decade younger than Ulfrik, he appeared older than Snorri who was the oldest man Ulfrik had ever known. He had forgotten how bitter life could be this far to the edge of the world. How much worse would Iceland be if it lay even closer to the edge?

As he rested in the cool darkness of his old hall, his mind filled with a dozen memories that threatened to overwhelm him. He began to think of his family and his closest friends left behind in Frankia. He wished someone would interrupt him, but he was nothing more than a totem to Eldrid and her people and no more than a broken slave to Nye Grenner. No one sought him, and so memories were his only companionship. It was not long before he felt the wet chill of tears leaking down the sides of his face and into his ears. The familiarity of the hall made it feel as if his family was near, but they were far away and believed him dead.

Hours passed and people came and left the hall. Voices were mostly happy and bouts of laughter punctuated the exchanges. However, as the day drew on, silence grew and then shouting began. Ulfrik raised his head, as if expecting his broken legs to be healed. They were not. Gunnbjorn stormed inside with several others following.

Audhild followed, hand on her chest and her eyes bright with fear. Gunnbjorn charged directly to Ulfrik's litter, hanging over him with a disgusted scowl upon his face.

"Look at me," he commanded.

Ulfrik swallowed, then smiled weakly. "You're not happy to see me, old friend?"

Gunnbjorn straightened and the men at his side looked expectantly at him. A woman with cratered, red cheeks clung behind Gunnbjorn and hissed.

"I don't understand," said Audhild, forcing herself to the front of the crowd. "I thought he and Hrolf were friends of yours?"

"Actually, I am jarl here," Ulfrik said, daring to name his title when obviously he could not enforce the claim. It was the truth, as he had never relinquished the title.

Gunnbjorn's laugh was like the bark of a dog. "Jarls left these lands years ago, and none are welcomed back. I can scarcely believe what I see before me, but it is true. I recognize your eyes, like the wolf of your namesake. You are Ulfrik the Unlucky, and I see the title still fits."

"I was thrown from a tower. A story for another time. I was hoping for a better welcome, and that you of all people would remember the sacrifices I made for this land and its people."

Gunnbjorn's scowl deepened and he curled his lip. He turned to Audhild, who now had Gudrod at her side. Both stared slack-jawed at Gunnjorn, who pointed his gnarled finger at them. "You may repair your ships and trade. But you must leave immediately. This broken man you placed in my hall is cursed. He brought us war and death and all for his own vanity. I'll not have him back."

He faced Ulfrik and squinted. "Never call yourself jarl here again, or I will have the grievances of the people brought against you, then you'll find out what it's like to be thrown from a cliff."

20

The door to the abandoned barracks wheezed opened, bright moonlight sliding through the crack. Ulfrik roused from half-sleep, barely lifting his head. "If that is you, Eldrid, you're too early. Audhild has not visited yet. You can torment me later."

The door closed as someone entered, returning the room to darkness. Ulfrik was awake now, hand searching for anything to use in defense. Nothing but old straw filled his hand. A spark flared in the blackness, then the pungent scent of burning touchwood hit his nose a moment before a candle flared. The sudden brightness was like a bonfire to his eyes, though in reality the shadow of a man husbanded the weak flame as he slipped past the stacked bags and crates.

Half the barracks had been converted to a storehouse, and Gunnbjorn had staged trade goods here along with Ulfrik. The shadowy man placed the candle beside Ulfrik's pallet, then searched around as if just realizing the crowded conditions.

"It used to house thirty men," Ulfrik said, his voice rough from disuse. "The crew of one ship."

"I know it, Lord Ulfrik. I was a boy then," the shadow said. He leaned over the weak candle flame; a smiling but unfamiliar face wavered in the orange light.

Ulfrik returned the smile. "Then your beard must be what throws off my memory."

"I am Bork Borgarson. I was a lad of twelve when you sailed away. You might remember my brother better than me, Helgi. He was supposed to sail with you and my Da, but he was too sick."

The tale knocked loose more memories, but Ulfrik could not place the brothers. "Borg was a good man. Did you get his blood price?"

Bork nodded. "When Toki returned, he made good for all the families of the dead. Did it in your name. People here seem to have forgotten that part of your legacy."

Ulfrik closed his eyes at the mention of Toki. His ghost haunted this place, and with days to idle he thought about him more than he wanted. "Toki lost all the gold I sent with him. He must have got it from his wife's family."

They sat in silence a moment, then Bork spoke. "These people you're with, they're strange. They've made you a slave."

"Not a slave, but not free. I don't know what I mean to these people, and their claims about me are stranger still. The blind woman, Eldrid, she's their seidkona, but she's more than a witch or a seer. She has them under her control."

"A spell." Bork's eyes widened as he whispered the words.

"A spell anyone can weave. Most of these folk are bondsmen to her family. The blind seidkona is sister to Audhild, and she has promised these people land and freedom as long as they accompany her to Iceland. She had a vision of me being a gift sent to them from the gods, and as long as I live with them they will prosper."

Bork's eyebrows drew together, causing shadow to flood his eyes. "Is it true?"

"True or not, I've no intention of dying in Iceland—if we even reach it. You see my condition and you've heard Gunnbjorn's scorn for me. I need help. Someone must get word back to my family in Frankia. They think I'm dead."

"That's a long way off." Bork reclined deeper into shadow, rubbing his chin. "But I've come to help. My brother, Helgi, feels the same as I do. You were a good leader to our family, and your wife cared for us when you left. It's not right for you to be stacked in this room like a bale of hay to be traded. Everyone else may choose to forget their oaths, but not us. My father raised us better."

A smile stretched across Ulfrik's face. "I feared I'd never find another honorable man again. Your courage warms my heart."

"Helgi and I will sneak you out. We own a fishing boat sturdy enough to deliver you to the Irish monks living north of here. Once they see your injuries and understand the injustice, they will admit you to their care."

"Don't underestimate the people keeping me prisoner. They will pursue us, and I don't doubt they'll kill the monks to get me back."

Shaking his head, Bork waved away Ulfrik's concern. "The monks are protected now. Jarl Hrapp the Cross has become a Christian, even if his people have not. He won't abide an attack and we'll alert him to the possibility. Gunnbjorn won't stand for it either. The battles you and my father fought against the northern families ended the time for wars in these lands. We will stand together to drive out any enemy."

They shared the silence while Ulfrik mulled the plan. This was the best he could hope to achieve. "When I am finally returned home, I will send such riches back to you and Helgi that you'll become jarls yourselves."

"It's not more than what I should do. Perhaps I will remain with you. There's nothing here for me. Stole my wife from a farm in Scotland and she's no prize. Hasn't given me children either. I can leave her behind."

"I'd be glad for the company. Now you must leave, for neither Audhild nor Eldrid have visited me yet. Audhild tends my injuries, and Eldrid later comes to demonstrate she's the stronger one. Once they've visited, then I will be prepared to enact your plans."

"Good, we've readied everything for tonight. The sky is clear and moon shining. No better time to do it."

Bork collected his candle and extinguished it before he opened the door to slip out. He whispered a promise to return, then disappeared. Ulfrik lay in the dark and imagined escape. Audhild interrupted his planning when she came to check on him. By candlelight she examined all his wounds, brought him scraps of the evening meal, and shared minor details of the day. Repairs on the ships were complete and Gudrod was going to float them the next morning to test for leaks. Everyone was optimistic for the last stretch of the trip.

For his part, Ulfrik attempted to act as calm as possible though his heart raced. At one point while checking his shoulder, Audhild noticed the fast throb in his neck. She had given him a quizzical look, but Ulfrik dismissed it with the only excuse he could muster. "I'm lonely in this room. Your touch is ... welcomed."

Audhild had laughed and continued with her ministrations. After placing a skin of water in easy reach, she left him. Now he awaited Eldrid's arrival, where she would inflict her minor torments. She never did anything overtly damaging. One night she had forced him to drink the entire water skin and then refastened his pants so that he urinated on himself all night. Most other times she rambled about visions and purpose, and intermittently prodded his broken bones until he cried out. He had learned to express his pain more vociferously than he felt it. That satisfied Eldrid's purposes while keeping the pain manageable.

Time stretched on and Ulfrik's pulse quickened again. Eldrid did not arrive and he wondered what would cause her to forget. She seldom missed a night to toy with him, though it had happened. However, tonight was made for desperate plans and her absence was troubling. At last the door opened again, but the lack of anything besides moonlight informed him it was Bork and not Eldrid.

Two forms flitted past the door to disappear in the shadows of the stacked boxes. Reemerging by his side, Bork crouched with a finger over his lips. Ulfrik nodded understanding. The other man, assumed to be his brother Helgi, merely patted Ulfrik's good arm in greeting. The two then spared no time in securing the ropes that held him to the litter before lifting him between themselves. They began to guide him through the former barracks with great care, but they knocked a stack of empty crates. Though none fell, they both cringed as if an anvil had crashed in the silence.

Passing beneath the door, the air was instantly fresher and cooler on Ulfrik's face. The salty smell of the ocean mingled with the warm, earthy notes of the grass that swished in the breeze. He had not been outside his prison for a week and it felt liberating to see the sprawl of stars above. Only scattered clouds glowed silver in the moonlight. The two brothers wasted no time, but jogged in a crouch across the field behind the main hall. Ulfrik had hosted games and feasts here, and had won a battle against his neighbor, Hardar, in this same place. Now it was painted in ghost-white strokes and empty of anything but grass and stones. They stumbled and tripped at points, and one would outpace the other and jumble up the litter. Yet they managed to transport him down to the sea, where a wide and low fishing boat leaned sideways on the thin strip of rocky beach.

Lifting his head up, he saw the lumpy outline of bags stacked in the hull.

Eldrid sat on a bench in the boat, arms folded over her staff and her blindfolded eyes seeming to meet his own.

Helgi stopped short with a gasp and Bork cursed as he stumbled. Gentle waves lapped the rocks, hissing when the water retreated back to sea. A rough voice came from the left, and all three turned to face it.

"Getting some night air?" Gudrod stood up from where he had crouched. Covered in his cloak, the moonlight had painted him as little more than a rock. Now his sword gleamed as it scraped across the wood of his scabbard. He pointed the tip at them. "Place Ulfrik on the beach and step away."

More noise from the opposite side drew Ulfrik's attention, and he saw a knot of shadows moving from behind a large rock toward them. Spear points gleamed a milky blue in the moonlit night. Both Bork and Helgi cursed.

"Be good lads and surrender. You're trapped between spears and sea, not much of a choice really." Gudrod stepped closer, his sword threatening Bork.

Ulfrik's mind raced, but there was no solution. He cursed his broken body. With a sword and both his legs mended he would cut the heads from all of these snakes in one pass.

"Don't trust them," Ulfrik warned. "They're all mad. The blind whore has them under a spell. You two have to escape."

"I don't see how," Bork said, and his brother agreed. The spearmen were now in reach.

"Throw me in the sea," Ulfrik said. "Then run. They'll have to save me."

Helgi looked at him as if he were mad, but Bork understood Ulfrik's plan. He shoved against his brother, but the plan spluttered out like a candle in a wind.

The litter collapsed sideways and Ulfrik's weight carried him over. He crashed into the sand, landing on his good shoulder but pain rocked him nonetheless. Bork had turned to flee and Helgi paused to draw a sword.

The brief fight ended before Ulfrik could shake the sand out of his face. Gudrod lanced his blade through Helgi's neck and he fell beside Ulfrik, clutching at his throat and bubbling blood erupting from his mouth. Bork made it ten strides before one of the other men threw a spear to pierce his side. He collapsed with a scream, and his pursuers followed on with their weapons. Spears pumped over Bork as his cries died and his body stilled.

Rough hands flipped over Ulfrik in the sand, and Gudrod's musky scent clogged Ulfrik's nose as he bore down over him. "You only have to be breathing for the magic to work. Gods said nothing about you standing up again."

"Enough," screeched Eldrid. Ulfrik could not see her but imagined her holding out her staff as she always did when shouting her pronouncements. "Get him aboard ship."

Defeat suffused Ulfrik's body, flattening him into the sand. Next to him Helgi's final breath gurgled in bloody foam. At least he died with his hand upon his sword. Gudrod and another hefted Ulfrik back onto his litter, where his legs still remained tied. Pain shot through his body at the rough treatment, particularly in his legs. A filthy rag tasting of stale beer was stuffed into his mouth and tied with a leather strap about his head. Gudrod's shadowy form playfully slapped his cheek. "Nice try, but you've got to stay with us. We need your good luck."

"How?" he managed to ask through the stifling gag.

Eldrid appeared as two other men lifted him. "What I've lost in sight, I've gained in hearing. Do not plot against me, or I will find out. Even a thought will be enough, for the gods let me hear your evil imaginings."

She grasped Ulfrik's leg at the break and squeezed, sending ice cold pain up into his brain. When he recovered, they were bearing him along to the two ships farther down the beach. Unlike Audhild's description, these ships were already at sea and a chain of people were relaying goods down a line that ended in Ulfrik's former prison. When they reached this line, Gudrod ordered Ulfrik placed to the side. "Watch him, and break his legs again if he tries to move."

A guard with a bloodied spear stood beside him. His eyes were wide with shock, and even in the darkness Ulfrik could see how pale his face had become. As soon as Gudrod left, the man vomited in the grass. He had probably never killed before, but Eldrid and Gudrod had forced him to it.

He remained staring up at the moon, trying to remember Bork's face. The man had sacrificed his life for him, and already his image was fading. Ulfrik squeezed his eyes shut as if to impress the vague memory of the man deeper into his mind. He would not forget the sacrifice. Such loyalty would guarantee Bork a place in the feasting hall, even if he had died fleeing, at least so Ulfrik convinced himself.

"What's this?" the voice ringing out in the night was Gunnbjorn's, and Ulfrik opened his eyes to find the jarl running down the slope with a shield and a drawn sword, but otherwise only wearing gray wool clothes. Men came with torches and spears, all in the same condition as their leader. Gunnbjorn's ugly wife waddled behind him.

"Gods curse you," Eldrid screamed, sweeping forward with her staff overhead. She had remarkable accuracy for a blind woman, and Ulfrik guessed she could strike Gunnbjorn's head if she desired. Instead, she ratted the staff at him. "You plot to steal our gift? This is your hospitality?"

Gunnbjorn did not answer, but looked to his men. Their faces were flat in the dancing torchlight.

"We'll be taking what we need for winter," Gudrod said, stepping beside Eldrid. His bloodied sword drew Gunnbjorn's eyes. "You can collect the bodies of your thieves down the shore."

"I don't know what you're talking about. These are my winter stores, and you'll return them or face death." Gunnbjorn raised his blade as if to signal his men, and they stirred to his command. Yet Gudrod's line did not hesitate as men and women alike handed sacks, casks, and boxes down the line to the foremost ship.

"Your daughter might disagree with that choice," Gudrod said.

Audhild came forward with a girl of no more than ten years clutched to her side. She held a knife to the girl's throat. Seeing this made Ulfrik's gorge rise. Could the woman who had tended his wounds so carefully murder a child?

"Bastards!" Gunnbjorn searched the crowd until he found Ulfrik lying on the ground. He stalked toward him, sword extended. The guard fumbled with his spear and set it at the oncoming attacker. "This is your doing. You brought these madmen to us."

Ulfrik wanted to agree with him, to admit his fault and apologize for the horror visited on this place, but the gag in his mouth turned words to muffled nonsense. Gudrod called Gunnbjorn to heel as Audhild bit the knife deeper into the girl's throat. He stopped.

"After we've loaded everything we need, we'll cast off. Your daughter is coming with us, and we'll let her off on one of these small islands with food and water. You can fetch her there, as long as you don't follow. Give us one day, and if we see any ship on the horizon behind us—even if it's not yours—your daughter goes over the side. Understood?"

Gunnbjorn nodded and his wife sobbed. His men shook their heads in frustration as he waved them back from the line stealing his winter stock. "You are killing all my people with this."

"But the gods have chosen us to survive," Eldrid said, straightening herself with evident pride. "And so we shall prosper this winter."

By the time dawn was staining the night sky, Ulfrik had been loaded aboard the ship like another piece of cargo. Audhild dragged the girl hostage with her, and avoided looking at Ulfrik. Without a favorable wind, the men were forced to row and he was glad they had to strain to escape their evil.

Fearing the worst for the girl, Ulfrik was surprised when Gudrod let her ashore the next day on an empty island. He hoped the tiny girl would survive the ordeal, but if her father hastened she would be rescued.

Then the two ships sailed for Iceland, replete with ample stocks for the coming winter.

Ulfrik wished the gods would send both ships to the ocean floor. Yet, after nearly a month of monotonous sailing, a lookout proclaimed land off the starboard side.

They had arrived in Iceland, Ulfrik's grave.

21

Ulfrik hobbled across the uneven ground on his crutches, following Audhild to the gathering of her people. After so long at sea with nothing more to do than accustom his legs to bearing weight, he was glad for the open spaces. Flimsy slave clothing had finally been exchanged for buckskin pants and a scratchy, gray wool shirt and cloak. A wet wind sliced through him as he trailed Audhild. She paused now, patiently smiling as he caught up to her.

"How does it feel to walk on grass again?"

"As if I'm always about to trip."

Her laugh was light and vanishing, but her smile lingered as he came to her side. He continued past, and she matched his pace. Ahead of him nearly sixty people congregated around a tall lichen-spattered stone. Two boys stood atop it, one of them dancing playfully. The rest of the crowd spoke in animated, upbeat voices that echoed off the fat clouds hanging overhead.

"I can hardly believe we have come so far," Audhild said. "I've dreamed of this day for so long. All the planning, the setbacks, and the fear, it's all over now."

"Winter doesn't figure into your plans? It will be a blessing if half of these people are alive come springtime."

Audhild's white hand grabbed the silver hammer at her neck. "Eldrid has foreseen success. You will ensure it for us."

Ulfrik had tired of asking how exactly he ensured success. Neither Audhild nor Eldrid could answer, and Eldrid became violent if pushed. He snorted and spit, rather than ask again. By spring he planned to have regained his former dexterity and worked out a solution to acquiring one of the two ships for himself. He would row with his own crutches if that guaranteed his escape. These people would have their god's-gifted winter and then he would be gone.

As he came among the crowd, it parted for him. A few people applauded and it began a reaction that spread across the circle. Frozen in place, he met their approving faces with wide eyes and a half-opened mouth. Lini and his friends clapped hardest and bowed to him. Even Gudrod, standing in front of the great rock, labored out a few claps. Ulfrik blinked, his mouth quivering with nothing to say. What had he done to deserve their praise?

"The people are grateful for the sacrifices you've made." Audhild lightly placed her hand upon his shoulder and drew him to face her. "You are the gods' gift to our people, and we all know you gave up your old life for our sake."

He wanted to scream in Audhild's face that he had done no such thing. He had fallen from a tower during a fight with his mortal enemy. He had depended upon Audhild and these people to aid him, and instead they had enslaved him to their bizarre visions. Yet the applause continued and Audhild's smile was clear and warm. Instead, he swallowed and faced the crowd.

Atop the rock, Eldrid now balanced with the aid of the two boys, each one hovering with arms outstretched about her. Despite her blindness she stood as if she was part of the stone. Her thin mouth bent in solemn approval of the crowd, and Ulfrik wondered if she thought the praise was directed at her. She began to butt her staff on the rock, the necklace of bones about her neck rattling. In moments, everyone turned to face her.

Her blindfolded gaze spread across the gathered families. The wind pressed her plain dress to her body, revealing the thin frame beneath and setting her unkempt hair flying. Behind her the shoulders of snow covered mountains loomed and the start of a sparse woods of birch trees shook their branches. Were it not for the waves rolling onto the beach, the silence would have been perfect.

Eldrid's voice broke the quiet like a rock dropped on a pile of shells. "Last night I slept under the birch trees and asked the gods for wisdom. A rabbit came to me and said this is the place the gods have made for us. Our long journey is at an end. My vision has proved true. The man I witnessed falling from the sky in my dreams has carried the gods' blessing to this land and will carry it with him for our prosperity."

More cheering ensued and Ulfrik wished he could slink away. He had never been shy before the admiration of others, but this was wrong. He had done nothing for these people. He feared them for their zealotry, despised them for their ignorance, and wished to escape. He would rather they all die than prosper. Their adulation only added to the sense of madness.

"What is more, your hope for freedom is fulfilled." Audhild shouted above their cheers, stepping forward to make herself clear. "Today, all bondsmen are now freemen. Whatever oaths held you to another are dissolved this day. You are free to live as you will."

Cheering turned to dancing and shouting. Two-thirds of the people who made the journey were bondsmen or slaves no longer. Freedom, even in this rugged outland at the end of the world, was more precious than gold. Ulfrik knew it only too well.

"And I suppose that doesn't apply to me," he said with a frown. Audhild's smile did not falter.

"You must remain married to the people, to fulfill Eldrid's vision and ensure prosperity."

His attempt at whirling away from Audhild to sulk nearly ended with him crashing on his face. The makeshift crutches that supported his weak legs caught on a stone and he barely prevented a fall. Pain radiated from his left shoulder as he recovered, growling away a young woman who had made to catch him had he tripped. That the girl could have borne his weight had he fallen on her was even more humiliating. The muscle and strength that had so long defied the decades were diminished after months of inaction. He left the celebrants behind, and did not turn back to face them.

Hobbling to the shore, he stared out at the gray ocean. Winter would come and ice would float in to lock them into their homes, which currently consisted of tents for the prepared and lean-tos for the less fortunate. Favoring his left leg, he stood at the edge of the water and tried to ignore the celebration back in the clearing. He fought the memories of his family that invaded his thoughts. Throughout this entire ordeal, he had staved off Runa's warm smile, the proud deeds of his sons, or the playful laughter of his adopted daughter. He chased away his army shouting in victory, carrying gold and spoils beneath his banner. All of it he pushed down, else he would collapse under their weight. Now standing at the top of the world where ice and snow reigned over all, he began to realize these memories were all he would have for a long time to come.

Memories were not for banishing, but for holding close and providing strength. Without his memories, he might actually become the weak, broken thing these people wanted him to be—some living token of the gods' favor forever tied to whatever scrap of land they chose to settle. Without his memories, he might surrender.

"I will not," he said, his grip tightening on his crutches. He swallowed hard, throat clicking with the effort. "I will not give up until I am dead. I will not stop seeking a way home. I will not forget who I am."

He faced the ocean, gusts of cold spray peppering his face, and studied the sea birds riding the high clouds. Sitting would have been more comfortable, but his legs needed to strengthen. Also, without assistance his attempt at sitting would end up more like a crash, and nor would he be able to stand again without Audhild to hoist him. So much healing yet remained. He shook his head at the thought.

The celebration had sobered and he recognized both Audhild's and Gudrod's voices addressing their audience. Soon ordered crews of men began to descend upon the ships that had been hauled to the edge of the grass. Ulfrik observed them under hooded eyes. Younger boys followed, bearing mallets and axes along with empty barrels that formerly held supplies. Gudrod shouted instructions to both crews, typical encouragements to work fast and not waste anything. The first crew began to straighten their ship, wedging large stones beneath its hull. Curious, Ulfrik approached.

The younger boys helped carry out the sail, handing it down to women who had arrived behind their men. It seemed everyone had arrived. Next, the men unstepped the mast and dropped it over the side into the grass.

Audhild now found him, with Eldrid picking her way behind her.

"What are they doing?" Ulfrik asked. "This is not like any repair I've ever seen."

Eldrid answered, feebly shoving her sister aside. "We need wood for houses and barns. We sailed in our homes across the great ocean, and now we will remake them in this land."

"You're taking apart the ships?" Ulfrik's voice did not register any of the fury welling up inside. He could not believe even these people were crazed enough to cut off any possibility of leaving.

"We need the wood," Eldrid said, her voice filled with finality.

"You just slept under trees last night. There's your wood." Ulfrik's voice cracked as he tried to control himself. "Ships are important to a new colony. Trust me on this. As your contact with the gods, I'm telling you they want the ships intact."

Eldrid screeched as if she had been branded with a red-hot iron. She dropped her staff and held her head, wailing in agony. Ulfrik recoiled in surprise as Audhild bent to her sister's aid. All the people stopped, and those nearby rushed to Eldrid.

"No one speaks to the gods but me!" She burst out of the small crowd, her face pulled taut with hate and fury. "You do not have the sight! You are a liar!"

The hostility surrounding him became palpable. Every face grew dark and scowling, and every eye regarded him with suspicion. Even Audhild, normally mild, bared her teeth in undisguised hate. She stabbed a finger at him. "Do not claim to know the gods' will. Whatever speaks to you is an evil spirit. Never say such a thing again."

The crowd was like a great boar ready to charge. Either Eldrid or Audhild only had to give the signal and boar tusks would tear him from crotch to throat. He raised his hand for peace, holding Audhild's hate-filled glare. Her chest was heaving with anger, as if the challenge to Eldrid's authority had knocked the air from her.

"Think about this. These ships are important to us. We will need to find our neighbors and trade with them. Your sons will need wives from other lands. Without ships, we cannot be found nor find anyone else. Use reason; leave at least one."

Eldrid stood as if barely recovering from the grievous wound. Ulfrik considered if his words could inflict such suffering on her, he would have spoken them sooner. Audhild whispered soothing words to her, though he could not hear them. She shook her head, then accepted her staff from a woman who had retrieved it for her.

"Continue with your work," Eldrid said, straightening her necklace of bones. "Leave no board wasted. Winter is at hand, and we need shelter. Be quick."

Gudrod repeated her orders and the crowd resumed their work. Audhild snarled at Ulfrik as she escorted Eldrid past him.

He stood watching the crews throwing oars, tackle blocks, benches, and boards over the side. Tears began to slide from his eyes.

The wood piling in the grass made him think of the funeral pyre that surely awaited him in this horrible land. There was no longer any hope of escape.

22

Ulfrik hefted the weighted club overhead, holding it at the apex until his shoulders burned, then sliced down. He stopped the club when his arms were perpendicular to the leaf-spangled floor of the woods. Sunlight played along its length and highlighted the sweat coating his forearms. The stone lashed to the end of the club pulled down on his wrists and threatened to break from his grip. He snarled and held it steady until the burn consumed him, then touched the rock to the ground. Blowing sweat from his mustache, he let the club drop from his calloused hands.

Leaning against a birch, the only kind of tree that grew in these rocky lands, he congratulated himself on his effort. Though his legs were stiff and his form poor, he had done better than yesterday. Yesterday he had done better than the week before, and better by far than he had in the last days of winter when he finally regained mobility. Though the forest air was cool, a V-shape of sweat penetrated his brown wool shirt. With only the merest of responsibilities to perform for his so-called family, he had plenty of time to exercise his muscles and regain his fighting form. With the ships completely stripped down to their last nails, no one seemed to fear his escape and Audhild had even encouraged him to practice his swordsmanship. However, trust did not extend to providing him an actual sword.

With winter releasing its grip, Ulfrik had expanded his world from Audhild's hall to the perimeter of the village and now to the outskirts of the birch forest. He hesitated calling it a forest, but given these northern lands held so few trees, this scratchy patch would have to do. He wondered how far he could expand before Eldrid or Audhild pulled his leash. The birch trees were about the limit, since he noticed a young man spying on him from behind a large rock.

"Hello," Ulfrik called out, waving to him. "You can see me better if you stand closer."

The man ducked back as if Ulfrik had shot an arrow at him.

Waiting for the man to peek once more, Ulfrik snorted his laughter. Do they imagine themselves unseen like forest elves, he wondered. He had known simple men, but none as dull and superstitious as these folk. Though they had shared the trials of winter, due to their provisions and the sturdiness of their homes, few people had suffered. They attributed it all to the luck the gods had invested in him, and would hear nothing to contradict that belief.

Hungry for a diversion, Ulfrik decided to test the limits of his minder's ignorance. If the fool thought hiding behind a rock could make him disappear, what would he do if Ulfrik himself was no longer where he expected once he finally dared to look?

"Time to challenge these legs," he said, patting his thighs. As soon as Audhild had removed his braces, he had begun strengthening his legs. They had withered from disuse, but he fought all winter to renew the muscle. Audhild had even helped, bracing him for his first days on his feet. Now he would test how well he had recovered.

He did not run so much as swiftly pick his way among the trees. The forest floor was rocky and covered in leaves still wet after the melting snow had retreated, so he did not dare speed. His body was fragile and a fall on rocks would be disastrous. Instead, he picked a zigzagging path through the trees. He laughed like a mischievous boy, and felt as wild as one. Flouting authority even in such a mundane way boosted his spirits.

Coming to where the trees climbed a rocky slope, he wondered if he should stop. The incline seemed treacherous to him given his current state, and he wouldn't want his minder to fetch someone without a sense of humor—like Gudrod. That evil bastard spent the winter being surly and jealous of Ulfrik for living with Audhild, and Ulfrik did not want to imagine what punishment he would deliver if he could justify it. Yet this incline was the farthest distance he had gotten from the village. Why not try for more? After today, what chance would he have to be let out of sight?

He heard his name in the distance, and laughed again. Carefully testing his steps, Ulfrik scaled the steep slope. Dark, wet rocks broke away under his feet or gnarled roots shoved up from the ground to catch him, but he still mounted the slope without an accident. Looking down, he now worried for his return journey.

"That looks a lot worse from up here," he said. Maybe he would let his minder carry him down. Leaving that worry for later, he turned to where the trees grew thicker. Sunlight flickered among the white trunks, inviting him to explore. Though his left leg grew stiffer, he decided to press on. His name echoed louder now, and it galvanized him to motion.

No longer running, content to let his minder catch up with him, he ambled from tree to tree, clapping his hand to the trunks and feeling the sturdy strength of them. He wanted to be like that, tall and strong, not feeble and hunched like an old man. If ever he were to escape this island, he needed to stand as straight as these birches.

Despite everything, he had not abandoned hope for escape. After the ships had been dismantled and their planks carried away to construct houses and halls, he had despaired of escape. Yet over the long winter with nothing more to do than eat and sleep, he had occupied his mind with a dozen possibilities for escape. Some plans were so fanciful a skald would be shamed by his imagination, while other ideas relied on boons of fate so difficult that only the rarest treasures could persuade the gods to grant them. Yet a few were plans he could enact if the right circumstances combined. For those plans, he prepared himself.

He wasted no time pushing deeper into the woods. The steep incline had dropped him into a flat stretch that led to still higher ground. He could see the rocky slope through the gaps between the trunks and decided to head higher. Surrounding their colony were steep mountains and bald cliffs, and if he could reach even one of these lower points he would have a good view of the area. That would be useful knowledge, and his game now turned serious. When he heard his name called again, he increased his pace. At the foot of the slope he found a less forgiving climb, and decided to search along its length for an easier path. His persistence was rewarded with what almost seemed a man-made path snaking up the side.

Following the path to the top, he discovered the birch trees still populated the area though lacking enough density to be even called a woods. Sweat rolled off his nose and his leg throbbed, but the excitement of getting a view of their colony surpassed the inconvenience. Audhild's hall occupied the center of about ten houses all built in the traditional design resembling a boat. Given that the wood mostly came from their ships, the resemblance was apropos. Size varied by function and family, but none were as large as Audhild's hall nor were any as empty. She kept no company besides Ulfrik and she had one girl attending her whose only relative had died at the onset of winter.

Scanning the outlying areas, he saw what he guessed to be Eldrid's hut, a stone building suitable for the witch she was. He wished it would collapse on her one night, but the gods would not be so kind. Men were constructing farms not much farther from her. The place seemed well established for having only been in place for half a year. Behind it was the iron gray sea rolling endlessly away to the edge of the world.

His legs were trembling and he decided to sit and await the arrival of his minder. He cupped his hands to his mouth as he called, "Up here. I need your help to get down. Hurry."

After a moment he saw the dark figure of his minder scurrying toward him. He decided to let him struggle to locate him, and walked farther away from the edge to a fallen birch log sunk into the grass. When he sat down, he nearly fell over in shock.

This was a campsite. The log had been a seat and in front of him was the ring of a campfire banked with gathered rocks. He leaned forward and touched the ash pile. Cold muddy ash clung to his palm.

He batted his hands together to clean them. This campsite had been beneath the snow all winter.

Someone had been here before Ulfrik and the others had arrived. Certain that if he searched around he would find more evidence, but he had no time to search. If his minder found this and reported back to Eldrid, there would be no guessing what she might do. Ulfrik wanted to find the creators of this campsite first, if that would even be possible. At the moment, he nervously brushed his pants and tossed about for something to cover his discovery. He heard his name called again, this time from the edge of the incline.

He strode toward the voice, biting back the pain and stiffness in his legs. The man was just scrabbling into view when Ulfrik nearly crashed right into him.

"And here I am," he said with a huge smile. "I was beginning to think you'd never catch up. Really, one old man with a bad leg can outrun you?"

Up close the man was smooth-skinned and dark-haired, with striking blue eyes ringed with dark circles, reminding Ulfrik the man was named Bresi Black-Eyes. His beard marked him for a youth, and his mouth was drawn into a frown. "You shouldn't have run off. Gudrod says you can't get out of our sight or you'd be up to no good."

"Gudrod is a good sailor, but a terrible judge of character. What trouble have I made up here? See, I'm even willing to follow you back. Let's go." Ulfrik took the man's arm, but he pulled free with a scowl.

"I'm tired from chasing you. Let me rest a moment before we start back. There's a log."

Ulfrik's guts burned as his minder started toward the log. To Ulfrik's eyes, the place now looked so obviously like a campsite he wondered how the man had not realized it at a glance. Yet he seemed not to notice as he removed his fur cap and scratched his head. The moment he sat down, he'd know.

"If you think I'm in trouble, I expect it will go far worse for you," Ulfrik said. The man stopped and replaced his hat.

"Gudrod won't be happy with your forest walk."

"True, but what about the man who let me take it? Look, you're a young lad and probably have no experience with this sort of thing. I like you, so let me fix this for both of us. Come here."

Bresi's frown deepened, but he returned to Ulfrik and left the campsite undiscovered. Ulfrik placed his arm over the man's shoulder and began to guide him toward the slope as he leaned in to speak as if they might be overheard. "I know you'd like to see me punished for putting you through this, but Gudrod will have you whipped for failing in your duty. Then he'll assign another to the job because you'll be what he'll call incompetent. You know what that means?" Bresi shook his head as they came to the edge. "Well, it means you'll be off to a bad start in your new home. You'll not be trusted with anything important again. So instead, why don't you and I make an agreement?"

"What kind of agreement?" Bresi pulled back, but Ulfrik was already seeking a foothold in the slope down.

"I'll go back with you and never speak a word of this, nor will you. No one is the wiser, and if anyone did see us we'll both agree you were with me the whole time. I just need to get out and explore once in a while. Let me come up here and no one has to know what happened. Gudrod will be happy and you'll not have to wear yourself out chasing me."

"I'll think about it," Bresi said, but Ulfrik guessed he was only covering his pride.

"That's all I ask." He suppressed a smile as he worked his way down the slope with his new friend following. He planned to spend a lot more time here.

23

Ulfrik checked over his shoulder, certain his minder would be chasing after him. Weeks had passed but the campsite was exactly as he had left it, the only difference being the muddy ash in the remains of the fire had dried to a clump. He kicked through the grass finding old bones from a meal, a stake buried in the ground where a tent had been pitched, and most telling a bent knife blade discarded by the fire. From the little rust on the blade he guessed the last visitors had left within the year. He searched the bright spring sky as if the answers were overhead, but found only the dots of distant birds.

His minder, Bresi Black-Eyes, called from the woods down the slope. Despite Ulfrik's intense desire to return and explore this campsite, he had deliberately waited weeks to slip away again. He had hoped Bresi would have forgotten the location, but he was doing an admirable job finding it. He also wanted to avoid eliciting Bresi's suspicions for this location by returning too soon. As it was, he wanted to lead Bresi away from this place to be caught elsewhere.

Bresi called again, this time closer, and Ulfrik stepped up his plans. Whether or not anyone would return to this place, he could not guess. He had hoped to discover a midden pit or something to indicate habitual activity. His minder left him no time to discover one, if one existed. However, the place was a natural spot for anyone to make camp in these woods. High ground was mandatory when selecting a location, and in this area the only higher elevations were unsuitable. Fresh water was nearby and a commanding view of the area would be welcomed by any traveler.

However, travelers would see the village below and either come down to it or remain hidden from it, and Ulfrik did not want either outcome. He wanted the campers to stay away until he could find them first.

Reaching into a pouch carried at his waist, he produced a flat stone he had procured from Audhild's hearth. In secret, during his almost limitless idle time, he had scratched a message into the stone. Not everyone could read runes, but most could recognize basic messages. His was simple, "Wait here." He set this in the center of the campfire remains, then threw a handful of kindling twigs next to the stone. Staring at them, he had the sinking feeling that this message only made sense to him and future travelers would be confused. He wanted them to make a fire and wait. With Fate on his side he would see the smoke before others and escape to this campsite. He would be the only one looking for smoke at this place and he knew how to find it faster than any other.

He heard his name again, and decided he had to set Bresi on a new trail or risk his discovering this setup. If he ever saw smoke rising here, it would have to be the work of fate. He clapped the dirt from his hands and hobbled off toward the far end of the slope. Once he had clambered down, slipping and scratching his leg on a rock, he yelled a challenge to Bresi. "You can't keep an eye on one old man? Try to keep up."

Waiting until he heard Bresi curse in response, Ulfrik darted toward the west. He had no plan to his route, picking the easiest paths that rolled out between the birches. Even in a mere two weeks his agility and stamina had increased, and he was covering far more ground than he had thought possible. Conversely, Bresi seemed to be fading into the background. Maybe he had given up or had stumbled and hurt himself. Ulfrik didn't care. He reveled in the motion, the pleasant pain of exerting his legs, and in the freedom of the forest.

Though not even at a fraction of his old strength, he still exhilarated in the power of his flight.

After what felt like an hour, yet was likely not more than minutes, that power fled him and he was doubled over against a birch tree. He gulped his breath, laughing. Here was good enough; let Bresi catch up to him.

Then he heard the singing.

It was distant, but high pitched and melodious. His skin tingled and he felt a cold trickle along his back. Had he disturbed the forest spirits or aroused the interest of an elf? In all his years, never had he experienced such a voice from deep in the trees. Yet this was a new world with new wonders. Common sense told him to spit for luck and walk backwards away from the enrapturing evil, but what if the singing was from a more mundane source? What if this singer could aid him?

"Bresi, I wish you'd find me," he said as he started toward the singing. His heart beat in both dread and anticipation. Having company would bolster his resolve, but alone he was free to worry.

As he drew closer, the voice resolved into a woman's. Her lyrics were indistinct, but some words rose through the distance. It was a mournful tune, but expertly sung and powerfully executed. He slowed his approach, half from fear of discovering a forlorn spirit and half from just wanting to enjoy the song. He had not heard such singing in many years, and it stirred memories he wished to enjoy a while longer. Even a sad song was a joy in this frozen land.

He came to glade bathed in sunlight and seated upon a low rock was the source of the singing. His mouth dropped open and he leaned against a tree when he recognized the singer.

Eldrid sat on the rock, staff leaning forgotten by her side, her face toward the sun. Her blindfold was unbound and lay spread across her lap. She smiled as she sang, though Ulfrik's ears registered nothing from the pure shock. Under this light, swaying to her own singing, hair floating with the breeze, she was nearly beautiful. However, as she turned her head in time with her song, Ulfrik saw the horrid wounds of her eye sockets. The one eyelid was heavily scarred with scabrous red flesh while the other was nothing more than an angry knot of twitching scar tissue.

When her gaze slid past him, Ulfrik stepped back. A branch cracked beneath his foot and Eldrid's singing stopped.

His stomach felt as if it had burst into flame. She shot to her feet, snatching up her staff as she did. Her formerly sweet voice had become shrill.

"Who's there?" She shot forward directly toward Ulfrik, her head tipped back as if she could still see out of one eye. He thought he saw a yellowish eyeball seeking him beneath the mangled lid. "I'll turn you into a frog and dash you on the rocks."

Her face was a mass of angry lines and she bared teeth the color of stale cheese and livid gums. Raising her staff overhead she charged him with a hoarse scream.

If she realized he had caught her in this private moment, Ulfrik feared what sort of visions she would begin to have about him next. Maybe the gods would ask her to have him burned alive or thrown from a cliff. Owing to Eldrid's blindness, she struck close to where he had been standing. He was already skittering away, yet she was uncannily accurate in following.

Having exhausted himself leading Bresi on a chase, he feared Eldrid might catch him, but he managed to put a gap between them that she could not close. She stumbled and he heard her indignant cursing.

"I'll pull out your eyes and cut out our tongue," she screamed. "You are cursed. Cursed!" She repeated her threats as Ulfrik continued to pull away. He slowed to a jog once he realized she would not catch up.

Then he was crashing into the dirt.

Sliding down a slope he hadn't even seen, scree and sand rushed down over his head and into his clothes. The scratch on his leg now deepened to a gash from another sharp, black rock that pervaded this area. He lay with his feet pointing toward the top of the slope, shirt hiked up over his face and pants torn. His body throbbed with pain, every old wound coming back to him.

Eldrid's shrieking drew closer. He tried to stand, but was not limber enough to regain himself before Eldrid arrived. She approached the edge, using her staff to tap out the perimeter. Her dead eyes looked down into the ditch.

Ulfrik lay still.

She inhaled deeply, like a hound tracking its prey. Ulfrik shuddered at the thought, for as she did a wide smile came to her face.

"So," was all she said, but the single word encompassed a world of meaning. Ulfrik heard the recognition and threat in it, realizing that somehow the infernal witch had known him by scent.

His hand gripped a sharp, black rock. If he had his former strength and accuracy he could throw it straight through her face. Men had named him a champion ax-thrower in his youth. Now, he doubted his strength, and in the moment Eldrid simply turned from the edge and left him. A slide of rock and sand marked her departure.

He remained on the ground long after she was gone, feeling the dank earth seeping into his bones and watching the clouds form shapes above him. He saw one in the form of a long dagger, and he imagined it would be much like the one Eldrid would use to cut out his eyes.

24

The hearth fire had burned low, casting Audhild's hall into a room of wavering shadows. Ulfrik sat at the opposite end of the table from Audhild, who quietly ate with her attendant —a sad-faced woman named Kelda. He slurped from his wooden bowl and avoided looking at either of them. He studied the murky broth, which suffered from too much salt and fish meat that had disintegrated from over-cooking. Nightly he remembered Runa's meals and the pride and care she took in them. Even in times of deep poverty she had prepared soups better than this puddle of salt and fish. Runa had been a perfect wife. He wished he had told her so more often, now that by all counts he was dead.

The sound of Kelda's bench pushing back from the table shook the room, such was the quiet. Most evenings were silent, for Audhild was taciturn with him and Kelda as well as her occasional visitors, of which Gudrod was most frequent. However, tonight the hall was morosely quiet and Kelda appeared eager to leave, eyes constantly flicking toward the door. Now she smoothed her skirts and collected their bowls into a bucket.

"Leave them for tomorrow," Audhild said to her. "You are free tonight. I would like a moment alone with Ulfrik, please."

"Of course." Kelda's pale face blushed down to her long neck. She smiled awkwardly, placed the bucket next to the hearth, and left the hall without a moment's hesitation.

Audhild stared at him across the table, her scarred eyebrow raised. He had been waiting for this since his encounter with Eldrid. That day he returned with Bresi, who had deserted the chase and waited for him to exit the woods, Audhild was shocked at his torn clothes and scratched leg. He had managed to deflect her concerns with excuses, but she would not be put off the trail. Instead of working him, she later sought out Bresi. Ulfrik did not doubt she had extracted everything she wanted from him.

"My strength grows each day," Ulfrik said, avoiding her stare while swishing the cloudy soup in the bowl. "By the end of summer I will be in full health. Thanks to you, of course."

He gulped the final mouthful of soup, a thin fish bone catching in his teeth. He spit on the floor to eject the bone along with the excess salt. When he sat up again, Audhild remained staring at him with her chin resting in her hand. They remained in silence until she leaned back and gave a tired sigh.

"And you'll put all that strength into leaving me. Is that repayment for all I've done for you?"

"Escape is my usual reaction to being held captive."

"I saved your life." She slapped the table, making his wooden bowl jump, then glared at him.

"To make me worse than a slave. At least slaves have work to do. You just want me to wander around like the village fool."

"You are no slave. You are a gift from the gods, as Eldrid dreamed it. Your life brings us fortune."

"This discussion bores me," Ulfrik stood, wobbled a moment as he balanced himself; his legs were still unsteady from his encounter with Eldrid. "I've heard this a dozen times and it is nonsense. You are right. I will put my strength into leaving this place at the first chance I get. I have a family waiting for me in Frankia."

He deliberately mentioned his family, knowing that for whatever reason it angered Audhild. It was as if he were not allowed to have ever had an existence prior to her rescuing him. She did not disappoint, for her face turned red and her fist clenched.

"Your family is here now. The people need you."

"Enough," he said as he held up his hand. "If this is what you wanted to discuss, I'm too tired for it."

"I want you to move out," she said, her voice sharp with anger. She folded her arms across her chest, as if to dare him to argue.

Ulfrik blinked in surprise. "Where?"

"A small home has been prepared for you, close to those woods you so love." She held her chin higher as she spoke. "I've done all that I can, and it would be unseemly for you to remain here any longer. People might misunderstand."

The sensation of loss that loosened his knees surprised him. All he had dreamed of had been escape, but now the threat of loneliness and isolation frightened him. Audhild had been a constant since he fell from the tower, and though he bore no love for her, she was the closest person he could call a friend. She was also young and easy on his eyes. He was already missing the woman's touch from his life.

"You are certain I can handle myself alone?"

"Your house will be far less difficult to run through than the woods." She smiled; so she had known about his run-in with Eldrid after all. "You will be fine. You'll be given a goat, cooking pot, and other necessities that the community can provide. They owe you their lives as surely as you owe me yours."

He frowned at her last statement, but she shook her head to warn him off the argument. He shrugged instead. "Very well. Is it ready tomorrow?"

"It is." They stood staring at each other until the silence became uncomfortable. Ulfrik rubbed the back of his neck and Audhild studied her feet. She broke the silence. "So you will go, then?"

"Well, you demanded it of me. I will make the best of my new home."

"Good."

More silence dragged on and Ulfrik decided that nothing more was worth saying. He turned to find his bed, but Audhild stopped him with a word.

"Eldrid may be blind, but she sees beyond what mortal eyes see.

She is more complex than you imagine, and more dangerous. Do not vex her when she desires to be alone."

"Are you warning me stay away from her? That is wasted breath. I've no desire to be near that woman ever again. Ease your mind on that score."

"Good. I cannot help if she were ever to curse you. Your death would be terrible."

Audhild's eyes glittered in the low light of the hall. Ulfrik nodded and turned away, certain she had just threatened to have him killed.

25

Ulfrik leaned against the door of his small home, scanning the wooded hills for signs of smoke. No hopeful smudge of gray stained the sky above the yellow-crowned birch trees. A fleet of clouds plied overhead, periodically hiding the sun. Nothing, just as it had been all summer long. No travelers had returned to find Ulfrik's messages hidden in the old campsite. He checked every day, a habit born from both hope and boredom. Though it was a foolish thought, he wondered if Runa or Gunnar or any of his family ever stood on the walls of Ravndal and looked hopefully for his return. Could they both be repeating the same tired, hopeless actions every day across the thousands of miles? From within the hut, he heard his table jolt and a wooden mug thump to the floor. His goat had bumped it as he did at least a dozen times a day. Were it not for the companionship the beast provided him, he'd kill it for its sheer stupidity.

Satisfied that help was not coming today, Ulfrik stretched and strolled around his house. The woodpile was well stocked, and a rabbit had been strung up by his door, an offering from one of the villagers. Despite living nearly a year among them, he hardly interacted with any of them. They all feared his supernatural powers, whatever those might be. They came with offerings in the early morning hours or at midnight when the never-setting sun was most dim. He prodded the rabbit, bony and small, not likely the best part of their catch. Yet, he appreciated their sacrifice. Carving a life out of this land was difficult, and carrying an unproductive man was a burden that could lead to ruin.

He decided to walk the shoreline this morning. Gudrod had left enough wood from their old ships to build several fishing boats, and Ulfrik enjoyed watching them at work. He also imagined seizing one for himself and making his escape, though without a destination he would either die at sea or be forced back to the coast. He needed an ocean-going knarr or longship if he were to ever have a chance.

Halfway to the shore he found Gudrod with his cronies leaning on the wood fence of a goat pen. Busy in discussion, they had not noticed his approach and Ulfrik was about to turn away when Gudrod spotted him.

"So where are you going this morning?" Gudrod shoved away from the fence and walked up to Ulfrik.

"Any place where the air is not fouled with your breath. Step aside."

Gudrod's smile dropped. "You're in a fine mood. Did the goat kick you when you tried to mount her?"

"You'd be the one to teach me about mounting goats, since you can't get between a woman's legs unless you beat her senseless. How's it going with Audhild? Her door's still closed to you?"

"You'd do well to remember who you're speaking to."

"A virgin?"

The barb drew a snicker from one of Gudrod's supporters, and it stopped Gudrod from releasing the punch he had aimed at Ulfrik. Instead he whirled around at the man. "You think he's funny?"

Ulfrik's punch collided with Gudrod's ear, and being that he was already twisted off balance, he crumpled to the grass. Pain flared in Ulfrik's hand but the violence released a killing euphoria he had forgotten. Reveling in his new strength, Ulfrik was atop Gudrod before he could recover. Conquering the urge to pound him, Ulfrik grabbed Gudrod's beard and yanked his face close.

"For each night that you've pulled your cock and dreamed of Audhild's bed, I've killed a dozen men with my hands alone. If you ever think to raise a fist to me again, I'll twist your head off." He shoved Gudrod back into the grass and stood. A dozen bones cracked and as many joints burned as he did, but Ulfrik suppressed it all beneath his dignity. He glared at the others surrounding him. Fortunately, their shock was plain in their slack-jaws and wide eyes; otherwise Ulfrik might have taken a horrible beating.

"Get your master out of the dirt. You had all better take the same lesson. The gods placed me here, and who knows what they really sent me to do? Be good to me or I'll make Eldrid's curses a pleasure."

They all stepped back and one bent to help Gudrod. Ulfrik did not linger to see what became of his display, but heard Gudrod's indignant roar. Without trying to run, he increased his pace toward the shore. His heart pounded and his hands itched for more fighting, but the pain in his body told him he was not yet ready for brawling. Gudrod had not been paying attention and so Ulfrik had exploited the moment. A straight fight would still not be favorable, and Ulfrik did not want that known.

A smile came to his face, even as he realized both Gudrod and Eldrid would punish him for his trespasses. Let them come at him. He had nothing better to do.

Until he saw the ships.

Three sails arrayed along the horizon, already close enough to see they were two fat-bellied knarrs and one a sleek longship. The strong wind carried them, and their oars were shipped. He could not tell if they had set beast heads on the prow, but on the longship shields were racked, a sign of peace. He checked over his shoulder, but the lazy village scene showed no reaction to the approaching ships. No warning shouts or blowing horns. Goats chewed the grass in spotty sunlight and people were away at chores or indoors. He looked back to the beach, and the three fishing ships were beached. For whatever reason, they had not put to sea this day.

Tears nearly erupted from his eyes. The gods were sending him a way home. They had blinded the village and kept the fisherman away, who normally would've intercepted any approaching ship.

These ships were undoubtedly traders, two knarrs for hauling goods and one longship for protection. They would send a party ashore before landing and Ulfrik would greet them. He wanted to dance, to run screaming in joy along the shore. He waved at the ships, but Ulfrik was already standing on the only sensible landing point. He did not need to draw any attention.

So he waited, constantly checking over his shoulders for someone to appear from the village. The ships stopped in deep waters, and he saw the white splash from the dropping anchor stones. Over his shoulder, the village idled. His heart throbbed until he became faint.

One of the knarrs released the ship's rowboat into the water, and five men scaled down ropes to leap into it. Over Ulfrik's shoulder, the grazing goats were joined by another but nothing else changed. Men crowded the forecastle of their ships, some waved and Ulfrik waved back. The small rowboat drew closer, bobbing with the gentle tide.

Behind, nothing changed. Ulfrik felt ready to explode. At that moment, he could've hoisted an anvil overhead and ran it the length of the coast.

The rowboat now came to shallow water, and two men leapt out to guide it safely ashore. Ulfrik waded out to assist, calling his greeting with a smile so wide it hurt his cheeks. Once the boat lodged on the sand, he helped beach it then stepped back to allow the visitors to clamber over the sides.

"Gods be praised," Ulfrik said, his arms thrown wide in greeting. "However you found me, I cannot be grateful enough."

Of the five men, three were armed with swords and girded with leather and fur. One fetched spears from the hull of the rowboat and distributed them to their owners. The two others were less well armed and lacked the killing edge Ulfrik recognized in the three sword warriors. All wore fur caps and were clad in wool cloaks stained white with sea salt. Their faces were rugged from sun and ocean spray, and the creases at their eyes spoke to their years of glaring into the horizon searching their next destination. All sea-roving traders were of kindred aspect, for the open sea bends men in certain ways. They swayed at the edge of the surf, revealing how long they had been aboard their ships.

"Well met, friend." The speaker wore a frizzy beard like a plume of smoke from a swift-burning flame. "I'm Heidrek Halfdanarson. These are my ships. We've come a long way in hopes of trade. Heard there were new settlers in the area. See we found the right place."

Heidrek stuck his beard at the village, and Ulfrik turned again to see people emerging. Gudrod and his pack were leading the group. Ulfrik's guts tightened.

"Listen, Halfdan, these people are dangerous. They're mad. A blind woman rules them with strange curses. You're not safe here and neither am I. Please take me with you and leave this place."

The traders frowned, and Heidrek looked him up and down. "Name's Heidrek. Calm yourself, friend. Trade's good for everyone. Never met a man this far north that didn't welcome news and supplies."

The group was closing in. Gudrod was waving as if he were reuniting with a lover. Worse still, Audhild was hurrying behind the crowd and guiding Eldrid by the arm.

"Curse the bastards," Ulfrik said.

"Say what?" Heidrek's lip curled and the spearmen stepped closer to him.

"There's no time. I know what I must look like to you, but I am a jarl where I hail from. I'm Ulfrik Ormsson. I served Hrolf the Strider. Surely you know that name if not mine."

"Jarl?" Heidrek's sneer filled in all the other words he did not need to speak. One of the traders laughed, more of a derisive cough.

Ulfrik checked over his shoulder. Gudrod was a dozen paces away and Eldrid was waving her staff overhead and screeching her miserable gibberish. He faced Heidrek and reached out to him. "These people will kill me."

Spears lowered, cutting off the rest of his words. Their faces were resolute. Heidrek glared at him. Ulfrik halted and his arms flopped to his sides, a lump in his throat threatening to choke him. He had rushed his chance and destroyed any hope of convincing the traders to aid him. Now he played the madman, all out of desperation.

"Stop!" Gudrod shouted from behind. For a moment Ulfrik hoped

Gudrod defended him against the threat to his life, since Eldrid's visions required him to live. "Get back from these good men, slave."

A rough hand at his shirt collar yanked Ulfrik back, causing him to stumble. The bravado of moments ago had fled him, such was his shame. He deserved the humiliation for his own stupidity. He landed on his side and Gudrod kicked him.

"Did he threaten you, my friends? He's a slave who's always trying to escape me. He hit me in the face a moment before you arrived." Ulfrik looked up to see Gudrod displaying the red side of his face to Heidrek.

"No, just wanted to join our crew."

Whatever else Gudrod and Heidrek said Ulfrik did not hear. As soon as Heidrek indicted him for an escape attempt, Eldrid howled as if she'd been speared. She leapt at him with staff overhead and began slamming his head and shoulders with force unexpected for her thin frame. "Unruly slave! Ungrateful cur!" Each strike landed with a new curse. "Faithless bastard! Uncaring pig!"

"You bitch!" Ulfrik caught the staff and tore it out of her grip. Fire pumped through his body as he raised it overhead. His vision clouded and ears pounded. He imagined Eldrid's eyes hanging out of her broken skull and the pink brains beneath. He roared.

Then he stopped.

He was surrounded, nearly half the village pinning him to the ribbon of surf. A few carried swords, but all carried a knife as matter of course. Eldrid cringed as if expecting the blow, but when it did not come she sprang back up like a sapling that had been stepped on.

"Get him," she screamed.

Half a dozen hands seized him, tearing Eldrid's staff away and forcing him to the ground. More crowded him so that he was lost in shadow, hands trying to force him down. He did not struggle. If Heidrek wasn't already convinced he was mad, further resistance would just make him look worse. The group parted and Gudrod stood over him with sword drawn. His gloating smile made Ulfrik's stomach burn with hate. "Stay still, slave. You've caused enough trouble for one day. Take him away."

Three men hoisted him up, forcing his arms behind his back. Eldrid stood with her head lifted in triumph and Audhild watched with her hand over her mouth. The man behind shoved and Ulfrik trudged forward.

He wondered what punishment awaited the gift of the gods.

26

"Make him drink it." Eldrid hovered behind the two men holding Ulfrik down. Arms already bound behind his back, he had no leverage but fought with all the ferocity he possessed. The bed underneath him rocked as he bucked, kicking out as far as his tied legs allowed. Eldrid and her followers had been thorough with him, now wary of his strength after the day's displays.

"Hold his head steady," said the third man. Ulfrik couldn't see him. The two pinning him down were from Gudrod's pack, one a long-faced man with sad eyes and curly hair who leaned in too far. Ulfrik head-butted him, hurting himself as much as his opponent. The long-faced man crashed into the wall of the small home, hands over his forehead.

"Make him drink it," Eldrid screamed again. Now he could see her, blind eyes somehow starting at him through the dirty blindfold. "It'll calm him."

The last man pressing his shoulder down was thin and lumpy with puss-filled pimples, and young enough for Ulfrik to be his father. That this child held him down shamed Ulfrik. Had he his normal strength, all three of these fools would be in twisted heaps. Now his joints were inflamed with fatigue and his breath ragged. The third man finally appeared over him, bearing a clay bowl in two trembling hands. Unkempt red hair framed a white, freckled face.

"Lini?" Ulfrik ceased struggling, staring at the inverted face appearing over him. "I thought we were friends?"

"Just drink this and you'll feel better." His brow creased with worry as he extended the bowl and he appeared on the verge of tears.

Ulfrik pitched up again, but the man he had head-butted threw himself over Ulfrik. Gray fluid that smelled like sweat splashed out of the bowl as Lini stepped back.

"You'll make me drop it," said Lini.

"Careful with that. I only have a bit of it left." Eldrid reached out with a blind hand as if she could catch the foul brew.

The pimple-scarred man draped himself over Ulfrik and now he was fully pinned. Lini grabbed Ulfrik's face with a cold, hard hand and pinched open his mouth. "It's for your own benefit. Don't be such a—ow!"

Ulfrik bit Lini's finger. Whatever the concoction, he figured it was some sort of poison to render him senseless. He did not want to guess what Eldrid planned for him. Her humiliation had been great, and she did not brook the slightest challenge to her authority.

"You goat-fucker!" Lini punched Ulfrik straight on his nose, bringing stinging tears to his eyes. In that moment, he shoved the bowl into Ulfrik's lips and upended the contents. The bitter liquid ran out the sides of his mouth and pooled behind his head, but he swallowed more than he wanted. He began to choke and gag on it, but Lini had done his job. "Last favor I do you," Lini said as he slammed the bowl beside Ulfrik's head.

The two men remained atop him until his vision began to haze and his arms grew heavy. They sensed his relaxation and peeled off, crouching back as if he were a wolf that might spring to the attack. Ulfrik was such a wolf, but only in his mind. His body was like lead, as dead to him as when he had been drugged in Audhild's home after his fall from the tower.

"I can't stay for the rest of this." The voice sounded as if it were underwater. Ulfrik recognized it as Lini's. The other two shared looks, and the sad-faced man nodded. They seemed prepared to remain.

"Go on, my son," Eldrid said in her falsely concerned voice. "I will remember what you've done."

The fire in Ulfrik's belly was the only thing he felt. Helpless before Eldrid, he recognized too late she planned to maim him. What else could she intend? he thought. I should've fought hard. Should've made them kill me, not cut me apart like a hog. You fool! He closed his eyes, having at least the power to do that much. Gudrod and his men had tied him up at sword point. He should have fled at that moment. Now he was tied down in someone's house, on a strange bed, the sunlight fading and no hearth fire yet lit. The dark crept across the room, brushing his feet as if to caress them before devouring them.

"Lini did insist we numb you for this," Eldrid said, leaning on her staff at the foot of the bed. The door behind hung open to let in the light, casting her into shadow. "You should not have bit his hand. You should not have bit my hand, either. You are the ungrateful dog from the stories, biting his master's hand."

The response that fell out of Ulfrik's mouth was a jumbled mess. His tongue was like water-soaked leather. Instead he growled his anger.

"If you'd have drunk all of the medicine you'd not feel a thing. But now I fear you'll be awake for it." She shrugged, twisting both bony hands on her staff. "Perhaps you will forget this. The brew has the effect, too."

The coolness of her voice was far more frightening than the insane ravings she normally spewed. She seemed normal and in control. She waved a hand at the sad-faced man as if shooing away the vile deed she had prepared for him. The man nodded and reached below the bed. The other man grabbed Ulfrik's left leg and pulled it to the side.

"I have to keep you from running, and punish you in the deal." Eldrid reached down and pinched his big toe as if playing with a child. Ulfrik could not resist, only grunt his rage. "There's only one way I know how. Boys, you know what to do."

The sad man brandished the stone-headed club Ulfrik had used to practice his sword form. He had lost the original one, or so he had thought. Now his enemy hefted it in two hands, the heavy stone head drooping in his grip. The man did not look at him, but touched the stone to Ulfrik's thigh as if marking the spot he intended to smash.

Ulfrik's body twitched, the best response to the mental struggle he suffered. His body felt shrouded under a blanket of iron. His eyes were wide with fear and rage.

The other man held Ulfrik's leg steady, just like chopping a log.

The stone club rose.

Ulfrik closed his eyes, bracing himself for the smash.

"Stop this!"

Audhild was in the doorway. Ulfrik could not see her, only a shadow framed in the rectangle of bluish light, but her voice was a clear note of sanity in this madness.

"What are you doing here?" Eldrid leapt like a frightened cat.

The stone did not fall, but hovered over the wielder's head as he stared at the two women. Sweat rolled into Ulfrik's eyes and his breath was short and hot.

"You two. Out." She swept into the room. When the man carrying the club did not lower it, she pushed aside Eldrid and forced the club down. "I told you to leave. This is not your concern."

"But Eldrid—"

"Will talk this over with me. Now go, as I've already told you."

Ulfrik closed his eyes in relief, listening to the men leaving. His head swam and whatever had been forced into his mouth now made him unwilling to open his eyes. Sounds became dull and echoing, but even as his breathing slowed and head swam he still followed.

"You would shame me more?" Eldrid said. "It's not enough to be threatened with my own staff?"

"He will pay, Sister. But not in this way. Does he sleep?"

Ulfrik felt a cool, smooth hand pull around his eyes and for a moment a bright light filled his vision.

"Most of the brew ended up on the floor," Eldrid said. "He should be asleep."

Words faded in and out, Ulfrik unable to hold onto much. However, whole snatches of their exchanges blasted his ears. It was like the singing of a skald that goes from a mere whisper to a roaring crescendo. The identity of the voices were lost to the muddy echoes. It was all just words flying through the black.

"He was to be mine. You promised."

"The vision was true. You know it."

"...Not a choice anymore. The gods have decided ...."

"...is dangerous ...will turn them ..."

"...worry not, if he does I will deal...."

The words became ever more disconnected, and Ulfrik's hearing ever weaker. At last nothing made sense and he felt his mind leaving him. Only one last phrase surfaced, bobbing up like a piece of cork released underwater.

"He remains mine forever."

Then Ulfrik slept.

27

Ulfrik awakened in darkness. For a moment he thought himself blind, but a thin bead of orange light edged a door frame. In the next instant his stomach flopped and vomit rushed into his mouth. He tried to flip to the side, but he was restrained. Turning his head, the watery vomit splashed onto the floor below. Spitting out the foul taste, he lay with his head to the side. Everything rocked and whirled, only settling after long moments of stillness.

He strained to hear anything, but nothing more than silence greeted him. He could not recall what had led to him being restrained in the darkness, then the memories flooded back. A horrible brew that smelled like sweat had overpowered him, forced down his throat by man who he thought was at least friendly. Ulfrik realized he could not count a single friend among these crazed fools. They called him a gift from the gods, then treated him like a slave and threatened to break his legs.

After what could have been an hour or only minutes, the light around the doorjamb flickered and then the door opened. Light rushed in, forcing him to squint, and Audhild entered with a candle in hand. With the darkness relieved, Ulfrik looked side to side and realized he was in the same room Audhild had lent him during his recovery. Nothing in the small cell had changed.

She paused at the vomit on the floor, set the candle at the side of the bed, and pulled up a stool. She sat close to his head. He could smell her fresh scent, and Ulfrik felt himself stir at her proximity. His face grew hot.

"You will have to eat lightly," Audhild said, indicating the vomit. "The potion is hard on the stomach."

"Not as hard as a rock to the kneecaps. I suppose you will want to add this to the many things requiring my gratitude."

She arched her brow, the white scar buried in it rising. Ulfrik faced the ceiling and studied the rafters. A brown stain had formed since he had last been here, indicating needed repairs.

"You were very foolish for what you did. Do you understand that?"

Ulfrik clenched his jaw and closed his eyes. Audhild waited in silence, but he was not going to relent even if she pried open his mouth with a knife. At last he won his victory and Audhild continued.

"Eldrid and Gudrod both consider that you might be more dangerous than we had thought. Are they right?"

"I've either been lame or restrained the entire time I've been your prisoner. How could they have judged my threat in that condition? Give me a sword and I'll carve a red path through this village of madmen. Your best fighters beat their wives and call themselves warriors. Not a man among any here is fit to challenge me. So, do you think I'm a threat now?"

Audhild sat back, cocking her head with a disapproving curl to her lip. "That kind of talk does not help your situation. I've negotiated your safety, but I've guaranteed you would not threaten anyone again."

"I won't threaten, I'll act. Even if you make me your slave, I'd rather die fighting than spend a moment allowing a blind whore to whack me with a stick."

Audhild's backhand cracked across his face, white pain radiating from his cheek. He absorbed it and smiled at her glaring back at him. "Then maybe you shall die after all."

"And so dies your sister's vision. Go ahead. Any knife will do. Drive it through my throat and have done. Send me to Valhalla. Dear friends are awaiting me there."

Audhild shot to her feet, both fists balled and lips disappeared into a thin line. Her eyes searched as if looking for the knife Ulfrik had suggested, but then she let her breath out and she slumped. Touching a pale hand to her head, she sat again.

"You are baiting me. I don't know why I let that anger me." She smoothed her skirt then smiled at him. "You can be as mad as you wish, but do not be so swift to ask for death. Eldrid for one has told me she will seek guidance from the gods again. She fears her original interpretation of your arrival might have been mistaken. If the gods tell her your life is no longer necessary, then you will need my friendship."

Ulfrik swallowed. He did not fear death, but did not seek it. Fate had other designs for him, he knew. Why had they placed him in Frankia under a great man like Hrolf the Strider? Just to die at the hands of madmen in a forlorn island at the edge of the world? Still, Fate could have woven a new pattern for his life.

Audhild leaned next to him, letting her soft breasts brush against his arm as she did. "I am your only friend here. I've saved your life before, and will save it again. But not if you fight me. Don't be like a wild rabbit that refuses to accept the clover from its protector. Don't bite every hand extended to you."

"What have you negotiated for me?" He tried to ignore the touch of her body, but her sweet smiling face was now mere inches from his. A lock of her hair tickled his cheek and he turned aside.

"You are lonely, yes? How could you not be when you fight your neighbors? You speak names in your sleep, old friends or lovers I don't know. None of those people are here nor will you see them again. Time to start anew."

Her breath rolled across his face and he felt himself stir. The bindings holding him to the bed bit into him as he squirmed. "What arrangement have you made?"

She retreated, a satisfied grin on her face. "You will remain with me, under my direct care. You will do the work of man in my hall. You will not be allowed to leave on your own."

"That's slavery."

"Not at all. You just cannot leave the bounds of the village without me or someone I appoint. You're to never threaten Eldrid or Gudrod again."

"And when Gudrod comes knocking, hoping to find his way to between your legs? You'll not want me chasing him off?"

Her smug smile vanished and color came to her cheeks, her hand touching her chest. "Gudrod is no worry. Why would you say such a thing?"

"Because it is well known what Gudrod wants. He only looks towards one door when he walks through the village. That'd be yours."

"Don't concern yourself with it." She straightened her back and her hand fell back to her lap. "Before I remove your bindings, I have your word? You'll abide by these rules and not attack Eldrid again?"

"You'll assure me Eldrid won't have a vision from the gods that throws me into a bonfire?"

"How can I control what visions the gods grant her?"

"Then you've no promise from me."

She stared at him and again he resolved not to shift. Eldrid would want him skinned alive and he knew too well if the gods don't say what a man wants then he says it for them. "I never realized how stubborn you are," she said with a shrug. "If you follow the rules I will protect you from Eldrid."

"I will follow the rules," he said. *Until I find a way around them,* he thought.

The ropes fell away and his limbs tingled from the improved blood flow. As he sat up, his head began to spin and she caught him. "Don't stand. Remain here a while. Kelda and I must prepare for the evening meal. Heidrek and his men will leave tomorrow and we will give him a proper send off tonight."

"So you'll steal his cargo and take him hostage?"

Audhild paused in the doorway but did not turn. Instead she

rested a hand on the frame and sighed. "Yet you ate the provisions we took. You slept happily under the wool blankets we carried off. Don't pretend outrage for your old home. You wanted to survive the winter as much as anyone."

She left him with the candle, and the door swung closed behind her. Ulfrik stared at the gray wood door, and shrugged off her accusation. He could not resist the barb, but lost no sleep for enjoying the spoils of raiding. Nye Grenner had grown soft under Gunnbjorn and so deserved their fate. He dismissed the matter and leaned on his knees while his head swirled.

Outside his door, Audhild and Kelda chatted while they prepared the hearth for cooking. The familiar sounds of clacking plates, sloshing buckets, and women's laughter took him back to his own hall and wife. He imagined Runa and her servants flitting about the hall, his children under their feet. Pressing a hand to his head, he forced the memories away. Instead he waited for the feast, when Heidrik would be available for one last attempt at finding help.

The hours never seemed to pass until at last he heard male voices beyond the door. Gudrod was among them, but in Ulfrik's state he avoided confrontation. He waited for Audhild to summon him, which she did by opening his door then leaving. Beyond it her hall was lit with the hearth but otherwise empty. The front door hung open and merry voices laughed beyond. He followed them outside, his steps still uncertain from Eldrid's poison.

A simple feast had been prepared with long tables set out for Heidrek and his crews. Ulfrik located Gudrod seated at the head of a table with Heidrek, both leaning into each other like old friends. Ulfrik counted that a good sign for his plans. Other traders were sprinkled among the villagers, the younger women entertaining more than one trader hoping for an amorous send-off before the night finished. Eldrid was not present, a great relief but a surprise. She usually overawed any gathering of more than two people.

Avoiding his own people was impossible, but he eschewed eye contact with them and they reciprocated. Audhild saw him and motioned him closer. She walked the line of benches to mingle with her guests and Ulfrik fell in beside her.

Keeping her voice low, she pulled him gently by his shirt. "Remember your promise to me. Their ships are guarded. So if you think to hide yourself in one, you will be disappointed to say the least."

"The thought never crossed my mind." It has been his first impulse but it was too obvious and likely to end with his capture. Eventually Heidrek would find him and either return him or throw him overboard. He had resigned himself to finding another way to use the trader's presence.

Audhild smiled and patted his chest. "Find a spot at any table, but do not drink heavily. Your stomach is not ready for it."

Looking past her, he saw Gudrod scowling at him as Heidrek offered a toast. Ulfrik fell back into the crowd, seeking the company of the trading crew. He located an opening on a bench with two men on the outside edge of the women. They had not witnessed his outburst and likely had not even heard of it.

"A fine night for celebrating your last days ashore. Can I share a drink with you lads?"

The older of the two, red-nosed and rosy-cheeked, gestured with his mug. "Was hoping for someone with tits, but you can warm the spot till she finds us."

They all laughed and Ulfrik sat. He then set about ingratiating himself. All he required was information from them, and after a half dozen toasts, a round of riddles, and teaching them a rowing song neither had heard before, he had their attention. Their faces glowed from the ale they had guzzled, but Ulfrik had been careful to spill his into the grass.

Amid the laughter and off-tune singing, Ulfrik pressed them for what he hoped to learn. "Well, lads, the night is growing late and my old bones can only handle so much. You boys have to find a girl before you leave."

The red-nosed man, who had given his name as Folkmar, scanned the scene and waved a disgusted hand. "Bah, they're all taken. Better luck at our next call."

"And where's that?" Ulfrik asked.

The two grew quiet and glanced at each other. Folkmar answered for them. "We can't tell you. It's bad luck."

"Yeah, no trader will say where he travels next. Brings ambushers and worse," said the second man, who called himself Geir.

"I didn't realize," Ulfrik lied. He did not expect them to divulge their next destination even after they had become drunk. "Still, now you've got me curious. We don't have ships, so we can't chase you or set an ambush. What's the harm in telling me?"

"Heidrek'll whip the skin off our backs," said Folkmar.

"All right, I won't bother you about it." Ulfrik sat back and they watched others at their merriment. Two men danced with a girl to pipe music by the bonfire, then one nearly stumbled into the flames. The ensuing laughter reopened Ulfrik's opportunity.

"This is really bothering me, now. I have to know where you're going next. Let's make it a bet. If I win, you tell me what I want to know. If I lose, I'll get the two of you a girl for the night."

They now leaned forward, Folkmar raising his brow to Ulfrik's proposal. "What's the bet, and can you deliver on the girl?"

"Yeah, and not a cow. A real woman," added Geir and they all laughed.

"The woman is none other than my own, Audhild. See her over there? She's a tough lass, but listens to me. I'll share her with you if I lose." The two craned their necks, Folkmar frowning in disbelief. Ulfrik continued. "The bet is simple. I can throw my knife in the air and make it land on its cutting edge right on this table."

The two stared at each other then at Ulfrik. Folkmar eyed him. "She's quite a woman. She's really yours?"

"As sure as the sun rises. What have you to lose but a little bit of information?"

"Let me see your knife first." Ulfrik handed Folkmar the blade. It was a miserable thing, dull-edged and pitted but useful enough for common chores. Satisfied, Folkmar handed it back. "We'll take the bet. This thing's not sharp enough to stick in the snow, never mind stick on its cutting edge."

Smiling, Ulfrik took the knife, grabbed the blade with his shirt, and bent it into a V shape. The poorly crafted blade had bent on him so many times he had to be careful not to snap it. He then tossed it loosely into the air and it landed on the table, edge side to the wood. Of course there were two cutting edges and the V shape ensured a careful toss would land it correctly. He sat back in triumph.

"So where are you headed next?"

The two stared incredulously, then burst out laughing. Folkmar picked up the bent knife and repeated the toss, getting the same result with even less care. "But I must remember this one. Such a bet is worth losing to learn it." Geir repeated the toss until Ulfrik reminded them they had lost.

"All right," said Folkmar. He put his arm around Ulfrik and whispered to him. "There's another settlement north of here. A day's sailing in the worst weather. Part of our regular trade route. That's our next call. Happy now?"

Ulfrik smiled, "A terrible itch has been scratched. Now that you've told me, you wouldn't mind giving a few other details? Do they have ocean-going ships of their own?"

Folkmar and Geir nodded at each other, as if confirming their understanding. "Last year they had two ships, one knarr if I remember."

"Thanks for satisfying my curiosity."

Ulfrik's smile broadened. He had found his way home.

28

Ulfrik slid along the roof of Audhild's hall, tying the newly laid straw thatch to the supporting slats. The leak in the thatch roof had grown into a hole by the time snow had melted, and being over Ulfrik's room he had to fix it. A cool spring breeze carried the ocean scents to his nose, and he relished clear days like this one. He paused to rest, shoulders sore from the repetitive work. He checked the row of thatch behind him, much of it still needing to be trimmed into line. That was the hardest work; his shears were not large enough for the job. He would be at this the rest of the day, but did not mind. After another restless winter, he was glad to be outside working.

"How much longer will you be up there?" Audhild called to him from below.

He crawled to the edge to answer. She shielded her eyes from the sun with one hand and braced a basket of wool against her hip with the other.

"If I had proper tools, I'd be faster."

"I asked how long, not if you liked your tools."

"The rest of the day. Would be nice of you to get me help. Running up and down the ladder wastes time and makes me hungrier."

"I'll be back before the evening meal," she said, ignoring his request, then turned and headed inland.

Ulfrik crawled back to his spot and stretched his legs. From the roof he could survey the entire village and beyond. Homes were scattered like feed thrown to hens, settlers having grabbed whatever plots they liked. Behind them the land jumped into rough hills of black rock. In the gray distance brooded mountains shrouded in snow. Ulfrik did not like the looks of them, for their conical shapes were unnatural and once during the winter everyone heard a rumble from them that shook the earth. Horrible frost giants must dwell there, and all eyes avoided the peaks for fear of what they might see.

Now that winter snow had released its grip, people were outdoors more often. In another life it marked a happy time for him, but now it meant encountering Eldrid and Gudrod more often. Both had made their rounds during the milder days of winter and had treated him as if he did not exist. However, with summer and the midnight sun a few months away they would become far more active. Ulfrik flung a handful of loose straw from the roof and frowned.

Children laughed in the distance and reminded him of a time when his own children had nothing better to do than play. A group of boys chased each other with leather-capped spears and enacted their mock battles. The comical death-throes of the boys that had fallen removed his frown. "A shame you are children of madmen," he said.

He glanced at the flat, gray sea and imagined the warm lands of Frankia. How had their winter been? Had the Franks united as Hrolf had feared, and did they threaten Ravndal? What did Throst's alliance to the Franks in the south mean for their safety? A year and a half had passed since those questions were pertinent. Still he had mulled them all winter and each time the answer was the same. It did not matter to a dead man. Until he returned home, there was no point in fretting for any of it.

With the arrival of spring he could enact his escape north to search for the village the traders had mentioned. Most of the coastline leading north was cave-pocked cliffs and mountains of jagged rock with ample places to hide from pursuit. He did not need to know the village's exact location, for the people owned ships and so their dwellings would be along the coast. Whether they would accept him or drive him off was his greatest danger and sole hesitation. Through the winter Ulfrik had rehearsed his pleas to the village of strangers. He had to be perceived as a freeman or else he would be sent back as an escaped slave. Worse still, they could take him as a slave of their own. Charity from strangers was a rare thing, and a land as rugged as this either sharpened a man's mercy or his ruthlessness. At the least he would be free of Eldrid's madmen and their determination to keep him prisoner. From guarded conversation with Audhild, he had determined no one knew of the other village. The traders had kept their routes secret. Had Audhild or Eldrid suspected help was only a week's overland journey distant, Ulfrik supposed he would not be left alone to repair this roof.

He picked up the next bundle of straw and turned to his work.

Then something caught his eye in the distance and he whirled so that he nearly fell off the roof. Grabbing a slat to steady himself, he stared hard to the northeast.

Above the thin line of new birch leaves a twist of white smoke climbed into the air.

The campfire was lit. Someone was up there, maybe woodsmen from the other village to the north.

He was down the ladder before caution caught up to him. What if those were Eldrid's people? If he answered the signal, he would incriminate himself and that would be a poor start to the summer he planned to make his last in this land. If they were outsiders, he not only had to avoid being caught on the way up but also not frighten them as he had with the traders.

The campsite had so long been out of mind that he had no plans for it. At best it had been a desperate hope, but now it was reality. He needed to get to the visitors before others saw the smoke. He thought of the children playing outside. Children were always gazing at the skies for shapes in the clouds or birds circling, whereas adults had no such idle moments. Would they report it to an adult? Habit alone still dragged his eyes toward the hill several times each day. He hoped others spent less time scanning the horizon for signs of outsiders.

He ducked into the hall and pulled on one of Audhild's rust-colored cloaks. At the height of his strength his shoulders would have never been covered, but now to his shame the cloak managed to disguise him well enough. He only needed to look like anyone else in order to slip out of the village. Pulling on the cloak and drawing it tight, he hunched over like walking into the rain and made it to the edge of the village. From there, he checked for followers, and finding none he jogged toward the woods.

Footing was treacherous but he had scant time to waste. He stumbled, but kept the smoke in sight through the trees. It was a thin, weak column, yet still plain against the light blue of the morning sky. He cursed the beacon, now certain others must have spotted it.

By the time he mounted the steep rise, following the path he had discovered earlier, his heart was pounding and his thighs aching. Recovery had progressed all winter, but still his legs pained him under exertion. At the top, he leaned on his knees to catch his breath. Nothing could look more desperate than his bursting in on a camp while red-faced and winded. He wiped sweat from his brow with the back of his arm, then approached the campsite.

Moving from tree to tree, the loose white bark cool against his skin, he peered out at the campers. A man and a boy of perhaps fifteen years stood by the edge of the rise, hands on hips and looking out at the village below. They were dressed in green-dyed wool shirts and hide pants. The man carried a sword, but otherwise was unarmed. Behind them a tent billowed in the wind and a campfire sputtered smoke into the air. Ulfrik straightened his back and decided to approach. He picked a branch from the ground and snapped it. The two visitors whirled to face him, the man's hand flexing to his sword.

"Friends," Ulfrik called. He emerged from behind the tree with both palms open. "I saw the smoke and came with all haste. Did you find my message?"

The older man halted as if expecting a wild boar to charge him. The boy jumped but relaxed the moment he noted Ulfrik's upturned hands. Freckles splattered over his nose and cheeks and rust-colored hair blew over his eyes. The two exchanged glances, and the boy produced the rune-inscribed rock Ulfrik had left by the old campsite. The boy offered a hopeful smile. "You wanted us to wait?"

"It was the only way for me to communicate my message," Ulfrik said, approaching with his hands still extended. "You've seen the village below. They're madmen, every one of them. They came to this place to be alone and would see you as intruders. I did not want you to stumble into this village unprepared. Please, you should douse the fire before others come."

"Too late for that," the man said. "We've seen people pointing up this way."

Ulfrik lowered his hands and cursed. The man drew his sword half from his sheath to warn him. "No threat from me. Still, put out the fire. Let's not make it easier for them. Only I know this exact location. We have time yet, but you should leave."

The father and son exchanged confused glances. "Then we'll go immediately. Thanks for the warning."

"Wait," Ulfrik cringed at the desperate note in his voice. "Now that we have met, let us introduce ourselves. I am Ulfrik Ormsson. Are you two from the village north of here?"

The father nodded, then gestured they should head to the campsite. "How did you know? We've seen no ships besides traders, nor any scouts. At least none we've spotted." He stopped suddenly and eyed Ulfrik.

"I'm no scout. In fact, none of the people below are interested in discovering neighbors. They want to be left alone."

"Something I understand," the father said. Now at the camp, he set his son to covering the fire with earth. "Anyway, you can put your hands down. I'm Lang Seven-Fingers and that's my boy, Finn."

Lang waggled his left hand, revealing the stumps of his ring and little fingers. Ulfrik raised his own left hand to display his missing little finger. "Between us we make a complete hand."

Finn flashed a smile, accepting and simple. Ulfrik felt an immediate kinship with the boy and hoped no harm would befall the lad from this encounter.

"So now we are introduced," Lang said as he pulled up tent stakes. Their gear was already packed as if they were prepared for flight. "I'll not travel this way again, now that you've warned me of the danger. I'll warn the rest of my kin to stay away. No reason we can't both have peace."

"No reason at all," Ulfrik said. "This will be a hasty request, but may I travel with you? I came to these lands expecting peace for me and my woman, but these people are mad. A hard winter has made them worse. If there's room for a farmhand where you're from, I'd be grateful for the opportunity."

Lang had pulled up the stakes and now rolled up the tent. Finn had doused the fire and was carrying two packs, watching his father along with Ulfrik. Lang rubbed his chin. "I'm not a farmer, but a trapper and hunter. Can't say if others would take you on. But you're a freeman, and if you want to follow me back then you'll have to settle for what you can get, which might be nothing. Your people won't follow?"

Ulfrik restrained his excitement, but immediately offered to take a pack from Finn. "They will not care for my disappearance. Let's not delay. You've got a boat nearby?"

Lang nodded. "What about your wife?"

"Died in winter. Let's be off."

Lang gave him an appraising look from head to toe, then scooped the rolled tent underarm. "Nothing at all to take?"

"I bring only the strength of my back and willingness to earn my way. Quickly now, the others must be closing in."

Finn smiled at him, as he shouldered the other pack. Lang grunted then headed toward the same path Ulfrik had climbed to get to this spot. "You're that crazy slave Heidrek told us about, aren't you?"

A coal fell into Ulfrik's gut. He winced at the tremor in his voice. "Who's Heidrek? I've no idea what you mean."

They continued down the path, leaning back as they slid downslope. Lang stopped against a cluster of birch trees, gathered Finn to his side. "You're not much of a liar. We're going to start a war with your masters if we take you north. Sorry, Ulfrik or whatever your true name is, but you're staying here."

"Do I seem a slave to you?" Ulfrik shouted, then remembered

himself and dropped his voice. "Is my head shaved or a collar about my neck? Do I seem starved?"

"Not every slave is mistreated," Lang said. Finn shifted his pack from one shoulder to the next, and gave him an apologetic shrug.

"Think you can tell my lies from the truth? Then hear this. These madmen captured me when both my legs were broken. They put me on a ship bound for this wretched place because they believe the gods have commanded them to do so. Now they won't free me for fear the gods will punish them. Do you know who I am? I am a jarl in Frankia, where hundreds of hirdmen knelt before me and gold flowed from my hall to my champions. I'm not meant to die on this frozen turd at the edge of the world. What part of that was a lie, my friend?"

Lang and Finn both stepped back at his tirade and Ulfrik chastened himself. Again he had overpowered a potential ally, and his shoulders sagged. "Never mind your answer, I know what you think. Truly, you had best leave before you're found. Think on what I've told you and consider helping me one day. Hurry, before you're caught."

"I believe you," said Finn. The boy stood straighter, as if challenging his father to deny him. Ulfrik shrugged and gave a weak smile. The boy's opinions mattered little.

"As do I," said Lang. His eyes glittered in the shadow of the woods. "The truth is in your voice. It has command and power, like a jarl's."

"Then you'll help me?"

"No. Who's to say these people are wrong? The gods have their own plans and I'm not one to cross them. Life's hard enough."

"They are wrong. People still get sick and die. The winter was still perilous. A baby was stillborn only a month ago. What am I doing that aids them?" Ulfrik's hands itched to grab Lang's shirt, but he mustered all his restraint to not destroy the burgeoning promise he felt.

"I don't know, but they store value in your life. That's enough for me." Lang hoisted the pack again, and Ulfrik's hand raised as if to grab him. He guided Finn away.

"You're leaving me to die."

"We're leaving you to fate." Lang turned to face him again. "Listen, I will discuss your story with my jarl. We'll see what can be done."

Ulfrik straightened and squared his shoulders. He extended his hand to Lang and they grasped forearms. "You will have my gratitude."

An ear-piercing screech came from behind, and Ulfrik whirled to face it, still clasping arms with Lang.

Four men had emerged from the woods, and Eldrid stood among them—blindfolded but her staff unerringly pointed at Ulfrik's heart. She bared her teeth and hissed like a snake.

The four men drew their swords and started forward.

29

Ulfrik watched Lang forfeit his life and could do nothing to prevent it. Lang released Ulfrik's arm at the sudden appearance of Eldrid and her underlings. Despite the warning he just received and the obvious hostility of drawn weapons, he stepped forward with arms raised in a sign of peace. Eldrid's lead henchman was Bresi Black-Eyes, his knuckles white around the hilt of his sword and his pasty flesh glistening with sweat.

His dull blade flashed a wan blue as it raised. Lang's hand reached for his own weapon. Finn shouted for his father.

Then Bresi's sword slashed up beneath Lang's neck, a poor cut that any prepared warrior could have stopped. Yet Lang had nursed his doubts for Ulfrik's warning and it had cost him. His hand flexed back from his hilt to this throat and he crashed down with both hands stanching bright blood that arced into the dead leaves on the ground, the jets of red in time with his heartbeat.

Another followed up Bresi's cut, stabbing Lang uselessly in the shoulder. Bresi stood over the body in bewilderment.

"Run," Ulfrik shouted as he grabbed Finn and shoved him away. The boy instead leapt for his father's corpse. Eldrid's underlings hovered over Lang's writhing body, swords shaking in their hands.

Eldrid stumbled after them, screaming. "Is that Ulfrik's voice? Stop him! Kill the raiders!"

Ulfrik caught Finn by his collar and whirled him around, sending his pack flying. "I'll cover you. Just get back to your boat. Your father's dead."

Finn stumbled forward and Ulfrik shoved him again, not allowing Finn the chance to return to his father. "Live to have revenge for him. Run!"

Now they were sprinting through the clumps of birches, following the natural trails between them. Finn shot ahead, and Ulfrik realized he could not keep pace and would not reach Lang's boat. Eldrid's insane screaming followed and a glance back revealed four black shapes charging toward him. He had a slight lead, but it would not last.

"Don't stop," he called to Finn, who was already fading into the shadows. Whether Finn heard, he still shouted. "Remember who saved you this day."

Then he ducked into underbrush that crowded a stand of three birches, dead leaves shaking into his hair. His hand swept the wet muck until his fingers curled around a palm-sized rock. He began to pry it out of the dirt. Heavy footfalls and panting breath drew closer.

When the first shape passed him, he leapt up and hurled the rock into the man's back. His forward momentum carried him to the ground with a thud. The next man was close on his friend's heels and Ulfrik whirled to smash his elbow into the man's face.

He heard bone crack, smelled the rank beer breath, and shoved the man onto the one following. Only Bresi managed to avoid entangling himself in the crash. As he skirted it, Ulfrik wasted no time.

Snatching the sword from Bresi's grip was no more difficult than taking it from a boy. Many of Gudrod's men were practiced with swords, but Bresi was not one. He rapped Bresi on the head with the hilt, then kneed him in the crotch before shoving him away like a broken barrel. The other two had regained themselves, one with blood flowing out his nose onto his beard and shirt. The injured man staggered aside and slumped to the dirt, surrendering. The other straightened from his fighting crouch, staring at the bloodied sword in Ulfrik's hand.

"Care to find out if I still have what it takes to kill four men at once? I've done it before, against better men. Come on. Have a lesson in using those swords you're so proud of. Be ready to lose a nose or eye in the bargain." Ulfrik ranged his sword at the pathetic group. Bresi was still holding his crotch while the broken-nosed man pinched his bridge to stop the blood flow. The other two lowered their weapons.

"Stop them!" The shrill, distant voice drew the eyes of the final two. Ulfrik did not fear Eldrid, not now with a sword in hand. In fact, he seized on the idea of taking her hostage. He would take her north, turn her over to the people there for justice and earn freedom for himself. This was yet another chance the gods placed before him. Only four men stood in his path, and two were already defeated.

His sword lanced out at the distracted men. He caught the closest one in the sword arm, slicing to the bone. The man dropped his sword and screamed in pain, his free hand clamping to the bloody wound.

As the enemy toppled, he revealed Eldrid stomping through the woods and navigating with her staff. She moved with surprising speed for a blind woman on uneven ground. Ulfrik ignored her continued screaming and did not waver in his attack. The final opponent raised his sword as if it were an extension of his arm. Ulfrik swept aside the awkward block with his sword and slammed a fist into the man's kidney. Fighting inexperienced and unarmored opponents provided a multitude of ways to eliminate the enemy. Ulfrik went with expedience, dropping the final man with a follow-up strike to his temple.

Four men now were laid out in the refuse of the woods, and Ulfrik confidently turned his sword toward Eldrid. She had homed in on his fight, cursing the entire way. She was going to charge straight onto the point of his sword if he wasn't careful.

"You've gone too far now," he said, his heart light with joy. He felt like dancing.

She did not pause but instead swept the earth before her with her staff and plodded ahead. The edge of her blindfold had darkened with sweat, and her teeth were bared in a hateful grimace.

"You are my prisoner now," he said, and raised the point of his sword to touch her body.

But rather than yield, she raised a fist to her lips. She slipped around his sword, glided up to an arm's length away. A small reed protruded from her fist.

"Shit!" Ulfrik realized too late, and Eldrid blew hard on the reed.

A red colored cloud exploded into his face, lashing it with itching fire. His eyes slammed shut, but it felt as if a fistful of sand had been ground beneath his lids. Snot rushed from his nose as he coughed and choked. He dropped his sword and scrubbed his face, only inflaming the itch to a crescendo. He doubled over with a furious scream, mucus and tears streaming over his hands. He felt as if he had inhaled fire through his nose. Something slammed across his back and he staggered. His eyes would not open and he could only cough and gag.

Another strike to his head sprawled him, and several hands dragged him a short distance before releasing him. He lay on the ground, heedless of anything but the fire in his eyes and nose. The feeling of sand in his eyes did not abate, but the burn wore off as he continued to rub. Someone grabbed him by the collar and hoisted him up.

"You're a long way from the village." Though Ulfrik could not open his eyes, the voice was unmistakably Gudrod's. "Time to explain yourself."

Blinded, Ulfrik stumbled back through the woods as Gudrod yanked him along by his shirt like a child being dragged to a whipping post.

30

Ulfrik's face still burned and his eyes watered for hours after Eldrid's powder had subdued him. He perched on the edge of his bed and stared at the shirt he had torn off. Red blooms of the powder clung to its collar still; the sight of it made his skin burn anew. Now he swathed himself in a wool blanket, blinking incessantly as tears leaked over his cheeks. A bowl of water left for him had only spread the burning when he had washed his face. The only solution was to wait out the poison.

"I've a dozen more powders, each one worse than the last," Eldrid had said after Gudrod shoved Ulfrik into his house. "If you test me again, I'll hit you with something harder. Behave while we decide what to do with you."

She had left with a cackle that continued to echo in his head. Now that he had recovered enough from the debilitating itch, his thoughts returned to Lang's death and Finn's narrow escape. He rubbed his face out of habit, but the burn flared and ignited his anger. Like a trapped bear he shot off his bed and kicked over the small table where the water bowl sat. It crashed to the dirt floor, and he kicked at the upturned table until the legs broke. He had been so close to escape, yet Eldrid's trickery had defeated him. How many more times will that conniving hag stand in his way? Picking up a broken table leg, he flung it at the door. It had been barred shut from the outside, but someone standing guard shouted.

"Be still in there!" The voice was familiar, perhaps Bresi's. Ulfrik didn't care. He flung another leg after the first.

"Come in here and quiet me, if you've got any balls!"

When no answer came, he snorted and returned to the edge of the bed. Smashing his meager possessions would not benefit him. Drawing a deep breath, he tried to focus on where the new situation would go. He had saved Finn's life; whether the boy had understood it was another question. He would lead men back to take revenge. There was no question on that point. Audhild and Eldrid would resist; another point without doubt. A battle with these northerners might be advantageous if Ulfrik could appeal to Finn. However, the boy was young enough that he might not accompany a war party. Ulfrik shook his head, realizing whoever sought revenge would not likely name him an ally. He would have to win them over to his side or find a way to compel their aid.

Yet before any of those concerns, he had to deal with Eldrid's vague statements about his fate. He had laid out four men, one with broken bones and the other with a harsh sword wound. In most places common law dictated a man was entitled to compensation for injuries from the offender, but Ulfrik could not guess what laws governed this strange group. They might forgive him owing to his status as the storm god's gift, or they may set him on fire and throw him off a cliff. Anything was possible from these madmen.

With a sigh he decided his only option was to see how things developed and to not antagonize anyone. He had to stay alive and intact while remaining alert for the chances the gods would set before him.

As if in answer to the thought, he heard the bar slide off the door and it opened. Audhild's slender shadow filled the door frame against the sun behind. Another man hovered behind her, but she warned him off with an upraised hand.

"How are you feeling?" she asked.

"Like I washed my face with hot coals."

"Despite her blindness, my sister has crafted a dozen or more hideous poisons. The gods guide her hands in that work."

"Too bad the gods did not send a wind to blow that red poison back into her face. Blind or not, her lungs would be set aflame."

Audhild smiled, then closed the door behind her. The guard protested as the wooden door thumped into the frame, but Audhild folded both hands at her lap as if she was on a social visit.

"I could grab you now," Ulfrik said. "Take you hostage and demand my way out."

"That has always been possible." She paused at the broken table, absently touching her chest, then faced him. "But you have nowhere to go with me. You think you've made friends with the village from the north? I doubt they will welcome you, even if that boy you let escape speaks for you. At best, you can expect to be turned away unharmed. Do you imagine scratching out a life in the caves along the shore, trapped between here and those enemies to the north?"

Ulfrik turned aside from her, remembering his decision to be contrite no matter how much he yearned to lash out. "Such a life has no appeal. But what of my life here? I put a sword to Eldrid's neck and I'd do it again if I could."

He bit his lip, silently cursing his threat. She gave a tired laugh, pulled up the single stool Ulfrik owned, then sat.

"No one other than the people involved know the details of what happened. Eldrid and I feel it is best no one else know your role in the boy's escape. No sense in creating conflict over your actions."

"What of the men I injured?"

"I've spoken to them. All will be laid at the feet of the spy we killed. Right now, I fear the boy will tell a story that leads his fellow villagers back to us. I want everyone focused on dealing with that threat and not arguing over what you did. I expect you to support the same story."

Ulfrik tightened the blanket around his neck and frowned. "No one talks to me anyway. When I speak it's as if only the wind blew across their ears. Do not fret for my story."

"All the same, that is the price for my speaking on your behalf.

Eldrid and Gudrod both are in a rage at your actions and had I not calmed them you might be in trouble."

A smile tightened his face, and she stared levelly at him. The scar in her brow raised as she awaited his answer.

"I will say what you want," he said at last. "You are right to worry for revenge. They will seek it and you must be prepared."

"Eldrid will beg guidance from the gods tonight. The whole community will be gathered to witness. Remain close, support what I say, and all will be well. We are in treacherous waters now that outsiders have found us. I fear they will undo all we have created here."

Ulfrik nodded. Whatever chance for escape remained was with these outsiders. He feared what Audhild hoped: that outsiders could not do enough to unmake the madness that trapped him.

31

Eldrid sat on a high seat, blindfolded head tilted back and swaying as if to unheard music. Her bone necklace clattered from side to side in time with her intensifying motions. Behind her, stars fought through the orange haze of the bonfire that lit the circle of villagers. Their faces were either rapt or turned aside in horror. Ulfrik sat in the grass as part of the circle, arms folded and face bent in a frown. The pile of driftwood and branches used in the bonfire could have built a bridge back to Ravndal. His face sweated, from the fire as well as the lingering effects of Eldrid's poison, but his back was cold against the night.

Audhild sat next to him, her eyes so wide he expected to have to catch them when they popped. In the wavering light, her smile and upturned nose made her a child held in the spell of a master storyteller. Seeing her so delighted eased his foul mood. Yet he only had to glance across the circle where Gudrod sat and glowered at him. Despite the exhibition of dark magic before him, he was more intent on grinding his hatred for Ulfrik.

Eldrid swaying more violently now, a young girl stood up from where she sat at the foot of the tall chair. She carried a skin of wine, and apparently Eldrid's increased activity had been her cue. Her gray skirt and white overdress were stained bright yellow from the blazing fire. Shouldering the skin, she placed her bare foot on the bottom rung of Eldrid's chair and began to climb. The chair rocked, and Ulfrik silently begged the gods to fling her from her high seat, but the girl made it to the top where Eldrid sat over the tallest man's head. Though blindfolded, one searching hand grabbed the skin and upended the skin to her lips.

The girl leapt down as Eldrid's cheeks bulged with ale. Discarding the skin, she stood on the chair, again rocking it but managing to stay balanced. She leaned out to the fire and sprayed the ale from her mouth as if having heard shocking news. The ale mist settled on the fire with no effect, but Ulfrik saw her left hand flick before a brighter flash erupted from the flames.

The circle recoiled and shocked cries went up. Audhild's hands flew to her chest and she squealed. Ulfrik flinched, his face warming in embarrassment. "She threw something into the fire to make that flash. How could you not see it?"

Yet Audhild paid no mind, both hands now clasped hopefully beneath her chin as if begging Eldrid to continue. Ulfrik touched the amulet of Thor's hammer at his neck and spit against evil, just in case Eldrid's powers were true. The rest of the circle had recovered from their surprise and Eldrid now stood poised at the edge of her seat, one hand outstretched to the fire and the other grasping her staff.

Her back arched as she wailed, head shaking as if trying to escape a trap. Her hair flew over her blindfolded face and the chair wobbled on the verge of collapse. Wide eyes twinkled in the light of the bonfire, watching Eldrid settle at last. Her head hung limp, hair concealing her face. Only the fire crackled and the breeze rustled the grass. At last she spoke. Her voice was hoarse and broken.

"I have seen what will be and what must be done. Blood will cover this land before the summer ends and bones will grow white in the grass by first snow. The northern folk, people of fiery tempers and evil intentions, will bring their swords south. Our sons will feed their hungry blades, our children shall be their slaves, and our women will be shared among their men before they join their men in death." Eldrid lifted her head and scanned the crowd with her blind eyes. No one moved, and even Ulfrik swallowed hard at the dark prophecy. "But the gods have shown me such terrible visions so that we may be warned. It's true. The northerners sent a spy among us only two days ago. But by my magic he was slain before he could escape."

Eldrid's lie broke the spell she had over Ulfrik. For a moment the images she had conjured had him believe she communed with gods, but now he knew this for the manipulation it was. He strained to see Audhild from his peripheral vision. She leaned forward, both hands over her mouth. Audhild must have known the fiction Eldrid wove, yet she seemed as enraptured as the others.

"We must prepare for war, my children. When the spy fails to return, the northerners will bring their wrath down upon us. We must remember why we are here. Do you value your freedom? Have we traveled so far to only be threatened again by a new jarl and new laws? No, all outsiders are evil. All see we are beloved of the gods and their jealousy drives them to attack us. These people must be destroyed or we shall never know peace!"

Eldrid paused as if expecting praise, but the circle remained frozen in amazed silence. Gudrod finally spoke, shaking himself as if aroused from a dream. "The gods have shown Eldrid a vision of what might be. We can stop this. We will defend our homes. All men of fighting age will prepare for battle. Who disagrees with this?"

Heads shook all around the circle, and hesitant voices spoke up. "Not our homes," said one. "I'm not going back to bondage," said another. Enough people voiced agreement that Eldrid settled into her chair, head tipped back with a smirk.

Ulfrik itched to speak against Eldrid, but knew the people would not listen. Truth has no power over what men wish to believe. Eldrid wanted her people closed off from the world so she could control them, and Gudrod abetted her. He stood, gathering men all while raving for the protection of their homes. A crowd formed around him, all anger and energy. If they could, they would march north this moment.

Beside him Audhild observed Gudrod with narrowed eyes. A smile turned the corners of Ulfrik's mouth.

"Gudrod imagines himself a great chieftain," he said, leaning closer to Audhild. "Eldrid's vision has the people ready to follow any promise of victory. Looks like they've elected a new leader."

Audhild regarded him coolly. "The people need someone. A woman cannot lead men to battle."

"But a woman may choose who does." Ulfrik folded his arms about his knees, as if the discussion was finished. For a moment, it seemed over. Eldrid slumped on her chair as if spent from her visions and Gudrod moved about the circle, encouraging men to violence.

"You think Gudrod oversteps himself?"

Ulfrik shrugged. "He has no ships to build nor any crew to command, so Gudrod would like an army."

Audhild studied Gudrod. Her lips were tight and thin as she considered. "You would like an army as well, no doubt. You'd have them build ships to bring the fight north, then sail off for Frankia without another thought for us."

Her eyes shifted to his, narrow and smug. Ulfrik held up a hand. "Attack is all wrong. We don't know their land, strength, or anything else about them. I'd prepare for defense. Draw them down to us, offer them what they want, then give it to them."

"Give it to them?"

"Along with a trap that will destroy them. That's not what Gudrod is barking about, though. Seems he favors attack, but without knowledge of the enemy the risk is great. Inexperienced men trying to ambush what could be seasoned warriors, I hate to think of that outcome. Seen it too many times."

She again grew silent while Gudrod now had a tight group of eager-eyed young men hanging on his promises to rip apart these meddlesome northerners. Her chin tucked down as she considered her options. Ulfrik decided he had to tip the barrel in his favor.

"Of course, should he be victorious I imagine Gudrod will stay in the north to consolidate control. He'll have to or the enemy will be back next summer. The conquered people will be folded into his own. It will be a hard thing to keep both communities united. He might even break off, and why not? He has all the swords in his camp. No reason to take orders from anyone else."

"That will not happen." She got to her feet now, and Ulfrik followed.

"Maybe not. Even if victory isn't so complete, he will be a hero. And when a hero comes knocking on your hall door, you may find it harder to resist allowing him inside—and we both know how much he would enjoy getting inside."

Audhild's lip curled, as if the words alone repulsed her. "I see it now. This is your destiny, why the gods chose you to come to us."

"If ever there was a point we could agree upon, it is this." Ulfrik inclined his head, hiding his smile. Audhild's eyes were searching a distant landscape known only to her. Cheers for Gudrod drew her back, and she stared at Ulfrik. He raised a brow. "It seems no one else shares our vision of my true purpose."

She strode to Eldrid's chair, chasing away the girl seated beneath it, and slapped her palm against its leg. Eldrid leaned over the side as if straining to hear.

Ulfrik watched the brief exchange with a mixture of hope and disbelief. Only two days ago he had threatened Eldrid with a sword and had escaped punishment only by Audhild's intervention. Now he wanted the sword returned and a warband in the bargain. He expected failure, and as Audhild spoke Eldrid shook her head like a fly had invaded her ear. Yet whatever leverage Audhild held over her sister—and by now Ulfrik knew it had to be powerful—prevailed, and she fell back into her chair with her head bowed and shoulders slumped. Audhild stepped back, arms folded across her chest.

Within moments Eldrid howled and stood once more on her chair. The clamor and chest-thumping died as she outstretched her staff for attention. She hovered in the silence, a scarecrow woman wreathed in golden firelight.

"That we must fight, no one doubts. But who shall lead? The gods have long ago prepared us for this day. They have sent one among us who is a king of the battlefield." She paused, and a murmur spread. Ulfrik watched Gudrod's eyes flash in the bonfire light, his smile replaced with a snarl. Eldrid slammed her staff down and half the circle leapt at the loud crack. "Ulfrik shall lead us to victory. The gods have granted me this vision."

Gudrod had lunged three strides before he caught himself. Ulfrik nearly laughed at the exasperation in the man's expression. "What are you doing?" His voice was raw with anger. "This isn't ..."

Clipping his last sentence, Gudrod glanced around at the confused faces. This isn't what the two of you planned, Ulfrik thought. Too late now, your witch has already made her prophesies.

Audhild stepped up, spreading her hands wide as she addressed the crowd. "Ulfrik was a great jarl and warrior. He led armies to victories over the Franks. You see him now as a humble man, but once he was a maker of the raven's harvest. We must not offend the gods by ignoring the gift they have given us for this purpose. He will lead us to victory over our enemies."

Every face turned to Ulfrik. Some stared in awe, others fear, and a few in repulsion. The scrutiny, something that he once sloughed off like a summer rain, was now a hailstorm. He had to summon more strength to stand straight than he ever had before. The judgment of these people mattered little to him, but their compliance was key to his plans. He needed them to believe they could win in battle, but only if he led them.

"It was not until tonight that I understood my true purpose here." He scanned the faces, skipping past the glares from the likes of Gudrod or Bresi Black-Eyes. "I have fought hundreds of battles, led men to victory, and saved their homes. I will do no less for you. Eldrid has foreseen it, and I will make it so."

Cheers met his speech that moments ago had been reserved for Gudrod. Audhild beamed with satisfaction, regarding him as if he were a long-lost brother returning home out a blizzard.

Across the circle a small knot of men clumped to Gudrod's side and stuffed their applause under their arms. Ulfrik finally smiled at them, anxious to get a sword and teach these bastards what a real warrior could do.

32

The heft of a sword and shield in hand once more infused Ulfrik with confidence. He watched his men, thirty-seven total, drill as he instructed. One line locked shields and another reinforced from behind. The heaviest men kicked at the wall and tried to dislodge a defender. Too often the wall broke, as it had now. A defender just barely old enough to be called a man crumpled and the wall breached.

Ulfrik leapt into the opening, shoving aside the attacker who had breached it. He slammed his shield into the left side, rolling up the defender's shield, and plowed through the second rank. The second rank defender's eyes were wide as Ulfrik pressed his sheathed blade into his guts to drive him back. He easily popped out behind the shieldwall and rounded on the men.

"Your shieldwall is breached and I'm now cutting up the rear while my friends hold the gap open. You're all dead." He dropped his shield to the grass and hitched his sword onto his belt. "Can you explain how I walked through this line like it was door?"

They studied their toes and the front rank man remained sitting on the grass. He dared an answer. "I didn't brace properly."

"Wrong," Ulfrik said. He grabbed the second rank man by his fur vest, then shoved him back into line. "You fell because this man was taking a nap on your back. If he had pushed back, I wouldn't have broke through. Try it yourself."

Ulfrik tapped the man's legs and he raised his shield. Ulfrik placed his own shield into the curve of the man's back and braced his legs. With a nod from him, the man on the ground stood and took a running kick. His foot thudded into the shield, and the man grunted as Ulfrik shoved forward with his own shield. They held ground, though, and the man kicked twice more before stopping.

"That's how it's done. Keep practicing. The front rank forms the wall but the second and third ranks keep it whole." Ulfrik clapped the shoulders of his men as he walked down the line, meeting their eyes with confidence he did not truly have. These men could not become true warriors in the time they had. Fortunately, his plans did not require it of them.

If he knew Lang's people better, he would consider using his newly acquired sword to take Eldrid captive and bargain for safety among them. Yet too much remained unknown. Would they accept him, and if they did, would they be strong enough to withstand the attack Gudrod would lead? He had to test the strength of these people before bargaining with them. No matter the outcome of the battle, he had plans to save himself.

He left the group to their drilling, noting the absence of Gudrod and his coterie. Over the last week Gudrod had grudgingly participated in basic drills. He made a pretense of keeping watch for approaching danger. Ulfrik could not deny it was important, but he suspected Gudrod used the time to plot against him. Now that Eldrid had endorsed him and gave him a sword, the village was seeing him in a new light. He was born a leader, and with his strength returned and weapons in hand, everyone saw him as such.

A fog hid the base of the distant mountains, icy blue teeth against a late spring sky. Sea air was crisp in his nose and the grass wet at his feet. As he crossed the open fields of the village center, his stride possessed a bounce it had lost since his fight with Throst. Though his legs were sore and his stride shorter, he was whole. All he needed was his family, and he would be complete.

At the next stop he found the women and elderly at their work,

Audhild organizing them. As he approached, she stopped and waved. Her skin glowed in the morning light and her smile lent her a gentle grace. Ulfrik reminded himself that she was his captor, and no matter that she was also a desirable woman. Yet during this week, when his goals aligned with hers, he had grown to appreciate her more. Throughout all of this disaster, she had been a foil to Eldrid's rabid madness. She was his caregiver and protector against her sister's wickedness. He no longer saw her as an enemy. As she crossed the short distance to him, he admired her slender form and stirred at the sway of her hips. Why had such a beautiful woman remained alone? Why had he blinded himself to it before?

"How are the preparations coming?" Ulfrik asked as she closed.

"Come see what we've done. I think you will be pleased." Her smile was sun-bright and a gull overhead called as if in agreement.

A cluster of women sat on stools or benches besides a pile of straw. Their calloused hands wove and tied with quiet intensity, each woman crafting their part of the overall job. Audhild nearly skipped the final distance to the stack of completed items. She hauled up one straw dummy, holding it before her like a child. "We've made ten of these already."

Ulfrik plucked at the straw man, admiring the craftsmanship of the tied straw bundles woven into a man's shape. "Put a shirt and pants on it and I'd swear I was seeing my own reflection in a lake."

The women laughed, and Audhild returned it to the pile. "This is the most incredible plan I've ever heard. Do you think it will work?"

"Why would I have you do this if I didn't? It will work—once. That's all we need."

He stood with Audhild as the women demonstrated how they crafted the dummies. One square-jawed woman held up the head she was crafting. "It's no more than making a scarecrow, really."

He attempted to tie a bundle on his own, but the straw came apart in his hands and fluttered to the ground. "I'll stick to fighting."

More laughter followed, though Audhild's laughter was weak and did not show in her eyes. Ulfrik felt his heart beat faster, wondering if Audhild was jealous. He turned away, making a show of searching the area. "Where has Gudrod gone? Haven't seen much of him or Eldrid."

"Eldrid must rest. Prophesy drains her." Audhild's voice flattened at the mention of her sister. She pointed lazily up the hill. "Gudrod is with the boys, digging the ditches you ordered."

"I cannot imagine Gudrod the Great digging ditches." The women's levity had fled and Ulfrik's face warmed at the collapse of their conversation. "I'll check on his progress."

He left them with Audhild to their silent work, the impatient cry of a baby marking their presence behind him. Walking the path he had plotted, he considered how much of his plan depended on the battle progressing a certain way. Battles never took the turns commanders expected. The grassy field he crossed was the only logical spot for battle, and a retreat to higher ground also made sense. A cautious enemy would not follow, and a rapacious one would turn on the undefended village. He needed a vengeful enemy for his plan to succeed.

The hilltop flowed away into a short field of grass and black rock. Much of the landscape was shaped as if it had been poured, layers leading ever higher. At the opposite end a shallow defile carved through the rocky shoulders rising out of the grass, clumps of it clinging like patches of hair on a balding head. The work parties of boys were digging ditches and stocking driftwood and branches. He did not find Gudrod among them.

"Not too deep," Ulfrik said to one group already up their thighs in the hole. "We want the smoke to flow out, not stay trapped in the hole."

The boys paused, two stripped to their waists and glistening with sweat. They nodded, too winded to speak. Ulfrik turned to a different group stacking firewood in a completed ditch. He asked for Gudrod.

"Gone into the ridge." One of them waved generally at the defile. "Hasn't come out for while."

"Took the ale skin with him, too," muttered a second boy, who received an elbow in the side from his companion.

"Keep up the good work. Don't tire yourselves overmuch. You've got shield wall drills tonight." The boys slouched. Ulfrik clucked his tongue at them. "When I was your age I'd swim the fjord in morning, drill all afternoon, and fight all night. Don't complain."

"You can swim?" both boys asked at the same time.

"Of course not. Makes my story all the more amazing, doesn't it? Now back to your work." He left them laughing and entered the defile in search of Gudrod.

Shadows engulfed him and the air grew colder in the narrow gap. The smile left over from his banter drained away, and a flutter grew in his stomach. Over his long years and many battles, he had learned to trust the feeling. He thumbed aside the leather loop holding his sword in its sheath and continued through the jagged black rocks. The defile was as if a dragon had dragged its tail through the lump of earth and stone. Looking up at the walls on either side the sun glared into his eyes. Perfect for his plans.

Perfect for Gudrod's ambush.

Two men stepped up to the ledge on his right, black shadows against the sun, and Gudrod blocked his path by standing in a dagger of sunlight straight ahead.

Ulfrik's hand flexed to his sword, but Gudrod did not move for his own. The two men above filed past him, and began to climb down behind. Ulfrik blinked impassively, but his gut tightened nonetheless. He had been lucky in his fight with Eldrid's dogs. Would the same luck prevail again?

"You waited here all afternoon hoping I'd wander into your trap?" Ulfrik's hand floated above his sword hilt, fingers loose.

"And here you are," Gudrod spread his arms wide, a yellow-toothed smile bright in the sun. Rocks crumbled behind Ulfrik and a man cursed. Gudrod's smile faded and his eyes flicked past Ulfrik.

"If you kill me, the people will rise against you. The gods have sent me here for this purpose, or were you not listening to Eldrid?"

"No one wants to kill you." Gudrod stepped closer. Ulfrik heard the crunch of rock behind him. "Merely seeking a bit of justice."

Ulfrik spun on the men behind him, kicking the loose, broken rock at them as he did. Bits of sharp, black stone sprayed up and they reflexively covered their faces. It was enough of an opening.

He charged the first man, plowing his shoulder beneath the man's outstretched arm. A warm, sweaty stench filled his nose as Ulfrik shoved into the man's torso. His feet caught on the rough ground and he stumbled. Without delay Ulfrik whirled on the other man, Bresi Black-Eyes, and landed a wide-arced, left-handed punch around Bresi's raised arm and clipped his head. It was not solid, but it distracted him. Ulfrik followed with a right-handed jab to Bresi's soft gut and folded him over.

But the time wasted was enough for Gudrod to catch him from behind. He heard Gudrod's feet scraping and crushing the loose rock as he ran, but he did not have the speed. His leg, already bearing too much of his weight, pulled tight with a pain like hot wire tied over his thigh. He faltered and Gudrod had wrestled his right arm behind his back. Off balance, Ulfrik staggered to the side and Gudrod pulled him along until he had hooked both arms behind his back. Ulfrik was pinned.

Bresi recovered as did his partner, who was the man whose nose Ulfrik had flattened. Seeing the two of them smeared with dirt, he laughed.

"You two fools. For a moment I was frightened. Now I'm relieved. Even with Gudrod holding me down, you'll probably miss me."

Gudrod jerked on Ulfrik's arms, and the old injury in his shoulder lit up with pain. Ulfrik gritted his teeth, but did not cry out.

"This is for breaking my nose," said the one Ulfrik now decided to call Flat-Nose. He balled a fist as if to punch Ulfrik, but he did not let it fly.

"Gods, lad, be a man about it and fight me fair." Ulfrik rolled his eyes as if he were disgusted. In truth, despite every manner of violence he had survived, he had never broken his nose. It had been a point of pride for him, and to have some angry farmer finally break it was humiliating. Still, pride dictated he goad the man.

"Do it, if you won't bust your fingers. What are you waiting for?"

Flat-Nose hesitated, lowering his fist. "What if he curses me? The gods sent him. Maybe this isn't a good idea."

"By Freya's tits!" Bresi shoved Flat-Nose away. "You wanted to kick in my stones? Have a taste of it yourself."

Ulfrik slammed his knees together and Bresi's kick failed to connect. Still, the jolt to his knees tightened the wire of pain he felt in his left leg. He had to end this before they seriously hurt him.

Tugging forward as if to break free, Ulfrik waited for Gudrod to pull back in response. When he did, Ulfrik plowed backwards.

The two scrabbled in reverse a few steps before the rough ground tripped Gudrod. As Ulfrik crashed atop him, he slammed his head back and bounced his skull off Gudrod's face. He screamed as he released Ulfrik, and he bound up before anyone could react. The lightning pain in his leg nearly sent him to the ground again, but he slammed it straight and clenched his teeth. His sword was in hand.

"No more foolishness. I'll make three fresh piles of stinking guts out of you then piss in them. You want revenge? Like this? Are you boys or men? Lay the hazel branches and deer skin. Make a ring and we will fight to first blood, then all will be settled. Do you accept?"

Gudrod flipped onto his back, cradling his face. Bresi and Flat-Nose traded glances, uncertain if they should draw weapons.

"I thought not. Too weak to fight me on even terms. Well, I'll remember that. When the enemy comes, you three will be standing at the front of my lines where I can see you. Let me warn you now. Come too close during battle and I might accidentally slice off your empty heads." He thrust his sword forward, and Flat-Nose jumped as if he had actually been pricked. "Now get out of my sight before I lose my temper."

Castling on his hands and knees, Gudrod hung his head. Spit and snot hung down, and Ulfrik guessed he might have broken Gudrod's nose. He smiled. That was a satisfying trend.

"What if the enemy doesn't come?" Gudrod said, his voice thick and muddled. "You're just keeping us all afraid so you become important. You'd have us act like cowards when our homes are threatened."

"You murdered Lang and witnessed the escape of his son. The enemy will come, and will seek revenge. Knowing how stupid the lot of you are, you'll not give them justice and they'll have to attack. Honor demands no less, though you scum know little of it. My tactics are the only way I can keep a bunch of simple-minded farmers alive. Now go before my patience is gone."

Gudrod stood, hand over his face and tears in his eyes. His smirk still managed to radiate arrogance. "You can't kill us. Eldrid would bring everyone down on your head."

"I can kill you and be gone before Eldrid finds out, which is beginning to sound more pleasing with every moment."

They did leave, backing away deliberately then turning to a jog. Ulfrik stood with his sword drawn, wondering if he should chance escaping on his own. He still had no idea where or how far north Lang's people were, nor if they would kill him outright as an enemy.

The thought had no chance to take root. The warning notes of lookouts blowing on their horns sounded in the distance.

Lang's people had finally arrived.

33

Ulfrik coolly greeted the man who would rescue him. He stood at the same strip of beach where the trader Heidrek had landed, the same surf lapping at his sealskin boots. The man was no sun-beaten farmer but the best vision of the warrior ideal Ulfrik had seen in this part of the world. His mail coat had been scoured, though orange rust clung to sections of the links. His helmet was dented from a blade, likely an ax, and the nose guard did nothing to conceal the fierce green eyes staring out from beneath it. His salt and pepper beard was interrupted at his right cheek, where a white scar drove up to his nose and furrowed down to his jaw. A gold band clasped his bicep over a red shirt, and a fat hand like an old root breaking apart a stone rested on the hilt of his sword. Arrayed beside the man were five others just like him, though younger and stronger. Their small ship leaned to the side and behind them at anchor was their high-sided knarr with dozens of men crowding its deck.

These did not seem like men to be led into traps.

"Be welcomed, friend." Gudrod stood beside Ulfrik and offered the greeting with little enthusiasm. His face was swollen and bloodied, and overall disheveled from the beating he had just taken. Still, there had been no time to wrangle over authority, particularly with Eldrid having become insensate in the moment of crisis. Audhild bade both he and Gudrod to represent them while she organized the defense according to Ulfrik's plans. They selected ten men to follow —Gudrod selecting Bresi and Ulfrik grabbing a bewildered Lini.

The man looked Gudrod head to toe with his mouth bent in repugnance. Ulfrik shivered with the pleasure of having such disdain directed at his enemy. It was about time he got a taste of it.

"We'll see about your welcome. I am Valagnar Dannarson, jarl of Reykjaholt. Who leads you?"

"We are all equals here," Gudrod said, his nasal voice grating on Ulfrik's ears. From the frowns of the others, he guessed they felt the same.

"Then who gives justice from crimes done to freemen? Looks like someone broke your nose, friend. Who will judge that crime?" Valagnar's comment drew a snicker from one of his companions. It was cut short with a curt glance from Valagnar.

Gudrod glared at Ulfrik, but did not answer.

Ulfrik found his sword hand itching. Everyone knew why Valagnar had come, so he decided to cut to the point. He stepped forward, the slight movement setting all of Valagnar's men reaching for their weapons. Ulfrik raised a hand.

"I am Ulfrik Ormsson. I know why you have come. A man called Lang died here."

"Murdered," Valagnar said, twisting the word like a dagger in the gut. "He was my wife's brother and my lifelong friend. He meant no harm to anyone, and you cut him down in front of his only son."

"He was here to spy," Gudrod said. "If the boy hadn't fled, you wouldn't be here with your army."

"You mean to say if you had not been caught, you could've escaped justice for murder? What is your name, so I might mock it after I nail your head over my hall door?"

"Gudrod Bone-Breaker."

His nasal voice diminished the grandiose name he had assigned himself. He was pumped up like a walrus defending its rock, arms wide and chest out. Ulfrik smiled at the childish inspiration, and if Gudrod had broken many bones it was likely from hitting his own thumb with a hammer. Still, Valagnar rose to the challenge.

"Well, Gudrod Bone-Breaker, I see you've had a fine start today breaking your own nose. I'll give you one chance to surrender the men who killed my brother. Will you grant me justice?"

"You are a beast come to steal our land. You'll get nothing from me." Blood began to flow again from Gudrod's nose, but he was so worked up he did not notice. Red flecks sprayed over Valagnar, who flinched as if hot coals had been thrown at him.

"Fling your bloody spit on me? Then you've made your choice. Call your men and name the place. We'll settle this with a fight and see who the gods favor."

"In that field." Gudrod stabbed a finger where Ulfrik had planned. "Bring your best, so we can stomp you roaches out all at once."

Valagnar and his guards stomped back to the water's edge and waved his ship forward. Ulfrik watched men begin to haul up the anchor stone. Despite the impending battle, he imagined himself on its deck, sailing from this madness. The thought shattered as Gudrod shouted through his broken nose. "Let's get ready."

As they marched up the field, out of Valagnar's hearing, Ulfrik halted Gudrod with an outstretched hand. He tried to bat it aside, but Ulfrik held it steady.

"Calm yourself and keep to the plans I've set. Remember I am the leader of this battle, sent by the gods for this purpose and prophesied by Eldrid herself. Go against me and you defy the gods. Your defeat at the hands of these men will be terrible. Do all of you understand?"

He stabbed his gaze at Bresi and others who seemed to drift into Gudrod's angry circle. None met his eyes. He dropped his arm from Gudrod's chest and let him pass. The others fell in, and he grabbed Lini's shoulder as he passed.

"Stay close to me. Gudrod, Bresi, and maybe a few others will try to kill me during this battle. Warn me if I don't see them."

Lini stared at him with eyes wide and mouth half-formed into a word. Ulfrik did not know whether he was shocked that Gudrod planned murder or that he had trusted him to guard him. In either case, he had no one else in the battle lines he could trust. Lini was the best he had for a friend, and he hesitated to call him one.

Despite the planning, the villagers were confused and scattered. Ulfrik shouted commands in the loud, arresting voice he reserved for his trained hirdmen. It succeeded in drawing order out of panic. Non-combatants scrambled off to their posts while the fighters assembled in the field. Eldrid vanished, as expected, and Audhild led her women with their straw men underarm. Ulfrik formed his ranks wide and shallow, more concerned for being overlapped than broken open. Once satisfied at the order, he took his place at the center. Lini stood directly behind him, and at his sides were the strongest men he had. He would have preferred Gunnar and Einar flanking him, but no such talented warriors stood with him this day.

"Do not fear death," he shouted to his rows of men. "To die in battle is to join the heroes in Valhalla. But if you remember what I have taught and do as I have planned, then we cannot fail. The gods are with us."

A cheer went up in time to meet Valagnar's men tromping into the field. Their haughty cries dwindled as they saw the front ranks of mail-clad warriors with freshly painted shields rimmed in iron. Ulfrik and his men carried old, leather-edged shields from Frankia that would not hold long in battle. The grim faces of the enemy stared out beneath iron helmets and not a one gave any hint of fear.

A man vomited in the rear rank, and others cursed him or joined him in retching. Fear haunted every shield wall, no matter how brave the men, and some prevailed against it while others failed. Ulfrik ignored his fear. Conversely, his pulse quickened and he felt light with anticipation. He would have to restrain his battle lust or risk undoing his own careful plans.

"This is your last chance," Valagnar shouted across the field, grass waving before him like a hand shooing away flies. "Give up the murderer and spare your people suffering."

"Crawl back to Reykjaholt," Ulfrik answered, "or fight if you can find the stones for it."

Now began the hesitant period before the clash. Insults hurled like spears between the groups, each side hoping to goad the other into moving first. Ulfrik had no interest in charging from his position, and restrained any man who seemed ready to pounce. Fortunately, not many were brave enough. Archers were needed to prod Valagnar, but the bows were set elsewhere. They held until the cursing became uninspired.

At last Valagnar raised his shield and trod forward.

"Brace for them." Ulfrik raised his own shield, hearing the satisfying clack of the front rank locking shields. Behind him Lini pressed his shield into the small of Ulfrik's back. Despite his grand appearance, Valagnar lacked tactical acumen. He charged in a flat line, rather than a swine head formation that would easily break the thin defense. Ulfrik felt a hint of disappointment, having hoped for a more challenging opponent.

At spear-throwing distance, Valagnar and his men roared and ducked behind their shields. Ulfrik widened his stance, pulling behind his own shield.

Feet thudded across the grass, shaking the ground.

The clash was as hard and satisfying as he remembered it.

Shield slammed into shield with a thunderclap of violence. Men cursed and screamed. Ulfrik's heels drove back, piling up cold mud at his feet. Pain lanced through his leg and he feared he had been stabbed, then realized it was the protest of his old broken thigh. The skid back caught as Lini remembered to shove back. Ulfrik's sword was an awkward length for a tight shield wall, but he thrust it beneath his shield. The enemy in front of him cried out, but a sword licked back at him. A nick on his forearm was the worst of it, and the burn of the cut flared Ulfrik's anger.

The battle-song was on him now, a tuneless melody of death shrieks, war cries, slamming shields, and clashing blades. All the fury dammed in his heart burst from the edge of his sword and flowed bright red. He shoved into the swell of bodies, coppery blood filling his mouth and the piss-stench of fear invading his nostrils. The dense heat of the fighters smothered him. He laughed. A head appeared above his shield. He slammed his shield into the shocked face, erasing it to reveal another equally horrified. He slashed this one, spinning the helmet around on the man's head as he fell with a red line carved across his eyes.

He stumbled on bodies. A spear pierced the meat of his thigh. It felt no worse than a bee sting though a hunk of flesh flapped over the running blood.

Deep into the ranks, he realized too late he had pushed the center of his lines deep into Valagnar's men. His wings were not as successful, lagging behind and threatening to leave Ulfrik surrounded.

Retreat was harder than pushing forward. His own men mindlessly shoved forward, their fear robbing their sense. Ulfrik shrunk behind his shield as swords shuddered on the wood. A triangle of splinters flew into his face and his arm went numb as the enemy hammered at his defense.

"Fall back," Ulfrik screamed over his shoulder. "I'm surrounded."

All resistance at his back fell away and he nearly stumbled. He yanked his shield close as he tripped, and it saved him from being speared as one leaf-shaped blade turned at the edge of his shield.

His men were fleeing.

Regaining himself, Ulfrik joined them. At least the majority were fleeing in the correct direction, though some headed into the village.

With a final slash, he disengaged from the enemy and followed behind his men. Smoke already climbed into the sky, premature but not glaringly obvious to men intent on pursuit. He heard the enemy howl with delight then smiled.

The scattered group of his men fled with genuine terror. Most had never witnessed battle, and a pile of guts that used to be a drinking companion was enough to make cowards of strong men. He only hoped they would stop and reform as he had planned and not continue running.

Gudrod and Bresi floated into view. Ulfrik searched for Lini but he was alone. So this is how fate wove this thread? he thought. Let's be done with you two now. I'm in a killing mood.

Yet neither Gudrod nor Bresi shared his battle lust. Gudrod, already battered earlier, was splattered in gore and where his flesh showed it was the color of ash. Bresi stared through Ulfrik, his black-ringed eyes threatening to explode from their sockets. As Ulfrik roared at them, shield up and sword low for a ripping cut to the gut, they broke from their fugue and fled. Bresi had dropped his sword and held his shield only because the straps had caught on his arm.

Now Ulfrik came to the defile which was filling with smoke from the fires built into the ditches. A stitch in his side slowed him, and he stole a glance back as a chance to catch his breath. Valagnar was leading his men for him, his face wild with anger.

A vengeful enemy, he thought. Thank the gods.

In the defile, smoke rolled and turned the sunlight brown. Men were coughing and staggering. Ulfrik skidded on the loose rock of the defile floor, then stopped.

"Form up! Archers! Hurry! Where are the reinforcements?"

The first of Valagnar's men ran shrieking into the smoke. Shadows of others loomed through the black cloud.

He turned back and now his men were pulling into ranks. Lini shouted at them, pulling them tight, and a few others aided him. Behind the small group, Audhild's women added their straw dummies. Through the eye-watering smoke they looked genuine enough with fur caps and old shirts for clothing and driftwood for spear shafts. Now he had replacements for the dozen men that continued through the defile to loop around and cut off Valagnar's escape.

Valagnar's men rushed in, whooping in victory. The archers on the defile, seven of the best hunters in the village, shot into the enemy. They had lined up their arrows in the dirt, and sent one after the next without pause.

The first line of enemies toppled with arrows shivering in their bodies. The next line hid behind shields, but caused those behind to collide with them. Ulfrik sought Valagnar and found him sheltering a fallen warrior beneath his shield.

He charged.

Valagnar leapt up in time to block the strike, though Ulfrik had not wanted the blow to land true. His plan had reached its end and was flawless. The smoke started to lift, carried away by a sudden wind that swept out the defile like a servant cleaning a hall. He occupied Valagnar with a follow-up strike and then a sweep of his feet to unbalance him.

Cries came up behind Valagnar's men, and a horn blew. The tears in Ulfrik's eyes were not from smoke alone. He saw the fear in

Valagnar's face at realizing he was trapped. For all he knew fresh men assaulted his rear and Ulfrik's force still arrayed before him.

"You've no way out but death," Ulfrik shouted over the crash of battle. "Yield or die."

"I'll die," Valagnar stabbed, but Ulfrik easily batted aside the strike.

"Your son might live if you yield. Yield to me and I guarantee you mercy. Will you make your wife a childless widow?"

He had only guessed the man Valagnar stood over was his son, for little else but injured kin could give a man pause on the battlefield. Valagnar tossed his sword into the dirt. "I yield."

He immediately went to the man at his feet and began to stanch the flow of blood. An arrow jutted beneath the collarbone and over the lungs, likely a fatal shot.

Raising his sword overhead, Ulfrik summoned his strength and called for his men to stop. Valagnar's men, bewildered at the sudden mass of enemy and the capitulation of their leader, first lowered their weapons then dropped them.

A shout of victory went up from Ulfrik's people, the sound of it warming his face with pride. He stood over Valagnar, certain to claim him a hostage.

The final part of his plan needed Valagnar's help.

Home might not be so far away now.

34

Ulfrik rode on the backs of jubilant men beneath a swath of stars. The bonfire roared at the center of the field, the flames fed with the debris of battle, and men and women danced around it. He could not meet another's eye without being toasted, nor could he take one step away from the celebration before a drunken reveler dragged him back to the fire. As the revelers lowered him to the ground, Ulfrik's legs wobbled in pain, though he had drunk enough to not experience it sharply. They slapped his back and named him a hero.

He staggered away, bumping from one merry group to another, receiving a hearty thump and thanks at each stop. He was like a pine cone kicked from tree to tree across the forest floor, finally coming to rest at the edge of the celebration. Gudrod and Bresi gathered their own crowds, doubtlessly inflating their heroism to those naive enough to believe. Once the battle ended, Eldrid had sprouted up like a weed after a summer rain. She gathered praise for her foresight in giving Ulfrik command. Perhaps the highest praise he had received all night came in the form of a word of thanks from Eldrid's thin lips. He had accepted it in quiet surprise.

Of all the revelers, Audhild's mood was strangest. She held herself apart from others, but looked on like a girl hoping to be invited to dance. Her face and clothes were still smeared with soot and dirt. She did not look at Ulfrik, but he caught her scowling when she must have thought him unaware. At last with a moment's peace, he decided to approach her.

"You frown as if we had lost the battle." She stood beside a bench dragged out of a nearby home. Ulfrik, his legs tired, sat next to her.

"It is not right to celebrate when men have died." Audhild lifted her chin and folded her arms, then looked down her nose at the celebration.

"Men die in battle. Once a sword is drawn in anger, it is never put away unblooded. Besides, our dead are in the feasting hall now. The Valkyries have collected them from the field. They died as heroes."

"And some live as heroes." Her brow raised, the white scar lifting with it. She still did not meet his eyes.

Ulfrik chuckled. "You are unhappy that I have lived?"

"Did I say that? You think yourself a hero?"

"The people say I am. Do you?"

She ignored the question and they both watched the villagers stumble through their dances and stutter through their songs. Lini danced with a tall, wide-hipped girl that made him seem no more than a stick. His lovesick smile drew out Ulfrik's own smile.

"We have captured a ship and more than twenty men." Audhild spoke as if addressing no one, the firelight sparking in her eyes. Ulfrik could see the vein throbbing in her neck from the hard shadows of the fire. "I suppose you expect to claim it as part of your spoils."

"A ship without a crew is little use."

"But you're a hero now. I'm sure some of our boys could be tempted to crew the ship. Then you sail off for home."

Ulfrik bowed his head as if the words stung him. In fact, he had considered the option but did not believe the villagers would support it.

"You have no understanding of what a journey home would require," he said. "It's leagues of trackless ocean across some of the worst waters known. Boys alone cannot hope to prevail, not even seasoned crews. You don't understand how fortunate we were during our journey here. That luck won't repeat."

Her mouth twisted into a smile and she faced him at last. "I do understand our fortune. You were the wellspring of that blessing, as Eldrid prophesied. The gods meant us to be here."

A nearby group's laughter overwhelmed them, drawing their attention. Ulfrik stared past them to the house used to imprison Valagnar and his men. Orange light rimmed the doorway where unlucky guards sat out the celebration. Inside Valagnar's son was dying and Ulfrik's plans were slipping away.

"You only ever think of what was," Audhild said, turning aside from the drunken laughter. "Why not about what can be?"

"In fact, I have thought of little else since this morning. This battle has changed everything. There is purpose here for me. Now there is an enemy to defend against, and men who need my leadership. You cannot understand this, but a bond is forged between men who fight shoulder to shoulder. Today all of us were made brothers in war and blood. Can you not see it in the men? My home is long gone, and all believe I am dead. I can rebuild here."

His wife, Runa, had named him a terrible liar. He hoped these lies could pass with one who knew his heart a great deal less than his wife. He turned what he hoped were soulful and thoughtful eyes on Audhild. She regarded him with a puzzled look, a slender finger tapping her cheek. He let the words settle, expecting her to laugh. Instead she laid a hand on his shoulder.

"Such words are a victory that I can celebrate. Do you mean it?"

"I swear it before the gods." He hoped the gods were not listening. They had not heard him since coming to this place, and he prayed they would ignore him a while longer.

Her hand lingered on his shoulder, and gently squeezed, nearly massaged. The smile that came to her face perplexed him. It was both coquettish and joyful, full of meaning that was misspent on him. "Then I am well satisfied with your answer. We should speak more of what this means."

"That we should," he said, bereft of any guess as to what she intended. He was decades out of practice in guessing a woman's heart. Runa was all he had to understand, and other women that he bedded while away at war had not been worth reading.

She broke the moment by artlessly wiping the grime from her face, as if she only now realized her slovenly appearance. Ulfrik was spared further embarrassment when the stab wound on his thigh flared in sudden pain. He had leaned his elbow on it while sitting, and now jerked back with a hiss. Audhild immediately bent to it, checking the bandage over his ruined pant leg.

"This is not properly washed. Have you learned nothing about caring for your battle wounds?" She shook her head, retying the bandage. "I'll look at this later."

"Valagnar's son was gravely wounded. I fear the boy will die without aid."

"Men die in battle, as you only just reminded me. What about our wounded?"

"Ours either died or suffered lightly. Gudrod had it worst, and that was from me."

Her eyes narrowed and her coy smile vanished. "All of those bastards should die for what they did."

"They are hostages and honor demands we aid them as best we can. That means caring for their wounds. No one will ransom a dead son, and we'll only make a more bitter enemy of them. Will you help?"

Audhild stood, transformed into a petulant child with arms folded and head turned aside in disdain. "They should have thought more carefully before invading our land."

Too much was wrong with her sentiments for Ulfrik to address. He rubbed his face, then stood. When he reached to touch her arm, she flinched away. He stared at her, a backdrop of revelers dancing behind her. "Then I will go to do what I can."

Gudrod paused in his bragging to watch Ulfrik leaving. He turned aside as Ulfrik flashed a warning glare at him. Others followed his leaving like puppies unsure why the master no longer wanted to throw sticks. Even Eldrid, though blind, sensed a change in mood and turned generally to face him. He shivered at the thought of how she could see him. Whatever lies she told about the gods, her senses were unnatural.

The guards at the building containing Valagnar's crew pricked up at his arrival. Ulfrik asked he be let inside, and the guards lifted the two bolts that had been fastened to the doors when converting the building to a prison.

"Will you be all right? Need us to stay with you?" asked one of the guards, a lanky man with a scabbed-over cut on his nose.

"They are weaponless and I carry my sword. I fear nothing." Ulfrik patted his hilt, enjoying wide-eyed admiration of the two guards. He also sought to exaggerate the myth of his fighting prowess. In reality, even with a sword he stood no chance against a roomful of unarmed men. One strong blow to the back of his head and he would be senseless and disarmed.

Stepping inside he found all of Valagnar's twenty-three men crammed around a hearth fire. The injured sat on the dirt floor or laid out on benches, red splotches bleeding through their bandages. Others stood as Ulfrik entered, all but one who remained on his knees by the fire and held the hand of a man laid out before it. It was Valagnar attending his son. The gray-fledged arrow protruded from beneath the left collar bone, buried a third of its length into the flesh. The son's face shined with sweat, and his skin was ashen. He otherwise looked at peace, as if he had fallen asleep.

The whites of the staring eyes were stark against the sooty faces regarding him. Only Valagnar did not raise his head, but remained focused on his son. "He has not awoken since taking the arrow. At least the gods were kind enough to grant him sleep before death."

"I have seen men recover from such a wound." Ulfrik declined to mention he had only seen one survive out of the dozens with similar injuries.

Valagnar's smile was thin and defeated. "The arrow must be pushed through the body. To do so, his shoulder blade will have to broken, then the shaft must not snap or splinter inside. Even if I could do all of that now, I lack the tools. He will slowly bleed to death from the inside as I watch."

Ulfrik swallowed, unable to deny the truth. Valagnar stroked his son's forehead, and Ulfrik felt a kindred twist of pain. His own son, Gunnar, had fought at his side and risked the same fate as Valagnar's son. Ulfrik remembered the terrible sense of failure he experienced when Gunnar lost his hand to the Frankish warlord, Clovis. His own missing finger suddenly ached in ghostly, sympathetic pain.

"I have come to discuss ransom," Ulfrik said, casting his voice back at the doors in case the guards listened.

Valagnar nodded. "The ship is my greatest treasure, but I have more. Send word to my wife and she will prepare whatever you ask. Gold, sheep, iron, wool, whatever other goods you seek. My men will have to speak for whatever they can pay, but I will buy their ransoms if able. I am not a poor man."

"Nor are you accustomed to losing a battle. I see it in your eyes." Ulfrik entered deeper into the house, the musky scent of sweat mixed with the stale iron tang of blood. Checking the closed door, he knelt beside Valagnar. "You may yet have victory."

His eyes narrowing, Valagnar eased back from his son. "What are you suggesting?"

Ulfrik licked his lips. "You were fooled into surrender. My straw warriors and the smoke made you believe you were surrounded. Had you pressed the fight, your victory was assured. These people you fought," Ulfrik waved a dismissive hand at the door, "are farmers and former slaves. If they had to fight again, they would fail."

The two men stared at each other as the others tightened conspiratorially around them. Valagnar's throat clicked as he swallowed hard. "What sort of game is this? You come to set ransom then seem to offer me battle again?"

"Both true," Ulfrik said. He struggled to keep his voice steady, conscious of how his overeager treatment of the traders had cost him his opportunity. "I have scant time to explain, as I'm sure Eldrid or Gudrod will burst in here any moment. Know this much about me. I set the trap that caught you, and I trained these fools to hold their shields together and flee on command. Without me to lead and organize, they become farmers and slaves once more. Their next best warrior is Gudrod, and he is not more than a ship-builder and coward. When I am gone, you will have no trouble reducing this village to cinders."

"Are you inviting me to kill you?" Valagnar chuckled, but a flicker of seriousness shined in his eyes. Yellow light danced along the lines of his face as he smiled.

"This is no moment for boasting. I am as much a prisoner of these people as you and your men. The blind woman, Eldrid, is a witch and holds a spell over these people. They've taken me captive all for a mad dream she had. You are my way out of this madness. Tonight, I will free you from this prison, guide you to your ship—and you will take me. Once we are in Reykjaholt, you will lend a crew to sail me to Scotland and give me enough silver that I may buy passage home. That is the ransom for you and your men."

Valagnar snorted. "An impossible promise. You are but one man."

"A man who led you into defeat. All I've planned has led to this moment. If I say you will be free this night, then it will be so."

Dirty, hard faces looked to each other then to Valagnar, who turned back to his son. "Did you plan to move the injured? Many of my men cannot run."

"I will carry your son myself, if I must." Ulfrik's heart pounded, fearing the opening door in the next instant. "You must seize what chances Fate provides. If it is for your son to live, then he shall. If not, he will join the heroes in endless feasting and battle. He will not have died a coward."

Valagnar bit his lip then nodded. "Deliver us from this place and you shall have your crew and ship."

Ulfrik exhaled in relief, as if he had set down a burden of heavy rocks. He reached into both of his boots and drew out two knives. "I will bring other weapons when I return. Accept these as tokens of my good intentions."

Taking the knives, Valagnar thumbed the edge of one and passed the other to the man standing behind him. "And when will you return?"

Ulfrik inhaled to answer, but a raised voice came from beyond the door, then it slammed open. Gudrod swept in, sword drawn.

35

"What is this?" Gudrod ranged his sword at the gathered men. If the stink of ale did not give him away, the glowing red of his face showed his drunkenness. The blade trembled in his grip, the hearth light shimmering along its pitted length. His teeth were bared as fiercely as if he had caught Ulfrik in bed with his lover. The shadows of the firelight deepened the black pouches beneath his eyes and heightened the twist of his broken nose.

Ulfrik's stomach dropped. He had to distract Gudrod before he noticed the knives he had just provided Valagnar. He shot to his feet, Gudrod following him as intently as a cat does a wounded bird. With a firm hand he pushed the sword down. "Don't charge a room with a drawn sword. You might hurt someone."

"That's what swords are for," he said, running his words together. His small eyes were lost to darkness, but Ulfrik noted the shift in his demeanor when Valagnar also stood and the other prisoners did not flinch. Gudrod lowered his sword against his leg. "Well, what are you doing in here?"

"I came to see their condition. Some of them are dying for lack of aid. Hostages deserve better treatment, and dead hostages provide no ransom."

"Don't expect me to weep for them. Got what they deserved, I say."

A small shift in the tension of the prisoners warned Ulfrik of impending violence. He had just stoked their hopes of escape and provided weapons. With Gudrod's posturing he might goad them into a premature attack. Too many villagers were still active and many yet carried their weapons from the battle. Now was not the right time.

Ulfrik shoved Gudrod back through the door, then turned a knowing glance to Valagnar as he followed. The jarl narrowed his eyes and gave a slight nod. Ulfrik turned and snapped at the two shocked guards. "Bar that door and keep a close eye. Our foolish ship-builder has aroused their anger."

Gudrod flapped his arms trying to keep balance as he stumbled. Ulfrik held his breath, hoping the fool would crash on his ruined face. Unfortunately, he regained himself. His sword lay in the grass by the door. One of the guards retrieved it and Gudrod snatched it away.

"No more talking to the prisoners alone." Gudrod's shouts drew looks from the distant celebration. Ulfrik only smiled.

"You've no right to make such a demand. Valagnar is my prisoner, and I will do with him as I wish. If you wanted some say in the matter, then maybe you should've participated in the fight rather than cower behind me."

Ulfrik nodded to the slack-jawed guards, then headed back toward the celebration. Gudrod remained silent until he was out of arm's reach. "I'm watching, you snake. You're not a hero, and all will know it soon enough."

Returning to the celebration, Ulfrik received the same scrutiny he had as when he had left. More cheering and back-slapping ensued. Even those who had lost family spoke in quiet tones of gratitude for saving the village. Eldrid departed without the spectacle she reserved for large gatherings. Had Ulfrik not been seeking her, he might have missed her slipping away with a young boy leading her by the hand. She prodded the ground with her staff as she went, apparently not trusting the boy, her blindfolded eyes pointed at the ground.

As the night progressed, Gudrod and his brood of sulky cowards disappeared. More people toasted Ulfrik's victory and he became warm-faced and dizzy even though he drained most of his ale into the grass when no one looked. He needed his wits for tonight, but the ale took the edge off the pain and stiffness from the day's exertions. He sat on a bench and watched others passing out in the grass, too exhausted to care where they slept. Others drifted off toward their homes as the bonfire burned down to a fitful twirl of flames, sparks spinning up into the night.

This was the last he would see of these people. Strangely, he felt a hint of sadness for it. They were good yet simple-minded folk. Eldrid manipulated them, but in the end Audhild had granted all of them freedom. He could not begrudge the common folk that desire; it was common to all men. Their only fault had been in clinging to the belief that Ulfrik was a magical totem given to them from the gods. Had Eldrid not been so set on making her dream become reality, he might have liked these people. Maybe, once he was back at his own hearth with his own family, he would remember them fondly.

He estimated a few more hours must pass before he could safely release Valagnar from confinement. Starlight and a slice of moon would be all the light he had to work with, yet it would be enough. Had Valagnar attacked later in summer, the midnight sun would have foiled this plot. Ulfrik took it as a favorable sign that Fate had sent them earlier. Their weapons were heaped at the blacksmith's forge, and he only had to steal a few to arm Valagnar. Their ship remained unguarded at the beach, but on the chance someone discovered them, Ulfrik wanted to be prepared to fight.

"It is time to end this celebration." Audhild approached from behind, and Ulfrik startled at the warm touch of her hand on his shoulder. He twisted at the waist to greet her. She had cleaned her face of ashes and her hair was curled and wet. She no longer smelled of smoke.

"I wondered where you had gone," he said. In truth he had only considered how to avoid her home tonight.

"Do you find my condition more acceptable now? You wrinkled your nose at me earlier."

"Did I?" Audhild's hand began to rub his shoulder. He carefully moved out from her touch, standing to face her.

Audhild drew closer, replacing her hand on his shoulder. She ran her tongue across her bottom lip, the wetness of it glistening in the dying firelight. Her fingers flexed on his shoulder. "What you said about making your home here, was it true?"

She looked up at him with doe eyes that made his breath catch. Without waiting for his answer, she took his hand and tugged gently. "Let's go home, and you can show me the truth of your words."

He followed her as if a rope had been tied to his neck, all thoughts of his plans fading behind the sway of her body as she guided him. Pausing at the door, she glanced over her shoulder. Ulfrik swallowed and followed her inside.

The hearth was cold and a single candle fluttered in the breeze from the open door. Her modest hall sat in cold darkness, but she lifted the candle off the table and pointed it not at Ulfrik's door but her own. Her eyebrow raised in question, the white scar clear even in the darkness. What he had once regarded as her sole detraction now blended with the clear and powerful appeal of her glowing face. Her cheeks were flushed as she turned back to her door, then pushed it open.

What am I doing? Ulfrik thought, knowing full well he would not restrain himself. How long had he been without a woman's touch? How much longer still before he would feel it again? In his youth, he had taken women while out raiding or shared them with his crew. They were spoils to enjoy. Yet as his beard grayed, he had lost his taste for such a fleeting release. He much preferred a willing woman. Audhild seemed willing. Her appeal was without compare to the other women of the village. How often during the long months under her care did he not stir at her touch, the scent of her hair, or the heat of her breath?

Audhild placed the candle inside the door of her room. She grabbed the collar of her dress, her delicate hand pale and filled with shadow, then tore it down to reveal her chest. A shadow caught the swell of her left breast, inviting Ulfrik to tear the dress further.

"Show me you mean to stay." Audhild's breathy words filled his head, and Ulfrik seized her by the arms. A quick squeal from Audhild, and then he snatched her forward into his embrace.

They kissed deeply, their hands exploring each other, seeking ingress to the flesh beneath their clothing. Ulfrik's skin tingled as the warm smoothness of Audhild's hands slid beneath his shirt. She led him to her bed, and she spread herself out atop the furs and blankets. Her skirts slid up, revealing strong legs so white they glowed in the darkness. Ulfrik smiled, leaning on the frame of the bed as she reached for his pants.

They joined together on the bed, naked to the night chill. Ulfrik marveled at the warm, smooth skin gliding beneath his rough hands. Audhild gasped as he climbed atop her. Ulfrik had been so long without the pleasures of a woman he had nearly forgotten the sensation. She stared past him, her eyes unfixed and her lips parted. He drew in her scent, bending to kiss her neck. She worked her hands into his hair.

Then she screamed.

It was not the scream of pleasure but of intense pain. His ears rang with it, then he felt an icy slash on his shoulders. She was dragging her nails into his flesh. He pulled back.

"What in the name of—"

She continued to scream, "Help me!"

Something slammed across the back of his head. He pitched forward, only to have Audhild shove him off.

Ulfrik slid onto the floor, naked and dazed. Something warm ran over his face. He absently touched his temple. Blood.

"I knew it, you dog!" The voice broke loud over his head, then strong hands grabbed his legs while another hand yanked him by his hair. "Get up!"

The candlelight shed scant illumination. He saw Audhild cowering on the bed, covering herself with a fur. People crowded the room, but he could not tell how many. A woman's voice cried out from the rear. The man who held him by his hair was lost in shadow, but he recognized Gudrod's voice.

Gudrod rammed something hard into his guts, knocking the wind from him. "Good thing I was watching you."

Ulfrik started to answer, but one of the others in the room

clubbed him across the head. He flattened out to the floor, catching old straw and dirt in his mouth.

"You poor girl," he heard the woman's voice. "Are you all right?"

"I couldn't make him stop. I ...I don't know what to say." Audhild's voice trembled and she began to sob.

A hand pressed his head to the floor while another used rope to bound his arms behind his back.

I don't know what to say either, he thought. When the bindings were tight enough for his hands to go cold, Gudrod lifted him off the floor and held him up.

"Hero? You think that allows you to rape whomever you want?"

Ulfrik knew better than to argue. Another candle was lit, adding more light. Gudrod had brought witnesses, and had been smart enough not to take his own clique. Two men and a gray-haired woman stared at him, eyes wide and lips drawn into a tight frown. One of the men held the rope that was tied to Ulfrik's wrists.

"Why?" he asked Audhild. She stared at him fearfully, but he thought a smile played on her lips. It could also have been the dancing candlelight. Gudrod shoved him toward the door.

"We'll be asking you the same questions at dawn tomorrow. Better come up with a good answer for it. I've got three witnesses to what you did here."

Ulfrik glared at him. Gudrod's ruined face leered at him in the wavering shadows.

They forced him out of the hall, hands bound, and he sent a long, forlorn stare down the field to the prison house where Valagnar and his men waited for a signal that would not come.

36

Ulfrik lay on his old bed in the house Audhild had granted him in what now felt years ago. The goat he had kept for company was gone, but its rank odor still clung to the place. No one lived here, but it had become a storehouse for a miscellany of unwanted or half-broken junk. He had watched them carry out anything he could use as a weapon: broken tools, plates, shafts of shaped wood, a partially woven coil of rope. They left him bound by the unlit hearth and he shivered on his side until the dawn.

Nothing he considered made any sense. Audhild had trapped him, and had planned it with Gudrod. Eldrid had not been part of the events, but perhaps she would weigh in now that the sun rose on a terrible night. No single moment defined the truth Ulfrik felt in his gut. Instead, a recollection of frowns, glares, and injured looks from Audhild combined with Gudrod's incessant jealousy formed the truth for him.

The admiration the people had shown him was a threat to Audhild's position. It was one thing to be the feared, mysterious gift of the gods. He had no friends, no definite meaning to anyone. He was as controlled as a hen in her pen. However, as a hero who led them to war, bled with them, and saved them from an enemy set on their destruction, he had risen above his station. He was no longer a chicken in the pen, but a dragon among men. If he had not been so intent on securing Valagnar's help, he might have seen that he now had men who owed him their lives and would gladly repay him. He might have wrested control of the village for himself.

Fueled with doubt and worry, Audhild plotted his disgrace.

"Beaten by your own plans," he said to the rafters overhead. "And by your own cock. Gods, Ulfrik, are you fifteen again? Couldn't forgo a romp in bed for the bigger plan? Bah, you got what you deserved."

"Who are you talking to?" The voice at door startled him. The early morning light seeping between the planks of the door was obscured in the shape of a man.

"The gods," Ulfrik called back. When he raised his head to answer, his bed slid and he jerked as if falling. He was still reeling from the strikes to his head the night before. His hands were cold from remaining tied behind his back, and his side ached from lying on it all night. He was miserable and decided not to waste strength taunting his guard.

Expecting to be dragged out before the village at dawn, he waited well past the moment when the morning light revealed all the gaps in the walls and roof. Eventually he sat up, if only to relieve his side. A commotion played out in the distance, and Eldrid's screeching voice was clear above all of it. Ulfrik closed his eyes at the horrid noise and slumped forward as he waited. A lice-ridden wool blanket covered his nakedness, and he studied the white bugs to keep his mind off what awaited him.

By late morning voices neared the door, and then it slammed open. A wave of old hay and dust blew out before Gudrod as he rushed in with Bresi at his heels. "Even tied up you still managed to make trouble for us."

Ulfrik stared at him.

"The prisoners escaped last night and took their ship," Gudrod said. "You were the last one to see them and must've helped them."

"What happened?" Ulfrik sat up straighter, new hope animating him.

"Don't know. The two guards were dead and there was a blood trail leading to where their ship was beached. I guess they tricked the guards into unbarring the door and they killed them. How unarmed men did that is my question."

Gudrod and Bresi smiled as if they had solved a master skald's greatest riddle. Ulfrik snorted at them. "My old goat was smarter than you. How did they kill the guards? Twenty strong men against two armed fools is no great feat. If you weren't too drunk to remember, I warned those guards to be careful. They fell for a trick even a child would see through. They worked for that fate."

"Their throats were slashed. The guards had spears. They must've had other weapons at the ready."

"And I provided these to them?" Ulfrik stood, wobbling on his feet. "Don't you have better lies to be telling about me today? Let's get on with this madness before I knock what I left of your nose through the other side of your head."

"Have a care for what you say," Bresi said, tipping back his head and dramatically touching the hilt of his sword. "You're in a lot of trouble."

"Even tied up and hungover I can slam you through a wall. Don't foul the air with the wind from your cocksucking mouth." Ulfrik glared into Bresi's eyes and walked up to butt against his chest. "Draw that sword on me and I'll take you apart one limb at a time. You can depend upon it."

"Enough of this, let's go. Give him the pants back." Gudrod stepped aside as Bresi produced Ulfrik's pants. He held them out so Ulfrik could get his legs through while remaining tied. He had a desire to kick Bresi in the face, but he needed the pants more than the temporary thrill. Finally Gudrod took Ulfrik by the arm and led him outside.

The day was fair and clear, but in the distance Ulfrik saw dark clouds piling up. A bad sign. Wind whipped the grass flat and the villagers gathered around the remnants of the bonfire. Women held down their skirts as the wind gusted and men looked skyward for the approaching storm. Eldrid stood at the center, leaning on her staff. Her bravado was gone. The wind seemed as if it could scoop her into the air like a dead leaf. The tied ends of her yellowed blindfold fluttered behind her, tangled with her thin hair. Next to her stood

Audhild, covered in a green blanket and head lowered as if she were too distraught to look at anyone. Ulfrik immediately wanted to tear out her lying tongue. The bitch was about to condemn him to whatever punishments these fools reserved for their gifts from the gods.

"Unbind me," Ulfrik shouted at the circle of villagers, drawing surprised looks as if they just noticed he had arrived. "I've not been publicly accused of a crime. I'm a freeman, like any of you."

His comparison drew a few notable flinches. He searched the faces of people who the night before had celebrated him as a hero. Most looked away, others stared back, and others seemed to plead with him. Audhild, still not looking up, flicked her hand as if agreeing to the demand. Gudrod grunted as he untied the binds, and as they came free he leaned in to Ulfrik. "No need to cut them, since I'll be putting them right back on you."

Ulfrik was only concerned about working the blood back into his hands. He rubbed his tingling palms together, massaging them and gritting his teeth against the sensation.

"You all know why you've been called here," Gudrod said. "Hear the crime committed last night."

Audhild did not look at Ulfrik, but instead placed a hand over her mouth as she struggled to find the words. Ulfrik wondered if she was not hiding a smile instead. After a moment, she composed herself and spoke to the crowd.

"Last night, as I prepared for bed, Ulfrik came to my room. He was drunk. So was I. I did not realize until too late what he intended. I cared for him for so long, healed him from terrible wounds, that I could not believe what was happening. We lived together in separate rooms without ever a worry. It all changed last night. He tore my dress." Audhild pulled aside the blanket to reveal the dress. People gasped, as if it could have been torn by no other means. "Then he forced himself upon me. I tried to fight, but how could I? He raped me and all I could do was scream. If Gudrod had not saved me, I dread to think what might have followed."

Gudrod stepped up to his undoubtedly rehearsed part in this performance. Ulfrik struggled to remain impassive, massaging his hands and wrists, but rage seethed beneath his careless demeanor.

"I was checking on the condition of the village before returning to my own bed for the night. I found Meldun, Thorkel, and his wife Thorberta also ready to retire. We walked together by Audhild's hall. When I heard the screaming, I rushed in to find Ulfrik naked and atop Audhild. She was fighting him and begging for help. See how he is scratched up."

Heads turned to Ulfrik, but he blinked and looked toward the mountains. Thunder rumbled in the distance. He noted how the sound made everyone peek at the sky then at their feet. Did they all know this to be the lie it was? Were these madmen fulfilling another of Eldrid's dreams? How weak-willed were these sheep? He shook his head as Gudrod pointed out scratches on his exposed skin, half of which were from battle and not Audhild.

"I clubbed him, dragging him off and wrestling him into submission." Gudrod hugged the air as if reliving the moment. "These people are witnesses. Do you agree with all I have said?"

The three nodded, sad eyes regarding Ulfrik as if he were a favored hound that had to be killed. The woman, Thorberta, added her own commentary. "Poor Audhild was mad with grief. I had to sit with her all night just to calm her down."

A murmur spread around the circle. Audhild buried her face in her hands, and Ulfrik swore she was laughing. Eldrid sighed and shifted her weight on her staff.

"What do you have to say?" Gudrod asked. He folded his arms before him, a snide smile on his face. Dried blood and snot was still in his beard from when Ulfrik had broken Gudrod's nose the day before.

"Audhild invited me to her bed, spread her legs, and it was all set up to shame me. She is threatened by my success, as are you, and so you both plotted to bring me down. Nothing I say is going to stop whatever you planned."

"How expected," Gudrod said, throwing his hands in the air. "Rather than answer for his crimes, he would distract us with his own accusations. Do you deny being atop Audhild, even with four witnesses to say otherwise?"

Ulfrik stared off at the distant storm clouds. He imagined a bolt of lightning splitting Gudrod in half.

"And Audhild, do you say Ulfrik was not welcomed to your bed?"

"I do."

"Then the crime is rape, and the punishment for that has always been death."

Before Ulfrik could gouge Gudrod's eyes and strangle him, Eldrid screamed. It was no ordinary screech, but a piercing spear of ice that slid into the ear and stabbed the brain. Her back arched as she threw her arms wide. Hands clamped over ears. Audhild jumped in shock. Ulfrik let his arms drop and waited for her scream to wind out.

When done, she pointed her staff at Gudrod. "What fool words did I hear? You speak with the tongue of a snake. I have foretold Ulfrik must live for the gods' continued blessings. Do not oppose me in this. You have no sight. You lack any wisdom. All must remember my words, for the gods speak through me. Ulfrik lives."

"But ...he has to pay for his crimes." Gudrod's demeanor was like a child who had his toy sword snatched away.

"There is another way," Audhild said, raising her hands between Eldrid and Gudrod as if separating them. Eldrid withdrew her staff, her part in the drama completed. Ulfrik narrowed his eyes at Audhild. She was playing both him and Gudrod, but he could not guess her final scheme.

The pause had drawn every eye to her, and she scanned the faces of the gathering before continuing. "I agree with Eldrid. Ulfrik is the living vessel of the gods' fortune. She dreamed of a man from the sky promised by the gods to bring us a new life and great success. Ulfrik is that man, and to kill him is to spit in the face of the gods' generosity. He must live, but does not need to be free."

A few nods came from the crowd. Ulfrik stepped toward Audhild, but paused when he felt a blade point into his back. Bresi had come up behind, now carrying a spear he leveled at Ulfrik's spine. She continued.

"There are caves all over this land, and one is close. We will build a grate of iron to contain him within it. He will be fed and cared for by all of us. But we will be safe from his rabid lust and violence."

Bresi's spear point pressed Ulfrik's back as he flexed toward Audhild. Gudrod drew his sword, and Ulfrik had to stop. He glared at her over Gudrod's shoulder. Her face had no expression. She had dispatched him as a challenge to her power. How had he not seen this? He had looked to Eldrid all along as the true ruler, but she was evidently jumping to Audhild's commands.

"You ungrateful bastards!" he shouted at the crowd. "I saved your miserable lives only to have you treat me worse than a slave."

"A slave'd be killed for rape," called one voice. A few others agreed.

"Shut up!" Ulfrik's voice boomed like it did over the battlefield. Even Gudrod's sword quaked in his grip. His father had been Orm the Bellower, and Ulfrik had inherited his vocal prowess. He blasted them with it now.

"I demand a trial by combat. Let the gods decide if I am truthful when I say I did not rape Audhild."

The stunned faces had no answer. Gudrod paled, and Ulfrik flashed a venomous smile at him. For an instant, Ulfrik thought his demand might bear fruit.

Then he noticed Audhild tap her thigh twice, and Eldrid launched into her scream once more. It was not as piercing this time, but no less arresting.

"The decision is made," she said, stretching her staff toward him. "For all the times you've threatened us with violence or tried to abandon your sacred duties, you must be imprisoned. There is no other way."

Gudrod straightened, his smile returning, and nodded at someone behind Ulfrik. Bresi's spear dug into him as another man retied his bonds. Any attempt a flight would end with the spear head through his back.

Thunder grumbled louder in the distance and the sky darkened. All looked nervously to the sky. Eldrid's pronouncements did not ease their tense postures. "The gods witness this and agree. It is the sound of them banging their tables in approval."

Lightning flashed and wind picked up. Ulfrik did not see approval, but instead heard his opportunity. If the gods needed a voice, then he would provide it. As his hands were again bound behind his back, he lashed out at the crowd.

"You think Eldrid alone knows the gods? I am their vessel. She told you herself. They are not pleased, and neither am I. I curse you in the names of all the gods. By Odin's one eye and Thor's hammer, I curse this rotten village to death. Each day I am imprisoned the stronger my curse grows. The pox take all of you to the grave!"

"Silence him!" Eldrid screamed. Gudrod was as still as the rest of the crowd. Before he could act, lightning flashed and thunder shook the ground. A few of the women cried out.

"The gods hear me," Ulfrik said, a smile on his face. "Audhild, may your cunt fall out and your tongue turn black."

Gudrod's spear butted him in the gut, driving the wind out of him. Bresi forced a rag into Ulfrik's mouth, a smoky and gritty taste to it. He did not resist, for the thunder pealed again and people scattered.

The gods had heard him.

But he was still a captive and doomed to die in a cave.

37

Ulfrik leaned against the cold iron grate that sealed the cave entrance. Each square was large enough for him to put an arm through, though nothing beyond was worth grabbing. He looked out on ground that rolled like an ocean frozen in black rock, patches of grass its sea foam. The corrugated landscape prevented him from seeing too far, though he could smell the salt air and hear the faint purr of the sea. The sky was a match for the gray iron that held him inside the cave. He hung one arm outside of it.

When he was a child, his father had taken him to the summer trading bazaars in Kaupang where he had once seen a black bear in a cage offered for sale. The beast's eyes were sad and confused and it leaned against the cage so square patches of its fur pressed out. Ulfrik had stroked the fur and the bear did not flinch. It had been a broken animal, no better than a skin to be thrown over a bed. The man selling it proclaimed it a mighty beast worthy of a mighty master, but Ulfrik remembered how his father had snorted in disgust and left it without a second glance.

Ulfrik imagined he was that bear now, pressed against the side of his own cage.

He withdrew his arm and pulled over the lice-infested blanket he had carried since the night Audhild had betrayed him. In the cave, he was not allowed fire and his sole warmth came from his clothing. For now, only the night was chill but he dreaded the coming of winter.

The thought gave him pause. Winter was months away. When had he resigned himself to living so long in this cave? After he had cursed everyone he set eyes upon, Gudrod and his thugs beat him senseless. They threw him into this cave within a day of the iron grate being forged from Valagnar's melted-down weapons. No thought had been given to his conditions. Over the days or weeks—he no longer knew how long had passed—villagers supplemented his living conditions with bare necessities: blankets and furs for bedding, a bucket for his waste, a bowl for collecting rain water. They came with food and ale once a day, leaving it in bowls outside the grate. If he tried to talk to them, they fled.

He lay on his fur bed, the lumps of stone beneath digging into his back. Above him roots hung between the rocks. He wondered if the cave would collapse or if a dwarf would crawl out of a crack in the floor and kill him. He had been pouring his waste bucket into a deep crack at the back of the tube-shaped cave. The smells of excrement and urine had drawn enough flies to the crack that the cave hummed with their buzzing.

This was it. All the grand victories, the glorious battles, the piles of gold and silver had led him to a cave and a shit bucket.

He regretted Throst had failed to kill him. He used to hate Throst for attempting murder; now he hated Throst for not finishing the kill.

He rolled on his side atop the furs and closed his eyes.

When he opened them again all was dark, though he could see clearly. Moonlight shined into his cave and filled the rough black walls with silvery highlights. He was still on his side, facing the wall, and decided to sit up. When he did, he discovered Runa sat beside him.

She was dressed in the gray wool dress she favored for sleeping, hugging her legs and leaning her head on her knees in an expression of loving patience. She smiled at him as he awakened. Her hair was full of tight curls and her skin was apple-smooth and radiant even in the dark, like she had been when they first met so many years ago.

Seeing her brought tears to his eyes, and he grabbed for her. Her giggle was the clink of silver chains and her scent was fresh lavender. She laced her arms around him as he rocked with her in his arms. "I feared I'd never see you again," he said, running his hands through her hair.

"Yet I am here. Have you forsaken me so soon?"

He shook his head, burying his face in her shoulder. "Let me hold you again. I've missed you so much."

"You must do better," she said, her voice a warm whisper that tickled his neck. "You are better than this. If you wish to hold me again, prove it."

When he pulled back to look at her, the darkness muddled her face. He sat back, peering against the gloom until he realized he was not looking at Runa.

"Toki?"

"Who else?" With those words Ulfrik saw him clearly. His eyes flashed with the youthful mischief of the first years they sailed together as brothers and raiders. The last time Ulfrik had seen him blood had poured from his mouth and his eyes rolled in death with Throst's treacherous arrow piercing his head. Yet now he was whole, strong-jawed and full-bodied, sitting cross-legged next to him. A silver cloak pin flashed in the night.

"How are you not dead?"

"A question I must ask you. Or rather do you seek it? Were you not hoping for it?"

"I didn't mean it."

"But you did." Toki smiled, a wicked twist to his lips that he shared with his sister, Runa, and had passed on to Ulfrik's son, Gunnar. The simple gesture made Ulfrik burn with shame.

"Why can't I open the grate and walk out of here?"

"Some gates are closed and some are open and some are neither. All need men to travel under them. Have you wondered how Throst knew you were coming? He ambushed you in the tower. But how had he known to be there?"

"I ... he ... Hrut told him. Yes, I remember Hrut and his treachery."

"How is it you were invited to the place where Throst dwelt? When you return home, think about that. We are brothers, you and I.

But not all brothers are as true and not all brothers hold each other dear. Some brothers would betray each other for trifles."

Ulfrik stood, Toki's words hammering at him. Something about them troubled him, yet he could not grasp it. The thoughts made his head hurt, and he pinched the bridge of his nose as he struggled. Then he understood, and clapped his hands.

"Ah, you said I will return home. How ..."

Toki no longer sat across from him. The rock floor was barren, filled only with a pool of moonlight. Then a shadow stirred at the grate. A figure leaned against it, regarding him from a drape of darkness.

The vague shape of the man did not stir and seemed to be staring at him; his head was so lost in shadow Ulfrik could not tell where he faced.

"Who are you? What have you done to my brother?"

"Don't you know me anymore?"

Ulfrik puzzled at the words and the figure pushed away from the grate. Moonlight caught him, revealing the strong lines of a smiling face. His straight teeth were as white as the moonlight. For a moment Ulfrik did not recognize him.

"Yngvar Bright-Tooth?"

"Your old eyes still see some things. I saved you once, in the forest. You were a boy then."

"How could I forget? Yngvar, open the grate and free me."

Yngvar shook his head, his smile vanished. "I already saved your life once. Some tricks are not so fair a second time."

Ulfrik grabbed the cold iron grate and shook it. The moon-brightened fields beyond rolled away to nothing. "I am trapped here with no way out."

"You fool," Yngvar said. He pulled him around by the shoulder. "Your eyes seek the wrong things. You know the way out, but have decided it is easier to die instead."

"That's not true. I'm tired and weak. Would you have me break iron bars?"

Yngvar's face crumpled in a frown. "Shame me no more. We who have shed blood for you are disgraced. Why are you behind these bars?"

"I was outwitted. I have no talent for these deceitful games and have paid the price for my ignorance."

"Don't play games you lack the talent to win." Yngvar suddenly held a sheathed sword in his both hands. His eyes blazed as brightly as his teeth, like two stars above a tipped over crescent moon. "You gave this to me to hold in the sea grave. Do you know it still?"

Yngvar held up the sword in its leather sheath. A grip in sharkskin wrap was topped in a pommel that held a glittering green jewel. Ulfrik's heart leapt in his chest.

"My sword, Fate's Needle!"

"Yes, when you grasp it once more, a king will find his crown and your fate reclaimed. Return to your hearth, take up Fate's Needle again. Make my death worth something."

"I don't know how," Ulfrik said, his voice cracking with desperation. Yngvar closed his eyes and clasped the sword over his chest, just as Ulfrik had placed it before dropping him into the cold bosom of the sea.

"You do know," Yngvar's voice echoed in his head as he faded. It was as if he were sinking beneath waves of night, growing fainter each moment. "Seek the way beneath. Find your path home again."

Ulfrik was again facing the wall and light filled his cave. He was not certain how long he had been sleeping, but once he realized he had dreamed he shot upright. His head was heavy with sleep and the room spun. Yngvar's voice still echoed as the vestiges of sleep fell away. He rubbed his face vigorously, then slumped forward.

"Now only ghosts speak with me. I am going mad."

He stared at the bucket at the back of the hall, a dance of flies leaping along its rim. Something about a gate came to mind.

Then he remembered his dreams.

He tore away his blanket and fell before the grate. The ground was stony but the dirt was pliable. He cast around until he found a rock he was able to prize out of the earth. With this tool, he began scrapping the dirt at the base of the grate.

"All gates need men to travel under them," he repeated. "Of course they do."

The simplicity of the scheme would have embarrassed him had he not been so excited to have a plan. It all came together now. Like a dog digging under a fence, he only had to excavate enough dirt to slip through. He could dump the dirt into the crack at the back of the cave where no visitor would see it. The hole itself could be disguised with any of the flat rocks scavenged from the cave floor. Time was not a factor. He had nothing else to do but dig. Then he would head north and take his chances with Valagnar.

The tiny scrapings weren't large enough to fit a mouse yet. However, he would work this hole until his entire body could slide beneath the grate.

A tear streaked down his cheek as he gouged his makeshift stone shovel into the dirt.

38

Ulfrik scooped the dirt into his waste bucket, patting off his hands over it, then carried it to the rear of the cave. Light did not reach the back and even in the noon sun he had to take care not to break a toe on a hidden rock. However, he had been traversing the same path dozens of times each day and knew every dip and rise. He dumped the dirt into the corner. He had no need to hide the pile when others could not see it. The air at the back of the cave was rank with fresh earth and waste, and flies landed on his face as he shook out the last of the dirt.

Back at the grate, the slight breeze was a welcome caress compared to the humid stench to the rear. He set the bucket down and wiped sweat from his brow with the back of his arm. He had been digging for three days, being careful and methodically excavating the area next to the grate. So many promising starts ended in stones he could not dig out without removing the grate. Those he had filled in again and picked a new area for exploration. He stared down at the most promising dig yet, a wide but shallow area he had cleared out the prior day. Another stone prevented further progress, but he judged the day to only be slightly past noon. He had ample time to trench around the rock and prize it out. The resultant hole would probably allow all the room needed to shimmy beneath the grate.

His stomach growled and he patted it. A single daily meal had been enough to sustain him when all he had done was lie on his back. With real work, the food was barely enough to keep him. Pausing too long brought a weak tremor to his arms and legs along with a faintness. If he concentrated only on digging, he fell into a waking dream where his motions seemed to come from another place.

Now he had rested enough and began to feel the weakness. He tested the gap, getting on his belly and feeling the sharp grit sliding beneath him. He could fit his arm up to his neck and then the iron bars caught his head. He needed to redouble his efforts, for the width and depth of the hole had gone beyond his ability to hide with rocks or bedding. Today was the day for escape. His meal would not come until just before twilight. That gave him several hours alone.

He dug with mounting vigor as the edge of the blocking stone emerged. Unable to lift it out yet, he worked along its edges, hoping it would not disappear beneath ground he had not yet cleared. His fingers plowed under the lip and he puffed his cheeks as he pulled up. Nothing shifted. He fell back on his rump and stared at the hole beneath the grate.

On the other side of it, a boy of ten or twelve years stood holding a wooden tray that held a steaming bowl and mug.

They stared at each other.

Ulfrik leapt, slamming into the bars. His arms shot forward to grab the boy, but he was too fast. The wooden tray clattered to the ground, soup and ale sloshing into the ground and a wedge of bread and cheese rolling into the dirt. Ulfrik roared at him. "What are you doing here?"

The boy turned and fled. Ulfrik cried out for him to stay, but the boy dashed over a crest of black rock and disappeared.

"It's not time yet!" Ulfrik had to get free now or his chance to escape would forever be ruined. He stretched for the bread and cheese, dragged them beneath the grate, then stuffed them into his mouth. The iron taste of dirt mingled with the food, but he needed all the strength he could muster. Grabbing the digging rock, he renewed his attack on the blocking stone.

The harder he dug the less progress he made. He flung dirt under his legs like a dog searching for a bone. Every few moments he dove into the hole and tested the gap. His head still caught. He tried to push through, but the bars dug into his skull with unrelenting pressure. He backed out, dug until he could wedge more of his hand under the stone. When he pulled, he felt it shift.

He shouted with joy, strength flowing back into his limbs. He pulled up again and the wide flat rock broke out of its earthen moorings. Dragging it into the cave, Ulfrik flung it aside and slid back into the hole again. His head fit.

Barely.

Dirt pressed into his face as he kicked and scrabbled beneath. The bars scored above his ear, drawing blood as he pushed. His hair and beard rolled up with earth as he pushed. His head was through but he had not cleared enough ground on the other side of the bars. It was soft and free of rocks, perfect ground for digging. Yet he had no time. He pushed again, but it was his face shoving against the world. With his free hand he clawed at the dirt to make space.

As he scrambled, he heard a boy's voice approaching. Before he could back out, he heard it right over his head.

"Be careful. He'll grab your leg." The boy's voice was filled with worry. Ulfrik, unable to turn toward the boy, tried to withdraw but his clothing caught again.

Then he felt a cold, hard touch of wood on his temple.

"He'll do no such thing. He'll pull back behind the bars. You'll see."

Ulfrik slumped in the ditch. The voice was calmer and clearer than usual, but unmistakable.

Eldrid had arrived.

39

Eldrid and Ulfrik faced each other through the bars. The boy who had caught him hid behind her dirty skirt, his small pink hand bright against the gray wool and a single wide eye peeking out at him. Ulfrik snarled at the boy and he ducked out of sight.

"Don't frighten the boy," she said. "He did you a good turn fetching me." Eldrid probed the hole with her staff, banging the edges and then tapping the iron bars. The dull iron ping was a tolling bell in Ulfrik's head. Her thin lips pressed in a smile as she estimated the size of the hole. "You almost made it."

"Get down in it and feel for yourself. I'll be happy to pull you through so you can experience life as an animal." Ulfrik wished his waste bucket were full. He would douse Eldrid with the contents. "Does your magical nose bring you the ripe smell of piss? Your goats don't even live like this."

He expected mad cackling, a string of invectives, or senseless babble. So when she sighed and nodded, all his words fled. Her thin, trembling hand gripped the iron bars as she searched with her staff for a place to sit. Finding a low rock by the cave mouth, she settled down. The boy guided her, shooting terrorized looks to Ulfrik. Eldrid shooed him after she settled. "Go, but stay near. Tell no one what you saw here." When the boy paused she smacked his leg with her staff. "Go or I'll turn you into a toad."

The boy flitted back over the rise, Eldrid watching him even through her blindfold.

Ulfrik retreated to the rear of the cave, hunching low. He feared Eldrid planned to kill him with poison, and standing too close to the grate would make such a murder too easy. If he hung to the rear, she would have to enter and he would be ready. He had piled up the sharpest and heaviest stones to be used for weapons.

"It's time you and I spoke," she said. "Everything is wrong. This was not supposed to happen."

Her voice held a rough edge, but it was clearer and smoother than Ulfrik had ever heard it. It was as if she had swallowed honey to soothe a hoarse throat. She set her staff aside and folded both hands in her lap, head bowed and her thin hair flowing across it. For a moment, she resembled her sister, Audhild.

"What was supposed to happen? Break my legs instead? But you tried that once, didn't you?" Ulfrik remained crouched at the rear of the cave. The sun lowered in the sky, casting Eldrid into a pale gold light. She almost appeared normal. All her bluster and posturing had vanished, leaving only a frail girl slouching on a rock.

She shook her head. "I know what I have done and regret it."

"What does that mean? You tortured me when I was helpless and dogged my every step since I could walk. Now I'm locked up like a pig, and just waiting for you to tire of me. How much longer before that day? How much longer before the people can't support a prisoner who contributes nothing? Will you be sorry when I'm abandoned to die of starvation? That's how you cowards will kill me. You don't think I know?"

"No, no, no!" She touched one hand to her eyes and raised the other in a gesture for him to stop. "I am not your enemy. I am not the mad one. Audhild is all that and more. You must know it by now."

The words were so cogent, so uncharacteristic, that Ulfrik had to pause. Audhild was controlling and jealous, but he had not seen madness in her. "Is this your new game? Are the gods speaking to you now? Telling you how to turn my mind upside down so that my torment grows? You and your people are sick. Worse than trolls."

"You understand so little," Eldrid said, then smiled. Her lips trembled as if she were either about to laugh or cry, and she covered them with the back of her hand. "You are as blind as I am, maybe worse."

Ulfrik finally stood. He held onto his digging rock and approached the bars. She turned to him and smiled.

"You appear to see well enough through the blindfold."

"After I lost my eyes, the gods sharpened my other senses. I can hear ants crawling over the floor. My nose rivals a hound for scenting a man. With my hands, I can see whatever I touch. It is part of the curse and the gift the gods have made for me."

"Along with the gift of song?"

Her smile turned sweet. "I was happy to let you catch me singing. Did you like it?"

"I've heard better from a dying walrus." He had found her voice charming, but a compliment for Eldrid was like complimenting an executioner.

Her smile fell and head turned aside. "I want to tell you the truth. I want to set this right."

"Then pull down this grate and let me go."

"No, it's not what the gods have decreed. Your life for the good of our people. You are a living sacrifice, but you did not need to suffer. Only give up your old life for the new." Her hand balled into a fist and she bit her knuckle. At last she tore it out and pounded the rock she sat on. "But you are too stubborn. You resist and fight and make everyone suffer."

"I thought I made everyone prosper?"

"You make me suffer!" She shot to her feet, face pulled into hateful lines. She stabbed a twig-like finger at him. "You are why I am this way. You made me Eldrid the Ugly! It wasn't supposed to be that way."

Ulfrik shook his head, but realized she could not see it. "I hardly believe that is possible."

She hung her head with her finger pointed accusingly and her teeth bared, then slowly she melted back onto her rock seat. She remained with her head lowered, then heaved a sigh. "I will tell you everything from the beginning. From the time Audhild and I were only girls. Then you will see Audhild's madness. Then you will know how you have hurt me every day of every season we have spent together."

40

"Audhild is my younger sister, though we are only a year apart. My trials have aged me to what you see now, but I was beautiful once. More beautiful than Audhild was. She was a plain-faced child, more like a boy than a girl. We had two older brothers that I don't remember. They died when we still lived in Hedemark, shortly after Harald Finehair proclaimed himself king. Norway doesn't seem like a real place to me now. Frankia was my home, and I hated to leave it. Oh, yes, do not be surprised at that truth.

"We lived a good life on the edge of Gunnolfsvik. My father built and repaired ships for Jarl Gunnolf among others. The Franks had called it Gerville, for the trees in the surrounding forests were straight as spears. I was happy there, until the gods began to show me things.

"It started one night with a dream. I saw a young girl riding a white horse through town. I did not recognize her but her eyes were black and jaw slack. When I woke, I knew I had seen a terrible omen. I told Audhild and she calmed me back to sleep. The next day, one of the village girls startled a horse from behind and was kicked in the head. She died. My first vision had been of death. Audhild was amazed at what I had seen. She wanted to do it too, but only summoned nightmares. I continued to see things, like where a lost lamb had wandered to, and where my father's ax had been misplaced. They came as dreams and were always of small things. No more visions of deaths came to me.

"My parents did not want to talk about my sight. I was twelve winters old, and my parents had planned for me to marry within a few years. If the gods truly gifted me with sight, then I would forever be alone. So I shared only with Audhild. She was ever eager to push the limit of my dreams and though I did as she bade, it greatly disturbed me. Finally, one night, she had a plan that would change everything.

"I remember it to the finest detail, like all the horrors of that time. My parents slept opposite us on the other side of a partial wall. It was little more than a board screen to obscure my parents' private moments. Though that night Audhild and I pulled blankets overhead to make a tent. We kept only a flap open to allow in air and wavering candlelight. We were two conspirators, leaning our heads together in grave secrecy.

"'Tonight you're going to have a great vision,' Audhild said. 'Demand the gods show you something grand. Something that will prove to Da that you're a true seidkona.'

"'I don't want to be a seidkona,' I had told her, and it was true. Such a life seemed more of a curse than something to desire. But Audhild never relents on what she wants.

"'Fate cannot be changed. So embrace it,' she told me. I agreed and we touched heads together, as if that would increase my power. I think actually Audhild hoped it would steal my sight. We kicked off our tent and giggled, probably the last time we ever would enjoy being sisters. My father hushed us from the other side of the wall and warned us Mother needed her rest, then I was asleep. And I dreamed.

"I dreamed something horrible. My mother had been impaled upon a spear, pinning her to the bed. Blood rushed out of her stomach, from her mouth, and her hands struggled with the spear. I could do nothing but watch. Her twisting stopped and her legs kicked out like a boy killed in a play-battle. It would have been funny if not for the blood. The gods showed me my mother's death.

"The next morning Audhild begged for the details. I wouldn't tell her, but could not resist her persistence. When she heard my dream, she cursed and slapped me. I made her cry and she left me alone on the bed. The same morning my father said Mother still needed rest. She never again rose from the bed. Blood vomited from her mouth and her bowels let go. A fever consumed her and she died within two days of my dream.

"Audhild blamed me for it. I tried to tell her I only saw what the gods decided to show, but she refused to accept it. Audhild was our mother's favorite. They spent hours together at the loom and if there was ever any extra food, Mother always spooned it into her dish. I think Mother knew Da was sweeter on me, and so she made up for him. When she died, Audhild lost her source of joy.

"I continued to dream, though most of the time nothing grew from it. The gods denied me visions in the weeks following our mother's death. I didn't care, but Audhild obsessed over it.

"'You let an evil spirit into the house,' she finally said to me. 'You killed our mother with a curse. Don't dream anything again, or you will regret it.'

"But I did dream again, and when she confronted me I angered. I threatened to dream that her tongue shriveled up so I would not need to hear her any longer. I had no idea she took me literally.

"She tackled me on the bed where we had giggled and made plans for my great visions. I was helpless and she was choking me. I think she realized I was about to die and stopped. I squirmed underneath her, trying to catch my breath. I thought she was going to let me go. Instead, she plunged her thumbs into my eyes. I don't remember much else. Hot blood covered my face, everything went white. I screamed, that I remember. The pain has vanished with the years.

"I gave Audhild a memory of that day as well. My thumbnail gouged her brow and the scar remains to this day. It is a hard and cold thing when I touch her face and it shames her to know it marks her madness so boldly.

"It took a long time for me to recover, and one eye was crushed to nothing. The other was ruined. I see only vague light and dark from it. Audhild had wanted to destroy my sight, and took the most direct approach she could imagine.

"Father hired a wise woman to live with us and heal me. It took years. That was how Audhild learned the healing arts, from the wise woman. It might have been the only good to come of all this blood. Though we both learned other things less fair. You've tasted much of those bitter lessons in the draughts we've fed you or the powders that blinded you.

"My father remarried no long after Mother died. Reidun was her name. Audhild told me of her beauty and her voice was high and her touch gentle. She was good for my father, but Audhild hated her. For years after blinding me, she did not ask for my visions, though I still had them. When Reidun joined our household, her interest renewed. I was fifteen and should have been married, but now I was useless as a wife. I determined if my dreams had cost me my eyes, then I might as well embrace them. Audhild wanted me to have visions of evil befalling Reidun. When these would not come, Audhild tormented me. She moved furniture to confuse me, tripped me, threw hot water on my face, anything she could think of until I began to have dreams that suited her. In my blindness I was helpless to do anything in my defense.

"I told my horrible visions to our father, but he rebuked me. Audhild decided to shift the dreams from evil befalling her to evil done by Reidun's hand. Audhild told me what to tell father I dreamed and she would ensure these visions came true. It was simple things at first, minor visions easily arranged like missing tools found among Reidun's things, a snake placed in their bed, milk left to curdle. Audhild wanted to drive Reidun away. The poor woman did not know how to fight with Audhild, and I frightened her. She also believed in my visions. And why not? I had the sight and what I dreamed came true.

"Reidun had spirit, though, and braved the run of bad luck. My father believed me as well, but stood by his new wife. This infuriated Audhild. We had to cook up something bigger if Reidun was to be driven out. Audhild told me to dream that Reidun would try to kill me out of fear. We made a careful plan of my waking in the middle of the night soaked in sweat. It was water hid in a bowl under my sheets. I screamed, begged for my father. Then told him I had dreamed of a woman like Reidun smothering me while I slept. It was the first time I had to act as if mad, and I would never stop from that day. My act was so convincing that Father confronted Reidun straight away.

"Though I was blind, I could see Reidun sitting up in bed still sleepy and confused. I heard my father drag her to the floor with a squeal, heard Audhild stifle a laugh. He confronted her and they argued. Reidun called me a blind hag and Audhild the village whore. My father strangled her where she sat. We had set him so on edge, filled his every day with visions of doom, that I believe we drove him to madness. I heard Reidun's last breath rattle and my father sob.

"I don't know how he destroyed Reidun's body. At first he told everyone she went to visit family north of the Seine. When months passed, he said she had to care for her sick mother. Then her brother visited. He figured out Reidun's fate and drove a shard of broken plate through my father's neck. We girls were spared. Our uncle came to handle the business and see to our care. He stayed for a year, but when he tried to find a husband for Audhild, he suddenly left. Whatever she did kept him away until the time we left for Iceland. She did not want marriage.

"Audhild wanted to rule Gerville. By the time our uncle fled, she was seventeen and a full woman. With me as her authority, she began manipulating the people. I had the visions she instructed, and made the predictions she wanted. She ensured they came true. People believe anything they are told. At some point she began to believe these visions herself. Madness had ever stalked her since Mother's death, but now it bloomed. She beat me, burned me, threatened to kill me if I ever reminded her that my visions were on her instruction. To save myself, I learned to predict the visions she most desired. I learned to listen to what people told me and then predict something from it. It's a skill that grew with time and practice. By now I've no belief that gods grant gifts or take any interest in our lives. We are to them as worms are to us.

"People had respect for Audhild, and for years she ruled Gerville and discouraged suitors with both guile and threat. Gudrod has been the most persistent, starting from the days my father still lived. But he is too frightened to court her and too stubborn to give up. I get ahead of myself. When the Franks crossed our borders and the protection of Gunnolfsvik faltered, Audhild decided we needed to leave. She wanted to hold onto what she had built with Gerville. Most of the people were bondsmen of our father or a few other families; escaped slaves learned they could shelter among us. Audhild promised freedom to all slaves and bondsmen and choice property to all freemen who would follow her to a new land. This was a strong draw, and you know how they decided and how rushed the exit from Gerville had been.

"Gudrod suggested Iceland and Audhild fell in love with his description of it. It sounded dreadful to me, though my life in Frankia would be no better. Then I had my dream of the man from the sky. Everything changed that night.

"I had been so long without a true vision, I'd forgotten the experience. But that night the dreams were real enough to touch. Thor the god of storms spoke in voices of thunder and promised a man to me if I obeyed my sister. Lightning flashed and a man fell from the sky, landing in a field I recognized from the abandoned tower. This man rose from the ground, naked, and lifted me into his arms. Never had I beheld such beauty, but today I cannot even recall his face. Well, I am never blind in my dreams, but with a swipe of his hand he made my eyes whole again. I cried with joy and the man kissed my head. He promised as long as I remained with him all would be well.

"When I awoke it was early morning. Audhild was still asleep, and had been exhausted from the preparations for leaving. So I ran from the house, eager to tell others of my dream. By the time Audhild awakened, all the women in Gerville knew my dream. Audhild celebrated for me in public, but when the doors closed she knocked me to the floor and drove a blade against my neck. I had prophesied without her consent and told others before her. I won't describe all she threatened to do to me. I was so certain of my vision that I resisted her.

"'The gods intend to send me a gift,' I said. 'He will appear out of the sky, wrapped in lightning, and land at the old watchtower. I am as sure of this as I've ever been. Let me have my gift, and I will be loyal to you forever.'

"She considered this for a long time, though the moment I pledged myself I heard the change in her breathing and felt the blade flinch. I knew she would agree.

"'If I find this man, then he is a gift from the gods and his blessing will ensure our success as long as he lives.'

"This was not my dream, but I recognized what Audhild wanted. She twisted the vision to suit her wishes. I agreed. You know the rest. Audhild was genuinely shocked when you were discovered, but still pleased. She needed someone to play off Gudrod, to keep him away but interested in the Iceland journey. Your injuries were a perfect excuse to occupy her time.

"You proved hard to handle, but Audhild felt you could be controlled if one of us treated you poorly and the other treated you with kindness. Since Audhild tended your wounds, she took the pleasant role and gained your confidence while my torments drove you closer to her. We expected this to make you more open to Audhild's desires, but you resisted even this ploy. But soon I realized the game was not being played for you, but for me.

"She never forgave me for going to the villagers with my visions. It was a threat to her power, and she decided I must suffer for it. She will never let me have you. When you challenged her prestige, she grew jealous and wary. It was time for her to remove you and punish me. I've been forbidden to speak about you ever again, and you will never be freed from this cave. She believes her version of my vision. But for me, I just wanted my man from the sky who would bring me happiness for the rest of my days. I found you, but you have remained beyond my grasp.

"Now, there is no hope, and you will die."

41

Ulfrik sat mute, back leaning against the cage as Audhild's voice trailed off. The sun cast long shadows into the cave mouth, cutting squares of brightness into the scattered dirt. He was cupped in the hole he had dug in his bid to escape, feeling the cool of the earth seeping into his hamstrings. The gash over his ear had crusted over, and an errant scratch drew more blood into his dirt-filled nails.

"That is an amazing story," he said. "I am without an answer to it."

Eldrid snorted a laugh. "What can you answer? I wanted you to know the truth before you died."

"You're going to poison me," he said. He remained staring into the blackness of the cave. "That will be your vengeance upon your sister."

The silence was his confirmation and suddenly his stomach lurched. He scrabbled out of the hole and faced her. "You've already done it. The food I ate."

She shook her head. During her speech she had removed the blindfold and now sat with her head leaning against the iron grate. Her ruined eye was a brown twist of flesh that twitched, but from the thick-scarred lid of her other eye a line of tears cleared the dirt off her cheek. "I have not dared yet. Maybe the gods will let us be joined still."

Ulfrik relaxed, slumping back to his knees. Eldrid remained crying silently, deep lines between her brows filling with shadow. He realized that she was probably no older than twenty-three, yet she wore the countenance of a woman twice that age. While he could not forgive her, he at least now understood the strange madness that ruled her.

If he had learned anything from Eldrid's confession it was that people caught between the two sisters ended up dead. He could count his life in days, and once Eldrid regained her composure she would find some way to kill him sooner. Never mind poison, but starvation would work or a blazing fire set at the mouth of the cave would choke him to death. His life was a fragile blade of grass and he was never more helpless in all his life than at this moment.

"Eldrid, my death is not the answer. Don't you see your vision has been true all along? I will make your eyes whole again. I will allow you to see the way to a better life. Free me from this place, and join me in my escape. We will be beyond Audhild's power as long as you stay with me. It is exactly as the gods showed you."

She lifted her head from the grate and sat upright. Ulfrik held his breath, unable to read her reaction. When she said nothing, he goaded her. "Don't let your sister steal the gift. Never has it been more clear what you must do. Take the bolts out of the rock and toss aside this grate."

"No!" She shot to her feet, grabbing up her staff. Her voice fell back into the scratchy hiss of her role as mad seidkona. "You are playing me for a fool. You only want to flee back to your family. We will never be together."

Eldrid stalked away, stumbling as she went. Her blindfold remained on the rocks, and Ulfrik dragged it into the cave then tucked it into his pants. He might have use for it. He did not ask her to stop. He never believed she would help him.

She was mad.

This whole land was mad.

He returned to digging.

42

When dawn leaked into the cave mouth, Ulfrik's hole beneath the grate had not increased over the prior day. Stone after stone had deflected his searching path beneath the grate, and nighttime blinded him. It was as if he had excavated darkness, flinging small handfuls of night behind himself. He scraped like a dog searching for a prized bone, unrelenting until exhaustion had reached like a hand out of the ground and pulled him flat into unconsciousness. Now he lay on his stomach in the hole, the ends of the grate hovering over him.

The tips of rocks poked up out of the soup of shadow and caught the morning sun. He had felt their round, hard shapes in the night, but seeing them in the day he realized he had spent his effort on the wrong spot. Sitting up with a gasp, he searched for his digging rock then renewed the attack. He had underestimated the effort and time needed to dig free and cursed himself for a fool. Part of him wanted to blame the strain of isolation and hunger for his error, but he knew he had acted too soon. The single resource Audhild had left him had been time, and he squandered it.

The digging rock cracked against another rock buried in the ground, a sharp sliver snapping off. He cursed and flung the digging rock aside, then pressed his palms into his temple.

Eldrid was going to finish him off. Why else reveal all that she had? She had all but promised to poison his food, which meant if he would not suffer murder by poison he could choose to starve. But in the end he would be so mad with hunger he would have to eat, then whatever torments she had mixed into her poison would grip him. Maybe he would vomit blood, go blind, or suffocate as his father had. His father had died from poison. Now he would, too. Looks like his brother Grim would succeed after all these years.

"What are you doing to yourself?" Ulfrik slammed his hands down, palms numb from pounding through rocks and dirt with nothing but another rock. A rush of breath escaped and he sank like a bladder of mead drained of its contents. He sat motionless for several breaths, collecting his thoughts. "Just dig, Ulfrik. You will survive this. You won't be poisoned. Just. Dig."

Fears of poison and starvation banished, he renewed the attack. When he focused on the work of digging, he found his mind blanked and worry disappeared. He slipped into a rhythm much like when he used to pull an oar on his ship. Before he realized it, the sun had already risen fully on a clear day. His stomach grumbled, the only sensation to bring him out of his trance. Then his throat burned in protest as well. A skin of water left over from a few days ago held only a mouthful remaining. Tipping the sour water into his mouth, it relieved the tacky dryness. By the end of the day, he hoped to be free and drinking from a fresh stream.

He dropped the empty skin, then heard the crunch of rock. Someone was approaching.

His first instinct was to fall back into the cave, but he took three steps back and realized the futility. If death was approaching, he would not face it like a coward. He grabbed the broken shard of rock that had flaked off his digging tool and hid it in his palm. It would be a poor weapon in any circumstance, so he grabbed a heavy round stone he had gathered to be his main weapon.

Gudrod appeared over the crest. Ulfrik blinked as if he could clear the image from his vision, but his ugly face broke into a smile as he neared.

"So it is true," he said, striding toward the grate. "You're trying to dig a way out."

He laughed and clapped his hands together as if he had heard the funniest joke ever told. Ulfrik paid no mind to him. If Gudrod had learned of his escape plans, then Eldrid or her boy had told him. This would bring Audhild and then he would not live out the day. He studied Gudrod for anything useful. He wore a brown wool shirt and buckskin pants. His sword slapped at his side, revealed when his green cloak fluttered aside. As he arrived at the grate, his eyes flashed with childlike glee.

"You've been busy," he said. "But the gods seem to have put a few rocks in your way. How bad for you."

Gudrod's knife hung loose at his belt. The hide strap securing it had snapped and the knife held only as long as the strip remained tight under the belt.

The gods place signs and tests before a man to see how clever he is. The more cunning the man's response, the more entertainment he provides the gods and, therefore, the more they love him. Ulfrik had long ago recognized this fact, which is why he believed he had survived his ordeals and why he still had years ahead of him. The gods loved the entertainment he crafted from their signs and tests.

Gudrod's knife was one such test. As the sheathed blade dangled, asking to be picked like a ripe apple, he understood what the gods wanted.

They did not want dirt and rocks. They wanted blood.

"I can't blame you for wanting to get out of this cave," Gudrod said, prodding the hole with his foot. "It's a rat's life. Come winter, I suppose you'll freeze to death in here. I've seen frozen men. Have you? Not something you can forget. Their noses and cheeks turn black and their beards are full with frost. You can snap their hair like a handful of twigs. See what you've got to look forward to?"

Ulfrik watched the knife jitter as Gudrod carried on about his impending death. It twirled and slipped, but did not release. Gudrod smiled and rubbed his hands together as he described bodies frozen in ice, warming himself against imaginary cold. Ulfrik focused on the knife. He couldn't grab it, and even if he could Gudrod would know. He needed a distraction.

"But winter's a fair time off," he said, wistfully looking into the distance. "More than likely you'll starve before you freeze. A starved man is something to behold, all bony and—"

Ulfrik pushed his face between the square of iron bars and spit into Gudrod's eyes. The glob of saliva rolled down the bridge of his nose as he stumbled back in disgust. Ulfrik left his face framed in the bars, then fed both arms through the frame. His left hand palmed the round throwing rock.

Gudrod brushed his face with both hands, and Ulfrik watched his loosened knife slip even more.

"You little pig-fucker!" Gudrod balled a fist and charged at Ulfrik. He grabbed Ulfrik's shirt through the grate, but he was so blind with anger he had not noticed the rock Ulfrik held.

He slammed it on the side of Gudrod's head. His face crashed against the bars. Ulfrik battered him again and he flattened against the grate with a moan.

Ulfrik's left hand swept down Gudrod's side and caught the knife. It broke free and fell into the hole. Gudrod struggled now, and forced himself out of Ulfrik's grip.

He staggered backward, tripped and fell on his back. Ulfrik used the moment to drag the knife into the cave and fit it into the back of his pants. "You had something to say to me?" He teased Gudrod. "Thought I'd help knock it out of your head, since you were so caught up on imagining my death."

Gudrod rolled over and touched the back of his head, pulling two fingers away to stare at the blood. He remained on hands and knees for a moment, then struggled up. A trickle of blood had flowed over his ear and now connected with his nose like a red line of paint. His eyes were wide with the dazed expression of disbelief.

"What's the matter?" Ulfrik asked. "Afraid you can't best me even if I'm caged and half-starved? Has anyone explained to you that shipbuilding and fighting are two different skills? You might not want to confuse the two. I'll beat you senseless on my worst day."

Touching his head again, he blinked until he discovered his words. "This is a joke to you? You think you're getting out of this cave alive?"

"I never said that. I was just pointing out that my wife is a better fighter than you and my goat was three-times more clever. You want to stick your hand in my cage? Then find out how the rat bites. Come close again and I'll break your neck on this grate. But you won't do that, will you? You're a raven-starver coward. You couldn't stand against me alone. You'll have to bring friends. Go fetch Bresi and bring the two of you here. Bring five more. Let me out of this cage and it will be me and my rock against anyone shameless enough to associate with you."

Gudrod frowned, his lip curling. He took a step forward but halted on it. "You'd love for me to pull the bolts out of this grate, wouldn't you? That's what this is all about? Getting out and making a run for freedom."

"The freedom would come after I killed you and ten of your man-loving friends with a single rock. I wouldn't need to run."

His laughter sounded forced, but Gudrod indulged himself in it, bending back with both hands holding his stomach. "Brave words for a little rat. But I'm not so stupid. You think your curses are killing people? You think the gods are taking revenge for you?"

Ulfrik stared at him, not understanding his questions. "I think Bresi treats you as his wife every night of the full moon."

"Your insults mean nothing to me! You'll rot inside this cave. From now on, no one comes with food. Let thirst dry out your foul tongue and see if arrogance will fill your stomach. You will be eating mud and rocks just to silence the pain of starvation and you'll die in that cave. Forgotten."

Gudrod spun on his foot and left. Ulfrik watched him go and, once returned over the crest from which he had come, drew out the knife. The sheath was of worn leather and tight against the knife. He tugged the blade out, revealing a bright iron blade with a single cutting edge and point. The edge was sharp and oiled, and the whole weapon was as long as his forearm.

"Let's hope your former owner will miss you enough to return for you," he said, sliding it back into the sheath. He did not know what he would do with this knife.

But the gods had given him a weapon, and when they granted men such boons they demand blood to follow.

43

Ulfrik sat with his shoulder and head against the iron grate, muddy water all about him, watching the last of a summer shower sprinkle into his water bowl. His stomach clenched with hunger pangs, but he had eaten the day before. A puffin had wandered to the grate, and Ulfrik had grabbed it. Only beak, bones, and a scattering of feathers remained, and the rank taste of its flesh and blood still filled his mouth. Now he gently pulled in his bowl and drank the collected water. It was cold and fresh, and demanded all his control not to guzzle it like fine mead.

Two days had passed since Gudrod had made his threat, and thus far it held. No one came. Placing the bowl aside he licked the last moisture off his lips, then withdrew Gudrod's knife from the waist of his pants. He turned the sheathed blade in his fingers, pondering the meaning of it. Maybe the gods had sent it to him so that he might kill himself before he starved. Maybe it was their mercy on him, that he might hold a weapon in hand when he died and join the heroes in Valhalla. He held it up to his nose, eyes crossing to see it. Was that it? This was a promise of escape, but not the kind he had desired. The feasting hall sounded like a much better idea now. More friends awaited him there than any alive in the world, and certainly more than in this evil place.

He tried to remember the dream that had inspired him to dig. Ghosts were not to be trusted. Their words had been so emphatic, their reasoning so infallible, that he had begun to dig the moment he had awakened. Yet dream logic broke in its collision with reality. At Ulfrik's feet was the wreck from days of exhausting labor. Beneath the dirt hid an expanse of stones too onerous to dislodge with the tools he had. Pits in the ground shimmered with muddy water running down the sides, washing dirt over the work of days. No hole went deep enough to allow him beneath the bars. Rocks held him at bay and he finally abandoned his plans to dig out. Maybe if he starved he would eventually be frail enough to slip beneath the grate. For now, he remained trapped.

The sun retreated and blanketed the cave mouth in shadow. The rain clouds closed the day earlier than usual, being thick enough to stifle the last light of the sun. He sipped from his bowl a final time, and crawled back to the drier reaches of his cave. The smell of his waste was heavier here, but it was an even trade to be out of the damp at the front.

He stretched atop the tattered furs and closed his eyes, listening to the random tap of dripping water.

"Ulfrik." A voice whispered sharply at the grate. Ulfrik's eyes fluttered open, his hand reaching for the knife. If death was near, he wanted to hold a weapon. The person repeated his name again. It was a man's voice.

Sitting up, he twisted toward the cave mouth. All was black but for a shaft of gray light broken into squares by the grate. A shadowed man hunched at one corner, his hand resting against the grate as if trying to feel Ulfrik's presence.

"It's Lini. Are you alive? I've got food and water here."

Ulfrik scrabbled toward Lini so suddenly that he jumped back with a small gasp of surprise. His normally wild hair was matted with sweat and stuck to his freckled face. "You've got food? Water? You're a true hero."

Lini unslung three bags and two skins, handing them through the grate. "This is from all of us. I can't be long, else I get caught here."

The weight of the packs filled Ulfrik with joy. Savory scents brought water to his mouth. Even if Eldrid had poisoned the food, he would take it over starvation. "I don't know who provided all of this, but I'm grateful. More than you'll know."

"Oh, I'm sure I have an idea. I went hungry for weeks after my parents died. I never had a steady meal until I ... well, never mind."

Ulfrik searched the packs, his black and muddy hands soiling the carefully packed food. He withdrew them, not wanting to foul something so precious. "Until Audhild gave you steady meals and your freedom. She's a wonderful woman right up to when she betrays you. What's in here?"

Lini passed through the skins. "Two of ale and one of water. Everything else should keep for you. Salted fish and meats, pickled eggs, goat cheese, and dried seaweed."

"A feast for a high king," Ulfrik said, then laughed. He unplugged the horn stopper on the ale skin and let the bitter fluid rush down his throat. If any ran over, he forced it back into his mouth with a finger. "That will give me strength again."

"Good to hear. I've been sent to make sure you survived. Audhild won't abide mention of your name, and Gudrod and his thugs keep people away from here. Eldrid has barred herself in her home."

"So you want to make sure the gods remain happy and you came to feed the caged rat. That's it?"

"Um, well, I came with a favor to ask."

Ulfrik sat back and laughed. "What? Maybe you want me to craft another battle plan for you? Is Valagnar back?"

"No. It's just, well, the curse you made. You must undo it."

Ulfrik blinked. "What curse?"

"The day you were ... um, taken here. You cursed the village to death. Already two people have died of fever and Thorkel Hairy-Ears had a litter of lambs all stillborn. Other folks have taken ill, at least three more. Little Norna Sigurdsdottir is stuck in fevered sleep."

Lini glanced over his shoulder, while the fingers of both hands laced into the grate. Ulfrik considered his words, not remembering what he had said in the fit of raw anger. Gudrod had mentioned a curse as well, so the people had heard something. Whatever he had done, he was glad for it. He took another drink from the ale skin, letting Lini hang on his response.

"Well," Ulfrik said, wiping his mouth with the back of his arm. "You were all content to let me die here until just today. Since I'm as good as dead, why should I care to lift a curse on your heads?"

"No, we had no choice!" Lini pressed against the bars. "You were caught by four witnesses."

Ulfrik struck against the grate with both fists, sending Lini falling back into the mud. "If you really believe I raped Audhild, then you deserve the fate your weak mind has earned. You are all half-wit sheep. You think Eldrid possesses real magic? What has she ever done but repeat what her sister demands she say? And you believe it! You betrayed me for a thin lie. I who saved all from death and slavery traded for the fears of two women! I should have joined with Valagnar and crushed you all for the worms you are. At least when I die I'll have the satisfaction of knowing the gods granted my revenge."

Lini wept, though consumed in shadow the errant light of sunset sparkled in the tears streaking his cheeks. "Not everyone believed, but what could we do? Gudrod had you locked away before anyone could say otherwise."

"I don't remember any protests at my so-called trial. You betrayed me, Lini. I'm half-dead already because you were too weak to speak the truth. You think you've got freedom? Ha! You traded one bond for another, and how much worse it is now. You're trapped in this land of black rock and bird shit. You couldn't leave even if you wanted to. You and everyone else are still slaves, and by your own hands."

His words echoed and Lini nervously checked for signs of anyone approaching, then he climbed out of the mud. He stared at the water-filled holes as if seeing them for the first time. "You've been digging?"

"You want to know about my curse?" Ulfrik focused instead on the curse. He did not believe that the gods acted on his command, but to hear that they had answered his calls for justice renewed him as vigorously as a feast of roasted meats and fine mead. The curse, which he did not believe qualified in the sense of dark magic, provided him leverage. First he had to embellish it.

"Yes, how can we end it before more die? Please, you see we're willing to risk Audhild and Gudrod by coming here with food. You must help us."

"For every day I spend behind these bars my curse grows in power. So feed me all you will, but more will die if I remain imprisoned. Kill me here, and my spirit will never be free. Within the year all will die and be dragged down to Nifelheim with me. I promise you this."

Ulfrik did not know if he overstepped the limits of his newly assigned magic powers, but his threats did not seem unreasonable. If the gods were listening, he hoped they drew inspiration from his hate. Lini sat with his mouth open.

"How are we going to get you out of here?"

"Stand up to Audhild and her new hero, Gudrod. Have no fear of Eldrid. Can you be cursed to death yet again? Besides, she is a liar to rival her sister."

"But Gudrod has gathered the youngest and strongest men to his side. Many would stand for you, but Gudrod's men frighten them."

"A curse of another kind plagues you, one I cannot help. Fear will rule you and unmake all you have achieved here. How much longer before Gudrod demands taxes and service? You will have to resist him sooner or later."

"But we don't want to fight. We fled Frankia to escape the wars there."

"Yet you brought swords with you when you fled. Here's wisdom. Where a sword is there is also violence and death. You don't want to fight? Throw your weapons into the sea. Just don't weep when other men treat you as their own cattle."

Lini put his hands on his head as if Ulfrik had shouted in his ears. Again he checked over his shoulder then glanced at the sky. "I have to leave now. What should I tell the others?"

Reaching through the grate, Ulfrik grasped Lini's shirt. He pulled him close so that he could see Lini's pupils widen in fear. "The only way to lift the curse is to free me. Gather whoever has any guts left and bring tools to open this grate. Do not waste another day wondering what to do. You already knew the answer, but have been too cowardly to accept it. Find your balls and free me."

He watched Lini scamper away, hunching down as he disappeared over the crest of black rock and patchy grass. Sipping from the ale skin again, he held the delicious drink in his mouth to savor it a moment. He set aside the skin and pulled out the knife from the back of his waistband. He weighed it in his palm.

"Not long now before I bury you in Audhild's black heart."

44

Ulfrik leaned on the iron grate, hanging both his arms through it. The cold iron pressed against his face as he squinted into the glare of the morning. Clouds formed a sooty blanket over the sun, which shined as a vague patch of brightness. The air smelled of rain and ocean. Two specks of gulls dueled in the air, each wheeling around and finding no advantage. Perhaps it was an omen. He did not care what the gods showed him now. Only one path remained open to him, and he felt the weight of it hidden at his back.

The voices traveled far ahead of the group. He had expected them sooner and his arms were already tingling numb as he waited. As the heads of the group came into view, he smiled. Audhild was first among them, her hair unbound and fluttering in the breeze. He had prepared for her to repulse him, but Ulfrik instead stood straighter as their eyes met across the distance. She moved with easy authority, though undoubtedly her appearance at the cave signified her defeat. The diffuse light lent a gentleness to her features, and the reality of her no longer matched the wickedly leering demon of Ulfrik's imagination. She stopped out of arm's reach, head tilted back and brow raised. The white scar through her eyebrow was prominent against her golden skin. She stood with arms akimbo.

"You don't look half as bad as Lini described." Her voice was hard but Ulfrik heard the hint of a tremor.

"You look wholly like the liar and betrayer you were at our last meeting." He withdrew his hands, nodding to Lini who arrived behind her with two other men, one carrying a spear more like it was an adder to be held at length rather than a weapon to wield. The food Lini had provided him had lasted the four days since their meeting, and he still had a portion prepared for his escape. He had stopped digging and just ate and rested. Today he felt better than he had in many months.

Audhild shifted in the uneasy silence, her eyes searching the holes under the grate. "They said you were trying to dig out. I knew the rocks would block you."

"I'm sure you knew. Audhild is always right, isn't she? She doesn't make mistakes."

She narrowed her eyes at him, her mouth bending in a frown. Lini stepped in for her. "We're going to let you out today. Remember your promise?"

Ulfrik shifted his eyes from Lini, scowling. He stuck his chin at Audhild. "Is that so? I walk out and am free to be my own man?"

"You will be let out as long as you lift the curse you placed on my people. They are dying, Ulfrik. Norna Sigurdsdottir drew her final breath last night. They say it's because you are being held like an animal in a cage."

"What do you think?" Ulfrik smiled then withdrew his hands through the grate. "I'm covered in lice. My beard and hair is one tangled mess. I smell like shit and sleep by puddles of my own piss. I saved your people and you all spit in my face. I rejoice at the news of your deaths. You deserve no less."

Lini and the others with him winced at his outburst, but Audhild wrinkled her nose at the description. "But you are an animal. You raped me, and who knows how many other women are in danger from your uncontrolled lust."

Ulfrik slammed the grate in anger. "Spare me that lie. We both know the truth. I know a good deal of truth about you. Eldrid visited me. Seems she has a guilty heart and some bitter disappointment. I know how she lost her eyes and where you got that scar. I know that anyone who gets between you and her is ruined. You have deceived not only me but all of these people. Why the gods have not struck you down yet is a mystery to me."

He expected Audhild to fly into a rage. Even Lini stepped back from her. Yet she folded her arms and squinted at him. Her jaw ground as she considered him in stony silence. Ulfrik bored his eyes into hers, unwilling to flinch. She was remarkably strong at holding her own, but he had stared down more fearsome enemies in his life. At last she abated and turned aside.

"As we were saying before, you are to be freed under certain conditions. The people have convinced me that your curse is real. If you will release us from it, then you will be allowed to rejoin us. Even though I still think you are a threat."

"How exceedingly gracious of you." Ulfrik gave her a mock bow, feeling the knife at his back pull tight as he did. "But we have a disagreement. I will not lift my curse while I am imprisoned. In fact, I cannot even if I wanted to. It was the condition I set with the gods. For every day I am captive the curse gains power."

Audhild sighed and shrugged. "Then you will be let out first."

"And allowed to leave this horrible place."

"Never. You will be allowed to move into your former home and you will be guarded."

"You can't guard me forever. Just end this pointless joke. Eldrid told me about her dream. I know—"

"Shut up!" Audhild's hands were balled into fists. "Do not speak about what you do not understand. Eldrid told you nothing."

Her face had turned purple and her eyes bulged like a frog's. Veins on her neck stood out, and if Ulfrik had not thought she looked mad before, he was now disabused of the notion. He held up a hand for peace, while his other hand felt for the knife at his back.

He did not need her blessings to flee. Once the grate was unbolted, she had only one purpose remaining: to serve as a hostage. He would hand her over to Valagnar as payment for his own guarantee of safety. All he had to do was agree with her and see the grate removed.

"All right, I am sorry. Being trapped alone in a cave for months has left me in an ill temper. You should understand that."

Her bulging eyes did not subside and her face grew darker. Lini braved her displeasure and gestured the other men to begin work on removing the grate. She did not restrain them, but remained fixed on Ulfrik. He withdrew into the shadow, slipping the knife from its sheath and laying it flat against his forearm. The cold iron pressed into his flesh. Patches of rust had formed on it, lending a rough touch to it. Without proper oils and rags to clean it, the blade suffered, but its edge would still cut.

Lini had taken the spear from one of the workers and the two men used tongs and pry-bars to work out the bolts that had anchored the grate in place. Of all the people Ulfrik had drilled in weapons, Lini had been one of the few who learned his techniques. He wondered now if it would work against him. He rolled the hilt of Gudrod's stolen knife in his palm as he waited, enjoying the press of the edge against his skin.

Rock crumbled and bolts clattered to the ground. First the grate slipped, then, as the last bolts were drawn, it collapsed into the earth with a thud. The two workers skipped backward to avoid the iron bars crushing their feet. When the grate did not topple, Ulfrik kicked it out so it slammed into the dirt, landing just before Audhild's feet. A puff of air lifted the hem of her skirt, but she did not budge. Instead she glared at him. He was glad for her stillness. Taking her hostage would be easier. He stepped atop the grate as he strode out of the cave. Spinning the knife around in his grip, he held it close to his leg but ready to strike.

Lini lowered his spear to Ulfrik's neck, stopping him atop the grate. "I don't want to do this," he said, the trembling of his hands vibrating through the spear to Ulfrik's neck.

Ulfrik's arm twitched to knock the spear aside but its blade drew a bead of blood from his neck. He relaxed his arm.

"Gudrod lost his knife," Audhild said at last. "And I see it pressed to your leg. Surrender it."

"Kill me and you'll all remain cursed." Ulfrik imagined closing the gap to Lini, knocking aside the spear and ramming the knife into his heart. Yet Lini, despite the sweat beading on his brow, only needed a moment's resolution to strike. Even an inexperienced fighter could make the kill without the blade already fixed in position.

"Drop the knife," Audhild repeated. "You've no need for it now."

Despite being surrounded, he fantasized Audhild's death along with Lini and the two workers behind him. The workers' iron tongs alone could bash in his head, never mind the cold iron at his neck. He sneered at Lini, then tossed the knife at Audhild's feet. It clanked atop the grate, light winking off the blade as if bidding farewell.

"I regret teaching you how to use that spear," he said to Lini. He pushed the shaft down and to the side. He thought of ripping it from Lini's grasp. A spear was a poor weapon for taking a hostage and with Audhild armed too much was left to chance. He decided to wait for another opportunity.

Lini swallowed and stepped back, sweat rolling off his nose. "I'm sorry. I don't want any more killing. Just lift your curse. Please."

Audhild's face remained bright scarlet as she studied the knife, turning it in her hand as if she had never before seen a blade. Ulfrik supposed she imagined what it would feel like rammed through her chest. He had been prepared to teach her.

Then a terrible screech tore everyone's attention to the top of the crest.

Eldrid stood with her staff raised overhead in both hands. A new blindfold of red cloth covered her eyes and her hair flowed free about her shoulders. Flanking her were four men, and at their front stood Gudrod. His sword was drawn and it caught a gleam of furtive sunlight from the cloud-laden sky.

Audhild swept toward her sister, a mad growl of her own filling the air. She held Gudrod's knife close to her side, her knuckles white around the grip.

"Halt!" A bowman emphasized Gudrod's shouted order. He nocked an arrow to his bow, but did not draw. Audhild was heedless, and with a flick of Gudrod's wrist the bowman drew and fired an arrow at Audhild's feet. She skidded to a halt where the shaft broke on the ground.

"What is the meaning of this?" Audhild's face, already red, now shaded into the color of a bruise. Ulfrik used the moment to draw closer to her, moving deliberately so as not to provoke a shot at himself. Lini and the others fell in behind, sticking close as if following him into a haunted tunnel. The bowman placed another arrow to the string and looked expectantly at Gudrod. Ulfrik recognized the man as Eskil, one of the few bow hunters in the village. He judged him an average shot, but at this range Ulfrik imagined even blind Eldrid could hit her target. Gudrod extended his hand to prevent another shot, lifting it barely off his thigh as if the gesture was too taxing.

"I have the same question for you," Gudrod said. He sidestepped down the crest and his men followed. Bresi Black-Eyes stood at his right. He smirked at Ulfrik and patted his sheathed sword. Eldrid followed, lowering her staff and being forced to diminish her glorious arrival by prodding a path down the slope unaided.

"You know the will of the people," Audhild said, stepping back as the dark crowd converged on her. "I came here about the curse."

Eldrid wailed again, placing both hands on her head as if in great pain. Ulfrik cringed at the performance. Only days ago she had revealed great remorse at living her life as something she was not. Yet today she acted no less mad than before. Maybe it had only been a moment of sunshine in the hurricane of Eldrid's madness. He had no time to ponder or care. She raised her staff again and pointed a bony finger at Audhild.

"The curse is a lie," she said. "Only I may speak with the gods of this land. The curse is mine! I have called it down upon the unfaithful and disloyal."

Audhild growled again and twisted her stance as if to hurl herself at Eldrid, who remained with her arms held high as if touching the spirits of the air. Gudrod, Bresi, and the others had gathered around them now. Ulfrik glanced at Lini, who stood shaking his head in confusion. His grip on the spear had slackened.

"Audhild, you have led the people of this community astray," Gudrod said. "Your actions have angered the gods. The people are clear on this. A woman is not a leader, and so they have asked me to assume the responsibility."

She did not move or cry out, merely flicking her eyes toward Gudrod as if he had only been a passing wind. Gudrod stared at her, and his gaze drifted to the knife in her hand. He nudged Bresi, who stepped forward and drew his sword.

"I have foretold this in a dream," Eldrid said, as if the rasping of Bresi's sword had been a cue. "The world is not balanced and must be set right. A man shall lead us, and the gift of the gods must be given over to me. Ulfrik must be mine."

"And you," said Gudrod, pointing with his sword at Audhild, "belong with me now."

His mouth opened to spew more drivel, but Audhild screamed and raised her knife. She pitched herself at Eldrid, blade flashing overhead.

The gods awaited their gift of blood.

45

A distant rumble of thunder accented Audhild's charge. It was a sign of the gods watching, Ulfrik was certain. He was not flat-footed as all the others, having expected violence from the onset. A knife in the hands of a madwoman would soon come to rest in someone's neck. Audhild's feet crunched on the gravelly dirt and alerted Eldrid. She danced backward but stumbled.

At his left, Ulfrik found Lini staring slack-jawed after Audhild. Without a second thought, Ulfrik snatched the spear and raised it overhead. He hated to surrender the weapon so soon after claiming it, but Gudrod had one supreme advantage that had to be neutralized.

Lini yelped in protest, but was powerless to do anything more. As Audhild scrabbled after her sister, Gudrod's sword still pointed to where she had stood. The rest of his men stood like children awaiting instructions for a new chore. Eskil kept an arrow resting on his bow but pointed at the ground.

The spear sailed out of Ulfrik's hand. After days of rest and eating his fill of Lini's provisions, he had regained some of his strength. His eyesight had never fully recovered after his fall from the tower, but today his aim was true. The spear traversed a short arc, its heavy shaft not crafted for distance. Its blade split Eskil's breastbone and plunged into the soft flesh. It sank through his body, piercing out his back. A red line of blood sprouted from the entry wound, but his flesh sucked at the shaft to prevent heavy bleeding. Eskil's eyes widened and he dropped his bow. He brushed the shaft with one hand as if to prove it existed, then collapsed onto his back.

Still no one acted. Audhild and Eldrid wrestled on the ground, a reenactment of Audhild's murderous rage of their youth. Gudrod's sword was finally lowering as he realized his ranged advantage had just been eliminated.

Ulfrik sprinted forward, aiming to hit Gudrod under his arm.

Bresi intercepted, knocking Ulfrik aside with his own body though he carried an unsheathed sword. Ulfrik stumbled away but caught his balance. Gudrod remained with his mouth agape as Bresi followed up.

He hefted his sword as if preparing to split a log. To Ulfrik it presented a target wide and slow enough that he could have sat down to adjust his boots before striking. Instead, he lunged forward and drove his elbow into Bresi's gut. He heard Bresi expel all his air as he drove his elbow just beneath the ribcage. He followed up with a knee to the crotch and Bresi crumpled. Ulfrik's hands swept up to wrestle with the sword.

They were both on the ground now. Ulfrik dug his nails into Bresi's flesh as he clawed for the sword. The longer he wrestled the stronger his battle madness grew. A red halo ringed his vision, and Bresi's straining face was inches from his. He bit down on Bresi's nose, biting off the tip. He howled in pain and his grip on the sword failed. Ulfrik spit the salty, coppery tasting bit of flesh into Bresi's face, then lurched up with the sword in hand.

Looking around, a brawl had erupted and combatants had paired off. Lini now had only a dagger and circled Gudrod. The two workers swung their heavy tongs at their assailants, who even with the advantage of swords could not get inside their opponents' defenses. He heard Eldrid screeching but had no time to see what happened. Bresi was thrashing beneath him.

"Thanks for the weapon," Ulfrik said, Bresi's blood smeared over his lips and beard. "We won't be meeting again. You're headed to Nifelheim."

He punched the blade into Bresi's stomach with no more thought than one had for skewering a rat. Giving the blade a twist made Bresi scream in pain and eject a stream of gore from his mouth. Yanking out the sword, he hacked it across Bresi's neck and spared him further suffering.

Thunder answered in the distance. The gods delighted in the blood and wanted more.

Now Lini knelt atop the grate, holding his side as bright red streams flowed over his hands. Gudrod drew his sword back to drive it through Lini's face.

In two bounds Ulfrik collided with Gudrod and slammed him to the ground. Both of them held on to their weapons, but neither was positioned to take advantage. Ulfrik rolled off and got to his feet. He turned in time to dodge one of Gudrod's men. One of the workers was facedown in the dirt and Ulfrik had inherited his opponent. Now that he had regained his stance, he crouched and studied the man. He couldn't recall his name, but did not want to. He was a dead man.

"Do you know what you're doing with that sword?" The man gripped it with both hands, pointing it accusingly at Ulfrik's face. "You're holding it too high. You know what can happen if you hold it like that?"

Ulfrik lunged and feinted high. It was poor form and any swordsman of experience would have sidestepped it. His enemy, however, was a fool and followed the feint. His right leg stepped back and exposed his left thigh. Ulfrik chopped down and carved open the man's inner thigh. He groaned and crumbled as his leg gave way. His pants blackened with a prodigious flow of blood. Ulfrik skipped past him without looking back. Such a cut to the thigh left a man counting his heartbeats on one hand.

In the flash of violence the scene had shifted again. Lini curled on the ground and the last worker knelt over him, whispering in his ear. The last of Gudrod's men sprawled out next to them, his sword lost and face obscured with blood.

Gudrod fled back up the slope.

Scurrying to Lini's side, Ulfrik leaned in to see his ashen face and eyes wide with shock. "Am I dying?"

The wound in his side hid beneath Lini's hands but the blood seeping through his fingers suggested a grave injury. "You'll be fine," Ulfrik said, then patted Lini's head. It was all the comfort he had time to offer.

Audhild and Eldrid had rolled in a frenzy of kicks and bites. Audhild bled from a rake across her face as she straddled her sister. Her dress had ridden above her waist and deep gashes showed on the sides of her thighs. Eldrid, now pinned beneath her sister, had lost her blindfold. A flap of skin over her forehead poured blood down her face painting her with a mask of red. She was clawing at Audhild's face with one hand and holding her knife at bay with the other. Both of their dresses were smeared with red handprints.

If he could get the spear, Ulfrik imagined killing both of them in one blow. It would be a dark irony bound to delight the gods. He dashed for Eskil's corpse, yanked on the spear but the flesh sucked against it. Watching Gudrod mount the top of the ridge, he abandoned the idea.

Eldrid's screech caught Ulfrik's attention. Audhild sank her teeth into her wrist like a wolf biting down a deer's throat. She tore sideways, ripping out flesh and breaking free of Eldrid's grip. She did not hesitate.

She slid Gudrod's knife into Eldrid's neck. Her screams gurgled with blood and frothy red bubbles poured from her mouth. Audhild laughed and stabbed again, slamming the knife into Eldrid's right eye.

Ulfrik wavered. Lost in her killing frenzy Audhild was easy prey, but he could not predict the villagers' reactions. Gudrod, however, would muster anyone with a weapon. Besides, Gudrod now claimed to be in charge of the village. If he returned to his men in time, then Ulfrik was as good as dead.

He glanced back. Lini and his companion huddled together, oblivious to the murder beside them. Audhild laughed as she plunged Gudrod's knife into Eldrid's corpse. The blade had become a red shard in her hand as it fell again and again into helpless flesh.

"A gift of blood," Ulfrik murmured. Thunder rolled and lightning flashed as the skies darkened. He darted up the slope to kill Gudrod.

46

For all the time Ulfrik had spent staring at this landscape, it should have been more familiar. Yet he crested the rise of black rock then stumbled for direction. He circled around, finding the ocean at his back. He could not see the beach but heard the waves breaking on the surf. That reoriented him on directions and he faced east where the village must lie. The plain of grass was like a lumpy blanket of fuzzy wool, punctured with curled and cracked clumps of black rock. He had never ventured this far from the village, but sure enough, in the distance he saw the white plumes of smoke rising over thatched roofs. Beyond that were the woods of dwarf birch trees and the rugged mountains beyond.

Gudrod had seemingly disappeared amid the flat terrain. Ulfrik jogged toward the village as no other destination made sense. He kept the sweeping mountain ranges at his left, their peaks lost in low clouds. The craggy earth brightened with lightning and several strides later the low rumble of thunder shook the earth. The gods demanded blood and were not sated. Ulfrik tightened his grip on his sword as he ran.

His heart pounded in time with his legs. He increased his pace even though Gudrod was nowhere to be seen. Dodging through piles of rock and leaping ruts, he threaded a path for the village. No wonder people had only visited him once a day during his imprisonment. The journey from the village was not only long but also over treacherous footing.

Like a ghost flickering into sight, Gudrod appeared ahead of him.

Ulfrik gasped at the sudden appearance, then realized he had been at the bottom of a rise. Surprisingly, the coward had enough sense to rest in a low-lying area to avoid being spotted. Now he scrabbled up the opposite side, sliding down as loose rock gave way. Ulfrik redoubled his pace, though his legs burned and the old wounds began to flash white streaks of pain at each footfall.

Gudrod mounted the rise and began waving at the village. A man waved in response. Gudrod did not glance back but began calling out, his voice weak in the distance. Ulfrik plunged into the dip where Gudrod had hid, and lost sight of him. With a curse against the pain in his legs, he leapt onto the steeper incline of the opposite side. When he scaled to the top, lightning flashed again.

The man was gone, and Gudrod as well. Thunder followed, and it was the laughter of the gods mocking Ulfrik.

"Gudrod!" he shouted the name as the wind picked up. "I'm coming, you fox-tailed coward!"

Assuming Gudrod had fled into the village, Ulfrik paused to catch his breath. He leaned on his knees and waited for the stitch in his side to subside. Anger was no substitute for conditioning, and the years of poor food and worse treatment had degraded his stamina. He spit and wiped the sweat from his brow. His hands slipped on the sword hilt and he wished he had a sheath for it. He decided to approach the edge of the village to listen for signs of alarm, then he would loop north into the hills and aim for the birch trees. From there, he would seek the eastern coastline and follow it north to Valagnar's home.

He listened at the village's perimeter but heard nothing. Gudrod could just as easily be cowering rather than summoning aid. Ulfrik was content to let him go. Escape was more important than revenge. He renewed his jog north. He had not gone more than six strides before he heard something at his back.

Throughout his years of battle, Ulfrik had witnessed the influence of gods and the Fates take a variety of forms. Winds batted arrows to the ground; enemy weapons bent and broke at key moments; warriors stumbled over fallen friends only to be saved from a killing ax blow; sunlight burst through clouds to blind a charging foe. A hundred times in a single battle Fate altered minor things to tremendous effect. Now was such a time.

The crunching of foot on rock might have easily been lost beneath the sounds of his own running. Yet something made him check behind.

Gudrod had reappeared and was charging with his sword held low.

Ulfrik sidestepped but did not avoid the blade. It ripped a line across his stomach, tearing his brown shirt so that it fell open like a bloody mouth. He screamed and staggered back as Gudrod charged past him.

"By the gods! Where did you come from?" Ulfrik instinctively clutched his wound and felt the warm wetness flowing from the burning cut though he refused to look down. It was not a serious wound or his guts would have been hanging on his lap.

Gudrod regained himself with a curse and held his sword toward Ulfrik. Grass fell from his shoulders and blades of it clung to his hair and beard. Ulfrik narrowed his eyes in understanding.

"You hid beneath your cloak in the grass hoping to ambush me," he said as he twisted his grip tighter around the hilt of his sword. "I wouldn't have expected it from you."

"Add it to the things you've underestimated about me," Gudrod said. He widened his footing and put both hands to his sword. "You think yourself a hero of some saga? No one can best you in a fight? Look at you now, bleeding over your pants. You'll die like any man."

"True, though you won't be alive when that day comes."

Their swords clanged as both struck in unison. The edges grated as the blades sawed down to the crossguards, sparks leaping. They locked a hand's breadth from each other, fierce eyes clashing. What Gudrod lacked in technique he bolstered with strength. Ulfrik shoved back but did not win the contest, and was forced to twist out of the lock. What Ulfrik lacked in strength he bolstered with experience. His blade spun beneath Gudrod's arms but only succeed in nicking his ribs. It drew an angry cry but nothing worse.

They pushed apart and circled once again. Thunder grumbled and a fat raindrop pelted Ulfrik's neck, its cold wetness trickling down his back. "You won't defeat me," he said. "This is your last chance to run."

"I'm done fearing you," Gudrod said, then struck.

He feinted low but Ulfrik read his true strike from his center of balance. He intended to cut up, and when he did Ulfrik hacked down on the unprotected arm.

It was a satisfying chop into Gudrod's exposed forearm. The meat of it parted and the blade sank to the bone, but did not pass through it. Blood welled up as Gudrod howled and dropped his sword. Ulfrik slipped aside and yanked his blade free, tearing a vicious scream from Gudrod who collapsed to the grass. Ulfrik spun to face him, but he huddled over his arm. His green cloak flowed over his body, demonstrating how he had evaded Ulfrik's detection. The color was a near match to the grass. Now, however, he shuddered as he sobbed and blood glistened on the tall grasses around him.

Ulfrik approached him with his sword out. "Die like a man. I've no guilt to run you through from behind, but if you expect to see the feasting hall then grab your sword and face me."

He waited but Gudrod only rocked over his partially severed arm. Lightning flashed, painting him with white highlights. Shouts came from the village, and Ulfrik decided he had no time to waste. He reversed his grip to plunge his sword through Gudrod's back.

Gudrod burst from beneath his cloak. He struck in a wide arc with his uninjured left hand. A sharp knife flashed in the wan light. Ulfrik kicked his left leg back in time, but the blade landed in the flesh of his opposite calf. It slipped into the smooth flesh below the bulge of calf muscle and passed out the other side. The fiery pain whirled up his leg as if he had stepped in a campfire. Unbalanced, his strike carried him forward and he crashed on his face. A rock drove into his cheek below his eye and he bit his lip to squirt blood onto his tongue.

He dragged himself away from Gudrod, hearing his grunting as he struggled to his feet. Iron scratched across stone as Gudrod retrieved his sword.

"My arm. You cut off my arm, you goat-shit bastard."

Ulfrik swept the grass for his sword, but he was lying atop it. It was easier to reach for the knife embedded in his leg. He scuttled away from the crunch of Gudrod's ponderous footsteps. He flipped to the side when he heard Gudrod inhale. The sword clashed against the ground where he had been.

"How many knives do you carry?" Ulfrik asked, then he struck.

Gudrod hung over his blade as if it was holding him up. His injured arm dangled useless and blood jetted from it in a weak arc. Even as Ulfrik drove the knife into Gudrod's kidney, he had been killed when first struck. He was bleeding out and collapsed beneath Ulfrik without protest.

"You should have run," Ulfrik whispered as he slumped over Gudrod's body. He pulled out the knife and felt hot blood flood onto his legs.

"You should have died," Gudrod said, his voice hoarse and wispy. Ulfrik felt the body slacken and the jet of blood slowed to a trickle.

He pushed upright. The voices were closer now. Two men were running toward him, and he assumed they would kill him. Though he had no time to spare, he pulled Eldrid's blindfold from his pant-waist and bound his leg. The gash across his stomach leaked blood but nothing could be done now. He clambered to his feet, hopped on his injured leg while he accustomed to the pain, and began to jog. The two men were almost to him now. He could see their fear-widened eyes.

He started running but the men caught up with him. He whirled on them. Blood coated him as if he had carved his way through an army of men. It stiffened on his face and melted where raindrops struck him. The two villagers recoiled as he ranged his sword at them.

"Go on, attack. You might have better luck than the last three fools." He spit frothy blood at them and one jumped as if it might explode.

"You are freed? Have you lifted the curse?" The man brave enough to ask had a face red with pimples and scars that obscured strong features and shimmering blue eyes.

"You're with Lini then?" The two men nodded, and Ulfrik laughed. "Then you better see to him before Audhild does. She's got killing on her mind, like the rest of you."

"But the curse. If you were freed, you were—"

"Don't tell me what I am supposed to do," he snapped, and the pimple-faced man stepped back. His companion wrung his hands like an old woman. "Let me go and I'll lift your curse. You want to test me, then I welcome it."

Both men stepped back again and Ulfrik jabbed his gory blade at them, drawing a yelp from the hand-wringer. Spitting once more, Ulfrik turned and loped north to avoid the village. The gods had favored him this once. They were too cruel to favor him twice.

47

Ulfrik reached the birch woods as the storm arrived. Darkness stretched across the land, relieved only by flashes of lightning. The thunder that boomed after it rattled through his chest, and wind shoved him at the trees. He lumbered toward the white trunks that looked like teeth in a black mouth. The closer he drew to them the more the illusion developed until he imagined he was running into the maw of a massive worm. He patted the loose bark and paused, shaking his head to clear the vision. Rain began to pelt the ground and galvanized him forward.

Blood steadily leaked from his stomach, soaking into the waist of his pants. His leg throbbed with every step and Eldrid's blindfold had darkened with blood. He wrapped his arms tight to his body as he fumbled deeper into the woods. The trees blocked most of the rain but what did reach him was a cold finger against his flesh, draining more of his precious heat. His heart beat as if he had been running at full tilt even though he merely had shambled the final distance.

"I'm bleeding out," he said to the trees, bumping one as he wandered through the underbrush. "Sorry about that," he said, and stepped aside.

After more wandering, a loud clap of thunder roused him from his confusion. In the moment of clarity, he realized he had been talking to trees and flopping around aimlessly. He put his hand to his chest, feeling his heart thudding. Blood loss was interfering with his thoughts. He had seen it hundreds of times on the battlefield. A man bleeding out grew cold while his heart thundered in his chest and his mind wandered to strange thoughts. Those who survived later described their thoughts being like a man deep in his cups.

If he did not stop the bleeding he would either die from it or from an accident brought on from confusion. He had to take action while he still had his wits.

The intensity of the storm had grown. Gusts bent the trees and blew leaves and twigs into Ulfrik's face while the rain splashed through the canopy to churn the dirt into mud. His first concern was to find higher ground or risk becoming flooded. Once on campaign in Frankia, he had found Frankish peasants facedown in a puddle no deeper than a man's thumb. A sudden downpour had caught them and the fools sheltered in low ground. He learned that day a man need not drown in a lake when a puddle would serve.

Maybe it was the direness of his situation, but Ulfrik marshaled his concentration and found a path up a steep incline. Water was rushing down it in three miniature waterfalls and confirmed his fear of flooding. The ground gave way under his feet and every time he slid back thunder seemed to echo in response. His plight was no doubt grand entertainment for the likes of Thor and Odin, laughing at him as men might laugh at a dolphin stranded on a beach. He gritted his teeth and mounted to another tier of underbrush and trees. The place was vaguely familiar but he could not place it. Nothing was clear anymore and he could not remember the direction he planned to travel.

He no longer felt pain at his stomach but his ankle throbbed. Sitting down on a rock, he unbound Eldrid's blindfold. The cut oozed black blood from both sides of the wound. He probed it with his finger and searing pain answered. Next he removed his shirt which now from the tear opened by Gudrod's sword to the soaking rain was useless. Placing it aside on the rock, he examined the stomach cut. Rain water turned the scum crust on his body to mud. He had not bathed in months and his skin was a mass of dirt and flea bites. The wound was not deep enough for serious damage, but a constant stream of blood mingled with the water rushing over his skin.

For the first time he noticed his ribs were visible. The thought staggered him, as if the body under his hands was not his own. Had he withered so badly during his time here? Again he dragged his wandering mind back to the matter at hand.

Using the rain water, he cleansed his body with a rough scrub. He found a flat rock to scrape down his arms and torso. He scooped out a hole to collect rain, which filled up as fast as he had dug it, and then cupped out water to clean the cut on his stomach. It was a large flap of skin and the water burned as he rinsed it, then he repeated the process for his leg. He dipped Eldrid's blindfold into the water and wrung it out, then applied it as a tourniquet. He tied in a branch to help twist it tight.

For his stomach wound, the only recourse he had was to apply pressure and not move. Being it traversed his midsection, every motion reopened the cut. His only hope was that Audhild had larger issues and would not seek him in the storm. Her madness made her unpredictable, and so he had to plan for the worst.

After a cursory search, he found heavy underbrush and a rock where he could conceal himself. The wind gusted through the forest and thunder roared across the skies, but the fury of the rain was already settling into a calm patter. Wringing out his shirt, he slapped it across the stomach wound, the wetness making it stick. He pressed it against his cut then settled to wait out the storm beneath the bushes. The mud was cold and sucked against his exposed flesh. He shivered to his bones and his heart still raced.

He lay down and closed his eyes against the rain falling into his face. Never had he felt more miserable. He was dizzy and his mind roved across a dozen different images. At times he thought someone was speaking to him, but then realized he was talking over the storm. Whenever he realized this he pressed harder on his stomach wound. I can't bleed out, he thought. The wound is not so serious. I'm just tired.

At some point he had fallen asleep, for he awakened to sunlight filtering through the trees and underbrush. When he could not sit up he panicked, thinking the worst had overcome him. Instead he found the suction of the mud bed he lay in held him down. For his efforts the bush he hid beneath dumped collected rainwater on his face. He heard a voice hush him to his left and he turned to face it.

Yngvar hid under the bush with him, his face strangely dry after the downpour. He placed a finger over his lips and warned with his eyes to look past him. His vision was blurry and it hurt to crane his neck, but he saw vague shapes moving cautiously. Only goatskin booted feet and green wool pants all thick with mud were visible. At least three pairs approached in a line.

He looked at Yngvar, who shook his head and kept his finger pressed to his lips. Ulfrik agreed with his assessment. He was in no condition to fight or run, but had to remain hidden and hoped these men passed him. Without a doubt these were either Audhild's or Gudrod's men seeking revenge upon him. He watched the feet avoid branches and puddles with care. The lead pair stopped abruptly and the other two continued another pace forward before also halting.

Yngvar was gone now, probably to scout the area. Ulfrik counted on his experience to lead him out of these woods alive. While he waited, he felt along his stomach at the tender edges of the cut. The area was warm and wet, but his fingers came away only with residual blood. As he struggled to examine his wound he shook the bush and more water trickled down.

The cold water snapped him out of the confusion. Yngvar was long in his grave, and Ulfrik figured if he was seeing ghosts then either he was dead or close to it himself. He did not want to find out until the men moved past, and all three of them remained still. He held his breath.

Voices were indistinct, but the hunters sounded as if they were in conversation. The boots all pointed toward each other, indicating they were not looking at him. One pair of feet turned and lightly stepped to the right and out of Ulfrik's view. The other two split apart and continued to pad cautiously through the brush. The pair eventually stopped only a few feet distant and now he could hear their hushed talk.

"Mud's thicker than cow shit," said one man, a voice smoky with age.

"Good for making tracks," said the other, a clear and youthful voice.

"Yeah, so why haven't we found any yet?"

The legs remained still and Ulfrik only heard the patter of rain dripping from the leaves overhead. A bird sang in the distance. Through the tangle of bushes he saw the profile of a man with a bushy black beard fringed with gray. He wore a wool cap, and his finger was thrust under it to scratch his head.

"I don't think he came this way," the older man said. "Egil said he was covered in blood. If that was so, we'd find a blood trail by now."

"The gods covered his tracks with the rain. Maybe they want him to escape?"

"Well, I don't want him to escape. Dalla's got the fever now. You want all of us to die like that?"

Ulfrik closed his eyes as if it could make him disappear. The two men grumbled and shifted. The older man was so close he shook the bush when he turned, and more water flecked onto his face feeling like pins of ice. The third companion called from a distance and the two left him alone.

He remained lying there for what felt like another hour. Rain plopped into mud and puddles with a maddening regularity, while birds screamed their indignation at the storm damage. The voices never left his range of hearing, but they were not close. He did not dare to move.

A splashing, sucking noise caught his attention. Now whoever moved cared not for stealth, but approached from the opposite side of the others. Ulfrik realized this was the path he had taken. He could not see the person without shifting and revealing himself. Instead he wished he could burrow deeper into the ground, lacking the strength for battle or flight.

The new arrivals batted around the area, shaking out the underbrush more thoroughly than the former searchers.

"Look at this," he heard a man say. "A bloody cloth."

Ulfrik could not think of what they had found, then someone

tugged on his injured leg. They had found Eldrid's blindfold tied to his leg.

"Hey! A body!"

A surge passed through Ulfrik's body, but the strength felt more potent than it was. The bush concealing him was pealed aside and two unfamiliar faces peered down at him. Calls were already going up in the distance.

"It's him!"

Ulfrik wanted to scream, but he only closed his eyes in defeat. Hands began to lift him out of the muck and the twist to his stomach made him open his eyes and cry out.

"Careful with him!" The voice was a woman's. Her visage made Ulfrik's blood run cold. It was Eldrid.

She laughed, but it was not the same. He peered closer as the two men fished him from the bushes like a sodden bag of grain. The woman wore the plain gray robes and the necklace of bones as well as leaned on her wood staff. But the face was Audhild's. She stared down at him, her pale hands wringing the staff.

"I had hoped to never see you again," Ulfrik managed to say. His voice was raw and cracked, thick with his torment. "This feels a bit too familiar."

Again she laughed, leaning her head back to reveal deep gashes on her face and the ragged scratches at her neck. "A storm sends you to me once more. The gods do not intend for you to escape your insolence."

A dozen rejoinders sprung to mind. He lacked strength for any of them. The men laid him out on the mud and at least half a dozen others converged on him. He recognized the older man's voice from earlier.

"What now? He looks almost dead."

"Take him back, of course. I will see that he is healed."

The answer satisfied everyone except Ulfrik. His mouth began to work in protest but he could say nothing. All his strength had been expended and it had not been enough to break free. He was as good as chained for these men, too weak to even crush a fly. They laid out a clean and dry cloak to serve as a litter, then two men lifted him into it.

He groaned as they hauled him off the ground, and the makeshift litter sagged to compress his stomach. Warm blood began to leak fresh from his wound.

Audhild sneered at him, her once pleasant features now scratched into those of a hag. Eldrid lived on, it seemed, though in a new body.

"Why?" It was the only question Ulfrik could form.

"I will make you whole again to remove the curse from our people," she said loudly. She leaned into him and kissed his forehead. Her lips were cold and dry.

Then she whispered, "And you will need to be strong to survive the torment I plan for you."

48

Waking from a shapeless nightmare, the familiarity of the room lulled Ulfrik into calm. The bed and its duck feather mattress embraced him like an old friend. Wolf fur pelts abraded his exposed chest, but he welcomed the warm dryness of them. Above him was no earthen ceiling dripping water, but rafters and straw thatch. The milky tendrils of hearth smoke formed lazy curls along its length. Warm light flickered from candles and throbbed from the opposite room where the hearthfire crackled. This was peace and beauty.

When he moved to scratch his nose, the illusion snapped.

Beneath the wolf fur pelts and all around the frame of his welcoming bed he was tied down. Scratchy rope crossed his chest, arms, and legs tight enough for his skin to feel cold and tingling where it pinned him. The fears of his dreams reignited in wakefulness as he pulled uselessly on the rope. He could raise his head and move his feet, but was otherwise immobile. His escape and resultant injuries had sapped him of all strength, yet even at his peak he would not have been capable of breaking free.

He lay in the gloom, not sure of the hour or day. Since his recapture all had become a smear of unrelenting boredom. He could remember five meals Audhild had supervised while her servant,

Kelda, fed him. The meals had been hearty, full of meat and blood, and he wondered if he were being fattened for the slaughter. He had been promised as much. Now he strained to hear beyond the walls, and voices were muffled and dull yet lost none of their strident tenor. Arguments carried on outside of Audhild's hall. The rise and fall of the debate was like the tide, at times loud and crashing and at others low but steady.

What if Lini survived his wounds, he wondered. Would he rescue me? Could it be an argument with those who want to free me?

The thought shamed him, but he could not deny it was his only remaining hope. Never in his life had he been rendered so helpless, and by a crazed woman no less. How much nobler it would have been to be a captive of a Frankish lord, dragged back to Paris to be hanged before all its citizens. No count could be made of the times he had wished Throst had killed him in combat. Any other death would be better than a knife stuck through his ear as he lay helpless on a bed. Would Odin welcome him to the feasting hall? Would the Valkyries fetch him or would they shriek at the sight of him dead and weaponless at the hands of a woman with arms no wider around than a new willow branch? A more unmanly and ignominious demise could not be imagined.

As he fretted over the circumstances of his impending death, the shouting outside had subsided. He only noticed the silence later, and then only by the immediacy of the hall door creaking open in the main hall. Audhild and Kelda murmured to each other, then he heard benches shifting across the dirt floor. Clacking sounds of some domestic chore reached him. Such a quaint life carried on beyond the open door of his room, and yet he remained lashed to a bed and awaiting his murder. He considered it true madness that such distinctions were so easily drawn.

Someone approached, and he raised his head to see Kelda staring at him. Her brown eyes were wide with fear and she flitted away before he could say anything. When he put his head back down, Audhild's voice came from the same place.

"You are awake?"

"If only this were a nightmare."

He closed his eyes as she padded into the room. Her skirts rustled as she sat on the stool beside him. She removed the wolf skins and pulled back the bandages wrapped around his stomach. Satisfied, she patted them down then examined the back of his leg. That wound did not disturb him, but when she pressed on it he flinched with pain. She replaced the furs and he opened his eyes. She was standing as if to leave, but he stopped her with a word.

"Wait. What was that argument about?"

Her back was to him, but she turned at his question. The bone necklace clacked as it rolled across her chest. In the shadows, the gashes on her face and neck looked like dark stripes. "What did you hear?"

"Nothing more than noise, but it was an argument. The people are not happy with what you're doing. They want to free me."

Audhild's smile flashed wide. She touched her cheek absently then began to laugh. "They want to kill you. I'm all that's preventing them."

"Why? That makes no sense. It should be the opposite."

"You've not lifted the curse. Thorvald's girl died of her fever last night. Now they believe you must die to end the curse. I say it is not true, and that you must live in freedom if you are to relent."

Ulfrik swallowed. "I think that is a lie. They know I will release the curse if I am freed. You want to kill me but can't without facing the rage of your people."

Again she tittered, hiding her mouth behind her hand. "Believe as you will. Again I am your savior and again you despise me for it. All I've ever done is to heal you and nurse you. What respect have you shown me for it?"

"I suppose falsely accusing me of rape and imprisoning me has vanished from your mind?" He expected his words to goad her ire, but instead she stared into the distance before answering.

"No, that was done to set you and Gudrod at each other's throats. He was never brave enough to challenge you fairly, and you couldn't kill him without good cause. It all worked out well enough in the end."

He blinked at her, mouth opening but forming no words. That

she used him to discourage Gudrod was understood, but that she designed a plot complex enough to both discredit Ulfrik and set him to murder for her was a shock. Had he been less occupied with his own worries he might have uncovered this layer. Now he wondered if his current plight had been planned from the start. It seemed impossible to predict his escape and recapture, yet he remained tied to the bed.

"Kelda is preparing the evening meal," Audhild said. "She will be in to feed you soon."

Again she turned toward the door.

"Why haven't you answered for Eldrid's death? The people should be your throat."

She lowered her head and touched the bone necklace at her throat. A low growl vibrated in her chest, and when she whirled on him her face had warped with hate. Baring her teeth like a rabid wolf, she grabbed his throat with her cold hands, nails digging into his flesh. She hissed and spittle flecked his face.

"You killed Eldrid! You killed everyone and fled. My sister was unmade because of your evil words, and died for it!"

Her crazed eyes bore into his, so close their noses almost touched. For an instant Ulfrik imagined head-butting her with enough force to smash her nose through her brain. He had witnessed it on the battlefield, and Runa had once killed an assailant in the same manner. What would it achieve? He would still remain bound and if she did not die then her revenge would be terrible. Her breath smelled faintly of onion as she continued to rant.

"You think you have a power to curse men? I don't believe you, though others might. I know true magic and did not see it from you. What is going to happen when you can't relieve the curse you set? No answer? Then let me tell you. The people will tear you apart in ways far worse than I can imagine. It is one thing to curse a man's luck and quite another to curse his children to die. Thorval was just outside this wall begging to carve out your lungs. He's just one voice of many. Can you imagine what others want to do?"

"If I die and the curse continues, they will hold you responsible.

You should ask yourself if you have the powers to remove the curse in my place. What then?"

Audhild released his neck and straightened up, a placid smile replacing the visage of madness. "You worry for me? I am touched."

"Release me from these bonds and I will end the curse. I might not possess the magic you expect to see, but it is clear the gods are angered at what you've done. There is no other way."

"I agree."

"The gods have—what? You agree?" Audhild closed her eyes and nodded. "Then what is this madness? Why must I remain bound? Set me free and the curse will be lifted."

"I shall."

"Yet you make no move to do so. There's more you're not saying."

Her head fell back in laughter and Ulfrik's skin tingled. "You wanted to know the argument from a moment ago. Here's the truth of it. We fought over the timing of your release. They wanted it to be immediate and I asked for more time. You are not ready for release yet."

The tingling on his skin gathered into a watery cold in his guts.

"We debated this, but I gave in to their demands. I can't deny this is an emotional time, with more death than our small community can withstand. I will release you tomorrow, though all may regret it."

Her smile reminded him of a time when he did not understand her madness, when he believed she was a healer. She began to rub his leg as she smiled.

"Why tomorrow? Why not now? Need time to prepare another prison for me. Confining me to a nice home is not freedom and will not fool the gods much less me."

"Oh no, you will be completely free. All of the people have agreed your imprisonment is the reason the gods have cursed us, and so must be reversed."

The cold in Ulfrik's guts spread from his core, emanating to his hands and toes. The words were all he ever hoped to hear, but he feared how the promise would be twisted. "What about Eldrid's visions? I am no longer a blessing to the people?"

"We all agree our actions have caused the gods to withdraw that promise. We don't need you here any longer."

"Then I may leave?"

"Any time after we are certain the curse is lifted."

Silence like a thick wool blanket fell upon the room. Even sounds of Kelda's work in the main hall stopped. Ulfrik stared at Audhild, who looked on the verge of exploding into laughter. "You are lying to me."

"Not in the least." She patted his leg again. "But I'm not telling you everything."

Sweat now beaded at Ulfrik's brow, and a cold droplet rolled into the corner of his eye and blurred his sight. He blinked it away as Audhild touched a finger to her lip as if in deliberation.

"Every method of preventing your escape relies on imprisonment, which means the curse cannot be lifted. If you flee and the curse continues, we've no way to bring you back. You see our problem? Your curse has created a difficult situation, but I've seen a way through it. After tomorrow, you will have total freedom but you won't want to exercise it. You'll need to stay with me for a while yet."

Ulfrik's mind flashed to Audhild's intention. He began to shake his head, and her smile grew with his realization. "No, don't do this," he whispered.

"It's the only way you left. I am not happy with it either, and I had hoped you could gather more strength. But the people are insistent."

Audhild squeezed the meat of his left thigh and sighed.

"I think one will be sufficient, though if you can stand it two will be best. Tomorrow I'm going to cut off your leg."

49

Three men arrived the next morning to move Ulfrik from Audhild's hall. Though he had regained strength over the past week of rest, they still overwhelmed him. He kicked but they were braced for his fury. Curses and shouts rose from the scuffle, and Ulfrik managed to gouge one's eye, but once he was released from the bed he could not break free. Held by his legs and arms, they carried him outside. He thrashed as he hung between them, tearing the wound on his stomach so the white bandages bloomed red. The men staggered and crashed against the doorway but they wrangled him outside.

The day was drab and cold as if winter were at hand rather than the start of summer. People gathered to witness the shame of his defeat. Suspended like a hunting trophy between two men, he surrendered to them. He had to conserve his strength for whatever chances the gods provided. The stern faces watching him pass did not flinch at his shame. Some even smiled, as if satisfied that justice was served at last. He kicked to loosen the grip of the man in front, but it only made him curse and pause to adjust. The third man whose eye had been gouged wrapped an arm around Ulfrik's midsection to steady him.

"Think this will save you from anger of the gods?" Ulfrik shouted.

"Fools! I pray the gods slay your children before your eyes. May you cry until your tears turn to blood!"

A hand covered his mouth, cool and smooth. Audhild now stood above him and smiled mournfully, as if she regretted everything. "Save your strength. You will need it."

They carried him into the blacksmith's forge, an open-air space covered by a roof of gray wood planks. The forge huffed sparks and the embers blazed yellow as Kelda worked the bellows. They hefted him onto a table and pinned him as the third man lashed him down with the rope from his bed. Again he struggled and swore, but they kept clear of his head and hastily secured him.

"Bind him tight," Audhild said above the shouting. "There's no telling what strength he might gather from the pain."

Ulfrik's mind raced with his throbbing heart. The moment had arrived and the gods had shown him no sign of escape. Angry faces fluttered around him as they tugged the bindings tight. To his left he saw a table laid out with tools that made his guts turn to water. Blacksmith tongs and hammers where shoved aside for a collection of axes, knives, and a long saw with a worn handle of dark wood. The teeth of the saw gleamed white from a fresh sharpening.

"Tie the leg here," Audhild said. Ulfrik felt cord shoved beneath his left leg above the knee. He would not look as rough hands laced it through several times before pulling it tight.

Tears began to leak from his eyes. Was this how Gunnar had felt, he wondered. Such a terrible, empty feeling. The helplessness unmanned him, and desperation filled his mind with the clutter of fleeting hopes. Maybe Lini still lived and would burst in to rescue him, or the gods would be so angered at his fate that lightning would strike dead all his enemies. Even more hopeless thoughts crowded his mind, but were short-lived.

A man braced his foot against the table and yanked the rope tight on his leg. Everything below his left knee turned to ice and began to tingle with numb pain. Secured at last, they stepped back. The table rocked and creaked in protest, but Ulfrik remained firmly bound to it.

The gods had showed their final gift to him at this last moment. He grew still as Audhild thanked the men for their help.

He gently pushed backward and the table creaked on unsteady legs. It had not been created to hold his weight or bear stress. It was probably donated for use in this crime because it was old and unwanted, and the blood from his amputation would ruin it. If he could collapse the table, the bounds would be loosened and he could slip out. The forge had plenty of tools that doubled as weapons. He needed a way to distract Audhild while he worked out of the bonds. Only his legs and arms had been bound, and with his struggling he guessed the knots were not well tied.

"You will not be needed," she said in answer to a question Ulfrik had missed. "Kelda and I are more than capable of the rest."

Now calmed, Ulfrik glanced at the three men. Their pasty faces glistened with sweat despite the cold. One refused to look at him, while the other two were wide-eyed with fear. All rushed out of the forge, leaving him to listen to the bellows pumping. Above him blue sunlight filtered between the roof slats.

Audhild came to his side, placing one cool hand on his face. "I have the sleeping medicine for you. It will greatly ease your suffering." She raised a wooden bowl in one hand, held it toward him, then let it fall to the floor. "Oh my, I lost my grip. I suppose you're going to feel every moment of this."

"You bitch," Ulfrik said through clenched teeth. He began to rock slightly, gathering momentum for his push.

She laughed at his curse. "My sister is dead and this community is falling apart all because of your stubborn refusal to accept defeat. I realize now, too late, that I needed to remove all hope of returning to your old life. Now I'm preparing to cut off the very leg I worked so hard to heal. Had I been thinking clearer, I should have removed it from the first. None of this would have happened."

Ulfrik narrowed his eyes and spit at her.

"Come now," she said with a pout. "Don't be that way. Let me explain what I'm going to do. I'll have to shatter the bone with a hammer first, then I'll use this saw to work through your flesh until the leg is removed. Kelda is heating an iron to cauterize the stump. By that time you will not be conscious, or will at least be wishing you were not."

"Is it not enough that you rule these people unopposed?" Ulfrik searched for any reason to delay. Audhild stood by the tools, selecting a hammer. If he broke free now, she could subdue him with one solid blow. She had to come closer. "Gudrod is gone and his supporters broken. You killed Eldrid—"

"You killed her!" she screamed, slamming the hammer back to the table. "She died because of you!"

"You'd like me to take the blame for it, but I'll tell everyone the truth. I won't hide your lies."

"I know a way to still your tongue," she said, then picked a knife from the table. "Maybe I'll take care of it after your leg."

"You are a murderous bitch."

She slammed the knife into the table by his head, so close he could smell its metallic oil scent. She held her breath, then let it out slowly. "Let's get started. That will steal the fight from you."

Snapping a piece of leather strap against her open palm she turned to Kelda. "Are the irons ready?"

Metal clanked as Kelda pulled one out of the forge. "This one glows orange. Will it be suitable?"

"Yes," Audhild said as she turned back to Ulfrik. She offered him the leather strap. "Bite on this or I won't have to cut out your tongue. You'll chew it off instead."

"Have you done this before?" Ulfrik began to shift himself for a push, hoping she would get closer.

"What's to learn about cutting off a leg? You won't lose enough blood to die. I've already made sure of it."

"Do it, then," he said with more resolve than he felt. It drew a poignant smile from Audhild.

"Just so. You do yourself honor at last. Now take this in your mouth."

She lowered the leather into his opened mouth. She was not going to give him a chance, so he had to enact his plan now. He shoved back as she turned away.

The table did not break.

It creaked and lurched, but nothing more. Audhild selected a hammer while Kelda continued to pump the bellows. Panic braced him, made his limbs go cold and stiff. He shoved again and the creaking drew an errant look from Kelda. Despite its flimsy appearance, the table required more weight to break. As Audhild weighed a hammer and nodded in satisfaction, he followed his first inspiration.

Spitting out the leather, he began to cry. "Please, don't do this. I'll do anything you ask. Just name it. I'll take back the curse, be your slave, anything. Just don't do this to me."

Tears came readily and shamelessly. He devolved into a blubbering cry that he feared might not stop, for the tears welled from the dammed up blackness in his heart. Audhild put down her hammer and laid her hands on her hips, the scar on her eyebrow raised along with it.

"Did I not just compliment your bravery? Now you sputter like a child."

"I can't help it," he said, hoping to appeal to Audhild the Healer rather than the butcher.

She huffed but bent over to retrieve the leather strap, disappearing from view as she knelt by the table. Standing again, she bent over him and laid her hand on his forehead. He continued to wail, forcing the intensity of his sobs.

"You're making it harder for me to enjoy this. Remember, you brought this on yourself, and no one else is to blame. You deserve no less. Now hold this in your mouth, and I will be quick. It's more than you deserve, really."

"F ... fine," he stammered. The tears abated but his heart raced with anticipation.

She leaned forward to kiss his forehead. Her lips were warm and wet on his skin, then she pulled back a hand's breadth to look into his eyes. "It could have been different between us, you know. Now, you—"

He struck with the speed of a snake, biting into the flesh of her cheek like eating an apple. Hot, salty blood flooded his mouth. She screamed and he dug his teeth deeper.

Now he pushed back and with Audhild's weight the entire table collapsed and the formerly tight bonds slackened.

His right hand ripped out from the rope and clamped over

Audhild's back. He thrashed his head side to side as blood gushed and choked him. Howling in agony, her hands raked the flesh of his scalp while trying to free herself.

He kicked free his left leg.

Kelda shouted but Ulfrik now had both legs free, his left arm still pinned to the wrecked table. Desperation lent him strength and he shoved Audhild aside like an old doll. She collided with the tool bench and hammers, saws, and knives clattered to the floor. Her face was painted red and she held her hand to it as she cried.

He worked out his last arm. Freedom! His left leg remained bound and was numb and heavy. If he did not restore circulation he would never stand a chance against the men who were certain to answer the screams. He snatched a knife from the floor, then cut the rope. A painful burst of needles exploded into his leg and foot. It had cost him time, but Audhild was still holding her face together and screaming.

Springing to his feet, knife in hand, he stood to run.

Then Kelda bashed him with a hammer.

50

The hammer clipped his shoulder and sent him stumbling back. He crashed into another bench, bounced off it and landed on the floor as a shower of iron bars, files, wood blocks, tongs, and a half dozen other tools landed atop him. Kelda stood staring at him, her face white and mouth agape. Her right hand wore a heavy leather mitt for handling the heated iron, the other gripped the hammer. A lock of hair had fallen from beneath her head cover and hid her left eye.

Audhild sprang up, hand clamped to her face as blood rushed from her fingers. "Kill him, you stupid bitch!"

She turned to run, crashed into the bench, then staggered out of the forge. Kelda blinked then raised the hammer.

Ulfrik jumped up but his left leg buckled, still numb. The wound in his right calf flared with pain as it bore all his weight. Lurching forward, Kelda's ungainly swing missed but the momentum of the hammer dragged her forward to crash into him. He used her body to steady himself, driving his left leg firmly into the ground and grinding his teeth against the pain. The two of them danced like drunken lovers, Ulfrik grabbing and Kelda vainly swatting with the hammer. When he regained balance, he shoved Kelda back.

She tripped over the broken table and landed on her rump with a squeal. He was content to leave her, but she discarded the hammer for another knife sticking out of the dirt floor. She blocked his way and he was not nimble enough to leap past. In his moment of hesitation, she scrabbled to her feet and pointed the knife at him, still in her left hand.

"Out of my way, Kelda. She's not worth it."

"She gave me my freedom." Kelda slashed but missed, her brows drawn in frustration. Ulfrik licked his lips, stood on the balls of his feet and prepared to rush her. She struck first.

It was a crazed, overhead strike that all but a crippled man could avoid. She hurtled at him and he sidestepped then shoved her past. He was already at the forge exit when he heard a hiss and scream. Kelda had landed on the forge, her hands and face splayed out on the coals. She fell away with her head and clothes aflame, flapping her arms like a speared seagull. The sweet scent of charred flesh enveloped the forge.

No time to waste, he left Kelda to burn. She had earned her fate. Outside the forge he expected a hostile crowd, but found nothing other than Audhild lying on her hip in the grass.

Her hair was tangled with blood from her cheek and stuck on the gaping wound. The front of her white overdress was drenched in gore and she no longer held her face. One hand supported her torso, and another reached for her leg. He loped for her, snarling in anger. Why she remained laid out did not concern him. He was glad Fate had held her down. As he loomed over her, she was sobbing.

Her other hand rested on the handle of a saw blade that protruded from the back of her thigh. It pinned the heavy blue cloth of her dress to her leg, and a wide dark stain glistened around it. The saw must have impaled her when she crashed into the tool bench. He laughed.

"Ah, but the gods know justice! The same saw you would use to take my leg has nearly done the job on you."

"I can't move," she said, then cried out and touched her face. Speaking apparently hurt worse.

"Perfect, let me help you."

She tried to peddle away from Ulfrik, but he scooped her up and clutched her before himself like a shield. One arm held her tight and the other jabbed the knife to her throat. He drove his knee into the back of her leg and she yelped. "Walk. Let's go meet your people."

The villagers had kept at a distance and dared not approach. As Ulfrik closed on them, several fled and the rest shuffled closer together. Audhild whimpered then screamed, finally going limp. Ulfrik surged with strength. At this moment he could have carried Audhild, the forge and anvil, and a horse as well. His moment had come and it would all end now. Either he would bargain for his freedom or die. There would be no half measures.

Setting himself in place, he shouted for the villagers to approach. Several men answered with spears and swords ready, others prepared to run in the opposite direction. He waited for them to gather, letting the armed men encircle him.

"Gods, what have you done?" The man who asked was one who had carried him to the forge. He brandished his sword with a measure of competence, and Ulfrik remembered him as Thorvald whose daughter had just died of fever.

"I am lifting the curse as you asked," he said over Audhild's shoulder. Her blood dribbled off her face onto his knife hand.

"What's that smell?" A man to his rear asked, and others raised their heads in response.

"Kelda flung herself on the forge trying to kill me."

"No!" Audhild began to struggle, but stopped with a shout of pain. The saw stuck in her leg bent against Ulfrik and she screeched whenever it moved. He had her in perfect control from that alone.

"What do you care for her?" Ulfrik asked. "You called her a stupid bitch last I remember. It's just what you think of all people, isn't it? We're all fools to dance to your crazed melodies."

She protested again, shaking her head. He barely had to force the knife at her throat to stop her. "This is madness. You must let me go."

Thorvald stepped closer and raised his sword. "Yes, let her go. You're a brave fighter but we've got you surrounded."

"Kill me and the curse remains. You've seen how the gods have judged. Think for a change. All who have opposed me are dead. All but Audhild and I say her life won't last till sunset. Do you think I am here as a gift or a curse? If you want peace, let me go."

Villagers shared desperate glances, but Thorvald did not waver. "You killed my daughter."

"I was locked in a cave. I killed no one."

"It was your curse. I heard you make it. We all did." He waved the sword at him. Audhild moaned and tugged at his grip, but he forced the knife at her neck and she stilled.

"Then let me go and the curse will be lifted."

Thorvald shook his head. His stance widened in preparation for a strike. Ulfrik nodded in understanding. "You don't care about lifting the curse. You want revenge."

"She was the last of my children." Thorvald's voice cracked and his sword trembled in his grip. Ulfrik felt the man behind him draw closer.

"He should die for what he did," Audhild said. "Don't wait. Kill him now!"

She bit down on Ulfrik's arm. Already slick with Audhild's blood, his own bubbled up as her jaws clamped into his flesh.

The scream exploded from his mouth though he had tried to endure the pain. Audhild still had use as a living hostage, or as a living shield against Thorvald's attack. She gnawed like a hungry dog, and he had to tear away his arm.

Before she could flee, he drove his knee into the saw and rammed it through her hamstring until it burst out the top of her thigh. Rather than scream, she gasped, then crumbled between him and Thorvald.

"You want revenge? She's the one who forced me to this island and held me prisoner. Kill her!" He pointed with his knife at Audhild's prostrate form. She lay in a pile, apparently unconscious from the pain. Thorvald wavered, unsure of where to focus his anger.

"How can we trust that you will lift the curse?"

"Only the gods can lift the curse. Are you foolish enough to think I command them? You've been under Eldrid's spell for too long. No man commands the gods. We plead and beg them to hear our wishes, nothing more. When I am allowed to go, the gods may see you have repented of your crimes. I was a freeman falsely accused and imprisoned. I saved you from enemies that would've overwhelmed you and was repaid with treachery. Who can say what price the gods will demand you to pay? All I can say is if I remain here or you kill me, then an even greater evil is done."

The group considered his words in silence. Audhild began to moan and stirred like a pile of bloody rags picked up by a stale wind.

"Let him go," said a man behind Thorvald, who had not lowered his sword nor taken his eyes from Ulfrik.

"He has never been good luck," said a woman. "Eldrid lied to us."

"Yes, look at all the death. Good riddance, I say!"

More voices joined and the consensus grew. Thorvald blinked and lowered his sword, nodding in defeat. His voice was a whisper. "Take what supplies you need and be gone. Never return."

Ulfrik opened his mouth to thank them, but Audhild let out an ear-splitting scream.

"You killed my sister! You killed Kelda! Murderer! You talk of injustice. Letting a murderer free is an offense to the gods." Audhild pulled herself up and attempted to stand, but her leg collapsed and she crashed to her side. She rooted around the ground, finally crawling to claw Ulfrik's pants and haul herself erect.

"You speak for the gods now?" Ulfrik grabbed her arm and pried it from his pants, but did not release it. He looked down at her, a pathetic mass of bloodied flesh for her face. Two eyes wide with madness and bright against the dark mask of blood stared up at him.

She winced with pain and hissed, one hand reflexively reaching for her wounded leg. "When I passed out, the gods showed me a vision of their vengeance. For every day Ulfrik is allowed to live, they will kill one of children. When they are all gone, then our wives and finally our men!"

"A convenient prophecy," Ulfrik said. He hauled her up with one hand, and let her dangle before him. "Your determination to kill me is wearying. You saved my life once, and so against everything my heart is begging me to do I will spare your life. I hold it in my hand." He smiled and prodded her with his knife. He wondered if she would not die of blood loss, but the cruel, crazed light in her eyes told him she would endure.

"If you love your children, kill him," Audhild shouted. "The gods have shown me a terrible fate if he lives."

Heads shook and Thorvald turned away. Ulfrik smiled, his heart lightened at the denial of Audhild's false prophecy.

She screamed for his death as he considered what to do. He had longed to kill her for all her cruelty, but now she was a ruin and her power destroyed. It would be like beating a crippled dog, and such an act was loathsome to him. Yet as she babbled about gods and visions, he thought of Eldrid's moment of clarity and the story she had told him. Audhild's life of cruelty demanded justice.

The gods had been provided their gift of blood, and now to complete their bargain they had placed their instrument of judgment in his hands.

"Enough!" he shouted over Audhild's raving. She stopped and the dispersing crowd paused. "You want to assume Eldrid's place? Who am I to say you should not? You'll need her staff to walk again. But there is one final touch to complete your transformation. One gift you gave to her long ago."

He placed the knife's edge across her eyes.

A quick slash across her face laid open her eyeballs and the bridge of her nose. He dropped her into a pile at his feet. She covered her face silently, her horrified scream sounding only after a long pause.

"Now you share her blindness." He dropped the knife next to her and shook his head. Eldrid had been avenged and his thirst to hurt her had subsided. If she survived the injuries of the day, then the gods had plans for her yet. If not, justice was done.

The villagers recoiled from him as if he were a snake. Maybe he was. He felt as cold as one, and no more welcome. He turned and staggered off to clean up and gather provisions for his journey north.

Valagnar's home was his only hope now, and whether they welcomed or killed him remained to be discovered.

51

The storm had delayed Ulfrik's progress along the coast. To his chagrin, he sheltered in one of the numerous caves that pocked the cliffs on the journey north. Rain had streamed across the cave mouth, spattering with angry snaps on the stone beneath, but he had sat at the back of the cave wrapped in his cloak to watch the lightning flash. The interruption had not been unwelcome. In his relentless drive north he had no plans for rest, though his wounds demanded it of him. At the risk of being whisked into the sea while traversing the thin strip of beach, he had to delay.

Now only drips of water pattered at the flat rocks of the cave mouth and a jagged cut of blue sky showed beyond. Seagulls landed at the cave entrance, peeked inside, then fled with a shout of protest. Ulfrik slung his pack of provisions over his shoulder, tightened the baldric that held his sword against his left hip, then resumed the final leg of his journey. His calf burned as he sidestepped down the ledges toward the beach, and he gritted his teeth against the pain. "If I never see another cave again, I will be a glad man," he said upon reaching the thin beach.

The trudge north continued, and he stopped only long enough to relieve the soreness building in his legs. The damp weather aggravated the old break in his left thigh, along with a dozen other old wounds. Progress remained slow but he did not mind.

He was free.

After blinding Audhild, he had been allowed to gather what he could from her home. Men had followed him to ensure he did not linger. He found food but little else of what he wanted. In the end, he claimed Gudrod's home and took a change of ill-fitting clothes and an old sword spotted with the beginnings of rust. The weapon would only last another week without proper oiling and sharpening. He hoped it would not be needed.

The morning wore away and his aggressive pace showed him to a natural harbor by midday. He had been following the puffs of smoke he had glimpsed over the cliffs, and now he saw a cluster of buildings huddled together, along with two boats tied to a short pier. Here was Valagnar's village, Reykjaholt. His heart pounded at the sight of it, and he felt a lump in his throat. The place looked as Nye Grenner had when he ruled it, though on flat ground. Memories flooded him, and he decided to sit for a moment and collect his thoughts.

He was responsible for the deaths of husbands, sons, and fathers of this community. They would not listen to excuses, nor attempt to understand why he had acted as he had. The slain were still fresh in their graves, and the people might slake a thirst for revenge upon him. Ulfrik had turned over the problem a dozen times in his mind, and in the end a simple and honest appeal for mercy was the best approach.

At the edge of the village, a woman carrying a basket spotted him. At first she disregarded him, but then paused and stared. In the next instant she was gone, disappeared between the homes. Ulfrik set his pack down and waited, hands relaxed at his side and sword in its sheath. He tugged it forward to make it more prominent, showing he meant peace but would defend himself. The sword would probably bend in the opening blows of a fight, he thought. But it was better than appearing like a beggar, even if he was.

Five men returned with the woman, who pointed at Ulfrik while holding her chest as if her heart might fall out. The men drew swords and marched along the water's edge to where Ulfrik waited. Their faces were dark and grim, empty scabbards dancing at their hips and sharp iron glinting in the afternoon sun as they strode to him. The man in the lead stood a head taller than the other four. A mane of black hair shocked with gray and a beard twisted into a point framed a squared head. His dark eyes glared out from expansive, black brows.

"I know you," he said in a voice like falling stones. "Ulfrik Somebody's Son. You took us captive."

"I'm flattered you remember my name." He had rehearsed that remark a dozen times in his head, but it never sounded as false as it did now. The man grunted while the others fanned into a semicircle around him.

"You've made quite a name for yourself here, none of them flattering." The man studied him up and down, nose wrinkling as if whiffing a stale fish. "Did you walk here? Your boots and pants are cut up."

"The rocks are sharper than I'd expect for a coastline. Yes, I walked here to see Valagnar. Would you take me to him, please?"

"Such manners. Well, as you've asked so kindly, I may as well admit you never had a choice in that. He'll demand to see you. Just need to surrender that weapon."

"As soon as you sheath yours," Ulfrik said with a smile.

The four were slower than their leader, who slid his sword into its leather scabbard without hesitation, but all withdrew their weapons. Ulfrik unhitched his baldric and handed over the sword. He slung it thoughtlessly onto his shoulder, then guided Ulfrik forward with a firm grip on his arm. "Walk between us and keep your hands up."

"Am I a prisoner then?"

"You're no welcomed guest, if that's how you expected to be greeted. Let's go."

They formed a box around him as they passed into the village. A dozen people came to follow him along the well-trodden paths that scored the grass between buildings. A clanging noise echoed in the distance where black smoke from a forge rolled into the blue sky.

Hens clucked and scratched in pens and a dog barked from inside a home. They passed a wagon loaded with hay and a young boy with a pitchfork who stared expressionless at him. He had lived so long in the strangeness of Audhild and Eldrid's vision of a community that he had forgotten the quiet and contented scenes of an established village.

Warriors stood outside Valagnar's hall, which was a simple building of stone and wood with a bright freshly thatched roof. The support beams leaning against the exterior walls were cream color of newly turned wood, a stark color against the gray of the main building. Two simple doors hung ajar, a stripe of black revealing nothing of the room beyond. One of the guards held a spear and wore a wolf pelt over his shoulders, and he stepped forward. "Who's this?"

"Take a good look," the black-bearded leader said. "Recognize that face?"

The warrior peered at Ulfrik, who smiled weakly as the warrior's expression melted into a frown. Without a word he disappeared through the hall doors, leaving one open to let out sounds of clacking plates and a man's laughter. The other door guards studied Ulfrik with equal disdain and the following crowd converged on him but held a safe distance. In the past he might have worried for their silent accusations, but after his experiences with Audhild, this was a light threat. Had they wanted to tear him apart, nothing would have stopped them. He fixed his eyes on the doors and ignored the staring.

When the doors swung open again, Valagnar stood framed within the dark rectangle. More men hovered indistinctly behind him. His eyes swept the length of him and his frown assumed notes of a sneer. He cupped his right elbow in his hand and stroked his beard. "Look who has paid me a visit. Did you bring an army of straw men with you or have you prepared another ruse?"

Ulfrik's mouth opened at the question but he did not have a response. He had not considered Valagnar would take his arrival as a trick, but it made sense now. His face grew warm from the anger of having missed this possibility. At last he shook his head. "No ruse. Do you still have the knives I gave you? I trust they aided in your escape from captivity."

Valagnar's expression softened but the frown remained. He addressed the leader of Ulfrik's guards. "Soren, have you disarmed him?"

"Got his sword. Haven't checked his body for anything more."

With a nod, Valagnar turned back to his hall. Soren nudged Ulfrik ahead and the guards parted. Once inside, his eyes struggled with the dim light. The smoke hole threw blue shafts into the center of the hall. Benches and tables had been cleared to the sides and a young woman paused in strewing fresh straw on the floor. Valagnar fluttered through the light and sat upon his chair at the high table. Soren gestured he should follow. The men inside watched him as one would a captured wolf, and more than one sword was unhitched in its sheath. Women shrank from him as he passed. Ulfrik felt a dozen eyes examining him from the darkness, but he kept his head up and stood beneath Valagnar.

"What does your presence here mean?" he said, holding out a mug that a young woman filled from a jug. Ulfrik watched the frothy ale spill over the sides.

"You remember my story?" Valagnar nodded again. "Then you know I have escaped, and in so doing I have slain all my enemies. And yours."

Someone behind him gasped. Valagnar paused with his mug touching his lips, then laid it aside without drinking. "Not all of my enemies."

"I am not your enemy, though we have faced each other in battle. You should also recall our bargain, and the weapons I gave you. You would not have escaped otherwise."

"Ha! Your knives were helpful, but the stupidity of your guards was all I needed."

"Did you consider who set those guards? Had I truly intended to keep you hostage, I'd have first separated all of you and put twice the guards on each of you. My only mistake that night was to not flee with you the moment we struck our bargain."

"I'll agree to that, since now we have no bargain. You missed your chance."

Ulfrik inclined his head. "So be it. Nonetheless, I hope that you will see how both my battle plans and the means of your brief capture were designed from the start to preserve your lives."

"Do not speak of saving lives!" Valagnar stood, hands balled at his sides. "My son died in that battle."

"He died a hero and warrior," Ulfrik said, holding Valagnar's eyes. "There is no better way for a man to leave this world, and we all must one day."

Valagnar glared in silence, then retired to his seat again. Now he took a deep drink from his mug. "What happened after the battle? Why do you claim my enemies are all dead?"

"It may only be a matter of months, but much has happened. It will take time to tell."

"If the tale ends with the death of my brothers' killers, then I have time to listen."

Ulfrik recounted the story of his betrayal and imprisonment and left nothing out until the moment he arrived at the edge of Reykjaholt. All listened with interest, for Ulfrik's retelling grew more dramatic and intense as his audience reacted to his tale. Soren pulled up a bench and he and three others sat to listen. As he recounted his final battle with Gudrod, a young man with a freckled face stepped forward. Ulfrik's retelling stuttered as he recognized Finn, and saw the formerly happy and accepting face now full of anguish. Yet when Ulfrik described Bresi's defeat and Gudrod's death, Finn closed his eyes with a weak smile.

"And so I have held nothing more from you. You can see every wound on my body to mark the truth of my words. I am sorry that the people of Reykjaholt had to become victims in this madness as well. Fate is strange and unknowable."

Valagnar exhaled and slumped. With this, the tension surrounding Ulfrik subsided. Now only he remained tight with anxiety and racked with pain from his wounded calf. He waited, hands at his sides, eyes downcast, attempting to look as contrite and helpless as he could. In the dark background, he saw Finn hug a woman who must be his mother, Lang's wife.

"It is a terrible story, made worse that I could not take revenge myself. Yet I see why Fate chose you to be the sword that cut this madness from our lands. Now, what are you here to ask? Our bargain was never completed, no matter what you say about arranging poor guards. Do not try to enforce it."

Ulfrik shook his head. "No, I only ask for a place to heal and recover. When the traders come, I ask you recommend me for their crews. I will work my way home to Frankia."

The hall filled with whispers and Soren and his companions stood again. Valagnar cupped an elbow in his palm as he stroked his beard. "It is not as easy as you say. There is a blood price to be paid for the dead."

"I have avenged those murders."

"Do not interrupt me," said Valagnar, pausing to let his silence gather attention back to him. "You say the leaders who provoked this war are all dead, but their people are not defeated. They should all be made to suffer, and honor requires me to stamp their village into the dirt. I will admit, your victory over us stung and has made us leery of returning to battle. But now you are gone, and if those people are as simple as you say, I can return to destroy them."

"They deserve no less," Ulfrik said. "But more fighting is not what this land needs. Before you rebuke me, listen. Even in victory men will die. It will be glorious but you've already suffered enough dead. I have been in your seat, and I know the bloody cost of fulfilling honor. I've no love for those people, but they were led astray. Some of them are good folk. The man from my story, Lini, may yet be alive. I do not know. If he is, he might be a leader to these people and he will be a reasonable neighbor. Do as you will, but consider the cost to yourself and the possibility for a truce."

Valagnar appeared to struggle with the thought, but Ulfrik knew he had wanted this chance to avoid another battle and still preserve his face. For his part, Ulfrik did not want to be swept into any more fighting until his body was healed. At last Valagnar spoke.

"Your words make sense, but I must discuss with the hirdmen before I decide. As for your request to remain with us, I must decline. You still bear the responsibility for the death of my only son. Soren, bind him."

Ulfrik stiffened in shock as he felt Soren's heavy hand grip his arm as he called to his companion. "Someone get me a rope."

52

"Wait!"

The word stopped Soren from binding Ulfrik's hands, and all searched for the speaker. The woman lurking with Finn behind Valagnar stepped forward. She wore a simple dress of green cloth and a white overdress smeared with dirt. The copper hair that fell from beneath her head cover was streaked with gray and the dash of freckles across her nose and cheeks marked her as Finn's mother. They shared a similarity in demeanor if nothing else, both carrying a natural openness even in their tense moods. She placed a calloused hand on Valagnar's shoulder and repeated herself. "Wait, I have a right to speak."

Valagnar twisted on his seat to face the woman. "Gytha, what are you doing?"

"It is my right," she insisted. Her eyes never left Ulfrik's. Tears shimmered at the edge of her fair lashes, and her voice trembled, yet she raised her chin defiantly.

"Then speak," Valagnar said, his voice a low grumble.

"You have avenged my husband's death, though it was not your intent." Her hands pulled back to her chest and she rubbed them together as if cold. "I will rest easier knowing the man who stole him from me is dead. I am grateful for that, but more for what you did for my son, Finn. You saved his life."

"It was the right thing to do. Lang and Finn should have been friends, not victims of murder. I was glad to see him live." He recalled his last words to Finn, a plea that he remember who had saved him. After all that had happened since, he had forgotten it himself.

"Then there is goodness in you," said Gytha. Her words drew grumbles from the crowd, indistinct but unfriendly. Valagnar turned again to face her.

"And my son is dead because of this one. Do you weigh one life more than another?" A few voiced agreement, but Gytha shook her head.

"Did he kill your son or was it another? Fate sent an arrow to him and he died bravely. Lang was cut down extending his arm in friendship. There is a difference."

"Enough of this chatter!" Valagnar shot to his feet and Gytha jumped back, clasped hands coming to her face. Ulfrik struggled against an urge to aid her, but Soren placed a hand on his shoulder and shook his head. Surprisingly, Ulfrik read a note of understanding in his expression.

"Ulfrik led good men to their deaths, all so that he might have cause to free the survivors later and earn a debt of gratitude. I heard the same stories you did, and all I heard was a man intent on using my son's death to enrage and manipulate me for his purposes. I will not have it. Ulfrik is cast out of Reykjaholt."

"Then I claim him," Gytha said, dropping her hands to her side. "Let him be made a slave."

Valagnar's mouth dropped open and Ulfrik hissed at the notion of becoming a slave. Soren chuckled.

"There is no precedent for such a thing," Valagnar said, tugging at his beard.

"There's a fine lie. Slaves are taken all the time. If Ulfrik is without a home, then I will give him one. He will be my slave, property of my family."

"If he's to become property, he should be mine."

"I still await the blood price for Lang's death. Your own sister, Valagnar."

His demeanor shifted and his face reddened. Soren chuckled once more.

Ulfrik watched his fate decided, and realized his supposed slavery was Gytha's way of protecting him. He did not know her, but he had little other choice in a harsh land without friends. A period of slavery would be acceptable, though he wondered at her intentions. Would he become a substitute for Lang, and forced to remain with her? This could be the same situation he had just escaped. He held his breath. Had he been in better condition, he would have grabbed the sword from Soren's grip and taken Valagnar hostage. Now merely standing so long pained his legs.

"Very well," Valagnar said, waving his hands in the air. He collapsed heavily into his seat. "I grant you this captive's life as payment for Lang's death. Do with him as you will, but under one condition. He must serve one year before you release him from bondage, though you may sell him at any time. I'll not have you free him under my nose, just to spite me."

When Gytha smiled, she became a woman ten years younger than the creases at her eyes indicated. She kissed Valagnar's head. "You are an honorable man."

People cheered for his generosity, but Ulfrik felt himself whither for it. Soren clapped his shoulder. "You'll like Gytha's hall better than those caves."

Ulfrik gave a wan smile and Soren continued to bind his hands.

"What are you doing?"

"You're a slave now. You rank slightly better than firewood."

53

Ulfrik laid the sheathed sword across the bed, next to his crisply folded winter clothes and a new sealskin cloak for rainy weather. He traced the hilt of the sword thoughtfully, pleased with the way the blade had been forged. His specifications had been followed in detail, and the blacksmith had called it some of his finest work. Upon seeing it, Valagnar had offered to buy it from Ulfrik, but he declined. This sword would be his closest companion for the next year or longer, and his life would be trusted to it. He shoved the clothes into a goatskin pack and fastened the flap with an antler button. A sigh rushed from his mouth and he glanced around the small room a final time.

The oil lamp lay where Gytha had placed it on the table. A knife sat beside bits of crumbled white cheese, and he swept these into his palm then ate them. He would not be eating as well after today, and now every final taste of this place was precious. Chill air filled the room, but the small space trapped body heat so that adding a few skins to the bed made it comfortable. With Gytha next to him, even the deepest days of winter had been pleasant.

He stepped into the main room where the hearth glowed and smoke prodded the ceiling. One of their goats stood chewing straw next to the table and flicked its ear at Ulfrik's appearance. Patting its head, he proceeded to the door where he heard voices beyond. Outside he stepped into a cool morning where Gytha waited for him. Finn stood beside her, and his two younger sisters clung around Gytha's skirts.

"You are the very image of a jarl," she said. Her smile trembled and he understood tears lurked behind it. "I would hardly know you from the man who came to this hall a slave."

Ulfrik laughed, cupping her chin, then kissed her. For all her strength and labor-roughened skin, she possessed lips as soft as goose down. "I will be happy to call myself your slave for the rest of my days."

"Then stay." Her voice was a shallow whisper, faint enough that Ulfrik could've mistaken it for the wind, but he understood.

"We both knew this day would come. I have stayed longer than I should have, and that for my devotion to you and your children."

Gytha nodded and bit her lip. Nothing would change Ulfrik's decision.

The year of so-called slavery began with a long period of Gytha nursing him to health. She and Finn both credited him with saving Finn and their men. Their positive views of him eventually spread to neighbors and by the time Ulfrik was hale again, many began to consider him a friend. His hair had been shorn at Valagnar's request to mark Ulfrik as a slave, but Gytha soon had him in her bed and his hair grew back thereafter. Both enjoyed and needed the companionship, and her children welcomed a man in their home. Even Valagnar proved to be more tractable than he first seemed, and relented on blaming Ulfrik for his son's death.

After the chaos of Audhild and Eldrid, life in Reykjaholt proved simple and pleasurable. Once Ulfrik's wounds had mended, he regained his strength through constant activity. He trained Finn and other boys in swordsmanship while he recaptured his old skills. He hunted with Soren and others, bringing home game to feed his building muscle. Ulfrik's father had remained a giant man until his death, which was about Ulfrik's current age. He had not inherited the mass from his father, but the strength and endurance came through the blood to him. By the end of the year he stood tall and strong once more, though he now had a slight limp and his hair had mostly turned gray. Both would be lifelong reminders of his time in captivity.

Still he remained sleeping beside Gytha, teaching riddles to her two girls and sparring with Finn. In the spring, traders came with news that Lini had survived and now led his band of farmers. He sent a message of peace, but reinforced it with nothing. Of Audhild's fate, he had heard nothing nor did he wish to think of her again. Ulfrik did not care what happened, so long as conflict remained at bay. An unadorned life of hunting and tending a hearth pleased him more than a hall full of gold. It was not until the dreams began where Yngvar spoke to him while sitting at the edge of his bed.

"This life is not yours, but another man's. It's not what I saved you for all those years ago," Yngvar would say, a reproachful smile on his lips.

"I know, but I must gather my strength for the road home. It will not be easy." Ulfrik always repeated the same excuse in every dream.

"Your real children have grown, and wish for their father's wisdom every day. Return to your hearth." Yngvar would fade with that last admonition.

These dreams soon haunted every night, then Toki joined Yngvar. Together they begged him to return to Frankia until he could hear their voices even in wakefulness. Worse still, Toki asked him once more how Throst had known to find him. It was as if Toki wanted to impart a secret he could not betray. The question frayed Ulfrik's nerves. Once the trader Heidrek Halfdanarson arrived at the end of summer, Ulfrik knew how to silence the dreams and questions. On Valagnar's recommendation, Heidrek agreed to employ him as a guard and rower. They had no plans for travel to Frankia, but he would earn enough silver to buy passage when he needed it.

"Take this," Gytha said, and pulled over her head a silver amulet of Thor's hammer strung on a cord. "It's simple but will protect you."

He held the warm silver in his hand, then kissed her once more. He put the amulet around his neck. "I have to leave."

"Let's go," Finn said, hefting his own pack.

Ulfrik frowned. "What is this?"

"I'm going with you," Finn said, a wide smile on his face. "You can't travel alone."

"Before you protest," said Gytha, "I have discussed it with Valagnar and we agree. Finn wants to see the world, and I can think of no one better to send him with."

"Do you know the risks? He could be killed or enslaved. It's no easy thing making a journey so far."

"I'm a man now, and I want to go with you." Finn shouldered his pack, and a newly made sword hung at his waist. "Two are safer than one man traveling alone."

"You filled his head with stories of battles and glory," Gytha said, tears streaming freely. "Now you see him safely to his destiny. His life should not be wasted tending goats when he could be building kingdoms with you."

"I can't say I'm not glad for the company. Thank you, Finn. And you, Gytha, I owe too much to repay."

They parted with a long kiss, then hugs from the girls. Finn and his mother embraced. Gytha's voice crackled with emotion. "I would accompany you, but my girls and I have a place with Valagnar. He needs family in his life, or I fear he would die like a calf in winter. Maybe one day you will return to us again?"

"I would like that. No man knows what Fate has planned for him," Ulfrik said.

Then he looped his arm around Finn and headed for the docks where Heidrek's ships awaited. The road across the oceans back to Frankia would be long and circuitous, but he would travel them in patience. His friends and enemies had counted him dead so long that another year would make scant difference. Though he yearned for his hall and his family, they would have to wait.

At the end of the sea road lay vengeance.

Throst would soon pay in blood.

54

"He agreed to meet with you," Heidrek said as Ulfrik helped him out of the rowboat to the deck. "You're guaranteed safety."

"Finn will come with me," Ulfrik said. "And I'd appreciate a few others."

"Finn will do," Heidrek said, eying him with a slight scowl. "Return by midday or I'll call back the rowboat and pull up anchor. So don't delay or you'll be trapped with these people again."

Ulfrik swallowed at the thought. He had faced death countless times, dodged spears and swords in the chaos of battle, but never had he felt so frightened. Looking across the iron gray sea to the shore, he saw Audhild's hall and wondered if she still held sway over these people. He feared he was volunteering to step into a trap, but the risks would be worth it to him. He laid one hand on his sword and tightened his resolve. *This time I am armed,* he thought. *Let them try to harm me.*

Both he and Finn climbed the rope down the short distance to the boat. The man there was red-cheeked, squint-eyed, and smiled warmly. "Your trip. You row."

Taking up the oars, Ulfrik rode the waves onto the beach as the red-cheeked man folded his arms and whistled. They ran the boat onto the beach, Finn jumping out to drag it ashore. Ulfrik nodded to Red-Cheeks and started up the slope toward the village.

His hands were like ice and his vision focused on Audhild's house. No one stirred, though somewhere a hearth chugged smoke over the village. He swallowed again.

"Coming here makes me angry," Finn said. "These people are the killers of my father."

Ulfrik did not respond, but continued to walk before stopping at the edge of the village. At last a lone figure of a red-haired man separated from the shadows of Audhild's hall. He stared across the distance without making a motion, but then he raised a hand in greeting. Ulfrik mirrored the greeting, then started toward Lini. His hand remained close to his sword. Once they stood arm's distance from each other, neither spoke but sized up the other. Lini had lost the youthful softness of his features and now kept his mouth pressed in a grim line. His hair was braided back but his beard curled out wildly.

"So you lived," Ulfrik said.

"As did you."

"Your tone sounds as if you're disappointed."

Lini glanced at the sword at his hip then slid his gaze to Finn. "You never lifted your curse. Half the village died from it."

The two men remained staring at each other in silence, a wind blowing hair into Ulfrik's eyes. He brushed it aside and decided to press his request rather than dwell on the past. "Thank you for meeting me and guaranteeing safety. Does Audhild know I am here?"

"She's dead. Hanged herself within the month after you blinded her. Swung from the rafters of her own hall until the stench got someone's attention."

"You are better for it. You saw who she really was, clearer than anyone."

"What have you returned for? People know you are here and are staying away for the sake of peace with Valagnar. But I can't guarantee some won't let a desire for vengeance rule them."

"I won't be long. Eldrid took something when I was first captured.

It is of tremendous importance to me, and I want to search her home. Perhaps I will find my belongings still there."

Lini nodded and pointed across the village to the general direction of Eldrid's home. "Her ghost haunts that place. No one dares go near it. Take what you will from it, and be done with us."

Ulfrik put his hand on Finn's shoulder and began to leave. He stopped and turned back to Lini. "Thank you for what you tried to do for me."

He shook his head and waved him off.

Wasting no time, he traversed the village and followed a trail to Eldrid's hut. It had been built of stone which had stood up to the weather, though white and green lichen splattered the gray rocks. The roof, however, had collapsed in places and laid bare the timbers beneath. Ulfrik hissed at that, hoping what he sought had not been ruined from rain.

"If it's haunted, I'm staying out here." Finn stepped back from the yawing black entrance, the door fallen from its hinges. "What are we doing here?"

"Planning for the future. Watch outside while I search."

Stepping inside, an owl screeched then furiously shot through a hole in the roof. Ulfrik jumped back in shock and heard Finn gasp outside. He paused while his heart thudded, then began to chuckle. "I flushed out the ghost. It's safe to come in now."

"I'm fine out here," Finn called back.

Where the roof had let in rain, everything was ruined. The bed was covered in rotten blankets and a mattress that had exploded wool stuffing from its seams. A table had collapsed and plates and jugs were in shards around it. Piles of rotting thatch lent a grassy scent to the stench of mold and the air did not move despite the openings in the house. Her cooking pot still hung over the hearth, bright orange rust clinging to the trestle that held it up. He began to poke around, first carefully, then with greater desperation. After Finn had checked on his progress a third time, he pulled out a small chest hidden underneath the fallen thatch.

Dragging it to the center of the floor he opened it to reveal a sealskin pack within. This he gingerly removed, then untied. He wore a pair of leather gloves for safety, then withdrew the clay jars from inside the bag. The cover of one had come free and spilled a dull green powder on everything. He held his breath as he set out three other jars, their lids tied with gut string. Undoing each one he revealed powders of different colors. The red one stung his nose just at opening it, and he quickly resealed it. At last he found a jar that held a fine powder the color of hearth ash.

This one he set aside, then removed one glove. The clammy smell of it already told him he had found what he sought, but he dipped his finger into it and raised the clinging powder to his tongue. A cold numbness spread into his mouth and the bitter taste was unmistakable.

"I knew you had more of this, you miserable hag," he whispered to himself.

He tied the jar, which was only half filled, then placed it in his own seal skin pouch which he had padded with cloth wads, finally tying it closed.

"Stay fresh for me," he said to the package as he slid it into his own bag. He kicked over the other powders, leaving only the burning powder untouched.

Outside the air was fresh and clean. Finn looked at him expectantly.

"I found what I needed. The gods have seen my plan and they are pleased. Revenge will be sweet, when it finally comes."

55

The scent of Frankia was of pine and river mud. Ulfrik stood on the deck of Heidrek's trading ship and inhaled. The balmy summer air pressed his face as he closed his eyes to listen to the birdsong from the surrounding forest. Oars gently splashed the water and men spoke in low voices behind him. He felt someone at his side, then looked to find Finn had joined him at the rail. His freckle-splashed face was bright with awe. Ulfrik had built up this land in the lad's imagination that he wondered if seeing it would disappoint. Now, more than year after setting out from Iceland, they were on the brown waters of the Seine.

"This is nothing like I've ever seen," Finn said. "It's beautiful."

"You've not even placed foot on its shore," Ulfrik said. "Don't judge yet."

They had passed through the forts at the mouth of the Seine, paying fees for safe passage inland. He was eager for news, but did not want to arouse suspicions through overly curious questions. During their stop, he had learned Hrolf collected these fees and so was still in power at least as far inland as Rouen. His lands seemed to still be intact. He had asked for news of Throst, but no one knew that name.

He and Finn rested on the rails until they were called back for their shift of the oars. Heidrek was anxious and pacing with his hands behind his back as he always did when thinking. Over the year, he and Heidrek had learned to respect each other. Ulfrik and Finn proved their usefulness when Orkney pirates had dared an open attack. Their bravery had saved Heidrek's cargo and likely his life. Heidrek had proved more than a fair employer and Ulfrik named him a friend. Some of the crew had been difficult company, but most were agreeable men who loved the open sea and the freedom it offered. No one stayed with Heidrek who did not wish it. He kept no slaves and paid a high wage.

At last Heidrek ceased pacing and came to Ulfrik at his oar. "You are certain this Throst fellow will treat a merchant with respect?"

"As certain as I can be. Reputation is everything in these lands, and he would not ruin his by stealing from us. That's only fair if he can catch us on the open sea."

Ulfrik laughed at his joke, but Heidrek's eyes were far away. He turned back to him after a moment of thought. "This makes us even now. My neck is bared for this bastard if you're found out."

"Relax, friend. Just make your trade and leave me behind. I will not press my plans until you are away."

Heidrek nodded and patted Ulfrik's shoulder. "You don't want to change your mind? I'll double your wages to stay."

The men rowing near him whistled or called out in surprise. "What if I threaten to leave?" asked one.

"You I'll gladly throw overboard and call it a profit. Keep rowing. I want to be done with this business. I've got real trade to do."

The travel up river went without issue, but soon they were navigating into the tributaries to where Ulfrik last saw Throst. These were Frankish territories, though trading ships were always welcomed as long as they did not hide troops. A new bridge had been constructed where none had been before, and after inspection by a local Frank ruler and paying a bribe, they were allowed to portage around it and continue. The delay cost them a day, which Heidrek cursed and blamed Ulfrik.

They said their farewells and settled payments for services before arriving at Gunnolfsvik. Heidrek slipped in a gold armband, and when Ulfrik balked at this, he pressed it back onto him. "If you truly are the warlord you claim to be, then let this be my first bribe for your favor. I've never come this far south, but if you reestablish your rule here, then I may add Frankia to my routes."

After this, they made a stop for Ulfrik to hide his sword and belongings along the river, all carefully wrapped in the sealskin cloak Gytha had bestowed him. It was now torn and stained white with sea salt, but it still had years of use remaining. Now it would guard his weapon and silver against the elements while he traveled on. Once back aboard, Ulfrik donned his disguise. He wore the plain brown and gray clothes of a traveler. His heavy wool cloak had a cowl that hung down around his eyes. He rubbed dirt onto his face to obscure his features. A well-worn walking stick was now in his hand, and he wore wool gloves to hide the missing finger of his left hand. A rope belt and small travel pack completed his disguise.

Finn was dressed the same as he, though he carried no walking stick but did have a sword hitched to his belt. He fussed with it, trying to get used to the dirty clothes. "Do we have to be so grubby?"

"The road does that to a man. Remember, you must act as if accustomed to leading me. Don't wander off and leave me stranded, or you'll raise questions."

"I won't," he said as excitedly as a child at a festival. Ulfrik smiled at his young friend's irrepressible cheer. Even on such a daring plan he gave no sign of worry.

They watched Gunnolfsvik emerge into view. It was unchanged in the five or more years Ulfrik had been gone. In the distance the Frankish tower was a purple rectangle over the treetops at the horizon.

"Are you nervous?" Finn asked.

"Of course. It's an ill thing to be unworried for battle. Overconfidence breeds deadly mistakes."

Ulfrik took a final look at the scene then tied the blindfold over his eyes, completing a transformation into a blind traveler and his servant. The loss of his vision except through the bottom of the blindfold was disorienting. Suddenly the rocking of the ship felt more violent and he had to brace the sides. He realized he should have done this earlier to acclimate himself.

He sat at the stern with Finn as he heard Heidrek negotiate with the men of Gunnolfsvik. They spoke Frankish at first, but a Norse speaker eventually filled in and allowed Heidrek's ships to dock. In his dark world, he sat on the deck and listened to Finn's prosaic descriptions of docking the ship. He and Finn sat aboard long after Heidrek had went ashore to discuss his business and pass on Ulfrik's message.

Finn grabbed his arm and helped him to his feet. "Some men are coming. Be ready."

"Halfdan the Blind and Finn Halfdannarson?" The voice was young and bent with a Frankish accent.

Ulfrik bowed. "At your service."

"Jarl Throst Shield-Biter will receive your news. You two are to be his guests at tonight's meal. Someone will fetch you. Remain aboard ship till then."

He bowed again and listened as the footfalls receded across the deck.

"I have to remember to call you Father," Finn said as he released Ulfrik's arm.

"Keep hold of me. Don't break the act from now until I have finished all I've come to do."

Finn guided him to a rowing bench and helped him sit. Ulfrik smiled. Tonight he would entertain the gods with a good show of bloody vengeance.

56

The voice tore through him with the fury of a winter storm. The self-satisfied laughter. The boasts. The haughty commands. Ulfrik felt each of Throst's words like a knife sawing through his bones. Though deprived of sight, the sweaty smell of bodies, heat, and the loud voices both Northman and Frank painted a vision of a full hall of revelers and Throst seated at the high table. He imagined him with a foot propped on the table, a woman strung across his shoulders feeding him, and gold glittering from every patch of open skin. Such a swine would have no dignity in his ill-gotten power, only vanity and a false air of power.

"The night is getting late, Father." Finn had maintained his act without fail, filling Ulfrik's cup and his guiding hands. Now he leaned into Ulfrik, who still sat at the far end of the hall with his cowl drawn. "Will we meet the jarl tonight, do you think?"

"Undoubtedly he knows my message and will be keen to hear it." Ulfrik disguised his voice with an aged strain. He groped for his cup though he could see it beneath his blindfold. Finn pushed it toward him.

"As you say, Father."

"We are merely travelers, not merchants, and far less than

warriors. He will want to entertain those worthy men before us. Have patience."

Ulfrik sipped the ale from his cup, careful to drink little but not insult his host.

The surroundings filled him with hate. The Frankish conversations reminded him of the depth of Throst's treachery not only to him but to his own people. He spent the first part of the evening marshaling his temper and reminding himself he had more than his own life to consider. Finn relied on his plan to carry them to safety, and so he had to stick with it rather than scrap it for a knife to Throst's neck.

Killing Throst was the easy part of his plans. Ulfrik wanted to learn who had betrayed him, to answer the questions Toki and Yngvar brought to his bedside each night. How did Throst know Ulfrik would be in Gunnolfsvik? Only Hrolf could have known, and only Hrolf had the motivation. In their last meeting he had noted Ulfrik might soon be called a king in his own right. Such a simple remark had gone unnoticed until Ulfrik had been forced to think on the reasons that led him to his fall from the tower. Had he become such a threat to Hrolf?

Only Throst would have the answers, and so he had to find out before he silenced Throst forever.

By the end of the evening, as he expected, a hirdman found Ulfrik and Finn and asked them to appear at the high table.

Trembling with what he hoped looked like infirmity rather than nerves, Ulfrik leaned on his staff and let Finn gently guide him along the path. He mimicked Eldrid's mannerisms in hopes he seemed authentic. When he stopped at the high table, he felt a dozen eyes upon him. He was confident his disguise plus the belief in his death would keep his identity hidden.

"Halfdan the Blind and my son, Finn, at your service, Jarl Throst."

"Be welcomed Halfdan and Finn," Throst said, his voice rough with drink. "I've been sharing news with your friend Heidrek all night, but he says you have a message for me. A secret message of great importance."

Two or three men chuckled and he heard the arrogance chime in

Throst's voice. Ulfrik's heart was in his throat now, for many men claimed he had a distinctive and commanding voice. He did all he could to reverse those traits, speaking hoarsely and as if in great effort.

"It is true, my jarl. A message I fear can be shared with none other than you."

He heard bodies shifting, the creak of benches and of leather. A few men whispered before Throst spoke again. "A cloaked and hooded messenger no less. The mystery only deepens. At least reveal your face to me. I might trust you better."

Sycophantic laughter chimed as Ulfrik did as directed. His gloved hands reached onto his cowl and he pulled it back. Finn dutifully smoothed Ulfrik's hair, which was now uncombed, thin and grizzled with gray. He lifted his head as if defying Throst to recognize him.

"That's better," Throst said, then swallowed whatever he held in his mouth, likely ale. "So what is your message?"

"I may be blind, but I do sense that we are not alone, my jarl."

"Really?" Throst sighed and Ulfrik heard him shifting on his bench. "Very well, we can meet in my room. Of course, you will be searched first. Safety always."

"Doubtless, my jarl." Ulfrik held his hands wide. As one who has too often delivered the knife to the back, he thought, you do well to be careful.

Rough hands searched him, lazily patting his sides and boots but finding nothing. A man lifted the staff from his hands and Ulfrik thought it realistic to protest.

"You would not deny a blind man his walking stick?"

"I would, and I am," Throst said. "A man is just as dead from a broken skull as he is from a cut throat. Your son will guide you, after all. Come."

Finn gathered Ulfrik's arm to his side and led him up the high table into a room that was once again filled with others. He guessed at least two more beside Throst. He did not want to peek beneath his blindfold for the risk of revealing his sight.

"Are we alone? I do not think so."

"Enough with these demands, Halfdan. If that's truly your name. I am as alone as I ever am. Your message?"

Bowing again, he licked his lips. "Jarl Hrolf the Strider sends you his greetings."

Silence.

He heard bodies shift, a low hiss to his right, yet from before him where Throst stood he heard nothing. Ulfrik waited, hoping for a sign that the two were allied. His next words had to fit their relationship or he and Finn might not live another breath longer. He sensed the same tension he felt in a parley just before battle, when each side tried to intimidate the other into surrender. Despite what he believed about Hrolf and Throst's alliance, Ulfrik decided on his approach.

"He wishes to discuss cooperation."

Throst exploded with laughter, though the others remained quiet. Ulfrik's gut tensed, expecting a punch. Instead, Throst clapped his hands together as he regained himself.

"The great Jarl Hrolf the Strider wishes to cooperate with little Throst Shield-Biter? My last message from Hrolf was a clear description of where he intended to display my severed head. Now he sends a blind old man and his so-called son as his representatives?"

"We are expendable and discreet rep—"

"Be silent!" He felt Throst draw closer. He smelled of ale and sweat. Ulfrik's hands trembled in a killing rage, but Throst continued. "What proof do you have?"

"I do not trust this one, Brother." The third person spoke up, a woman's voice. Ulfrik recalled a plain, shrinking girl who had been Throst's sister. "There is something not right."

"It's the blindfold," said a man to Ulfrik's left. "He's hiding something."

"His sightless eyes, is all," Finn said, protectively grabbing Ulfrik's arm.

"I have proof," Ulfrik said, diving into the pause. "With your permission, I will reach into my sleeve and then into my shirt, or you may have your man do it if you prefer." When no one answered, he slowly drew the gold armband Heidrek had bestowed him from his left arm, then reached into a pouch held in his shirt and produced a piece of antler with Hrolf's mark on it. Heidrek had collected it as proof he had paid his river fees then gave it to Ulfrik.

"He bade me deliver this armband and his mark as a token of sincerity."

Someone grabbed both from him. The girl, a vaguely sweet smell surrounding her, stood before him now. "You are a familiar man, Halfdan. There is much about you that speaks to me of deceit."

Ulfrik bowed his head to conceal the swallow. His left hand trembled. "Hrolf chose me for my discretion. I do not know the mind of my lord, but only that he wishes a meeting with Throst. He has asked I secure a time and place where both could safely discuss mutual concerns."

"I fight for the Franks," Throst said. "If Hrolf has forgotten what happened to the last band he sent to Gunnolfsvik, I'd be happy to remind him."

"No need for threats, Jarl Throst," Ulfrik shrunk as if in fear, but he wanted to recoil from the scrutiny of the sister. "Send whatever reply you wish and I will ensure it gets to Hrolf. Please, I've spoken all I know. Do not kill a messenger who has come in peace. Heidrek and his crew are expecting to return me to Hrolf before setting on their way. Do not have them say Throst kills old men for their messages. Your reputation does not deserve such a stain."

Throst grunted and the woman before him snorted. "I do not trust him or his message, Brother."

"May I suggest a compromise?" Ulfrik said. "You have heard my message. Tomorrow I will be gone from your hall with whatever reply you wish to make. For tonight, allow me to sleep on Heidrek's ship and take my son as a hostage. Release him to me when we cast off. If my words cannot allay your fears that I bring danger, then let my son's life be forfeit if I am false."

"Very well," Throst said. "I am satisfied with that arrangement. I will have an answer for your master come morning."

"Thank you." Ulfrik bowed again. Finn squeezed his arm. They had not discussed his becoming a hostage, but it was the only way Ulfrik knew to quell the doubts.

"Will you be all right without me, Father?"

"Master Heidrek will see to me. It is only for one night, and all will be well. The night will progress all the same no matter where you sleep. If this settles suspicions of my purpose, then we shall adjust accordingly."

Throst grunted, but he heard a short sigh from his sister. Ulfrik trusted Finn to understand the deeper meaning of his words. The progression of their plans had changed, but not the execution.

Finn guided him to the door and patted Ulfrik's arm as he released him to Heidrek's care. He seemed to understand.

Throst now counted his doom by the journey of the moon across the night sky. Ulfrik pulled his cowl overhead to conceal his smile.

57

Ulfrik dragged the corpse of the guard who had dozed off watching Heidrek's ship onto its deck. One of Heidrek's crew draped a sheet across the body as Ulfrik wiped his knife on the guard's shirt. He had transformed from blind man into a leather-clad warrior armed with a long knife, all dark gray and brown for concealment in the night. He clasped Heidrek's arm as the crews of his ships untied their moorings and began to shove off.

"We'll drop this body around the first bend, where the current will carry it away." Heidrek shook Ulfrik's arm. "I pray you succeed tonight and that when I return in a year I will hear your name spoken along the Seine."

"Depend upon it, friend. Now be away while these fools sleep." Ulfrik picked up his large sealskin bag and slung it across his shoulder, then let himself to the docks as the ships sloshed away into the current.

He did not look back, but bent low as if running into a wind and headed for the hall.

The moon brightened the grass with silver light, but Gunnolfsvik was asleep and at peace. Despite being a border town, these men must have been uncontested since turning to the Franks. Vigilance was lax and the few points of orange torchlight did not move, suggesting the guards had set their brands and fell asleep at their posts. Ulfrik smiled at the ease he anticipated, even with Finn being held in the hall.

The only defeat of the night had been the obvious disconnect between Hrolf and Throst. It seemed as if Hrolf had actually threatened revenge upon Throst, and that they were not allies was as clear as the moon. If Hrolf had not betrayed him, then no other suspects remained. Had it been Fate's plan? It seemed the only answer, but the entire debacle had the scent of man's bloody hands upon it. As he glided across the grass, he put the thought from his mind. A guard stood at the hall door, a brand smoking in a sconce set on the wall. He was wrapped tight against the night chill, his spear leaning against his leg.

Ulfrik approached from the side, and when the man noted him, he pitched to the ground with a moan. "Help me. Gods, it hurts!"

The man grabbed the torch rather than his spear and rushed to his side. He spoke in Frankish. "What happened?"

"Two of the merchant guards. They caught me outside my house." The guard was over him now, pulling Ulfrik around to see him.

"Where did they go?"

"To Nifelheim." Ulfrik's knife plunged through the man's leather jerkin and deep into his belly. He bowled the guard over in the grass, clamping his hand over the man's mouth as he struggled for his own knife. Pushing on the blade with his body, the guard spasmed, struggled, and his muffled screams turned to a death rattle. Ulfrik lay still a moment, then grabbed the fallen torch before it guttered out in the grass. He left the corpse where it lay, taking the second long knife for himself, then replaced the torch. He carefully opened the hall door.

Inside, the hearth fire had died to pulsing embers, filling the room with a throbbing, eerie light. Men slumped over tables or beneath them, drunk and snoring after a night of feasting. Here was the hardest portion of the plan: navigating the sprawl of bodies in various stages of sleep. The front room contained surrendered weapons, and he located Finn's sword immediately among the stack. The main hall had to be crossed to enter Throst's rooms, and Finn would be kept in one of them.

His heart sounded like a pounding rock as he selected his path through the hall of men. An exit at the far end had come into his sight, and he supposed another guard would be posted outside it. That was his escape route. He padded up to the high table, where a man sleeping at it awakened with a snort, looked directly at him, then returned to slumber. Ulfrik finally let his breath escape as he sneaked past the man to the door beyond.

It opened into a small hall with three doors. One was barred from the outside, and Ulfrik smiled. He lifted the bar and opened it.

Inside Finn sat placidly on a plain frame bed, wrapped in a fur against the night chill and a candle casting a weak light across his smile. The tallow candle filled the room with a scent like burning garbage. He stood when Ulfrik entered, received his sword and strapped it on in silence. Stepping into the hall, he pointed at the far door.

Ulfrik tested it, finding it barred from the inside. He had expected as much. From his sealskin bag he withdrew a short iron pry bar he had purchased from Heidrek in expectation of using it to force entry. He fitted it between the hinge and door frame and began worrying the door off the hinge. The wood cracked and snapped, but the nails popped free and the top hinge broke. He did the same for the lower hinge while Finn guarded the main hall. At every crack they paused in fear, but nothing more than snoring replied. When the door was free, he pulled inside to remove the bar. It fell from his grip with a thud, but again nothing responded. With Finn's help, they leaned the door against the opposite side of the hall.

Ulfrik's heart shuddered and his hands trembled. Throst lay sprawled out on his bed, his white skin barely visible in the dark. Finn entered with his candle, spreading a yellow pool of light into the door.

"It's time for revenge," Ulfrik whispered. He set his bag down beside Throst, who snored and smacked his lips in sleep. Finn placed the candle nearby as Ulfrik drew out the jar he had carried from Eldrid's home a year before.

With a nod to Finn, he broke the gut string holding the lid shut.

Finn held open Throst's mouth, and still he only murmured in his sleep.

Ulfrik shook the musty gray powder into Throst's open mouth, dusting his face and beard with it. He knew from experience only a small amount was needed to induce paralysis, and he limited the powder to what he guessed would debilitate Throst for an hour. Throst began to struggle and cough. He awakened but Ulfrik had already filled his mouth with powder. Finn clamped Throst's mouth shut.

With lightning reflexes, Throst seized Ulfrik's neck, the grip crushing his windpipe. Ulfrik did not resist, preferring to maintain the silence of their deed. In a dozen heartbeats, Throst went limp and his eyes fixed on the ceiling. His hand fell to the bed.

"Did we kill him?" Finn whispered.

Before Ulfrik could answer, there was a gasp behind them. Both he and Finn whirled to find a woman standing in the door. Her eyes were wide and mouth pulled back in horror. She inhaled to scream.

Finn piled into her and knocked her against the wall, expelling her breath as a gasp rather than a yell. With wicked efficiency, he slammed her to the ground and straddled her, pressing his hands over her mouth. She kicked and struggled, her voice a stream of muffled curses.

Looking up white faced, Finn whispered hoarsely. "What do we do?"

The woman's free hand rose behind Finn, and the knife she gripped flashed as it pointed at the back of his head.

58

Ulfrik snatched at the knife, grabbing it before it could pierce Finn's skull. He crushed the girl's hand until her grip released, then he stood back to assess.

His heart pounded, feeling as if it were punching the pit of his neck. A girl had not figured into his plans. Guards he could kill without compunction, for they understood the risk in their duties and could expect a seat in Valhalla for their deaths. But a woman had no such expectation, and he could not bring himself to kill this one even if she was Throst's sister. The cold, predatory eyes glaring at him were the same as her brother's. Finn struggled to contain her resistance.

"Are you going to kill her?" he asked. She kicked harder and her free hand grabbed Finn's hair. Ulfrik pulled her hand away.

"Open her mouth, and I'll give her the powder."

As Finn pressed open her jaw, Ulfrik sprinkled the gray powder into her mouth. She spit and coughed, but it dusted into her eyes and instantly the fight drained from her. Finn continued to press her to the floor.

"I am sorry to leave you alone in the world," he whispered to her. "But your brother's life is forfeit for his crimes against my family and me." Ulfrik tapped Finn's shoulder to indicate he could stand back.

Whether Throst's sister could hear him anymore, he was not certain. When Eldrid had fed him this poison, it left him in a dream world where words were disjointed and muted.

"Bind and gag her," Ulfrik said. "No telling when the poison will wear off. I'll get Throst ready."

Finn nodded and began to tear Throst's bedsheets to make a gag and bindings. Ulfrik had rope prepared for Throst.

"You probably can't hear me now," he said as he worked the rope beneath the body. "But when you awaken you're going to be far from the safety of this bed."

Ulfrik trussed Throst, tightening the rope by backing a foot against the bed as he pulled. He wanted the bastard to feel the pains he had endured. He worked quickly, knowing time fought him through this final stage in his plans. For a moment he considered cutting Throst's neck and completing his revenge. Yet questions remained to be answered and the gods would not be satisfied with murder alone. He would not be satisfied. The killing of his enemy would be a cold, hard lump in his heart for the rest of his days. Yet Throst's death rendered by the Fates themselves would not only satisfy but also deliver justice. The knife remained sheathed at his side, and he would not draw it on Throst.

When brother and sister were both tied, Ulfrik grabbed a spear from a rack. He leaned into Finn's ear as he spoke. "The exit beyond this door will be guarded. You will run out of it and draw him away. I'll finish him, then we come back for Throst."

The operation took only a moment. Finn opened the door, and kicked the sleeping guard before running off. The guard stood, presenting his back to the open door, and Ulfrik ran a spear through him. The man cried out, but Finn had turned to cover the guard's head with a blanket then drag him away from the door. Inside, the moonlight streaming inside revealed heaps of white skinned men snoring and shifting in their dreams.

Leaving the girl tied and on the floor, Ulfrik shouldered Throst and they crept away from the hall into the surrounding fields.

They did not know the paths through the village but Ulfrik recalled the general direction well enough. He followed the dark shape of the tower on its high cliff. Before long they came to the incline outside of Gunnolfsvik, where they rested from the burden of carrying Throst. Without time to spare, they used the bright moonlight to pick a path to the tower.

"No one is in it?" Finn asked.

The door had been removed from the bottom floor. "The Franks made a mistake building here, and stopped after the tower was completed. Looks like it's become a wreck now. Hopefully the stairs won't break under our feet. Come."

Together they carried Throst to the top of the tower, the final act of shoving him through the trapdoor being the most arduous. Once there, Ulfrik set Throst against the wall where he had broken the railing in his fall from the tower years before.

"I wish it were day," Finn said. "We could see the whole world from here. You really fell from this height?"

"Memories of it haunt my nightmares still. I fell and lived, if it can be believed. Now we wait for Throst to regain his senses."

They passed what felt like half the night, Ulfrik checking Throst incessantly. He slapped and shook him, but nothing roused him from the glassy-eyed state of helplessness until the moon was ready to set. Finn had even fallen asleep, nestled into his cloak in the shadow of the low tower walls.

At last Throst began to mumble. Ulfrik roused Finn, then bounded to Throst's side.

"Time to wake up and face justice," he said. Throst's eyes rolled as he tried to fix on Ulfrik's voice. Ulfrik remembered how quickly the haze fell away when the poison had run out of strength. It felt like a lead weight being pulled off his chest and a cloth yanked from his eyes. Throst seemed to experience the same thing, pulling violently against his bindings.

"Who the hell are you and what do you want? Wait, you're the blind man!"

"Am I? Look closer. Look at where I've taken you. It should help revive your memory."

Throst searched both sides. The beginnings of dawn were lightening the sky, chasing away the darkness. He snapped back to Ulfrik, staring deeply into his eyes. "No. You look like him, but you are not."

"But I am. Here's more proof if you need it." Ulfrik held up his left hand, revealing his missing finger. "You chopped it off right here. Sent me falling to my doom. Who am I?"

Throst shook his head and turned away, but Ulfrik gripped it between his hands and forced him still. "I am Ulfrik Ormsson. I never died, my old friend. I survived that fall and all the shit that came after it. And we're here together again in the same place."

"I saw your body."

"You saw a dead slave with his face bashed in dressed in my clothes. I was found and taken away to heal in secret. I believe it's because the gods wanted us to have this meeting today. Don't you think?"

Throst shook his head again. "This is madness. You've been gone for years. No one remembers you and you have nothing. But wait, I see what you want. A ransom, of course. I'm jarl here now, and I'm worth something to the Franks. You're hiding me here, and will set terms for my release. My sister will negotiate with you. Do you want gold?"

Ulfrik struck him with his backhand. "Gold? From you? You cost my son his hand, and cost my brother his life. You cost me everything. Gold can't fix what you've done to me."

They stared at each other. The sun was crawling into the eastern sky, and soon dead guards, missing traders, and broken doors would all be discovered and Ulfrik's escape would be hampered. Time was running out.

"What do you want?" Throst's voice was a whisper, trembling with fear. The haughty jarl was reduced now to a pig tied up for slaughter. His eyes glittered with tears and his mouth quivered. The bold, young man who had kidnapped his child and killed his brother now wore the fat, red-nosed face of an over-indulged laggard.

"I want to know what Hrolf took in trade for me."

Throst frowned at him. "I don't understand."

"You may not have an alliance with him, but he certainly betrayed me to you. You were ready for me before I arrived. What did he want for giving me to you?"

The scared visage vanished and the haughty Throst of old returned. He regarded Ulfrik with hooded eyes, as if he were not bound hand and foot. "You think Hrolf betrayed you?" He began to laugh.

Ulfrik slapped him again. "Who else would? He feared my power grew too strong, so he gave me up to you."

Laughing harder, Throst shook his head. In the distance horns began to blast.

"We're out of time," Finn said, placing his hand on Ulfrik's shoulder. "That's from Gunnolfsvik."

"They'll check the tower," Throst said in a singsong voice. "You really have no luck in this place."

Drawing his knife, be put the point beneath Throst's left eye and gouged the flesh. "Who betrayed me or you lose the eye."

"I don't respond well to torture. I'll just scream until my men arrive. Do you want to—"

Ulfrik sliced the skin beneath Throst's eye and he screamed, more in shock than pain. Eldrid's poison was still in him and he was likely numb. Beating the information from him would not work, and he had no more time.

"Who gave me up to you? It was not Hrolf?"

"No, look much closer to your hearth. Your wife is the reason you're here. How's that for a hard truth?"

"Liar!" He punched Throst's face, but he only continued to laugh. The sun was rising and Finn shook Ulfrik's shoulder when more horns sounded again.

He paused a moment as Throst chuckled. Whatever his motives, Throst was not going to provide the truth. If anything, Hrolf could still be the culprit and Throst was protecting that secret.

"What to do? She's forgotten you by now, being dead all this time. I wonder who she's sleeping with?" Throst babbled, delaying as the horns continued to sound.

"Forget this," Ulfrik said. "It's time for your judgment."

Throst's face fell and turned white. "What does that mean? You want to ransom me, of course."

"You threw me from this tower, yet I lived. Today I give you the same chance. I won't kill you, but let the gods decide."

"No, I'm worth gold to you!" Finn grabbed Throst's arm and looked to Ulfrik, who took up the other.

"Justice and revenge is all I seek. Now see the world as I did when I fell from this spot. If the gods love you as they did me, we'll speak again at the bottom of the cliff. Otherwise, may worms eat your guts for all time, you dog-shit bastard."

Throst screamed in protest as Ulfrik and Finn hefted him to the edge. "You can have everything. I'll tell you whatever you want to know."

"For me, my sons, and Toki, here is vengeance."

They released Throst and he plummeted head first over the side. Ulfrik could not bear to watch but heard him thump against the cliff rocks before smashing through the trees. In a moment, his shrieks diminished and a final thud sounded.

Then all was quiet but for the horns in the distance.

59

At the bottom of the tower they found Throst crumpled in a bloody heap. His neck had been broken and his head faced over his back. Dozens of other bones protruded from his shirt and pants. A broken branch impaled his side. Ulfrik spit on the corpse and Finn stared at it with sober dispassion. They left the body without a word, disappearing into the surrounding forest.

As they skirted Gunnolfsvik, Finn asked how Ulfrik felt. It was a numb sensation, yet still satisfying. He had avenged himself and his family, paying back Throst for the years of pain he had brought them. The gods had watched Throst fall, and let him die in shame. It was a fitting end for the coward. Yet doubt still gnawed at Ulfrik. Despite all his grand deceptions, he had come no closer to learning who had betrayed him to Throst. Perhaps the gods would forever mask the truth from him. With Throst dead, he would never know and decided it did not matter. Now, only the future was important.

They located their belongings and wealth at the riverbank before the end of the day. Gunnolfsvik was now behind them as the sun set. Finn stretched and yawned.

"I need a good night's sleep," he said.

"I'm afraid we'll be under the stars for a while yet. No great halls are in our near future. We'll search for a place to make camp tonight. I saw a spot on the way here I think will serve."

"Reminds me of scouting game with my father."

Ulfrik had a witty retort prepared, but a thoughtful look clouded Finn's normally sanguine face. Instead Ulfrik patted the young man's shoulder and the two began to retrace their steps into the forest. After a dozen paces in silence, Finn spoke again.

"Where do we go now?"

"North."

"Do you believe what Throst said? Hrolf is blameless?"

"What else can I believe? I want to find my family. There is nothing more important now than reuniting with them."

Finn nodded. "I can't wait to meet your sons and Snorri and Einar. I want to see Ravndal where you tricked the Franks. I'm looking forward to seeing every person and place from your stories."

"As am I." He looped his arm around Finn's shoulder as they took their first turn north. Toward home.

AUTHOR'S NOTE

Iceland was first settled in 870 C.E., shortly after being discovered by a Norwegian named Naddodd. Naddodd had been aiming for the Faeroe Islands but missed his mark and thus discovered a new shoreline. A few other accidental discoveries occurred until another Norwegian, Floki, made a deliberate trip to settle and named the place Iceland. He eventually despaired of settling and returned to Norway with his companions. He did not have many good things to say about the land. Yet despite his complaints, he would eventually return to Iceland and live the rest of his life there. Others were not far behind him.

What followed is known as the age of settlement, which lasted until 930 C.E. During this sixty year period all the available land had been settled, with anything from fifteen to twenty thousand settlers calling Iceland their home. One of the more famous settlers was Aud the Deep-Minded. Aud was the second daughter of the Norwegian Jarl Ketil Flatnose. She married Olaf the White, who was a son of a self-proclaimed "King of Dublin." A series of catastrophes which included Olaf's death in battle led Aud to build a ship hidden within a forest. Her reasons for this were never completely clear. She personally led this ship which was crewed by many slaves and prisoners whom she promised to grant freedom and property once landing safely in Iceland. Upon arrival she was true to her word, and claimed a large tract of land for herself in addition to what she granted to her followers. By now you will note where I borrowed from Aud the Deep-Minded's tale for my own character of Audhild.

While Audhild's story drew inspiration from a historical figure, Eldrid is entirely fictional. She is what was known as a seidkona, which can be loosely translated as a witch. Like the traditional namesake, powers ascribed to the seidkona include all sorts of black magic and prophecy. These seidkona were solitary and did not practice in covens as later European witch traditions would. Also, not every seidkona performed evil deeds but also knew healing magic and could use powers for good. These practitioners preferred to call themselves spa-kona, which separated them from their darker sisters.

Looking back to mainland Europe during this time, Frankia was entering a new period of unity that would prove troublesome for the Viking invaders. After the death of Charles the Fat, King Arnulf of East Frankia used problems in West Frankia to seize Lorraine for his own. His machinations finally resulted in King Odo of West Frankia recognizing the superiority of Arnulf in 888. This lasted until 893 when Arnulf decided to back Charles the Simple over Odo. The ensuing wars benefited Arnulf, who again grabbed more land for himself. During this time, the Vikings consolidated their grip around Rouen and the Seine River in West Frankia. They exploited the chaos but found Arnulf a difficult foe. After initial success, the Vikings were soundly beaten by Arnulf in 891 at the Battle of Leuven and Viking ability to make further progress in East Frankia was shattered.

By 895, Arnulf summoned both Odo and Charles to an audience in Worms, but Charles sent a representative rather than attend himself. Odo shrewdly attended in person and was careful to lavish gifts on Arnulf. This insult ended Arnulf's support for Charles. Odo was once again in favor and awarded the West Frankia throne. This was the situation when Ulfrik last lived in Frankia. With the infighting finished in West Frankia, Odo could turn his attention to the pressure of Viking invaders and perhaps do something about their encroachments on Paris.

Now that Ulfrik has returned to Frankia, he will find a new landscape and the Franks better organized to resist. The establishment of Normandy is still over a decade away and much uncertainty remains in his future.

∼

If you would like to know when my next book is released, please sign up for my new release newsletter. I will send you an email when it is out. You can unsubscribe at any time, and I promise not to fill your mailbox with junk or share your information. You can also visit me at my website for periodic updates.

If you have enjoyed this book and would like to show your support for my writing, consider leaving a review where you purchased this book or on Goodreads, LibraryThing, and other reader sites. I need help from readers like you to get the word out about my books. If you have a moment, please share your thoughts with other readers. I appreciate it!

ALSO BY JERRY AUTIERI

Ulfrik Ormsson's Saga

Historical adventure set in 9th Century Europe and brimming with heroic combat. Witness the birth of a unified Norway, travel to the remote Faeroe Islands, then follow the Vikings on a siege of Paris and beyond. Walk in the footsteps of the Vikings and witness history through the eyes of Ulfrik Ormsson.

Fate's Needle

Islands in the Fog

Banners of the Northmen

Shield of Lies

The Storm God's Gift

Return of the Ravens

Sword Brothers

Descendants Saga

The grandchildren of Ulfrik Ormsson continue tales of Norse battle and glory. They may have come from greatness, but they must make their own way in the brutal world of the 10th Century.

Descendants of the Wolf

Odin's Ravens

Revenge of the Wolves

Blood Price

Grimwold and Lethos Trilogy

A sword and sorcery fantasy trilogy with a decidedly Norse flavor.

Deadman's Tide

Children of Urdis

Age of Blood

Copyright © 2014 by Jerry Autieri

All rights reserved.

No part of this book may be reproduced in any form or by any electronic or mechanical means, including information storage and retrieval systems, without written permission from the author, except for the use of brief quotations in a book review.

Printed in Great Britain
by Amazon